Her Cree grandmother called it the gift of seeing, but for Petra "Pete" Orvatch, knowing things in ways that defy explanation has made reality and fantasy blur in a world where the clocks literally go backward. Her fascinating and clairvoyant mind is a riddle that many doctors have tried to solve with medication. Love comes her way unexpectedly when she meets Fiona Angeli, a stunningly beautiful single mother. A risk-taker by nature, Fiona is not scared off by her new lover's psychic abilities and eccentricities.

The two of them share passion and secrets on a magical and surprising journey, and their torrid love affair takes them to thrilling new places until betrayal divides them. Both these women fight battles within themselves; Fiona must gain control of her dangerous compulsions, and Pete's onerous gift ultimately puts her at risk of losing herself in the gap between delusions and the real world.

Published by
NineStar Press
PO Box 91792
Albuquerque, New Mexico, 87199
www.ninestarpress.com

**Warning:** This book contains sexually explicit content, which is only suitable for mature readers, and brief references to childhood abuse.

Print ISBN # 978-1-945952-49-4
Cover by Natasha Snow
Edited by Elizabeth Coldwell

# PEOPLEFISH

Medella Kingston

# DEDICATION

For Harry, who was with me when I began writing this, and now only visits in dreams.

# ACKNOWLEDGMENTS

This book would not be worth reading if it weren't for the help of many. Deepest gratitude to: Cyndi, Amy, Lynda, Bob, Tena, Scott, Michelle, Ravensgate Editing, Michael, Melissa, Patti, Jason, Pam, and to Mr. Frevola, the first teacher who told me I could write well.

# Chapter One: The Waiting Room

*May the holes in your net be no larger than the fish in it.*
*~ Irish Blessing*

Pete looked up from the mystery she was reading and scanned the faces in the waiting room. There was Tired Pinched Mom, with faded blond ponytail and dark roots coming in. She had one kid under control and was now quietly negotiating with the other. Next to this trio sat Man Too Large for His Seat, who seemed to be staring at his shoes or sleeping with his eyes open. In the corner was someone so nondescript she couldn't instantly name her—then it came to her: Any Woman. This woman was neither thin nor large, short nor tall, and had a slightly exotic yet familiar face. She looked as if she could be from many different places, like Greece, Morocco, Central America, or New Jersey. She was text messaging so quickly, Pete half expected her thumbs to spark and set fire to her phone.

*Doesn't anyone people-watch anymore?* Was she the only person left who liked to read faces and create narratives? Maybe so. She'd never stop doing it. She'd been spinning this stuff since she was little—much to the annoyance of her mother. Instead of acknowledging the creative gifts of her child, or at the very least being entertained by them, she'd say, "God will punish you, Petra Marie, for thinking bad thoughts about people and making up lies."

Some traits must skip generations, because Grandma Sweets had the right attitude. She'd join right in and embellish her granddaughter's rough outlines of strangers' lives with additions that could only come from a seasoned mind. If Pete said a passenger on the bus looked guilty, Gram Sweets would say, "Of course he looks guilty, he ought to! Instead of cooking a turkey for Thanksgiving, he cooked his wife!"

Her reminiscing was perforated by the staccato ring of a telephone.

"Cambridge Holistic Health and Wellness Center, please hold."

*Please hold? No one else is on the line; is this receptionista just fucking with the caller?* Pete dog-eared the page in her paperback, closed it, slipped it into her bag, and decided to devote all of her energy to observing. She was just about to make up a story about the receptionist when her eyes landed on something strange. She hadn't noticed the cheap plastic clock on the wallpapered wall before, but now she couldn't take her eyes off it because the second hand was moving backward.

At first she thought she was seeing things, since her imagination was such a well-developed muscle. So she did something that made her feel seven instead of thirty-seven. She closed her eyes to reset, inhaled a long, slow breath, and then opened them, hoping this simple act could alter what she saw, or make things feel right again. She didn't return her gaze to the clock right away, but rather avoided its face like you would dodge direct eye contact in a volley of flirt-and-stare with a stranger who'd caught you looking.

She panned her eyes evenly over all she had just taken in. Now the previously obedient child of the two was acting petulant, Man Too Large for His Seat actually was asleep, and Any Woman had stopped texting and was staring back at Pete. This startled her a bit. She looked away and then forced herself to look at the clock again. The red second hand was still moving backward and now instead of 2:27, it was 2:26, and the room seemed brighter to her than it had been just a minute ago.

"Petra Orvatch?"

She heard the automaton call her but she couldn't move—she felt obligated to monitor the clock and confirm that it was in fact going backward, but knew she shouldn't say anything about it. It was one of those times when she couldn't expect people to understand her. These occurrences had happened ever since she could remember and could be confusing, amusing, or even downright dangerous.

Pete put her bag on her shoulder, straightened her jacket collar, and walked up to the counter. "It's Pete, actually."

"Your doctor is running late, and you'll have to wait another hour, until 3:30. We're sorry for the inconvenience but it's either that or reschedule. She's dealing with an urgent situation." The receptionist's words came between snapping and chewing that actually revealed the pink gum. Her voice was nasal, and she seemed completely unconcerned. *Shit,* Pete mused, *she couldn't be more stereotypical if she had a beehive hairdo and cat's-eye glasses!*

"Uh, I suppose that's okay." Pete thought about it and decided it would give her time to figure out what was up with the clock—or if she couldn't, perhaps she could calm herself by reading her book until she could see Dr. Percy. She turned around and headed toward her seat, but saw that it was occupied by a woman who must have just come in. She was a stunningly beautiful redhead, about the same age as Pete or slightly younger, and when she saw Pete leave the counter, she left her coat on the chair and headed over to check in with Gum Snapper. Pete's first impulse was to move the woman's coat and reclaim her seat. She liked her seat. It gave her an optimal view of almost every person in the waiting room, and it faced the mysterious clock. She very nearly did move it but stopped herself when she felt two little eyes on her back. It was one of Tired Pinched Mom's kids staring mutely.

Petra Marie Orvatch had never been someone who cared much about what others thought of her, but for some reason this little girl's gaze stopped her from behaving rashly. Pete glanced up at the clock and saw that now the second hand had stopped altogether. Then she sat down across from her former seat. With her back to the clock, she started feeling anxious. Her cell phone told her it was 2:31. That was reality. It was what she focused on as she crossed her legs, removed her book from her bag, and opened it to the dog-eared page. Her mind flooded rapidly with the printed words as images played in her head. Pete was such a fast reader that she was at the bottom of the page before the redhead sat down.

As she walked past, a faint scent of lavender striped the air, which Pete enjoyed because it instantly reminded her of Grandma Sweets' backyard and all the happy times she'd spent there. She closed her eyes and inhaled more deeply, and when she opened them, the woman was looking right at her. With large, clear eyes that looked to be a greenish blue, flawless skin, high cheekbones, a regal nose, and a wide mouth hinged with full lips, this woman was a knockout.

She definitely seemed like one of those women who was beautiful but didn't fully know it. Well, all right, she knew she was pretty but didn't seem to capitalize on it. She didn't have a fancy haircut; hell—her hair wasn't even really styled, just sort of loosely arranged. She didn't appear to be wearing any makeup, and Pete thought that if she had been wearing it, she would look as good as any of those women in the beauty magazines. Red the Seat Stealer did not wear any fingernail polish and had on fairly inexpensive clothes from head to toe, except perhaps for her red cowboy boots. They looked pricey and made her taller than she was. Pete had met a fair number of women who wore boots, and they not only liked power, but weren't afraid to wield it.

As she continued the fantasy about Red, she distinctly smelled lavender. Pete uncrossed her legs, squeezed her thighs together ever so slightly, and became aroused as she continued studying the woman, who was reading an issue of *Popular Mechanics*. The fact that she chose to read this magazine instead of the homemaker magazines Pete knew were in the stack was a turn-on in itself. Red was definitely not a homemaker. She was an adventurer, but not in the obvious ways. She didn't have a dangerous job; she had a scientific job. She didn't drive a sports car; she probably owned a hatchback. She lived on the edge by doing things like mixing painkillers and booze, masturbating on trains, and having sex with strangers. Red the Seat Stealer came from a broken home, had a high IQ, and owned a predatory libido. Pete realized that while she was staring she'd been fiddling with the corner of her book cover so much that it was now frayed. *Shit. I'm sexually frustrated. I haven't touched anyone but myself since July. Maybe Red can help me change that.*

"Fiona Angeli?" the receptionist called through her nose. "I forgot to give you your insurance card back, hon. Sorry." Pete caught the term of endearment from Gum Snapper and wondered if Fiona's beauty had somehow subdued her, bringing out her gentler side.

Her name was Fiona. Pete thought that was an awesome name to say in bed. *Fi-on-a.* Each syllable hung musically suspended in Pete's mind like chimes. Fiona got up to reclaim her card, and Pete turned to study her ass. A little too big for the rest of her: perfect. Suddenly Pete felt guilty, or not quite guilty, but distracted from her purpose. Her purpose was to figure out what the hell was wrong with the clock, not have girl-on-girl fantasies. Her last lover had been a man who wasn't particularly skilled in bed, just energetic and fun to be with. Having sex with him was a bit like throwing a ball for a dog. Being with this woman would be more like driving a race car or playing a cello; it would require skill and focus. It never occurred to Pete that Fiona might be as interested in having sex with a woman as she was in the stack of untouched magazines with smiling women and baked goods on their covers.

"Mom!" one of Tired Pinched Mom's kids sang out abruptly. "How much loooooonger do we hafta wait?" She grabbed the small boy's wrist forcefully but not abusively, and he began to calm down, but then some unseen hand wound up his little sister, who started poking her mother in the arms, the belly, and the legs over and over without saying anything. *Poke, poke, poke,* until her frustrated mother took a wrist in each hand and brought them together, then leaned her face very close to the girl's as she said something very quietly, slowly, and deliberately.

Pete got the feeling this woman had acquired a special skill set for managing this behavior and that she had to manage it often. Some of the other people began staring in their direction; even Man Too Large for His Seat woke up and knitted his brow as he looked at the family. His furrowed forehead relaxed, and his eyes enlarged when they landed on Fiona. Her looks had woken him fully. Pete thought she saw his pupils dilate with desire as he eyed her up and down, knocking his knees toward each other like a boy with a hard-on. Fiona must have been a lighthouse since she was a girl, and Pete wondered how it would feel to grow up with that kind of magnetism, to call all those ships into port no matter what cargo they carried.

When Pete landed her gaze briefly on Fiona, she noticed a slight smirk on her face and wondered if they were in cahoots or somehow testing the waters for a mutual opinion of the family drama unraveling in front of them. Their eyes met, and Pete curled her lips too, then self-consciously smoothed her hair back, but it was so thick and willful that it just sprang back to where it was before she attempted to tame it. *Crap.* Now instead of just fantasy, Red was reality. Pete didn't always trust reality, not just because of this clock with its drunken second hand, or that time she saw a fish with a human face, but because there had been so many times in her life when she came by information in inexplicable, magical, and sometimes crazy ways. Like the time her dog spoke to her, and no one in her life believed her, except maybe her best friend.

This was four years back, when Turtle was still a puppy. Overnight he went from a healthy, active pup to a sickly, lethargic one. Pete woke to find him dull-eyed, listless, sick. He wouldn't eat, was vomiting, and had diarrhea. Pete had a much smaller salary back then and, usually, before deciding to take him to the veterinarian, she would consult her canine health book. She stroked his wiry fur with one hand and flipped through the pages with the other. The list of possible ailments was too long for her to sift through, and she felt a flash of panic. Turtle was so young, and pups this little could easily die from something like this. She was not going to let him suffer when he had already been through so much in his short life. He'd been found in a parking lot, so thin his ribs protruded, cowering inside a cardboard box, shaking and terrified of people. Pete had heard about him from her best friend, Sheila, who worked at an animal shelter. It was love at first sight when she met the little mutt. He looked like a combination of every terrier in the book with his scruffy coat and small features. He was mostly white, except for a circular patch of brown on his back and sides that reminded Pete first of a saddle, and then a turtle shell. And so she named him Turtle.

He'd come a long way in the month since she'd adopted him. His belly had rounded out, and he was much less afraid of people. And now he was ill, and she was about to take him to the vet when she got an idea. She would ask him what was wrong. She stared at the little guy and asked sweetly, "Turtle, boy, what's wrong with you? Why are you sick?" After Turtle heard those words, he stared at her intently, and Pete had an experience like she'd never had before: she heard him talking to her in her own head. Their eyes were locked the whole time, and he communicated to her that he had chewed some of the wooden trim in her apartment, and it had lead paint on it. He had lead poisoning and would need to go to the vet for treatment.

"Okay, boy," she said. She took him to the clinic immediately. She had a high limit on one of her credit cards, so she was not too concerned about the bill. When she arrived, she told the person at the front desk that it was lead poisoning. When he asked her how she knew this, she didn't think and blurted out, "My dog told me." The vet tech looked at her the way people do when shock prevents them from finding words; he opened his mouth in silence and then found something to say. He simply asked her about the pup's symptoms. Pete then sat with him and waited just a few minutes to be seen. She decided not to tell the vet about how she knew what was wrong with Turtle. She'd sit on that information so she didn't have to endure another scrutinizing glare. She knew what she knew, and she also knew that reality, as other people described it, was not to be trusted.

The treatment for the poisoning was fairly simple and inexpensive. Turtle would make a full recovery. This was a tremendous relief. She'd adopted Turtle a few weeks after her breakup with Robin, and the dog was a huge comfort to her. Walking him three times a day kept her connected to the world outside her pain. People came up to her all the time to pet the puppy, and in the months following the split, this was often the extent of her social contact for the day.

She turned away from Fiona and looked back at the clock. The second hand was still frozen. No wait, now it was moving! She blinked and hoped it would have a windshield-wiper effect, that she would see more clearly. The second hand was moving all right, and the time on the clock was the same as the time on her cell phone. She wasn't sure what had happened, but she was sure that Fiona was trying to get her attention, and that was exciting. *Forget the book, I have less than an hour until my appointment, and I don't know when she will be called in, so I have to connect with her somehow. There's something between us.*

Robin. She hadn't thought of Robin in a while. They'd almost married and had talked of raising children together. They had been together just about four years, and after the breakup, Pete had had recurring dreams about her for almost as long as the relationship. These visits through the sleep channel had been torturous; Pete would see Robin's deep blue eyes brimming with desire, the way they had when things were good between them. Their first three years had been filled with passion and connection, and then everything had fallen apart. She knew that people parted ways more than they stayed together, but when something whole became jagged shards of memory, it had stung Pete hard. Robin had been the only lover she could see herself with indefinitely.

Her stomach growled, and she realized she hadn't eaten a proper lunch. It was so loud, she half wondered if anyone near her heard it. Again came a thunderous roar from her belly. Fiona looked up at her and grinned slightly.

*She must have bionic hearing,* Pete thought. She smiled back and let out a small laugh.

Fiona reached into her bag and produced an apple. She held her arm out in Pete's direction with the shiny, red fruit in the palm of her hand. It was quite an unexpected and generous offering. How could Pete say no? She got up from her seat, took two small steps, and took the apple from Fiona's hand.

"You sure you don't want it?"

"I'm sure. You need to feed that beast you've got in there."

*Don't I know it. Looking at you is making me hungrier and hungrier...* "Well, um, thanks. A lot. My name's Pete," she sputtered quietly as she extended her other hand to the woman.

"Hi, Pete. Fiona," she responded as she shook Pete's hand. Her words were infused with her smile, so much so that if you only heard them and couldn't see her, you'd hear the smile like you sometimes can with radio announcers. They were several feet apart, and Pete didn't want to continue their conversation at that distance, so she decided to ask the older woman next to Fiona if she would move.

"Excuse me, ma'am?"

The woman paused her knitting and looked up. "Yes?"

"Would you mind terribly trading seats with me? I've just run into someone here, and we'd love to talk without shouting across the room. I'm really sorry to ask, but if it's not a problem..."

The knitter glanced first at Pete and then at Fiona, and her eyes seemed to soften as she soaked in Fiona's radiance. "No problem, dear. I don't mind moving."

"Thanks! Very kind of you," Fiona said to the lady as she shifted her weight and faced her body toward the empty seat, looking up at Pete to take her in. The old woman got up, moved, and settled herself quickly back into knitting.

"Hi. That was cool of her. You never know," Pete offered quietly.

"Yeah, most people are kind. Wish I knew how to knit. Do you knit?" Then her eyes trailed down to Pete's hands, which, like her voice, seemed too big for the rest of her. Those big paws had not been designed for knitting. Changing oil, maybe, but not knitting.

"Uh, no. My grandma tried to show me when I was a kid, but I didn't have the patience for it. This apple looks great. Thanks again," she answered as she tore into the red skin with a crunch.

"Happy to share. I almost forgot it was in there, but then that can happen when you carry around a bag this big."

Pete looked at the bag and saw that it was in fact really big and fairly full. It was well-worn and had once been a shade of orange, but the patina of time had turned it to more of a brown.

"What else have you got in there?" She raised one eyebrow playfully, almost flirtatiously. Fiona leaned in closer to her. More lavender.

"You really want to know?" Pete nodded. "Okay—but don't judge me too harshly..." she said conspiratorially. She unzipped the canvas behemoth, turned it to face Pete, and pried open its jaws briefly for her to see its contents: pepper spray, a battered old leather wallet, a pale blue scarf, a pair of handcuffs, a balled-up pair of panties, something that looked like a small bottle of lube, and a miniscule, shiny object she couldn't make out the details of. Before she could get a closer look at the contents, Fiona zipped up the bag. Pete thought she should be startled, or at least on guard, but instead she felt an adrenaline rush like the kind she got when she used to exceed the speed limit on her old motorcycle. Yes, Red the Seat Stealer was in fact a dangerous woman.

"Fiona Angeli?" the receptionist's voice sounded, this time without the perforation of gum chewing. "We're ready for you now."

"Oh, sorry, Pete—got to go. It's my turn," Fiona said with an apologetic smile. Pete fumbled in her jacket pocket, took out her wallet, produced a business card, and handed it to Fiona.

"In case you want to know what I think about all that stuff in your bag," she said provocatively. Fiona took it, gathered up her things, smiled at Pete for a few seconds, and left the waiting room.

Pete breathed in her scent like an animal as she watched her walk away. She hadn't felt this intrigued and captivated by anyone before. With those panties, handcuffs, and a distinct air of mystery, Fiona was a puzzle she wanted to solve. Fate had just put them in the same place at the same time, and though reality was not her most loyal friend, Pete did trust her own instincts, and they were telling her she'd see Fiona again very soon.

Forty-seven more minutes until her appointment. She was grateful for the apple, which had quieted her stomach. All she could think about was Fiona. Even though she couldn't be sure Fiona was into women, she did know for certain that she was bold, incredibly sexy, and utterly unafraid of social risks. Pete felt a butterfly flap its wings inside her gut as she imagined kissing her. Her mouth was fabulously inviting, and Pete had found it difficult not to stare at her ample lips as she spoke. Pete had been with many women who didn't know they liked women until they met her. Maybe it would be like this with Fiona. She closed her eyes, leaned her head against the wall, and fantasized about Fiona.

With her cowboy boots off, they were almost the same height. Fiona was just a bit taller than Pete's five foot seven. She didn't mind tipping her chin up to kiss this woman because the kissing was so amazing. Those delicious, padded lips absorbed hers completely. Their tongues met as equals; neither dominated, so the kissing was more like dancing than fencing. Her mouth was the perfect wetness, and even though they were both incredibly turned on, they couldn't stop kissing to engage in more adventurous activities.

Pete longed to be naked with her; she imagined the curves awaiting discovery beneath all those clothes. She crossed her legs and, feeling warm, undid a button on her blouse.

Her arousal made her too restless to stay seated, so she got up, looked at the clock one more time, and left.

After walking out to the parking lot while eating the last few tasty bites of apple off the core, she enjoyed how much warmer outside it was now than when she'd arrived. She removed her jacket and draped it over her arm. She was about to get in her truck and drive somewhere because she craved movement, but stopped when she remembered there was a little park nearby, and decided to take a walk. The sky was a cloudless, crystal-clear blue; it was one of those crisp and gorgeous early-September days that New England was famous for. Pete inhaled deeply as she ambled and felt a surge of energy. She had been sitting still for too long, and her legs were happy to move.

She was an abnormally fast walker, so she reached the park quickly. Some mothers, or possibly nannies, with young children were gathered around the play structure, and a handful of children clambered all over it. The toddlers reminded her of astronauts; they walked clumsily, as if their limbs were encumbered by some unseen bulky spacesuit. They teetered as they bravely attempted to walk without falling down.

She found an unoccupied bench and sat on it. Scanning the park, she toyed with the idea of making up stories about the people, but she didn't really feel like it. Her burst of energy left as suddenly as it came, and her eyelids drooped. She felt warm, relaxed, and almost sleepy, so she closed her eyes and meditated on the exquisite Fiona. Pete held her image in her mind as she fantasized about their next conversation. Fiona would dial the number on Pete's business card as soon as she got home. No, that seemed unrealistic, almost desperate. She would wait a respectable time period, like two days, and then call her. Pete would not recognize the number, decide to let it go to voicemail, then remember that it might be Fiona and grab it on the third ring.

"This is Pete," she would say confidently.

"It's Fiona. You know, the woman from the waiting room?"

"As if I could forget," she'd respond. "The nice girl who heard my growling stomach and gave me her apple." Fiona would laugh, and they'd make small talk for a short time. Talking came easily for them. Pete longed to know if not talking would come just as easily. The sun beamed down on her face and made her feel warm all over. Her thoughts drifted, and her head began to bob as she dozed a bit.

She woke when a dog barked three sharp, playful yaps. *Shit!* She didn't know how long she'd been drifting, so she dug her cell phone out of her bag and saw that it was 3:15, time to get back. As she moved down the sidewalk, she thought about the clock in the waiting room and wondered if it would betray or affirm real time. Either way, she should mention the experience to Dr. P today. She wondered if Fiona was still there and if she would hear from her. *I have to. We couldn't have been a random collision.* Fiona had been so genuine with her, and so open. Christ, she'd shown her what was in her bag! Pete and Robin had been together for years, and Robin had never liked her to go in her bag. She would see this stunning redhead again. It just had to be that way.

She was at the entrance to the parking lot when she spotted Fiona approaching a scuffed-up blue hatchback. "Hey," she called out.

"Hey, Pete! I'm all done. Is your appointment over too?" The two started walking toward each other. Fiona appeared luminous even against the ordinary backdrop of cars.

"No—mine is now. I wish it was over, though."

"Well, why don't you reschedule it and let me take you out for a proper late lunch? That little apple couldn't have filled that big, growling stomach of yours, and I need some food too." She smiled at Pete, and they were only about two feet apart now. Lavender. Heat. There was definitely heat between them. Pete surprised herself and responded boldly.

"I can't think of anything else I'd rather do than grab a meal with you. Let me run in there and reschedule with Miss Thing. I'll be right back."

"She is a piece of work, isn't she? I'll be right here," Fiona said with a little bite in her voice. Pete smiled and walked briskly into the office. Rescheduling took a few minutes, and Pete thought about Fiona the whole time. A late lunch. A meal meant sitting across from Fiona and looking into those amazing eyes. She thought she might explode from excitement. She suddenly couldn't remember if she'd shaved her legs. She subtly reached her hand down along her jeans to lift her pant leg, tug her sock down, and feel: *smooth. Thank goodness!*

"Okay, does next Tuesday at 4 o'clock work for you?" the receptionist said.

"Sure," Pete responded.

"And normally we charge a fee of twenty-five dollars for a last minute cancellation, but since we pushed your appointment back that doesn't seem fair—so we will waive that, okay?"

"Um yes, sure, good—sounds good. Thanks." She was surprised at how pleasant the receptionist was, and sailed out of the waiting room jauntily. She had a proverbial spring in her step because she was going to spend more time with the amazing *Fiona. Fi-o-na...* The name played slowly in her mind; each syllable was delicious. She took one more look at the clock, and it had stopped at 3:00 even though it was now 3:35. Pete convinced herself the clock wasn't working right and shifted her focus to the delightful situation at hand: sharing a table with a woman whose description could use up every synonym for beautiful.

"There you are! All set?" Fiona beamed.

"Yup, done. So how do we wanna do this—I mean, with the two cars?"

"Well, do you like Thai? There's this amazing Thai place a few miles from here that's open now. Want to just follow me there?"

"Thai food is my favorite! Sure, I'll follow you."

☆☆☆

When they entered the restaurant, they were greeted by the enticing aroma of the food. Pete's stomach spoke to her in anticipation. Besides two other couples, they were the only customers. The decor featured paneled walls of dark wood with intricately carved figures and decorative elements. The quiet made it cozy and intimate, which appealed to Pete so much she wondered why she hadn't known about this restaurant.

Oddly, their server looked very much like one of the women in the painting that hung over their table, and both of them noticed this at the same time when they ordered their beers. "Weird, huh? Do you think she recognizes herself in traditional Thai garb?" Fiona mused playfully. Pete loved that she had used a word like "garb." This woman's cup overflowed with sex appeal, and the way she moved her lips as she spoke made her extremely kissable. Pete studied the painting. In it, a group of four Thai women were walking down a city street wearing brightly colored, flowing dresses.

"I think it's totally random and, no, I doubt she sees herself. People have a funny way of not recognizing themselves. You know what I mean?" Pete asked.

"I do, actually."

"Wow, amazing. I usually have to explain myself to people but—I make sense to you?" Pete asked and then looked at the table for something to sip before their server returned seconds later with two cold Thai beers, which she poured for them. When she asked if they were ready to order their food, Fiona took the lead, ordering a salad for them to split. Pete suggested mussels, and Fiona approved.

"So far, yes, you do. Now the question is—do I make sense to you? I mean, there is some pretty crazy shit in my bag, and you didn't even flinch when you saw it. What's up with that?"

"I don't know. I—" Pete fumbled with words, which didn't happen to her very often. "I just trust you. Yeah—" She lowered her voice. "—I just trust that there's a good reason for everything you're carrying around right now, or at the very least, a saucy explanation."

"Nice." Fiona then pressed the glass to her lips for a long sip, keeping her wide-set eyes on Pete, who was completely rapt. Pete smiled, looked down at the table, and smoothed a small wrinkle in the tablecloth before returning the gaze. She ran a hand through her hair and looked right at her, trying to mold her eyes into their softest, most receptive shape. Fiona didn't blink and continued to hold her new acquaintance under a spell. "I do have my reasons, but I'll spare you those details now if that's okay with you. But, for your information, I was definitely going to call you..."

"Oh," Pete said. She didn't know how to respond, so instead she drank some beer.

"Well, you have a painting business, and I do have a room that needs to be painted."

"Really?" Pete asked.

"Nope. I was going to call you because I like you." Pete smiled, but before she could reply, the rose petal salad they ordered arrived.

"Fiona," Pete managed after her pause, "I'm really happy that we bumped into each other. You're something else."

"You're a real charmer, Pete. Hey, is Pete short for something, or a nickname, or—?"

"Petra," Pete cut in. "My given name is Petra, but it didn't stick past my teens. I like Pete better. This salad is too pretty to eat, almost." She gestured to Fiona, asking for her dish, and then scooped half of the salad onto it. Fiona dug into it enthusiastically.

"I like it," Fiona said.

"The salad?"

"Well, yes—but I meant Pete." Just then, the large, steaming plate of coconut curry mussels arrived.

"Oh thanks," Pete said. "I love the salty sweet mix of textures and tastes in Thai food. Don't you?"

Fiona nodded and moved her salad to accommodate the platter before blurting out, "Did you know that *Thai food* is a code name for sex?"

"No, actually, I didn't." She used the small fork to pry some delicious flesh out of its shell, put it in her mouth, and instantly oozed an, "Mmmmm..."

"Yeah, my friend Calvin likes to read the Urban Dictionary and share his findings with me." Fiona leaned in and smelled the mussels before taking one and eating it slowly. "Thai food means fun, hot, spicy sex."

"I get it. Makes total sense to me."

Conversation flowed easily from one random topic to another and, as they finished their last few bites, Pete found herself wondering when their time together would end. She had nowhere she had to be for a few hours because Turtle didn't need a walk until the usual time of 6:00.

Her answer came as Fiona spoke. "Well, Pete, just because lunch is over doesn't mean we have to part, right?" Pete nodded, searching for something witty to say, but Fiona's beauty had a way of stealing words from her. "You can have me for about an hour, but then I have to pick up Mack from school."

"Mack? You have a son?"

"Yeah. My little guy. He's in third grade over at Adams Elementary, and he stays after school a few hours for this special program. For gifted and talented kids."

"Oh wow—so you don't just have a kid, you have a have a smart kid, huh? Good for you."

"Yeah, he's pretty amazing, actually. I have to remind myself he's only seven going on eight when big words and massive ideas come flying out of his mouth." They got up, pushed their chairs in, and started heading toward the door.

"Well, Fiona, I've talked with you enough now to get a glimpse of where those brains come from..." Pete held the door open.

"I was smart enough to ask you to lunch, right?" Fiona bit her bottom lip slightly and looked at her suggestively. Pete just about melted on the spot.

"So what now?" Pete asked as they walked out into the street. "Want to—?"

Fiona cut her off.

"Want to come home with me? I live close by, and you still didn't hear the stories that go with the things in my bag..."

"Yeah, I'd love to—yes. Should I just follow you?"

"Sure, I'm about six miles north of here. Let's go."

They arrived shortly, and Pete took in the details of Fiona's home as she walked behind her up to the front door. It was a small house, almost a cottage, with a tidy front yard. The paint was fading but the colors were pleasing: a bluish gray with black trim. There were a few toys scattered in the yard and hanging baskets of flowers dangled over the porch. All in all, it was an inviting place.

When they got inside, Fiona quickly removed her cowboy boots and jacket, then tossed her bag onto a big chair near the entry. She stepped in close to Pete, slid her bag off her shoulder, and removed her jacket in one fluid motion. Both items fell to the floor. Pete leaned in close and kissed her. Fiona pressed against her, hard, and then put one hand on either side of Pete's face and returned her kisses passionately. Their lips fit together perfectly, and they stayed like this, locked together, kissing for a long time. Hungry, they made out in the entryway until they became too aroused to stay upright. Fiona pulled away from Pete, took her by the hand, and led her to the bedroom.

Still kissing, they fell onto the unmade bed; Fiona was on top of Pete and paused before saying, "Let's see what we can make happen in under an hour..."

Pete grinned and pushed her hips up into Fiona's. Her body surged with energy; their chemistry was pure electricity, and Pete thought she could easily become addicted to it, to Fiona. Now the two women were arching their backs, grinding, and speaking to each other in moans. Fiona started unbuttoning Pete's shirt, and Pete tugged Fiona's blouse out of her jeans. Then she reached her hand beneath the fabric and caressed her back, which was incredibly soft and moist with a very light sheen of sweat. They were both so excited. Out of the corner of her eye, Pete saw that the time on a clock radio next to the bed read 5:08. They had much more ardor than time.

Fiona started undoing Pete's buttons, but not fast enough for Pete, who rolled Fiona off her and started rapidly taking her own clothes off. Fiona did the same, revealing skin so flawless and creamy that Pete's hands looked almost brown on her. Fiona seemed to like being on her back, but was not at all passive. She undid Pete's bra deftly and then tugged at her belt. Jeans were wrestled with and discarded, along with Pete's damp panties. Fiona wasn't wearing underwear. In moments, they were naked and drenched with longing, their thighs locked together. Pete was so turned on she actually felt lightheaded. Fiona made noises—wonderful noises, loud and feral. Pete wanted to taste her, but when she started to slide down the length of her body, Fiona pulled her back up and whispered, "No, stay here..." Pete did, and the two of them found a rhythm and rode it fiercely until they came hard, first Fiona then Pete right after. They looked into each other's eyes, and it seemed to Pete that they saw all the way into each other. Fiona was incandescent; her cheeks were flushed, and her lips were parted slightly as she panted. Her dark red hair had become tousled and flowed around her head like seaweed. Their bodies still trembled as they lay there together, glistening with sweat. The room smelled like sex but felt like something bigger.

They were both on their backs now, and gradually their breathing returned to normal. Pete was staring at the ceiling. She felt spent, satisfied, and as if she had just played with fire. Fiona rolled onto her side and faced her new lover. She traced her index finger from Pete's damp collarbone slowly down the middle of her chest. "I'm still throbbing," she told Pete. "Feel." She took Pete's hand and placed it gently between her thighs. Pete rolled to her, gazing at her for a moment before speaking.

"Hmmm, I am too. That was intense."

"God, I wish we had more time right now! There are so many more things we could do, Pete..."

"I'm not complaining. I know you have to get going. I'll take off," Pete said softly.

She moved a strand of Fiona's fiery hair gently off her forehead and noticed a faint, crescent-shaped scar there. It was old but fairly large.

She almost asked her how it happened, but then thought better of it since time was working against them.

"Well, do you want to meet my son? I mean, I understand if you don't want to spend the evening with a seven-year-old, but he's a good kid and I—" She hesitated and stared hard into Pete's tawny eyes before continuing, "I'm just not done with you yet today."

"How can I refuse an invitation like that? Will Mack mind having company tonight? It's a school night too and—"

"Pete, I know it might seem irresponsible of me to introduce someone I just met to my son, but I wouldn't invite you over here if I thought it would be any kind of problem. He knows I'm social, and he also knows to tell me if he's uncomfortable around anyone. I have a strong hunch you two will get along just fine. He goes to bed early..." Her voice was confident and sultry; Pete was sold.

"Okay, it's settled then. I like kids. And I'm not done with you yet today either."

Fiona smiled and sat up. Pete couldn't believe how perfect her breasts were and let her eyes linger on them boldly. Then she remembered Turtle.

"I have to get my dog out for a walk and feed him in a bit. How about I go home and do that and then meet you back here?"

"Why don't you bring your dog over here?" Fiona said warmly. "You can't stay over if he's home alone, now can you?"

"Oh." Pete was caught off guard but recovered quickly. "Right. I could do that. He loves kids. Is Mack okay with dogs?"

"More than okay; I'll make us dinner, you just bring yourself and your dog over when you're done."

They kissed for a little while before getting out of bed and then got dressed. Pete suddenly thought about the contents of Fiona's bag. Later. She would ask her about it later. For now, there was the dog, the kid, and a whole night with this amazing woman.

Turtle's happy yips started the minute he heard Pete's pickup in front of the warehouse. She loved coming home to him because he always exploded with enthusiasm when she came through the door. She grabbed his leash and out they went.

It was still beautiful outside, and Pete took in a long, deep, delicious breath of fresh air and sighed as she exhaled. As they walked around her Cambridge neighborhood, Pete kept having sex flashbacks. The sensations of Fiona's touch washed over her, and her excitement built as she contemplated getting into bed with her again. Turtle sniffed excessively, leaving his yellow signature in all the usual spots. When they were a block from home, they ran down the sidewalk together; these moments with Turtle made Pete feel like a little girl again.

She gathered her thoughts around what to bring. She would need food for Turtle, his bowls, a chew toy, and dog bed. For herself, she just grabbed some toiletries. She had the urge to bring something for Fiona, but didn't know her well enough to know what she would want, so she decided to head over there empty-handed.

Turtle had his nose out the window, reading the scents in the air as they rode to Fiona's house. Pete got a twinge of anxiety: What if Mack didn't like her? Kids generally did like her, but what if it didn't go well? Pete knew that any mother worth her salt put her kid first, and even if Fiona's feelings matched her own for this amazing, crazy new thing between them, Mack came first. She had to click with this kid. Turtle sneezed, reminding her that he was her secret weapon; few children did not delight in the company of a loving and playful dog. Turtle would be her ambassador if need be.

After about fifteen minutes, she turned onto Fiona's street, parked in front of her house, and felt her trepidation shift to anticipation and longing.

## Chapter Two: Upside-Down Kisses

*L'amore domina senza regole.*
*~ Italian: Love rules without rules.*

Pete had Turtle's leash in one hand and pushed the doorbell with the other. The chime had barely stopped when the door opened to reveal a small, dark-haired boy in a striped shirt and overalls who had only one shoe on. His face was shaped like his mother's, but his coloring must have come from his father. He looked up at her briefly, and then his eyes went right to the dog, who walked inside with his tail wagging. Turtle licked his face from chin to forehead. Mack giggled. Pete announced, "This is Turtle, and I'm Pete. You must be Mack."

"I love, love, love dogs!" he declared as he took the end of Turtle's leash and walked him all the way inside to the living room, where he immediately played with him. Fiona was in the hallway, radiant, braless; she was going to drive Pete crazy all night. Before Pete could say hello, Fiona greeted her with a kiss. She tasted of wine, and Pete wanted to drink a glass of her.

"Did we really just meet a few hours ago?" Pete asked softly.

"No, I think we met a few lifetimes ago," Fiona teased back. She was sexier than anyone had the right to be, Pete thought. She wondered if this woman really believed in past lives or was just playing on her remark. Her mind flooded with big questions she wanted to ask her in the small of the night: *What do you think happens after we die? Where do you think we were before we were born? Do you think anything is random? Do you believe in luck? Fate?* Fiona led her by the hand into the kitchen, where she smelled beef and spices simmering. "Taco night," Fiona announced. "Mack's idea. Do you like tacos?"

"Sure. I wanted to bring something, but I didn't know what you'd want," Pete admitted.

"I think you know what I want," Fiona said. "Get over here quick." She slipped her hand into Pete's jacket pocket and pulled her close for a delicious kiss while they had privacy.

"Those two have hit it off," Pete said as she let go of Fiona and leaned against the doorframe between the kitchen and living room. Now both of his shoes were off, and the little boy was showing Turtle his toys one at a time, explaining what each one was called, and what he did with it. Turtle sat at attention with head cocked and scruffy white ears lifted. He sniffed them all and licked a few. Fiona smiled bigger than Pete had seen her smile yet. She could get used to that smile. "Turtle is bulletproof. With people, I mean. He's four and has never even lifted his lip to anyone. I—"

"I'm not the least bit worried," Fiona interrupted gently. "Any dog you raised is fine by me. As for the kid, he's not bulletproof. In fact, lately he's prone to tantrums. But he's always been sweet to animals; he's never lifted his lip."

"Turtle!" Mack's high voice trumpeted. "Come see my room! Can I take his leash off, Pete? It's hampering him."

"Sure thing, Mack," Pete answered. She turned to Fiona with, "Hampering? That's a mighty big word for a little boy."

"He's smarter than I am. That's nothing. Wait until he tells you all about a particular topic with more detail than you thought a little kid possibly could. You'll see…"

And Pete did, in fact, experience this later on during dinner. At school, they were studying dinosaurs, and Mack was particularly interested in the stegosaurus. She learned that the stegosaurus had a brain the size of a walnut, came from Asia, and that its spiked tail was called a thagomizer. Mack was amazing. If she or Fiona asked him for more information about anything he mentioned, he could supply it. His enthusiasm rivaled his appetite. Pete had never seen a skinny kid shovel in quite so much.

"Sweetie, Mack-meister," his mom cooed, "you're having thirds? Why are you so hungry? Do I have to feed you an entire stegosaurus?"

"Mom, that's not even funny or even possible because there aren't any—they're extinct. You know that." He paused to swallow some rice. "I guess I'm hungry because of the lunch incident."

"Lunch incident?" Fiona queried tentatively, the corners of her mouth threatening to tug her face into a grin. Pete suppressed a giggle and directed her gaze toward her plate so she wouldn't laugh at the little guy, who seemed very serious.

"Yeah. I traded my lunch for something. But I'm not going to do that again, because my stomach was growling all afternoon until they gave us snack in the extended day program." Then in went still more mouthfuls of rice.

"May I ask what you traded for?"

"Aw, you wouldn't understand."

"Try me," Fiona shot back, exchanging glances with Pete briefly. Under the table, Fiona's hand rested tenderly on Pete's thigh.

"Information," he offered.

"Information? About..." She paused, leaving space for Mack to respond.

"The stegosaurus. The most interesting of all the dinosaurs. Suzanne Kim said she knew something about the stegosaurus that wasn't in any book or on any website and that if I gave her my ravioli, she would tell me. I couldn't resist, Mom. You know? Have you ever just, well, wanted something so much you kind of ached?"

Fiona looked at Pete ever so briefly, her eyes flashing with desire. "Yes, Mr. Mack, I can definitely relate."

"Me too, Mack, totally," Pete inserted.

"But how could Suzanne know something so mysterious? That doesn't really make sense," Fiona questioned.

"That's what I thought, but she had this really convincing story about how her uncle was a paleontologist and knew about a new discovery that hadn't been published yet." He paused to crunch the last bite of taco. As Pete listened to him speak, she wondered if she'd get used to those large words coming out of such a small person. "Well?" he asked while crunching, "do you guys want to know what it is?" His face was earnest, which Pete found endearing.

"Well yes, of course, especially if it cost you my famous homemade spinach ravioli!" Fiona sassed.

"Well, if it makes you feel better, Suzanne really liked it. She licked the container when she was done."

"Hey, Boo, before you reveal this amazing fact, can you tell me if your teachers saw? I mean, did they notice you weren't eating?"

"Sort of. Toward the end of lunch, one of them, Miss Carol, asked about my lunch and I—" He paused, looked down at his empty plate briefly, and then back up at her. "I lied and said I ate it already."

"Well, I'm not happy that you gave your lunch away and—"

"Traded!" he interrupted her.

"Well, yes, traded your lunch and then lied about it."

"But I'm telling you now, and I'm trying to share what I learned about the coolest dinosaur ever! Can you please just listen? Like Pete is doing?"

Pete got a little nervous at the mention of her name. It took her by surprise. Was he genuinely appreciating something about her or was he using her to manipulate his mother? She didn't know how to respond and ended up producing a small equivocal noise in her throat.

"Yes, Mack. I can listen," Fiona said gently. "Go ahead."

"Well, scientists never knew why the stegosaurus had plates." His face was so serious that, for a split second, he seemed like he was thirty-seven instead of seven. He licked his lips and continued. "But Suzanne's uncle's research team has a theory about the scales based on some evidence they just found. They might soon have conclusive proof that the plates were a temperature-regulating device; they soaked up the sun during the day and gave off the heat at night!"

"Wow," Fiona said with slightly forced enthusiasm, "that's extremely cool, and almost worth my spinach ravioli." Pete wondered how much longer they'd have to listen to dinosaur talk, and just like that, it stopped.

Mack gave a small giggle, and drank his last sip of milk. "Do you like games, Pete? Not video games, but board games? Because I really like them, and Mom plays them with me all the time, but some games are way more fun with three people."

"Yes! I do like games—all kinds of games. What do you guys have?"

"Mack, why don't you show her the game cabinet, and I'll clean up," Fiona instructed.

"I want to clean up," Pete offered.

"Forget about that, go on," she said with an alluring smile. Turtle, who'd been lying on his bed in the kitchen with them, got up and scampered after them with his tail wagging. Mack grabbed the end of it gently to try to stop it from moving, but couldn't quite capture it. Turtle seemed to be playing keep away with his tail, and Mack giggled. Next he was on his knees in front of the cabinet, opening it up slowly and carefully, scanning the various boxes with something akin to reverence. Pete loved the thought of Fiona and Mack playing games together; she respected her for interacting with him in the evenings when many parents and kids these days were just parked in front of glowing screens. Pete noticed a wooden cabinet and assumed there was a television inside, and that it was not on all the time.

As Mack read out the names of the games they had, Pete scanned the room, eyeing an art corner with a drafting table and shelves full of paints, colored pencils, and markers. She began to appreciate more fully the kind of upbringing Fiona was giving Mack and fell a little bit more for her. She heard the sounds of dishes being washed and Fiona singing softly. Pete had stumbled into their lives and didn't want to get out.

They decided on a game called Stump Me that involved lots of clues, guessing, bluffing, and deduction. Mack scurried into the kitchen and squealed, "We're going to play Stump Me, Mom! Isn't that great? We haven't played that one with more than two people in a long time!"

"That's awesome, Mackster. Just so you know, it's 7:00 now, and you have to be in bed in an hour and a half."

"Yeah, yeah, I know, boss," he responded with a smirk. "Can we have ice cream?"

"You mean to tell me you have room for dessert in that belly of yours after eating three plates of tacos?" she challenged as she reached out and messed up his already messy hair.

"Definitely. There's a special part of my stomach reserved just for ice cream. Come on, bring it, and let's go play!"

Pete came into the kitchen with Turtle's leash in her hand and told them she had to take him for a walk. Fiona kissed her and told her rousing family fun and ice cream would be waiting.

☆☆☆

The temperature had dropped significantly since she arrived, and she zipped her jacket all the way up. "Come on, Turtle boy, how's about a quick poo and pee so I can get back in there? What do you think of those two—pretty special, huh?" Turtle cocked his head to one side as he looked up at her, the way he always did when she talked to him, as if he was really trying hard to understand her. Sometimes she swore he did comprehend the question and answer back with his eyes. This was one of those times. His eyes spoke approval. Pete thought about Fiona as she breathed in deeply and exhaled, her breath making puff clouds in the crisp, cool dark. Based on past experiences that involved jumping into bed with someone hastily, she would expect the connection to be limited to sex, but there was no escape from the enormity of feeling she already had for Fiona. Pete and Turtle walked to the end of the block and back, and as she looked up at the lit windows of the houses she passed, she found herself woolgathering and counting down the hours until she and Fiona could turn out the lights.

She let herself back in and tossed her jacket and Turtle's leash on top of a few items on the armchair that seemed to be their catchall. She saw Fiona and Mack sitting down in front of the large low coffee table that was set with a colorful board and game pieces. Mack slapped his hands against his thighs for Turtle to come to him, stood up, and asked her if she wanted chocolate chip ice cream. She answered with an "mmmmmmm" sound followed by an enthusiastic affirmative.

"Okay. Mom, can you serve us all or do you want me to?"

"I got it. Why don't you explain the rules to our guest so she has half a chance of beating you?" Fiona winked at Pete over Mack's head as she got up and headed toward the kitchen.

"I'm always the orange piece, and Mom is always the blue piece. That leaves you yellow, green, red, or purple! Which do you want?" All of the available pieces were in his cupped hands, and he offered them up to her excitedly. *This kid really does love games.*

"Red!" Pete answered as she took it from him.

"Like your truck," Mack chirped. He was an observant and curious child who was making a great first impression on her. Apparently Turtle liked him too, because he was coiled on the rug next to him.

Pete enjoyed the game; Mack flexed his considerable intellect and almost beat them, but Fiona pulled ahead at the last minute and won. Pete wondered if she'd ever let Mack win when he was younger, because she sure wasn't dumbing it down now. He got so giggly and wound up after the game that Pete doubted he would go to bed on time.

"Do I really have to go to bed at the regular bedtime? I mean, we have a special visitor, and I should be able to interact with her more," Mack pleaded as he yawned. Pete savored not only his vocabulary, but also his Machiavellian streak.

"Macintosh, honey nut, you know the agreement: bedtime on a school night is 8:30. Nonnegotiable," Fiona responded with warm firmness. Mack got up from the floor, came over to Pete, and threw his arms around her shoulders. His hug caught her off guard in the best of ways, and she could swear she felt her heart expand. This was why she loved kids.

"Turtle can sleep with you if you'd like," Pete offered, looking at Fiona.

"Yay! Really?" He glanced from her to his mom, who nodded. She got up and led Mack down the hall. Pete urged the dog to go with them. "Goodnight, Pete," he called as he disappeared into his room. Turtle followed, and Pete heard Fiona instruct him to get up on the bed. Pete put the game away, brought the ice cream bowls into the kitchen, and washed them.

It took about another half hour to get teeth brushed, pajamas on, a story read, and a goodnight tuck-in, then the lights went out, and the door was shut. Fiona walked around the cozy house and switched the lights off one by one. When Pete emerged from the bathroom, she was thrilled to see Fiona there in the flickering light, sitting on the bed, a button undone.

"Hey, special visitor..." Fiona purred softly.

"Well, I do feel special walking into this scene, seeing you now. I could just melt right here on this spot," Pete responded and then giggled awkwardly. "Did I really just say 'melt right here on this spot'? What is wrong with me? Is that a line out of some old movie? I think—" Fiona cut her off.

"Get over here, Petra. You could say just about anything to me right now and I would think you're sexy..." Her voice trailed off like the last drops of sweet, thick brandy rolling down the side of a glass. Pete walked to the bed and stood facing her. Fiona reached out and took one of her hands in hers and then pressed it between both of her hands firmly while looking into her eyes. Pete was surprised hands could say so much; the resultant warming effect radiated throughout her whole body. Then Fiona guided Pete's hand to her cheek, and left it there. Pete let both her hands wander, stroking Fiona's face delicately, and working her fingers into that thick, wavy red hair. She grabbed a handful with a slight tug, which seemed to arouse Fiona the way rough petting might excite a cat to the point of biting. But she didn't bite; that could wait. Instead, she leaned her head against Pete's belly, wrapped her arms around her waist, and breathed in long and slow. They rocked a little until Fiona pulled her down to the bed. The breeze picked up outside, came in through the open window, and made the candle flames stutter, painting dancing shadows on the walls. The night air felt good to Pete, who had grown warm. She started removing her blouse.

"These clothes have to come off!" she announced.

"Hold it, baby, we're doing this slowly, since we had such a small slice of time this afternoon," Fiona asserted.

"Well, who am I to argue? I can last. Can you?" She put it out there as a challenge.

"Oh yeah, I can." Fiona rolled on top of Pete. Their bodies fit perfectly; they were drawn together like molecules that attract one another. Pete pushed her hips into Fiona as they kissed deeply. Fiona bit now, pressing her teeth into Pete's lower lip, leaving her somewhere between pain and arousal. There were also the corner kisses: Fiona put her cheek against Pete's and slipped her tongue into the corner of her mouth, ever so slightly. This made Pete throb.

They continued kissing until they were interrupted by a knock on the door. Luckily, they were still clothed. Fiona unstuck herself from her lover, apologized with her eyes, and walked to the door. She opened it partway. On the other side of it was little Mack with an upset face and his pajamas buttoned incorrectly. "Yes, Mack? Do you need something?"

"I can't sleep."

When Pete heard this, she sat up and called out to him. "Is Turtle keeping you up with his snoring?" For a relatively small dog, he had a colossal snore.

"No, it isn't anything like that," he answered. "It's monster mind. I can't shut my brain off. Mom does things that help. Can you help me, Mom, please?"

"Yes, honey, you go back to bed, and I'll be right there," Fiona said. Mack complied and padded down the hall. She turned to Pete and explained, "He's got an active mind, and sometimes he gets insomnia and I have to walk him through some progressive relaxation."

"Can I do anything?" Pete offered.

"No, but it might take a little while. I'm sorry, lover," Fiona said before kissing her.

"Don't be. You're a mom, and this is what moms do. I'm not going anywhere."

Their eyes locked, then Fiona rubbed Pete's shoulder before leaving the room. Pete thought about taking her clothes off and getting into bed, but decided against it, since Fiona wanted to wade into the waters rather than dive in. She lay down on the bed and stared at the ceiling, then let her eyes wander, taking in the details of the room: it was neat and sparse with three different plants. The walls were a warm turquoise, and the room smelled of lavender. A large, framed photo of an old barn hung on the wall by the door, and closer to the bed was a child's drawing that

Mack must have made. It too was framed and depicted a night landscape with a tiny house and several stars in the sky just above it. The whole room had a dreamy feel to it. Pete felt deeply relaxed despite her keen sexual arousal.

Fiona returned about twenty minutes later. Pete was still on her back, but was now lying diagonally with her head toward the foot of the bed and her bare feet near the pillows. Pete remained belly-up and arched her neck back to see her inverted lover. Fiona said nothing as she got on her knees in front of the bed and began kissing her. Upside-down kisses. They stayed like this for a little while, enjoying the new perspective, until Pete moved to welcome her onto the bed. They continued kissing until she pulled away and asked, "Mack okay?"

"Yup. Sound asleep with Turtle curled against him."

"Good. How often does he get like that?"

"A few times a month, sometimes more. There's just too much crammed in that cranium. He says he sees pictures of everything he saw that day, or even years ago. Photographic memory. His father had it too."

Suddenly, Pete had so many questions about how Mack came to be, but they weren't questions that needed answers right now.

"Interesting. I really like him, you know. Great first impression." Pete smiled and received a smile in return. The items in Fiona's purse popped into Pete's mind, but she pushed the thought out as quickly as it had come because it just wasn't important right now.

"He likes you too, and he's picky." Fiona propped herself on one elbow and continued. "I know they say not to introduce your child to someone you're seeing until you've been dating them a while, but I just—I don't know..." She paused and stared at Pete.

"What, Fiona?"

"I live on instincts. and it just felt right to have you meet him."

Pete liked the sound of that and reached her arms out to her. Fiona crawled into them. More kissing. Buttons got unbuttoned, and clothes fell to the floor. Then the virtual noiselessness of skin on slick skin filled the room. They moved passionately as their limbs entwined and their hands searched the landscape; they groped for each other as only new lovers do. Something smoldering since the afternoon now caught fire, and the idea to take it slow was shed not long after their clothes were. Breathing got heavier, and Pete got so turned on when she heard their bodies smacking together, sticking and sliding.

"I've got to taste you," Fiona breathed into her paramour's ear before placing her face between Pete's breasts, where she lingered briefly. She then dragged her hair across Pete's belly, making her way lower slowly and teasingly. Pete arched her back the moment she felt Fiona's mouth on her and experienced her expertise. Fiona's kisses were just as thrilling below the waist as they were above it, and Pete gasped, grabbing at the sheets as her pleasure built. She wanted to cry out, but restrained herself in the face of several progressively more intense waves of ecstasy. Fiona brought her to the brink several times, but didn't want her to climax just yet; she stopped and crawled sensuously up to where Pete was, and then rolled on her back before emitting a satisfied "Mmmmm…"

Pete got on top of her and kissed her, enjoying the salty spice of herself in Fiona's mouth. Their chemistry made Pete throb as she put her mouth on one perfect pink rose of a nipple, then on her flat stomach, which she kissed before discovering a completely shaved Fiona.

"When did you have time to get yourself all pretty like this, what with picking up your kid and making dinner?"

"I made the time. I like surprises."

"Ah…so do I," Pete sighed. "So do I." Fiona was unbelievably soft against her lips and beneath her tongue. She took her time and relished the sounds coming out of Fiona. Making love to her this way was like playing some instrument from another world. The more aroused Fiona became, the more Pete pulsed and ached. Pete caressed her tummy and breasts and enjoyed watching her. Fiona opened her eyes a few times, and they held each other's gaze in a place that was new and dangerous. Fiona grabbed Pete's short hair roughly with both hands. Her orgasm was building now; Pete could feel her clit swell and become a plump, helpless hostage.

"Fuck, Pete. You're making me crazy."

"Likewise," she managed to breathe. Pete used her lips and tongue skillfully, matching Fiona where she was, and then, without warning, slipped three fingers inside her while licking her clitoris. This was more than Fiona could take, and she came hard, putting her fist to her open mouth to mute her volume. Then she gasped and squeezed her eyes shut, making small vulnerable sounds that sounded to Pete like they might turn into sobs any second, so she returned to her arms, and they held each other for a long time. The wind blew one of the candles out, and, for the first time in a while, Fiona opened her eyes and seemed to notice her surroundings.

Pete looked at Fiona and saw that her eyes were moist with emotion and her face was flushed. She looked perfect: not quite innocent but definitely unguarded. Fiona lifted her chin, and they kissed tenderly before slipping beneath the blankets. Their breathing slowed, and they both drifted into a sleep that lasted until just before sunrise.

☆☆☆

Fiona stirred and opened her eyes to the dimly lit room.

She was disoriented, but when her mind focused, her first thought was of Mack and whether it was time to wake him for school. She looked at the clock, which told her in a green glow that it was 6:03. There was one more hour before the weekday routine would press creases into her amorphous, dreamy state of mind. She got out of bed as quietly as she could, slipped on her old, fuzzy brown bathrobe, and went to the bathroom to empty her bladder. When she returned, Pete was in the same position: lying on her side with knees bent and both arms outstretched in front of her. As Fiona got closer, she noticed Pete's face; the corners of her naturally upturned mouth defied gravity, giving her a blissful expression.

Fiona got back into the warm spot she'd left behind and wrapped one arm around Pete's waist. Spoons. She put her face against the back of Pete's head, breathed in, and began to nuzzle her neck, leaving kisses behind her ear. This woke Pete up, and she started to roll toward her, but Fiona held her firmly in place. Pete sensed she had a plan and relented. As the nuzzling and kissing continued, Pete got excited, but could do nothing except receive. Then Fiona's hand left her waist and caressed her hips, outer thighs, inner thighs, and slid nearer to Pete's waiting pussy. She was moist, warm, and receptive to Fiona, who used her fingers in all the right ways. Pete threw her free arm behind her, grabbed Fiona's ass, and pressed their bodies more tightly together. Pete's sensations were getting more and more intense. As she neared her climax, Fiona suddenly moved her hand away. She brought her fingers back where she'd just been and slipped her wet thumb inside Pete's ass. Fiona really did love surprises, and Pete couldn't hold out any longer; she came spasmodically, throbbing for a long time against Fiona's fingers and thumb. Double victory. Then Pete relaxed and went limp.

They stayed like that, silent, for a little while, and then Pete spoke. "What a way to start a Thursday. Wow, Fiona..." She stopped talking and rolled over to face Fiona.

"I'm not sure that's all we've started, baby," Fiona cooed back.

They stayed on their little passion planet as long as they could there in each other's arms, until the clock radio made a clicking sound and Robert Plant and the Honeydippers serenaded them with a blast from 1985: *Come with me, to the sea of love. I wanna tell you just how much I love you.*

They stayed spooning as the song ended, not saying anything until Fiona invited Pete to shower with her and stay for a quick breakfast. The morning routine left them little time, so bathing together was more sensual than sexual. When they were done, they toweled each other dry, dressed hastily, and got ready to face the day. Fiona woke Mack, who was delighted to see Turtle still snuggled up with him. The dog licked Mack's face, jumped off the bed, and left the room in search of Pete, who took him out for his morning walk.

☆☆☆

When she returned and sat for the coffee and toast Fiona served her, Pete noticed the bag Fiona had opened up for her in the waiting room, and she thought about its contents as she sipped and crunched. Before Pete could ask about any of it, Fiona joined her at the old wooden table and talked between bites.

"We have this deal, my son and I, that every other day he can dress himself. It's our compromise. So when you met him, his clothes matched, but today I am not responsible for the fashion sense that comes out of that room," she exclaimed good-humoredly.

"Oh, he'll look good no matter what; he's your son after all." Pete turned on the charm. "Hey, Fiona," she ventured, "are you going to tell me about any of what I saw in that enormous bag of yours? "

"Oh shit—yes, yes. It's not that mysterious, actually, or I mean it's nothing to worry about. Remember how I told you I started off as an office paralegal and then started doing field investigations as part of background checks?" Pete nodded, marveling at how dazzling she looked this early in the day. "Well, I just feel safer having pepper spray with me in case I need to scare someone off."

"How dangerous do these investigations get?" Pete asked, searching Fiona's face with concern. Fiona ran a hand through her hair, as if thinking of the best way to answer.

"Family law attorneys like the one I work for handle a number of different issues. I've worked on a lot of divorce cases, ones involving child custody or abuse, neglect, or endangerment, but the ones that make me the most nervous are the ones where domestic violence has been alleged, like the Bradshaw case that I'm working on right now. Shit, I wasn't supposed to say the name. Pretend you didn't hear it. My work often underscores how truly ugly people can be to other."

"Wow—that's pretty interesting, actually. How long have you been doing this work?"

"Since Mack was about two. Flexible hours, pays well, and rarely bores me. I'd rather be dead than bored." Their quiet conversation was suddenly ruptured by Mack's exuberance.

"Mom! Turtle's a morning person too!" He came in beaming, with his hair as of yet untamed for school. He was clad in a blue-and-red-striped shirt, lime green pants that were a little too short, and mismatched socks. *Kind of awful and kind of great*, Pete thought. The dog was at his side, his white tail wagging against the boy's pant leg.

Before leaving, Pete asked Fiona when she could see her again. They made a plan for Friday evening, and Fiona said she'd try to have Mack stay with her friend Calvin. Pete said she was happy either way—just as long as they could be together. Before she and Turtle left, there were good-bye kisses from Fiona and two hugs from Mack, one for her and one for her dog.

Pete drove home; changed her clothes; set Turtle up with fresh water, public radio, and a new chew toy; and then got in her pickup, but texted her pal before turning the key. She figured Sheila would be out walking her four dogs at this hour and unable to write back, but she had to tell her about Fiona. In a way, things weren't real until she told her best friend.

*Met a woman with turquoise eyes yesterday and woke up in her bed this morning.*

Pete thought that would catch her attention. She and Sheila had been in constant contact for the last fifteen years. They'd met one summer on an all-women house-painting crew. Sheila was extremely lean and six-foot-two tall, so she stood out to people whether she wanted to or not.

What drew Pete to her at first was her sense of humor; she could make anyone laugh. Unbeknownst to the crew boss, Sheila did a spot-on imitation of her that had all the girls in stitches when they went out for beers after work. That summer, Pete had acquired valuable painting skills and a great friend, because it was a quiet trade, and the two of them had hours to talk about themselves, other people, and the big and small stuff life is made of. Sheila enjoyed hearing Pete's detailed stories of experiences going further back than most people could recollect when reminiscing about childhood. She also liked to get Pete talking about her sculptures and collages. Pete listened with interest to Sheila's comedic, mildly self-deprecating and sometimes tragic tales of, as she put it, the love life of a female giraffe. Sheila was four years older, and by the end of summer, she had become Pete's big sister and best friend. Pete's phone vibrated in her jacket pocket, and she pulled it out at a red light to read her friend's speedy response.

*OMG! So much more exciting than picking up dog shit for four dogs! Free tonight? Want details!*

Pete smiled and texted back. They would meet up at Sheila's favorite vegan dinner spot: Veggie Heaven. It was cheap, tasty, and quiet enough to have a real conversation in. Pete couldn't wait to tell her about Fiona and the insane chemistry the two of them had. What Pete didn't want to tell her friend about was the clock in the waiting room, because she knew that would worry Sheila.

After about twenty minutes, Pete arrived at the house she'd been working in for the past week and a half. She'd been an interior house painter off and on for the last dozen years and loved working alone, but today was one of those rare days she wished she had a colleague, someone to tell her she was glowing and pump her with questions. She felt distinctly different than before she met Fiona, and even though her heart felt tumescent in the best of ways, she wasn't sure it was vessel enough to contain the joy Fiona just put there.

☆☆☆

Back in Cambridge, Fiona had returned from Mack's school and sat at her computer, trying to get her brain dialed to work. She'd gone into the office every day this week, and today she had to write up some notes from her current investigation. She squeezed her thighs together absently and realized she was still aroused from this morning. Her recent encounter with Pete had turned her inside out, not just sexually, but emotionally. The speed of their coupling didn't scare her; she'd always leaped into things because she trusted her gut, but the intensity of their dynamic definitely caught her attention. She wondered if her insides were showing, vulnerable, there for Pete to know. Fiona had never been comfortable when exposed and tried to imagine how it would feel to be seen so out in the open by her new lover.

She fought the urge to call Calvin. He was rarely awake before ten unless he was with a client. Most of his tricks were later in the day or in the evening, but occasionally he had an early riser. She worried about him and wished he would stick to less risky ways of supplementing his regular income. He was handsome and fit enough to model or act, but lacked the inclination and confidence to pursue such work. When she expressed her concern and lectured him on the dangers of being intimate with strangers, he pointed out some of the inherent risks she took in her work and in her personal life. He had her there. At least he used condoms, but still she worried.

Fiona and Calvin had met when she was pregnant. It had been a challenging period in her life, and he had fit right in, taking the chaff with the wheat. He had waited tables at the same upscale restaurant as her former lover of seven years ago, and when Fiona would sit at the bar drinking sparkling water, waiting for her lover's shift to end, she'd talk to Calvin, and he'd chat back as much as he could while working. They gravitated toward each other, and words flowed effortlessly between them. She had instantly recognized in him a recklessness that mirrored her own. Calvin had been completely charmed by Fiona, and when her affair with his coworker fizzled, he'd admitted to her he missed seeing her.

A week later, Fiona had come back to the restaurant to return an earring she'd found which belonged to her ex, and Calvin told her she'd quit to move back to New York. Fiona had jokingly offered him the gold hoop and he'd surprised her when he'd said yes and then offered to serve her a drastically discounted meal. She couldn't refuse. It was a slow night, so when it was time for her dessert, he joined her, and they talked their way into a lasting friendship. Calvin loved Mack before he even left the womb. He was crazy about that kid. He'd always looked forward to being a "queen funcle" or, as he had explained, a fun gay uncle.

Even though Fiona had been having some financial troubles at the time and the pregnancy was hard on her, she never complained unless Calvin pulled it out of her. "Bitch about the bad stuff, Fi," he would say. "It's bad for your health and the baby's to bottle it up." She'd respond with something along the lines of redheads being born stoics, which he always waved off with a flourish.

Fiona managed to settle into her first hour of work and promised herself she wouldn't ring him until 10:30. That ought to give him enough time to get an espresso in his tank and be suitably animated when she told him about her chance meeting with a really hot woman. Try as she might to concentrate on work, she had difficulty focusing. She contemplated masturbating, but decided that would take her down the wrong track. Fiona could never sit for too long, so she got up, and paced around the house. She noticed some wilted plants and decided to water them.

Finally, it was time to call. As she reached for her cell phone, it rang. Ironically, it was Calvin. She answered it and heard the caffeine in his accelerated pace of speech.

"Fi! I had this bizarro dream about you last night, and I have to tell you about it. You were wearing some thin, gauzy gold-colored dress and standing on the edge of a moor. Very United Kingdom. It was way too cold to be wearing so little, but you didn't seem to notice. Your eyes were kind of blank—"

"Blank?" she managed to insert quickly.

"Yeah, like expressionless, but the kind of expressionlessness that has a feeling all its own. Is that a word? Expressionlessness? Anyway, so you were standing there. I wasn't in the dream; I was just watching it all like a film. Then you looked down, and I could see what you saw: cold, crashing, angry-looking waves. The toes of one of your feet were sticking out over the very edge, and suddenly you took a step and just fell straight down with your arms at your sides."

"Do I die in this dream? Cause I've just experienced something amazing, and I don't want any doomy-gloomy bad dream to shit on my buzz..." She said it sweetly and wasn't surprised that he didn't stop to ask. Espresso.

"No! You didn't die, that's the wonderful thing; you plunged into the sea with your arms at your sides the whole time, and when you sank, I could see underwater like it was lit, brightly lit. Your hair flowed up around you like some angelic Medusa and you smiled peacefully as you landed in a net. It looked like a big fisherman's net. That's when the dream ended. Weird, huh?"

"So, I might have died in the net after you stopped dreaming this dream?"

"No. No way. This was a very positive dream. I know it was. Okay—I shouldn't have had a double shot; I can't shut up!"

"Yes you can, darlin', you have to. I have to tell you about this amazing woman I met yesterday!"

"Yay! A woman! The boys never last, and you never fall in love with them. I—"

"Time for you to listen, Cal." She cut him off.

"Right. Yes. Of course. This is the sound of me listening."

Fiona giggled and waited a bit for something else to come out of him, but nothing did. He listened attentively to the account of his friend's latest conquest.

☆☆☆

Today would be Pete's last day on the job site. She had a few more doors to paint and then had to put the switch plates and outlet covers on, fold the drop cloths, tidy up, load out her gear, and go. She was a meticulous worker; she used the same precision painting interiors that she did constructing sculptures and assembling detailed collages. Her clients had a four-year-old boy, so she'd taken extra precautions not to leave anything out that would be dangerous for him to get into. She loved it when a job was done—not just because it meant a check for her, but also because of the simple satisfaction she took in leaving a place more beautiful than she found it.

This Brookline job had been pretty straightforward once the couple decided on a color for the living room, which for some reason had eluded them for a week despite Pete's consulting and putting up many swatches of color. The woman was pleasant enough, but her husband's personality was stiff, almost mechanical. When she was out and about, Pete habitually invented narratives about strangers; her mind couldn't help itself. Clients' homes were so replete with information that the highlights of many a workday were the tales she spun in her overactive brain. She never went in a room she wasn't hired to paint, she resisted the fabled allure of the medicine cabinet, and didn't even open the refrigerator to put her lunch in it. She didn't have the inclination or the time to snoop and instead fed her imagination with what was in plain sight and crafted stories with material that would be imperceptible to most.

Mr. Robot, as she'd come to think of the client, struck Pete as someone going through the motions of his own life; he was a man whose decisions happened in the realm of "shoulds." She couldn't fathom how he'd ever attracted Mrs. Robot, so Pete decided that she liked the money and must have a secret life she enjoyed outside their big house. She didn't cheat on him, but did thrill-seek. Once a week, she did something dangerous, something the mister wouldn't approve of or even show any interest in if he heard a story about it on the news. This week, it was racing out on the amateur track in Braintree. Pete knew she liked racing because she had a model of a 1964 Shelby 289 Cobra in her office that she had assembled. She had told Pete about it when they were choosing a shade for the walls.

When she wasn't thinking about clients, she crafted elaborate fantasies that occupied her mind hour after hour while she painted in silence. Today went quickly, and before long it was time to move furniture back. As she slid a leather love seat back to its original position, she noticed a tiny toy gun on the part of the floor she'd just revealed. It must have belonged to a diminutive action figure of Robot Jr.'s. She inspected it briefly, then slipped it into her pocket.

Over dinner with Sheila, Pete revealed just enough juicy details to whip her friend into a froth of whimsical jealousy. Sheila reminded her that she hadn't fallen asleep next to another human heartbeat in almost six months and sarcastically declared she was on the verge of donating her lingerie to Goodwill. When Sheila heard about the contents of Fiona's bag, she raised her left eyebrow and waited for the perfect moment in the conversation to put a fork into things. "So, it was the pepper spray that caught your attention, not the handcuffs and the undies?"

Pete laughed and said of course those items were noteworthy.

Sheila offered cautious optimism, telling her dear friend that she wanted the best for her and gently reminding her that her perceptions sometimes worked against her.

This dose of big sister truth couldn't kill Pete's Fiona buzz. In fact, she felt so bold she told Sheila about the clock in the waiting room, knowing this would raise more concern.

"Oh my, Petra, that hasn't happened in a while. I wonder what triggered it?"

Pete wasn't up for analyzing the whole situation or revisiting past problems. She promised Sheila she would hash it out with Dr. P next week, and steered the conversation back to her friend, asking her about her latest online dating efforts.

Apparently Sheila wasn't up for figuring out her own puzzles either and dodged the question with humor, saying with an exaggerated sigh that men were taller online than in person.

☆☆☆

After talking with Calvin for quite a while, Fiona managed to sink her teeth into her workday and get tasks done. She had to do some investigating in the field for a particularly complicated custody case, and then get back in time to pick up Mack from school, so she made herself a grilled cheese sandwich for lunch and headed south to Wellesley. She tapped her fingers against the steering wheel as she listened to loud, fast techno music. Her thoughts wandered to her new lover, and she caught herself speeding while projecting images of a future together, which extended beyond the bedroom. On the short drive, most of the traffic lights were green when she came up to them, but in her mind flashed a yellow light—*be careful*, she told herself—then a red light. *Stop.* She would make herself stay in the present tense; avoiding romantic time travel might be her best defense, since she was already thinking of Pete as more than sex.

Her investigation today was a mixed bag: some people were cooperative, some doors never opened, some opened partway and then were closed again, and still others were slammed in her face. Based on the look in people's eyes when she mentioned the client's husband's name, Fiona believed he had, in fact, physically abused her—or at the very least, screamed at her loudly enough for the people in nearby houses to hear. All in a day's work, she told herself. She finished earlier than expected and had time to kill before going to Mack's school.

The concupiscent state she'd been left in after making love last night and again this morning had never really gone away. It was a backdrop for the whole day, and she found herself in such a carnal state as she drove that she decided to take a detour through Brookline and hit a sex toy shop she knew of there. She found parking right out front, pushed open the door, and ambled in. The smell of Good Vibrations always turned her on: cyberskin, lube, and a faint trace of leather. Her panties were damp and clung to her shaven parts, which rubbed pleasantly against the center seam of her jeans as she walked. She took in the shelves and floor displays full of glittering temptations, not sure what she wanted to add to her collection. She recognized one of the clerks from the last time she'd been in and smiled a wordless hello. The young woman had short, spiky, dyed red hair and wore a black leather dog collar studded with spikes. Fiona imagined her look stood out amid the good people of Brookline.

She wasn't finding that special something to treat herself to and noticed her gait became predatory as she rolled her hips past the handful of patrons, boldly assessing them with her magnetic gaze. It was as if the other customers could sense on an animal level that she was someone they should look at. Maybe it was simply a matter of pheromones, but in any case, the shoppers looked up from whatever packaging they were reading and made eye contact with her. She still didn't see anything she wanted until she came upon a couple about ten years her junior who were having a conversation about which type of lube to buy.

"That one in your hand," Fiona interrupted assertively, "is the best I've ever used. It's great for boys or girls." Her provocative remark did what she intended it to, and the young man's eyes panned slowly from her head to her boots before he replied.

"Good to know. Thanks for the info. What, exactly, do you like about it?" His female companion looked up at him, her expression a mix of shock and intrigue, and then she surveyed the outspoken woman in front of them.

"Feels good, tastes good, is good." Fiona took a step closer to them and extended her hand to the woman, who was considerably shorter than her male companion, full-figured, and pretty. "I'm Fiona. And I'm sure I've just interrupted something very private."

"How private can you be in a sex store? I mean, if you want private, order online, right? I'm Sophia." She took Fiona's hand and held it warmly before introducing her lover. "This is Mark, and we literally just ran out of lube." Her dark eyes flashed with invitation.

"Yeah. Hi," he offered as he shook her hand. Fiona was standing close enough to smell the sex on them. He was tall and lean with sandy-colored, curly hair and a short beard that accentuated his full lips. He didn't seem to know what else to say, so Sophia took the lead.

"I'm going to buy this. You two just hang and talk. I'll be right back." She looked at Mark, then at their new acquaintance, before turning to go to the register. Since he seemed at a loss for words after his initial daring question to Fiona about the lube, she didn't speak to him and chose body language instead. She took a step toward him and, since his back was practically against the shelves, he had nowhere to retreat to, even if he'd wanted to move away from her. Then she tipped up her chin and kissed him. He was receptive. His lips were warm and luscious, his beard was soft, and the feel of it against her face sent shivers through her body. He kissed back and pushed himself into her. When he slid his tongue in her mouth, Fiona captured it by sucking slowly, which made him instantly hard against her. She throbbed, getting even wetter than she'd been when she'd arrived at the store. Before long, Sophia came up behind her and put a hand on her shoulder, then up on the side of her neck, which she stroked lightly. Fiona turned around, and Sophia kissed her. Mark moved in close behind Fiona, his erection against her ass.

"Our van is parked down the street," he said. Those words, along with the kisses and the feel of them both, were intoxicating to Fiona.

# CHAPTER THREE: SEEING THINGS

*Those who dream by day are cognizant of many things which escape
those who dream only by night.*
*~ Edgar Allan Poe*

Fiona awoke the following morning with a vague feeling of regret as flashbacks from her sexual escapade with the couple from the store played in her mind. She never planned these encounters with strangers, which was part of what made them so exciting. She reflected on a passage from the Sex Addicts Anonymous green book: *Being hit with the obsession to act out is like being engulfed in the bubble. We are powerless and carried away by the all-encompassing power of our compulsions.* Fiona liked the bubble; looking out at the inevitable ordinariness of everyday life through its slick transparent film, the world seemed more exciting to her. She reasoned that having sex with strangers would always hold her interest; it would prevent her life from feeling like a series of routines. She stretched her arms out as she pondered this and looked up at the ceiling for a moment before waking Mack and starting their weekday morning drill.

Mack was fussy and determined to pick out his own outfit for school.

"But it's my turn to pick your clothes out, Mack—you know what our agreement is," Fiona said sternly to her son, who stood with his arms folded across his chest, wearing only his briefs and one sock. His face was clenched in more defiance than one would expect from a seven-year-old. But, as Fiona was reminded on a daily basis, her child was a unique bird.

"But it's Friday free day at school, and it doesn't feel too free to have you tell me what to wear instead of me telling me what to wear. It's just not right for Friday free day."

"Mack Theodore Angeli," she cautioned, "the way the math works out is that every other Friday lands on a day you dress yourself, and the ones in between fall on my day to tell you what to wear. So your once-a-month special Fridays at school can fall either way."

He relaxed his frown a bit as he considered the logic of this before responding. "I accept the reality of this, Mom. I just don't like it today."

"I know, honeybug. Tell you what—you can pick the restaurant tonight, okay?"

"We're eating out? Any place I want?"

"Within reason, yes. And we have a special guest; my new friend is going to join us and stay over again."

His heart-shaped face bore no trace of dissatisfaction now. In fact, it was bright. "Her dog too?"

"Yes," she answered as she bent down and started helping him into clothes that matched.

"Yay!" He studied her before he spoke again, his brown eyes just inches from her face. "I can dress myself."

"I know, Mack. Moms just like to do stuff for their kids because we're used to helping, and it's just the giant love we have inside our hearts showing on the outside—you know?" He answered her in tickles to her midsection. They laughed together and then made their way to the kitchen for breakfast. After she poured the milk in his cereal, she sat down and sent a tender text message.

*Less than twelve hours till my lips puzzle piece with yours...xo Fi*

She wished she had a picture. She'd almost taken one yesterday morning while Pete was sleeping. Fiona closed her eyes and tried to frame her image from memory but pixels kept shifting. She daydreamed about this intriguing woman while Mack slurped his food, paying no attention to her. The toaster popped, snapping her back to reality.

She buttered her toast, poured half a cup of coffee, and before long saw Mack holding the bowl to his mouth with two hands, tipping his head back to drain the last drop of milk. Her phone vibrated on the counter with a response.

*Many Xs and Os await us!*

"Done!" announced Mack. He handed her his empty blue bowl and tucked in his chair as he'd been trained to do. She may have an unusually conceived child with a high IQ and a wild woman for a mother, but she was bound and determined to make sure he had good manners.

Fiona finished eating and then drove Mack to school, where she walked him past the other kids and parents. She loved how involved families were in general at Adams Elementary, and was grateful to have her son in a charter school with a program that could handle his mental bandwidth. "Have a blast, Professor MacProfessor," she said before she bent down and kissed him good-bye. He threw his arms around her neck and kissed her cheek; he smelled like milk and excitement.

Since she was working at home again today, she had the option of grocery shopping for the weekend now, rather than in the late afternoon before grabbing Mack; it would be less crowded. She loathed food shopping. The lights were too bright, and the air too cold. She dreamed of having a sizable vegetable garden, some beehives, and maybe chickens. She wished she'd paid more attention all those years her mother was canning fruits and vegetables. Fiona wanted Mack to grow up with a connection to his food that looked different than a reusable grocery sack full of packaged goods. But her yard in Cambridge was tiny, and this sustainable kind of life was too ambitious for a single mother; she needed a partner.

She finished the shopping, and on the drive home, thought she heard her faithful old Honda talking to her with a strange new knocking noise and wondered if Calvin was right about her needing a more modern vehicle. She didn't want to think of the cost right now, so she did the exact wrong thing and turned the radio up over the sound. Fiona liked the beat of the high-energy dance music and tapped her long fingers against the steering wheel; this station always made her speed. The singer oozed some dirty lyrics that made her think of sex and how amazing it felt when bodies collided.

It was only after she'd brought all the groceries in that she saw a missed call on her cell phone from her big brother, Anthony. He'd left a message, which she played on speaker.

*Hey Fi, it's me. Call me when you get this. I got some shit goin' on and I need to talk to my baby sis. Love you, big top.*

His usual jovial baritone was heavy with sadness; only the Maine accent sounded like him. That big heart of his was aching, she could tell. He was the firstborn, just two years older than Fiona. Her parents had taken turns naming their children to represent both their heritages: Anthony, Fiona, Francesca, and Liam. Fiona was closest to Anthony, who'd always been loyal, generous, and affectionate. She adored her little brother too, but like the boys in the family, she couldn't connect with her sister much at all. Growing up, they exhibited none of the closeness many sisters seem to have. Fiona marveled at how different their sister's emotional hardwiring was, compared to the rest of them.

Even Francesca's looks seemed to underscore this contrast; she didn't resemble any of them. Everyone but Francesca had some physical trait that connected them to the Angeli/McCauley line. Anthony had the same turquoise eyes as Fiona but with black hair and dark skin; Liam was blessed with the red hair he shared with his mother and older sister and had brown eyes. In contrast, Francesca had light brown hair that hung limp and straight, her complexion was freckled, and her eyes were gold and green. She actually resembled a neighboring family in their southern Maine town enough that teachers used to ask her if she was related to them. Their father would say Francesca was an exact replica of a great-aunt from Torino, but truly she was the odd girl out in every way. Fi and her brothers used to joke that their mother stepped out on Anthony Sr. and Francesca was the result of some affair. The older they all got, the more Fiona wondered if there was any truth to this. One day, she would have to get up the guts to ask her mother about that, or at least drop a hint and test the waters, since her mother could deflect any insinuation with her perfected impenetrable denial.

After she put all the groceries away, she called her brother.

"Oh, I'm so glad you called, Fi. You got time to talk? This might take a while."

"Of course I have time for you, big bro. Spill."

"You sure? I know it's a workday for you."

"Yes. I'm all yours," she said sweetly. She walked out into her backyard and sat in an old metal chair on the deck. She watched one squirrel chase another along the top of the fence. They moved like drawings in a flipbook, with herky-jerky stop motion. The neighbor's tabby cat slowly climbed a maple tree near the fence for a better view.

"It's Dawn." He let the words out like air from a deflating tire. "She's leaving me."

"What the *fuck*?"

"I know, that's what I said. Hit me like a brick. We were in the kitchen cleaning up after dinner, and I went to kiss her, and she pulled away and just said *don't*. So I stopped and asked why. Then she blurted out that she was leaving me."

"Oh Anthony. Jesus. Fuck. Why?"

He went on to explain in full detail how his wife of ten years had been cheating on him with their mechanic. The affair had apparently been an off-and-on thing throughout their marriage. It devastated him not because he himself had always been faithful to her, or because he was still very much in love with her, but because he thought he'd made her happy all these years, and his contentment with her now felt counterfeit. He felt like he was sleepwalking through his own life, or living it with an imposter. He didn't know who he was anymore. Anthony had chosen to stay in Cundy's Harbor and help his parents with the family fishing operation and restaurant. He'd lived there all his life. He was the steady guy, the reliable one, the man who married his first love and would have stayed by her side for the duration.

"Are you going to fight for your marriage or end it?" she asked softly.

"What marriage? As far as I'm concerned, I was the only one in a marriage. I love her but I'm not going to try to save something that she killed a long time ago..." He ran out of words shaped like his pain.

"I'm sorry you're hurting. If I were there, I'd give you a great big hug and bake you your favorite chocolate cake."

He chuckled. Sweets were his downfall and had contributed to his weight gain. Anthony was far from fat, but he'd lost the swimmer's physique that had the girls calling the house regularly when he was in high school. "That sounds great, but I've been cutting back. I didn't like seeing the number thirty-eight on my jeans."

"But you're six foot three. You need some meat on you! Besides, any guy as sweet as you needs his sweets. Hey—you should come visit Mack and me. He'd love that. Come!"

"I don't know. It's still our busy season for another month or so—"

"You're coming for an extended visit—I decided," she cut him off. They talked about it, and he said he would drive down in October and stay for a few weeks; he agreed it would be good for him to get away while the divorce ran its ugly course through the small town and the small talk.

Fiona finished folding the laundry while talking with him on speaker. She took the large basket to the bedrooms to put the clothes away. On the way out of Mack's room, her eyes caught a family photo in the hallway that featured her and Anthony side-by-side and grinning, sitting in a small rowboat. He was a tall ten, and she just a skinny eight. Her hair was long and unruly, and his was not as wavy as it was now. The pink-and-green flowered bathing suit she wore in the picture was the same one she'd almost drowned in the summer before.

Their mother had been pregnant with Liam, and they were at a McCauley family reunion in Connecticut. It was late afternoon, and the various adult cousins, aunts, uncles, and second cousins were mellowed from alcohol and lax about childcare. An hour earlier, Cousin Ted's pool had been filled with family splashing about in the July heat, but now it was empty. Fiona's small feet were hot, so she walked away from the yard where everyone was sitting and wandered out of view. She sat down on the edge of the deep end and kicked her legs slowly in the cool water one at a time, making a happy rhythm in the blue. She liked how the water distorted her feet and was staring at them, trying to wiggle more to make them look weirder. Suddenly, she heard her younger cousin, Christopher, running on the concrete along the pool. He had chocolate ice cream in the corners of his mouth and was laughing to himself about something. Fiona had been Francesca's big sister for a while now and so felt a sense of responsibility for this little guy too. She told him authoritatively to slow down and then turned to look back at her feet.

Without warning she felt his hands push on her back. "Swim!" he commanded with a giggle as she hit the water and sank down below the surface in the part of the pool where her feet couldn't touch. Her mouth gaped to call for help and filled with water. Fiona's eyes stung as she opened them and tried to reach for the edge of the pool. Her limbs flailed in violent panic, and she was terrified of dying. Thrashing hard, she opened her eyes in blurred blue panic and swallowed some of the water because she was too terrified to close her mouth. She was about to give up and just sink to the bottom when she felt hands on her back again; this time they were her brother's as he swam beneath her, pushing her from behind, then shoved her up toward the air. The cloudless sky looked like life itself to her as she coughed and gasped. Anthony had one arm around her chest and, with the other, paddled to the edge of the pool. She remembered landing hard on the warm concrete and him reassuring her over and over: "You're okay, Fi. You're okay. I got you."

Her memory then flashed forwards seven years to when it had been her turn to save his life. Like most teenagers, Anthony had discovered alcohol and hadn't yet learned about safe limits of consumption. Francesca and Liam were sound asleep, and Fiona had been left in charge while their parents went out on a rare "date." Anthony was supposed to be home by 11, but it was almost midnight when he stumbled in the front door singing off-key. Fiona shushed him and saw he was drunk. Their parents weren't heavy drinkers—they'd only ever gotten buzzed on red wine around their kids—but she knew what drunk was from seeing it on television.

He smelled like sweat and whiskey, and she couldn't believe he'd even made it home on his bicycle without having an accident. His voice was too loud as he told her about the party and how his buddy Carl's older brother had bought them whiskey and beer. He lamented that there weren't enough girls there, and was mumbling about someone named Melanie Kurzweil. Apparently, she was his *objet d'amour* and was expected at the party but didn't show. He must have said her name four times before they even left the kitchen. Fiona listened and walked with him as he went upstairs to his room, staggered in, and then flopped down on his bed. He lay on his back with his hands clasped behind his head and looked up at the ceiling. "Those glow-in-the-dark stars up there need to go. I'm too old for them now," he slurred before he closed his eyes and promptly fell asleep.

Fiona went downstairs to finish cleaning the kitchen before her parents returned home. A Nirvana song was playing from a small radio the family liked to have on while doing dishes. A few counters to wipe down, then up to bed. She was about to go into her room at the end of the wallpapered hallway when she heard the gagging. By the time she got to him, his face was covered in vomit and he was semiconscious, making piteous muffled sounds in his throat. Fiona knew he could choke to death on his own puke and immediately got her hands underneath him to prop him up. His deadweight was heavy to lift, but somehow she managed and kept him upright for several minutes until it was all out of his system. It took her almost an hour to get him cleaned up, his bedding changed, and the odor cleared out of the room. She sat on the footlocker at the end of his bed and watched him sleep on his side until she heard her parents' station wagon in the driveway.

She loved her brother so much, and never took their history or connection for granted. Her thoughts then shifted to Pete.

She thought Anthony would like her new lover. He might not get her, but he would probably see why Fiona and Mack did. She'd tell him about Pete when the shock over his impending divorce wasn't so new, before he visited them. *Yellow light*; she caught herself assuming they would still be together next month, and her flight response spoke from a corner of her mind. She would shed the embarrassment of hope by throwing herself into her work for the day.

After several hours of sitting still in front of the computer, she couldn't bear it anymore and got up to stretch. Stretching led to pacing, pacing led to silent dancing. Fiona was dancing her ass off to an inaudible beat—it was just something she'd done since she was a kid. Mack had been initiated into the silent dancing club years ago, one evening when she and Calvin started boogieing spontaneously at the same time, refusing to stop until Mack joined in. His reluctance gave way to curiosity, and after tapping his feet for a minute, he just went for it with some dramatic dance moves that were slightly behind the beat she and Calvin had found together. Now Fiona gyrated and bounced wildly as her arms flailed and her ass shook. She realized she was way ahead of schedule, so she decided to vent her restlessness by visiting Calvin before his shift started.

He loved when she just dropped by. She was his only friend who did that and the only one he would want to stop in unannounced. He greeted her with a hearty hug and immediately asked about her recent adventure.

"How's the lady with the man's name?"

"Funny. I don't think of it as a man's name, but it is. Well, my friend, she is all curvy, delicious girlie..." Fiona sat on the couch, squeezed her thighs together, and savored a flashback from yesterday.

"You're tainting my afternoon with vagina," he said in mock disgust.

"You'll live."

"I know. I'd just prefer to live in a world less vaginal..." Calvin was so Calvin, which was why she loved him. "So, could this maybe be something more than sex?" He arched his brows in anticipation of her answer and stared at her with his eyes wide. She stared right back, wondering why men always seemed to have the longest eyelashes, before answering.

"All I know is that yesterday morning she stayed in my mind after she walked out my front door. And maybe a little in my heart..."

"Wow. Hope I get to meet her. If you two keep hooking up, I know you're going to be cocooned for a while, but if you want to toss her into some social salad—I'm there."

Fiona tried to imagine Pete and Calvin meeting for the first time, knowing the best-friend test was one that not all new lovers passed. It wasn't that Fiona needed Calvin's approval; the only person in her life who must approve all new residents of her heart was her son. And so far, so good on that front.

"Hey—I was just going to make a turkey and Swiss cheese sandwich. Want one?"

"Yes, actually. I forgot to have lunch. I think my brother's call distracted me. He's getting divorced."

"What? He and Dawn are splitting up? I thought they were in it forever. What happened?"

Fiona unfolded the short version of the sad tale while Calvin listened attentively. He could see that she was sad about her big brother and tried to take her mind off him.

"Wanna hear the latest adventure from your local male prostitute?"

"Oh, why not! Please share," Fiona commanded.

"I was paid ridiculously well to pretend to be a high school football player for an older client of mine out in Newton. For sixty, Bertrand sure is a horny guy!"

"Good for him. I mean—was it?" She giggled.

"He got his money's worth. Finally turned the corner on a fantasy about a black jock giving it to him. He's wanted that since high school. He's intense about details, so it had to be a maroon-and-gold uniform from the late sixties, I was not to have greasepaint under my eyes, I had to be a little sweaty, oh, and get this—he had a carpenter build him a wooden bench on his back patio just like the one in his high school gym locker room. That's where I did him. Trippy, huh?"

"Some people truly know exactly what they want," Fiona marveled.

"Yeah. Enough work talk." He set the sandwiches and two glasses of sparkling water down on the table and sat next to her.

"So, Mack is super excited to see the dinosaur exhibit! When can I bring him by tomorrow? What works for you?" Fiona asked.

"Let's see—gym in the morning, client, shower, clean the house... How about noon? That gives us plenty of time in the museum. But I have a thing on Sunday at 11, so can you get him at ten? Does that work for you?"

"Work? It's wonderful. That means I can spend a whole afternoon, night, and a bit of a morning with Pete without having to be a hands-on mommy. I'm so grateful that you're his queen funcle. Is your Sunday thing a volunteer gig?"

"Yeah—the soup kitchen in Dorchester. It's kind of a regular thing right now." On one side of the Calvin Campbell coin was a sex worker, on the other a volunteer extraordinaire. When he was growing up in New

York, his parents were active in their church and exposed him and his sisters to volunteer work from an early age. He didn't know any other way to be. Soup kitchens, homeless shelters, hospices—his work varied widely, but the common denominator was people. He cared deeply about human beings and yet could seemingly turn his emotions off when interacting with his tricks. Fiona was pretty sure he'd fallen in love with one long-term client last year, but he repeatedly denied it. At thirty-two, he'd probably helped a thousand people but hadn't lived with one lover. She knew he had her and Mack, but wanted him to have more.

"Very cool. When do you think Mack might be old enough to start doing volunteer work?"

"Now. I was younger than he is now when we went to that veterans' hospital in Brooklyn. With Mack, it has to be the right sort of work, because he thinks too much. He might get too upset by people's situations, or have so many logical questions about the illogically tragic stories some people live that he's too overwhelmed to help. Maybe his first volunteer experience should be really simple and straightforward. I don't think he should work directly with people. Maybe do something basic and instantly rewarding like a beach cleanup, instead of getting tangled up in people."

"You're a wise man, Cal. That makes a lot of sense. Maybe we can all do a beach cleanup together." She enjoyed a few bites of lunch before speaking again. "And hey, those decorating magazines are paying off. This place looks fantastic." She scanned the newly painted walls of his sunny living room, letting her eyes linger on some encaustic paintings he'd recently purchased and hung. They were three small pieces depicting birds on wires. The background colors harmonized beautifully with the gold walls. She spied a small bird sculpture on his bookcase that hadn't been there the last time she was over. She was in complete awe of how a man who kept his place so consistently clean and beautifully appointed could so freely welcome a kid with sticky fingers and a fondness for piling things up on the floor.

They talked a bit more, and then Fiona left. She didn't hear that knocking noise as she drove home, so maybe whatever it was had fixed itself. That was her magical thinking on the matter, anyway. She did a little bit more work before straightening up around the house. Then it was time to pick up the Mackster and think about their evening plans.

☆☆☆

A job completed, a check to put in the bank, and a Friday off before her next job started next week all gave Pete a feeling of satisfaction. She decided to spend the day playing outdoors with Turtle and working on a sculpture. She'd slept later than usual because she could, and because she had been up finishing her latest mystery. Losing herself in the book kept her from obsessing over whether or not to call Fiona. After swinging back and forth a few times, she'd finally settled comfortably enough into the knowledge that they'd made a real connection, and she didn't want Fiona to get a false impression that she was high maintenance, needy, or expected a nightly phone call. Their good-bye Thursday morning had held the promise of more nectarous time together. Pete decided to take Turtle to the dog park early, since the forecast predicted rain in the afternoon.

Once his nose told him where he was walking to, the little guy strained at the end of his leash in a valiant effort to speed up his owner's pace. Windsor Street Dog Park was a favorite spot for Pete and Sheila to meet on weekends. Sheila liked the place because, unlike many parks for canines, it was completely fenced. Romeo, her whippet, was a real wanderer, and the enclosure kept her from getting gray hairs worrying over his whereabouts. Pete liked it because of its moody, industrial surroundings and the fact that most of the dog owners who went there were cool and kept their dogs under control.

Once the gates were closed, Turtle darted in to sniff the two other dogs who were there. Pete nodded a hello to a regular who stood smiling, holding a cup of coffee in her hands as she watched the trio romp in the brisk late-morning air. Although Pete felt slight pressure to be social with her and the other dog owner who sat on a nearby bench, she resisted and, instead, did what she really wanted to: walk around, watch the dogs, and relax without having to interact with a human pack. The gravel crunched under her boots as she walked the perimeter, hands buried in her coat pockets. In her left one was a ball she took out and tossed for Turtle. He let one of the other canines take it from him, but then reclaimed it and brought it back to Pete for more. Times like this calmed her mind, and slowed her racing thoughts. As she threw the ball maybe two dozen times, Fiona's face flashed in her mind. Though she relished the memory of their time together, Pete tried to guard against obsession by consciously thinking about the sculpture she would work on when she and Turtle returned home.

As she circled back toward the entrance, she caught Bench Guy looking away from his chocolate lab and checking out Coffee Girl. He was slouched a bit, extending his legs out to the sides and knocking his knees together the way some guys did when they had hard-ons or some type of sexual restlessness. His eyes were fixed on the girl, but she didn't notice because her gaze was still on her athletic, shaggy-haired mixed breed. Pete knew he was taking her out of the dog park to his nearby loft and undressing her. Hell, they both apparently had Friday mornings off from whatever they did for a living, so they might as well share the time slot and cheat on their spouses together. Pete seldom missed little things, especially if they were shiny, like the wedding bands they each wore. When she was little, she earned the nickname Eagle Eye from her mother after she'd found a five-dollar bill, a silver half dollar, and a large gold ring all in the same week. Eagle Eye Orvatch saw the distinct gleam of lust in the man's large, dark, almost brooding eyes and marveled at how oblivious the female park-goer was.

Other shiny things, like Mrs. Robot's spark for life, the cool metal handcuffs in Fiona's bag, the minuscule but lustrous toy pistol she'd taken from the job yesterday, and the polish of Fiona's impossibly turquoise eyes claimed her full attention. Fiona's face was filling her mind again now, so she aggressively returned to her narrative. One morning, perhaps even this one, Bench Guy would approach Coffee Girl to talk about their dogs, and he would stand too close, maybe lick his lips a few times while speaking, weave witty remarks, and slip in an innocent yet flirtatious compliment. She would be flattered, and though he was not her type physically, she would be drawn to his attraction for her. She would soak in the attention, and his charm would evolve into something more potent over the course of their conversation. She would find herself asking him to point out which of the nearby loft complexes he lived in and imagining what the inside looked like. He would say how their dogs got along great and would probably like to spend more time together. They would leash them up and leave together, having decided to shed their own fetters by committing adultery.

Turtle's panting snapped her back into the moment. He'd had enough exercise for now and studied her, his intensely intelligent terrier eyes in stark contrast to the cartoonishly long tongue hanging out of his mouth. It was time to go. As she latched the gate behind them, Pete saw the man walking up to the woman and smiled to herself.

On the walk back to her warehouse, Pete's camera brain revisited the other items in Fiona's bag: pepper spray, a worn old leather wallet, a light blue scarf, a balled-up pair of panties, what looked like a bottle of lube, and something small and shiny that she couldn't quite figure out. The pepper spray meant Fiona wanted to be able to protect herself, the wallet said she didn't mind the patina of age and wear, the blue scarf was to accentuate her eyes, the panties perhaps had been taken off for comfort? For recent sex? Sex involving handcuffs? Maybe they weren't even hers... Fiona might have been a woman with a real and potentially dangerously predatory libido.

These thoughts replayed in various versions and folded in on themselves all the way back. Pete approached her workbench, where the partially completed mixed-media three-dimensional piece was. It was about three feet high and roughly triangular in shape. Its frame was made of dozens of pieces of silverware welded together, and attached to most of that skeleton were old book covers and random small *tchotchkes*. Scattered around it were various objects, including the weapon Robot Jr.'s tiny action figure would never fire again. She enjoyed how it fit into the piece, and wondered if the little boy would even notice it was missing.

☆☆☆

"This was probably one of the better Friday free days so far this year, Mom," Mack chirped from the backseat.

"What made it good, sweetie?" Fiona thought she heard the knocking noise start again.

"The choices we had were fun ones. I spent the morning in the build-a-room, and after lunch, I was in the science lab doing experiments with light. You know how Harry Potter has an invisibility cloak?"

"Of course!" At almost eight, Mack had finished all of the books. The first few Fiona read aloud to him, but the others he dove into voraciously and inhaled with surprising speed.

"Well, we did a light-bending experiment that taught us about refraction, which is how a cloak like that maybe could work."

"That's very cool, babe." As she drove through Cambridge, he described in detail how they used a jar of water, a shoebox, and a flashlight to bend light. He explained with expertise that when light enters the water it slows and bends, and when the light exits the water it speeds up and bends again.

"What were you making in the build-a-room?" She knew it was dangerous to take her eyes off the road to look at him for too long in the rearview, but guessed that every parent did this occasionally. She exercised restraint, enjoying the sound of him, and waited until she was stopped at a red light to study her animated little boy in the mirror. Mack was the joy of her life, and having him was the best decision she'd ever made.

"We had to design and build birdhouses. But I had to work with other kids when I just wanted to do my own. They *made* me do group work," he lamented.

"It's good for you, Mackles. We talked about this. I understand that you have your own ideas about how to do things, but we are all surrounded by people throughout our lives, and we need to know how to listen to suggestions."

"But what if their ideas won't work and you *know* they won't work and *your* ideas *will* work and their ideas are just a waste of time?" His pitch rose as he asked this.

"Sometimes even ideas that won't work are worth hearing. All information is useful. You'll understand this more as you get older." *He may be smarter than his mother*, she reasoned to herself, *but he needs my wisdom*. She wanted to change the topic, because he was getting stuck, and she didn't have the energy to unstick him. "Have you thought about where you want to take our new friend to eat tonight?"

"Yes," he said, "Patrick's Pizza. We haven't been there in a while, and it's so delicious!"

"Sounds great. I'm sure she likes pizza. Who doesn't like pizza?" There were so many things she didn't know about her new companion and, being a detective at heart, she wanted to discover as much as she could about her; she longed to look in every corner, even the ones where the light didn't shine. Fiona had resisted the urge to use her work access to background information, but she did search on Facebook and a few other social media sites yesterday. No one with Pete's name turned up, and Fiona wondered if she used a different name, like she herself did, or had chosen to opt out altogether.

They pulled into their driveway, and Mack jumped out. "Backpack? Lunchbox inside?"

"Yes." He was surprisingly agreeable when Fiona told him he needed to take a bath before they went out. He told her all about the birdhouse he wanted to build, and when she asked about the one his group built, he said it wasn't interesting enough to talk about. Fiona filled the tub and went into his room to lay out some clothes for him. The glow-in-the-dark stars on his ceiling caught her eye, and she thought again of Anthony. She wanted to call Dawn and serve her up a slice of nasty but knew it wouldn't make anything better. The only thing that would heal him was time. It was time to text Pete and make a plan.

*When can you come out and play with us?*
*Hi gorgeous! Earliest I can b at your house is 6:30.*
*OK. Come then and we'll go out for pizza and a stroll. Sound good?*
*Yes.*

Now it was Fiona's turn to shower and change. At thirty-six going on thirty-seven, she had the body of a twenty-five-year-old. Pregnancy hadn't changed her figure, only left behind a few stretch marks on her belly and breasts. She took pride in her appearance and, if pushed, would admit she liked the attention she got for her looks, but never put much time into it all. She liked to think of herself as a wash-and-wear girl. When she was growing up, her mother pressured her to emphasize her beauty, to capitalize on it, to manipulate her fate with it. Audrey McCauley had been a stunner in her day, and her brush with glamour was that she had been Miss Connecticut, 1968. Raising four kids and working hard in the family business had faded her around the edges, but her bone structure was striking, and there was no denying her beauty. At sixty-three, she still turned heads with her tiny waistline, flawless skin, grace, and infectious smile. The last time she was visiting her folks, Fiona teased her mother about a waiter who couldn't have been older than forty, who was flirting with her shamelessly. When Fiona was young, her mother's fuss over her looks bothered her, not just because it wasn't who she wanted to be but also because Francesca never received the same consideration.

She wanted to look good tonight, but not like she was trying to. It was another mild day, but the evening would be cooler. She chose a long-sleeved, gauzy white blouse, the jeans that hugged her ass just right, and her favorite cowboy boots, which she'd worn on that fateful Wednesday. Fiona sat at the edge of her bed, looked into the large mirror on the wall, and put on some small silver hoop earrings and one of her many heart necklaces. Her mind flooded suddenly with romantic thoughts. She lay on her back, stretching out for a while as fantasies played in her head. The reverie was cut short by the call to parent.

"Mom? Can I bring my scooter for the walk? I can't decide if I want to have my scooter or my yo-yo with me. You know how I don't like to just plain walk. I gotta be doing something."

"Even if you have a dog to walk with? You still need something that moves?" She sat up and opened her arms, signaling him to come for a hug. He walked to her and leaned in.

"You smell nice," he complimented.

"Good, I try!" Every time she bathed, she scented herself with natural oils, and tonight's fragrance was orange. Mack buried his nose in her tresses, sighed, and looked up at her thoughtfully.

"Mom, I *really* love you."

The words surprised her. The two of them hugged for close to a minute before she offered a solution.

"Why don't we put your scooter and your yo-yo in the car, so you have choices?"

"Okay. And my helmet." As he shuffled out of the room in bare feet, she asked him to get his socks and sneakers on and comb his hair. It was six and soon her mysterious lover would arrive. Fiona couldn't wait to feel those big hands on her.

☆☆☆

It was Mack who greeted Pete and Turtle at the door, because Fiona was in the bathroom. He hugged the dog to him and squeezed lightly until Turtle wiggled free to circle around him a few times, tail wagging rapidly. "Hi, Pete! Mom's in the bathroom. She keeps going in there. I think she's trying to do something with her hair. She does stuff, but it always looks the same to me." Pete chuckled and didn't know whether or not to hug him. Her answer came in the form of two small arms reaching out to her.

"How goes it, Mack?" Pete asked warmly. Her face was bright, emanating joy. She, too, had spent a little extra time on her coiffure. She'd let it grow longer than it had been in months, and it needed a little styling; she managed to subdue it tonight with ample product. Grandma Sweets used to say her hair was where the Cree blood in the family ended up, and that she had to make peace with the stubbornness of it.

"It goes. I go, you go, he, she, it goes. *Yo voy, tu vas, él, ella va.*" Following this unexpected burst of Spanish, he scampered off after Turtle, who'd let himself outside through the open sliding glass doors.

Pete slipped her jacket off and put it on the back of a kitchen chair. She was standing there watching the boy and dog play when Fiona pressed into her from behind, her arms around her waist. She squeezed tightly, and before Pete could turn and face her, she nibbled her earlobe lightly and kissed her on the neck.

"Mmmmmm," Pete turned to take her in. Fiona was delicious, perfect; she wondered how she could be this lucky.

"Hey, you, give us a kiss," Fiona requested with a smile. They experienced the gravitational pull that lovers do, gazing at each other's eyes and mouths longingly before flesh met flesh.

"You look even better than I remembered," Pete oozed, "really. Did you fluff up your hair a bit? It seems more wavy, I like it." She cupped Fiona's face in her hands and let one wander in the cascades of dark red silk.

"Looks like you did a li'l somethin' somethin' with your hair too, huh?"

Pete laughed softly in response. "I got a great hug from that son of yours."

"I'm not surprised. He took to you right off the bat, which is usually not his style." She pulled away, but let her extended index finger trail down the length of Pete's arm until their hands met and clasped. Then Fiona led her out to the yard. "Hi, Turtle boy! How's my good boy?" The sweetness in her voice made Pete melt. Apparently, she had the same effect on Turtle, who ran to her and placed his scruffy white head under her outstretched hand.

Before long, all four of them headed toward East Cambridge in Fiona's car. Turtle leaned against Mack, who was perched atop his booster seat, and sniffed the air coming in the back window. In the front, Pete's hand was on Fiona's thigh. When she could, Fiona stole side-glances at her date. Pete was aware she was being keenly observed, but kept her eyes forwards, enjoying the subtle scent of orange; this woman was a garden.

"How was work today?" Fiona ventured.

"Had the day off, so I played with Turtle a lot and finished a sculpture," Pete let her hand move lightly over the curve of her lover's leg. Mack started humming a tune that seemed familiar to Pete, and she tried to place it as Fiona spoke.

"When do I get to see these sculptures of yours?"

"Anytime you want to come over. But I'm warning you, they're an acquired taste," Pete said with a trace of self-consciousness. They were at a red light near Mass Avenue, so Fiona turned to face her full-on.

"Well, I've definitely acquired a taste for you..."

"Lucky me," Pete teased. Then she finally figured where the tune was from, an old Band-Aids commercial from the late eighties, and started humming with him. So random, she loved this kid. Where the hell did he hear that?

"I feel left out—I don't know the tune," said Fiona. She tried to catch on, but never really got anchored in the melody, and then it ended. Pete turned to look over her shoulder at Mack and gave him a thumbs-up. He returned her gesture. Fiona glanced at him in the rearview and then back at Pete with visible satisfaction.

They left Turtle in the car with a chew toy Pete pulled from her bag. The air had cooled, and they parked him in the shade with the windows partly down for his comfort. He'd rejoin them for a nice long walk along the river after dinner. Fiona remarked on what a well-trained and easy little dog he was.

Patrick's Pizza was a large, festive restaurant in an old brick building like so many in Boston. Its prominent arched windows, high ceilings, and interesting decor were inviting; vintage racing bicycles were suspended in the air and anchored to the walls. Mack memorized the names of all of them after his first time eating there and liked to sit by his favorite Bianchi. The owner was a friendly baby boomer named Patrick Rizzo, whose passion for cycling was second only to his love of cooking. Unlike many restaurateurs, he actually cooked there often, making the pizza himself and chatting up customers. The first time Fiona and her son came in, he had guessed that, like him, Fiona was half-Italian and half-Irish, and joked about this particular cultural hybrid being crazy from the Irish temper and the Italian passion.

"My favorite table isn't free," chimed Mack. "Can we wait?"

Fiona didn't miss a beat. She was an attentive parent who loved her son, but she tried not to be indulgent. "Nah, we're hungry and besides, you can see that Bianchi from other tables."

Mack just stared at her.

Pete took a chance. "Any table is a good table to eat pizza on!" She smiled down at Mack, whose expression remained neutral.

"Actually, our usual table is the best one, but you don't know that because you haven't sat there. It's right under the 1965 Bianchi Mr. Rizzo was riding in the Tour de France. The one he had an accident on—it has scrapes in the paint..." Fiona looked at Pete as if to apologize with her eyes, and Pete wondered if he was headed to the land of tantrum, as his mother had warned about.

"Mack, while we are standing here discussing this, we're keeping an awesome little dog waiting in the car longer. He's okay in there, but he'd like us to come and take him for a walk sooner rather than later. That's why we're going to sit over here," Fiona said as she led him by the hand.

"Oh. I don't want Turtle to get lonely..." He studied the blue Peugeot on the wall. Pete wondered how mothers found the energy to manage children, and noticed with admiration that Fiona's patient expression remained unchanged.

During dinner, the women heard in detail about the different tools Mack had used at school today. But he didn't dominate the conversation, Fiona didn't let him. She inserted questions for Pete, trying to shift focus. She hoped her modeling of a polite verbal exchange would not go unnoticed by her son. He joined in with questions and wanted to know what Turtle was like when he was a puppy, or as he put it, *when he was my age*. The conversation flowed smoothly, and the pizza was so delicious they easily finished the whole pie.

The dog was thrilled to see them return and thumped his tail so hard his whole body wiggled. Pete gave him water from a container she'd brought and then let him out of the car while Fiona opened the trunk and asked Mack, "Scooter or yo-yo, sir?"

"Yo-yo. Then I can stay close to Turtle better. The scooter would be too fast."

They made their way from Mass Avenue to Memorial Drive to walk alongside the Charles River. Pete caught herself walking fast and made herself slow down. Turtle trotted out in front happily, and Mack walked beside him with the women a few feet back. He paused his yo-yoing to pet Turtle and talked to him, not seeming to mind that it was a one-sided conversation.

"So," Fiona mused. "What's your favorite color?"

"What leads you to ask this random question, my dear?"

"I don't know much about you, and I thought it was as good a place as any to start." The sky became more dramatic, and the last pink sunlight of the day painted her face as she spoke.

"Gray. I know that might seem like a weird favorite color, but I'm weird."

"No, I get it, goes with everything. Neutral. Also—there are all kinds of grays: green-grays, blue-grays, and brown-grays."

Pete smiled and buttoned up her denim jacket a little, fussed with her collar, and ran her hand through her hair. "Does he take after you or—" She paused and searched for the right words. "Or the other half of his DNA?"

"The brilliance must have come from his father, but that's a long story—besides, I'm focusing on you right now. Gray. Mine is brown; it's so earthy and unsung. Black gets all the attention, but brown is better. So, you grew up in Springfield, but came here for college and then stayed because you liked it? Did I get that right?"

"Yeah, Springfield to me just felt like a dead end and not the greatest place to be different in, you know?"

"I know. Maine was beautiful to grow up in, but not cosmopolitan by any means. Boston's got more layers to it than most people know about, and we're not too far from the folks, right? You said your mom is a widow?"

"Yes, my dad died from a heart attack when I was ten, and my mother never remarried, or dated much, for that matter. But she's a bit nutty," Pete said before looking down at her boots, noticing their strides extended in perfect rhythm with each other. Turtle paused to pee on a tree. "I'm not being unkind. It's one of *my* long stories."

"Sorry about your dad; that must have been hard on you and your brother." Fiona reached for Pete's free hand and held it. "Rudolph, right?"

"You've got a good memory," Pete said as she leaned in a little bit just to inhale her. "You have three siblings, correct?"

"Right. Two brothers and a sister. Actually, my big brother, Anthony, is coming for a visit next month. Poor guy called me today." Fiona lowered her voice even though Mack was clearly lost in dog land. "His wife is leaving him. Their whole marriage was a sham because she was hooking up with another guy the entire time. I can't believe it. I really love Dawn too, but now she's just as bad as some of the people I investigate."

"That's sad. Don't get married if you're going to cheat. Some people are selfish and want what they perceive as security, but not at the cost of their freedom, I guess. Ouch."

"Yeah, wait till you meet him. He's a sweetie, and the family member I'm closest to. He's a rock."

"Does he look like you?" Pete asked.

"Yes and no. He has black hair and gets brown in the sun, but people say our eyes are the same."

"Lucky guy." Pete planted a tender kiss on her cheek without missing a step. The sun was lower now, and the Cambridge sky was beginning to turn that special blue that happens as day trades places with night. Many people were out strolling, enjoying the mild evening. Mack said something to a baby in a stroller, but Fiona and Pete couldn't hear. He turned around and spoke to them.

"That's a smart baby. Special powers, I could see them." They nodded.

"You'll get used to him," Fiona said to Pete under her breath.

"Yes, but will you two get used to me?" Pete quipped. Fiona laughed in response and continued with her questions.

"Are you close to Rudolph?"

"No, we were tight when we were little kids, but after my dad passed, he became fixated on being the 'man of the house' and got overly involved with Mom. It's like he went from thirteen to thirty overnight. Right now, I'm fairly sure he's forty going on seventy. He just got so serious and staid and, well... I probably sound harsh, but he's sort of an automatic person."

"You mean he lost his instincts?"

"Exactly," Pete affirmed, taking note of Fiona's penetrating insights. "I was close to my dad. We were sort of alike. He's the one who introduced me to making art. After he was gone, my Grandma Sweets moved in and helped us carry on. My mom and I don't really get each other, but my grandmother got everything about me. She was a mother, a mentor, a friend, and full of surprises. She was always teaching me things, like how all living and nonliving things that make up our natural world are connected. She worked hard to pass her ways on to my brother and me, but it was almost as if Rudolph had been vaccinated against them. And Mom *really* clashed with Grandma, just about any way two people could clash. They argued over everything from politics to what color celebrities' eyes were, though they somehow managed to get along well when they cooked together. There were some really colorful arguments. Just imagine a half-Cree under the same roof with an ardent

Catholic..." Pete stopped herself and wondered if she was talking too much. Fiona's eyes looked eager for more.

"Now this is getting interesting," Fiona announced. "So you're part Cree? That explains your fabulous hair!" She let her hand slip out of Pete's and reached up to stroke the back of her head. "I love it! So thick and proud. How did your mom get to be so Catholic?"

"Well, her father's parents, my great-grandparents, were Irish Catholics who felt it was their duty to bring the faith into the home their agnostic son and his First Nations wife were raising their kids in. But it's weird. My mom didn't even get all religious until after my dad died—kind of like the old seeds that were planted in her childhood could finally take root and grow. My dad was culturally Russian Jewish, but didn't believe in any god. Maybe getting all Catholic helped her grieve; all I know is that she was always strange, but she really stopped making sense to me after she hung a picture of John Paul II in the kitchen..."

Just then, an older man walked by and glanced at the three of them, but rested his gaze on Pete before they passed each other. Mack turned back and caught this.

"He's dying," Pete said almost inaudibly. As she looked at him, she saw a large shadow that surrounded his body and obscured his face.

"What?" Fiona asked.

"He's dying," Mack offered with a sympathetic tone. "I see it too, Pete. And I think he knows it."

Pete hadn't even realized she'd said that out loud. She tried to read Fiona's face and thought she saw openness.

"Hey guys, sorry. I didn't mean to say that out loud. I just..." She groped for words, balancing on a tree limb she couldn't know for certain would hold her weight. "I see things..."

"Like baby superpowers?" Mack's face looked almost angelic to Pete as he asked this.

"Yes. Like that. You see stuff too, huh, guy?" Pete asked.

Fiona looked at Pete quizzically and then back at her little boy. He just smiled, turned his face away from them, and resumed his yo-yo tricks contentedly.

"Scaring you off, am I?" Pete said to Fiona tentatively.

"No, I don't scare easily. I'm just taking all this in."

Pete could hear no trace of judgment and would have to take her at her word. Still, she felt exposed and wanted to move forwards from this spot. And that's what they did, the three of them, walking until it was dark. When Fiona asked Mack if he was halfway to tired he responded with a yes, so they turned around and made their way back to the car. Boy and dog both fell asleep on the way home. Mack was so completely out that Fiona skipped the nightly rituals and just carried him to bed, where Turtle was all too happy to join him.

Pete was hoping Fiona wouldn't bring up the incident with the old man, and, as it turned out, talking was not on her agenda. She led Pete by the hand to her room, closed the door, and smiled with delicious hunger. They embraced, leaning into each other so hard they began to sway. They stayed like that for a few minutes, melting into each other, and then began to kiss, first softly, then hard and deep. Clothes came off, and the two women fell onto the bed, but still no words had been exchanged; the only sounds were those of skin meeting skin. Their arousal made them stick and glide with the heat of friction, and they moved against each other so long into the night that they were soaked in each other's sweat.

☆☆☆

The morning light was dim in a cloudy gray sky. The first thing Fiona and Pete heard was Mack singing a song he'd made up about robots:
*Robots will be everywhere, there will be robots to spare.*
*Big and small, they'll work for you, doing what you don't want to.*
*Shiny and smart, they're works of art, but they don't have hearts.*

He sang it several times in a row, louder each time as he got closer to the bedroom door. Fiona pulled the covers tight to their necks because she knew their privacy had ended. "Good morning, Mom Fiona and Miss Pete. Time to get up!" He plopped down on the end of the bed, his shaggy brown hair wild from sleep. "I let Turtle out to do his morning business."

"Thanks, Mack. Very good of you," Pete said groggily. They had only gotten a few hours of sleep. She looked at Fiona and was again astonished by how good she looked in the morning. Her own face was puffy when she first woke up, and her eyes usually got bigger an hour later. Amazingly, Fiona's face showed no signs of fatigue. She was sunshine standing out in the dim light of a day that promised rain.

"Mackenheimer, are you hungry?"

"*Yup!*"

"Why don't you go to the kitchen and take out what we need for pancakes, okay, sweetie?"

"Yeah!" he replied enthusiastically while he slid down from the bed and jogged out of the room, leaving the door wide open behind him.

"Mack? Please come back and close the door. And be careful on that step stool." He popped back in, barked like a dog, and then closed the door. Fiona rolled on top of Pete, kissed her, and said, "Welcome to a mommy's life."

"No complaints here, gorgeous." Reluctantly they dragged themselves out of bed, appreciated the sight of each other briefly, and then talked as they got dressed.

"So, are you tired of me yet?" Fiona nudged.

"Read my mind," Pete said as she stared at her.

"So, I can come over to your place today, then? Because I will be kid-free for almost twenty-four hours and I'd like to spend them with you."

Pete showed how she felt about the prospect with a hug and a kiss.

When they made it to the kitchen, all the ingredients for breakfast had been taken out. Pete was impressed with Fiona for involving her young son in food preparation. He told her he packed his own lunch every morning before school, and he seemed to enjoy cooking with his mother.

"Mom?" Mack said. "Can I play with Turtle outside before it rains?"

"Yes, go. Enjoy!" They fell into an easy rhythm of cooking. Pete sliced the bananas; Fiona made the batter, and then did the flipping. After each one was done, Pete added it to the pile they were keeping warm on the dish in the oven. "So, I'm excited to go to your place today, Pete; we single moms don't get alpha liberty that often," Fiona mused as she handed her the last one.

"*Alpha liberty?*"

"Oh sorry, my brother Liam was in the Marines, and that's the term for when the new recruits can leave base and stay somewhere else overnight."

"Oh, I get it. Well, it's nothing fancy, and not cozy like your place, but I like it." She was somewhat nervous about bringing Fiona home, but didn't want it to show. Fiona whistled, and it was Turtle who made it to the kitchen first, with Mack close behind. They sat and enjoyed breakfast while the clouds outside darkened and gathered more closely together.

"Perfect museum weather, Mack. You and Uncle Calvin can spend hours looking at dinosaurs and not even miss being outside, huh?"

Mack's cheeks were stuffed with food but he managed a muffled "yup" before swallowing and asking a question. "Do you have people fishing work today, Mom?"

"*People fishing*?" Pete asked with curiosity.

"That's what he calls my investigating," Fiona answered, "don't you, honey?"

"Yes! Because the work you do for Sharon helps her catch people like fisherman do."

"Actually, I don't have to work today, so I'm going to spend some more time with Pete. While you're having a boy-time slumber party, I'll be at Pete and Turtle's house. I'll pick you up tomorrow morning—sound like a plan?"

Mack kept taking bites that were too big for his mouth while Pete finished her last pancake before saying something. "I like people fishing, Mack. Very cool term."

"Um-hmm." He took a gulp of milk. "I'm not as interested in dinosaurs as I was, but I still want to go." Fiona had told her that Mack's passions could be obsessive and linger for months, or be just fleeting and last only days.

After breakfast, Fiona asked Mack to pack an overnight bag, telling him she would double-check that he had everything he needed. Calvin kept some basics for the boy at his house just in case, but Fiona was training her son to plan ahead and take charge of some of his own needs.

"I love how much you encourage his independence, Fiona. Impressive," Pete said as she gathered up her things.

"Well, he can depend on me now, but the sooner he doesn't have to, the better I've done my job." Fiona quickly stuffed a few items of her own into a backpack. Pete made the bed, then sat on the edge of it, watching her lover. Fiona pushed an errant strand of hair behind her ear, then bent to her for a kiss. "Almost done. You don't have to wait for us. I have to drop Mack off before I can come over anyway."

"Oh, I'm in no rush. I'll go in a little bit." Pete couldn't help but smile. She felt no trace of the heaviness that sometimes hung about her. She couldn't be weighed down in Fiona's presence. "Were you raised like that too?"

"Oh hell yes, are you kidding? In the Angeli household? I was the oldest daughter, so not only did I have to take care of myself but I also spent a fair amount of time babysitting Francesca and Liam. My parents had four kids and two businesses to run so—yeah, I was always independent. Sometimes I feel guilty that Mack doesn't have a sibling, you know? Someone else to help him figure out what was weird about his childhood later on in life—but then I swing around to the other side and feel so happy that he can have what I didn't: enough attention."

"He seems to have it good from what I can tell so far, Mama Bear." She wrapped her arms around Fiona and held on tightly. "I'm gonna say good-bye to the little guy and then take off. It'll give me a chance to do some last-minute tidying up." Rain announced its arrival with a steady patter of drops on the windows.

"Don't do anything special for me, babe," Fiona said before kissing her neck. They both walked to Mack's room, where they found him explaining to Turtle why he was packing a flashlight.

"Me and the mutt are gonna take off now, Mack. We'll see you next time." Pete bent to him and opened her arms, and he wasted no time returning the hug. He kissed Turtle on his head, a gesture the dog responded to by licking his face.

"You'll see them again soon, Moo. I'm gonna walk them to the door and then come back to check on your packing," Fiona said tenderly before leaving the room.

☆☆☆

They kissed good-bye and parted. Shortly after that, the Angelis were headed to Calvin's apartment. On the way there, they both sang the robot song to the rhythm of windshield wipers.

☆☆☆

After Pete stepped inside her place, she wondered how it would look to Fiona. She set about straightening up a few things. Her home was generally tidy and clean, but could be pretty interesting, depending on what projects she was working on at the time. *Well*, she reasoned, *I've already opened my soul to this woman. Now I just have to relax about opening my home to her.*

For the first time, she noticed things that weren't childproof if Mack came over. Granted, he was seven going on thirty with his prodigious IQ, but he still had the naïveté and curiosity of a little boy. The hot glue gun on her workbench, X-Acto knives, and various jars of paints and finishes were just the start of it. Well, she would worry about the hazards of her domicile another time. For now, she quickly mixed up some of Grandma Sweets' cornbread and put it in the oven. She thought it would be a nice in between breakfast and lunch snack for the two of them. Turtle went to his basket of toys, rooted around, and produced his favorite: a stuffed monkey with one eye, which he took to his bed, where he lay down and groomed it lovingly.

"Did you miss Mr. Monkey, boy? Good dog." She was petting his wiry head when his ears pricked up and he emitted a muffled bark due to the stuffy in his mouth. He leaped up and went to the large metal front door.

☆☆☆

Outside on the North Cambridge street, Fiona pulled up in her scarred Honda, stepped out, backpack over one shoulder, umbrella in hand, and surveyed the building. It was a large, handsome two-story brick structure. Somehow she wasn't surprised that Pete occupied a live-work space. There were four enormous red doors set in painted black wooden frames and two rows of large windows. Fiona took a deep breath, then ran her free hand through her hair.

On the opposite side of the door, unknown to Fiona, Pete was checking her hair in a small mirror in the entry. She let a few seconds go by after the buzzer sounded so it wouldn't seem like she had been watching and waiting. Turtle barked a few short yips, but stopped when the door opened, and Fiona entered. "Hey, you—cool place," she said before planting a kiss on Pete. Turtle did what most smaller dogs seem to get away with and jumped up on Fiona's leg to greet her.

"Thanks. It's one giant room, basically, but I can give you the tour," Pete offered. Fiona's big eyes looked up at the dramatic high ceiling and then moved all around the place.

Beyond the entry to the right was an alcove with desk, chair, and computer. Above the desk was a large bulletin board with several drawings, articles, and photographs pinned to it. A few feet past this was a minimal but efficient-looking kitchen with a large metal table half-covered with stacks of papers. On the back wall was an ample leather sofa wrinkled with time, an antique lamp, and an armchair. Against the adjacent wall was a television and a cactus with many expressive arms reaching up for the light that poured in from the row of high windows above. In the corner was a large loft platform with dark gray curtains above and below. The upper curtains were open and revealed a railing around a low bed. On the front wall was a massive workbench that had three high shelves filled with tools above it. Several clamp lights were clipped to the shelves and aimed downward toward the bench, which featured a triangular sculpture surrounded by a colorful assortment of small household objects and toys, books, coils of wire, various hand tools, and hardware. The center of the place was large and open, and the concrete floor was bare except for the living room rug and a runner at the foot of the loft steps. Fiona felt as though she'd just stepped into her lover's mind.

Pete took her backpack and jacket, which were both damp with rain, and then reached for her umbrella and put it in a wicker basket by the door. Fiona knew to take her boots off without being asked and put them on the shoe rack. "What smells so yummy?" she asked with that mile-wide smile of hers.

"Grandma Sweets' cornbread, I thought it would make a nice snack."

"You baked for us? Awwww. Tell me about your place!"

Pete took her by the hand and explained she'd lived there for the past four years and loved it because it gave her the space she needed to work at all hours without bothering her neighbors. "It used to be an ice cream factory. You're pretty much seeing it all except for the closet below the loft I built, the bathroom, and the laundry room."

"You made that loft?"

"Yup. And the workbench and table were made by my dad." Turtle walked behind them with Mr. Monkey in his mouth while Pete described her home. "As you can see, I have more random shit than I do furnishings."

"Oh, I doubt it's random. I'd love to know what you're working on, but only if you feel like explaining it," Fiona said before she inhaled the scent of the bread in an exaggerated fashion. "When will that deliciousness be ready to consume?"

"In about ten minutes. Do you want tea? Oh, and I'll tell you anything you want to know about my mad piles of stuff around here..."

"Tea sounds nice. I think we need the caffeinated kind, huh, lover? We didn't sleep much last night, did we?" She sat down at the kitchen table and scanned the cluttered side of it.

"Yeah, but this is the sweetest kind of tired," Pete answered as she put a kettle on. "Make yourself at home. The bathroom is right over there if you need it," She pointed to a door near the corner of the work area.

"Oh my goodness, is that you as a little girl?" Fiona asked as she got up for a closer look at the photo that had caught her eye. Behind the glass was a picture of Pete with an old lady by her side.

"You know it. Petra Orvatch, age eleven. And that's Grandma Sweets. I still miss her, but we talk sometimes in dreams." Pete took a few steps and stood next to Fiona while she examined the photo. It showed a happy girl with long, black hair who was barefoot and wearing overalls. She had a bunch of flowers in one hand, and she and Grandma Sweets were linked arm in arm.

"You are too fucking cute! Look at that hair, and those big paws! And your grandma is amazing. Those cheekbones... Yours are a bit like hers." Fiona turned her gaze from the picture to Pete and just stared at her for a while. The rain pounded harder against the windows, but the downpour wasn't as torrential as the flooding of love Fiona felt in her heart.

They kissed until they were interrupted by the shrill whistle of the old kettle, which cut through the air and seemed to sound all the way up to the rafters. Two Earl Grey tea bags steeped while butter gave up easily on the hot squares of cornbread Pete set before her guest. Pete set two cups down and picked up some cornbread, which she held to Fiona's mouth lovingly. Fiona took a bite and oozed an "mmmmm."

"Wow, Pete. Delicious stuff. Go Grandma Sweets! Hey, how did she get that nickname?"

"It started with my brother. He always said our grandma was sweet, so it turned into a name, and ever since I can remember, she was just called that."

"Nice. What was her actual name?"

"Nadie. Means wise in Algonquian. Nadie McNally."

Fiona smiled before saying, "I want to get a closer look at that sculpture of yours, you mind?"

"Not at all, come on," Pete answered as she led her over to it.

☆☆☆

Fiona's eyes got even larger when she examined something; Pete watched her closely as she took in every part of the piece.

"It's wild," she announced. "It's telling a story, wait—actually, it's telling many stories, huh?"

Pete could tell she wanted to touch it and admired her restraint.

"Yeah, you could say that. I just have to make things. Always have. My dad was like that, and he got me started down the maker's path when I was really little."

"Is there a picture of him around here somewhere? I'd love to see his face."

"Yes, actually. Come." She led her over to the little alcove. Just to the right of her computer was another black-and-white photo, but Pete wasn't in this one. It depicted a handsome man in his late thirties clad in an old work shirt and a driving cap. He had the same brow line and naturally upturned mouth that Pete owned. "This was taken about a year before we lost him."

"What was his name?"

"Lev. Our last name was broken and reassembled American-style at Ellis Island when my great-grandparents came here from Russia. I've never met another Orvatch who wasn't related to us."

"You've got his eyebrows and his mouth. He's beautiful."

"Oh, thanks—yeah, he was a good guy. He always made sense to me, and helped me make sense of things. You know?"

Fiona nodded, and the two of them went back to the kitchen table. "I do know. Families are weird places."

"Yup, and no one lifts you up and knocks you down quite like family, huh?"

"Listen to us, we sound like bad bumper stickers," Fiona observed and then laughed at her own joke. "Tell me more about your father, Pete."

Pete obliged her and described with love in her voice how, from an early age, she used to avoid kitchen duties with her mother and slip into the garage where her father worked. Lev supported a solidly middle-class lifestyle for his family by working at an insurance company. He didn't love it or hate it; he said it was complicated enough to engage him when he was there, but simple enough that he never thought about it outside work and that left room in his head to think about what he wanted to make next. He designed and built furniture and made sculptures too. But he preferred materials like wood or rock to the found objects Pete used.

"Yeah, where do you get all that stuff anyway? Flea markets?"

"Some of it—the rest I just sort of come across." Pete eyed the hodgepodge and wondered how it looked to Fiona. She started to feel a little uncomfortable, so she continued with her narrative. "My dad and I used to work side by side out in the garage all the time. He used to tell me, '*Look around you, Petra, most of what you see is made by Mother Nature, the rest is made by humans, but not all of it has to have a purpose. Some things we make can just be children of our brains, things for people to look at and think about long after we're gone.'*." She went on to say how he'd gently warn, "Don't make thunder before you have lightning." In other words, wait until you have an idea that lights you up before you pound away at it.

Pete suggested they finish their tea on the couch, where they sat talking while the storm intensified. At some point, Pete got up to use the bathroom, and while she was in there, Fiona grabbed her backpack and went up to the bed, where she waited. When Pete returned and saw only her dog on the couch, she paused. Turtle looked at her and then up at the loft. Pete smiled at him, telling him with her eyes that he was a good boy. She ascended the steps with the excitement of someone about to unwrap a present. Their passion was a gift in both their lives, and it could be heard over the thunder that seemed to hurl itself against the walls that held them while they held each other.

# CHAPTER FOUR: SNOW IN SEPTEMBER

*Imperfection is beauty, madness is genius, and it's better to be
absolutely ridiculous than absolutely boring.*
*~ Marilyn Monroe*

The noise of the ringing phone near Pete's bed startled her awake. She expected it to be Fiona giving her an update on Mack. They'd fallen asleep early after a long, passionate Saturday afternoon together, but Fiona had to leave hastily at sunrise when Calvin called, explaining that Mack had experienced a terrible nightmare and wanted to go home early. Instead, it was Sheila's voice on the other end.

"You still in bed after 9:00? That's not like you. Shit, do you have company?"

"No, not currently," Pete managed through a yawn. "What's up?"

"What's up with you?" Sheila asked while Pete dragged herself out of bed, reached for her faded old blue robe, and descended the steps to make her morning brew. "How did it feel to have her at your place?"

"I was nervous before she came over, but once she was here, it all felt really natural. How are you doing? Wanna catch up in person? Meet for bagels?"

"Wish I could. Gotta cover for a half shift at the shelter from ten to two. But tell me about your time with the new girl."

"Well, we had dinner out on Friday, and I stayed over, then she came over here after she dropped her son off."

"More sex, I take it?"

"Is it gonna break your lonely, horny heart to hear about it?"

Sheila emitted a laugh as deep as she was tall before responding. "No, any details you feel comfortable sharing would be words of encouragement, because I just saw that my inbox has seventeen emails in response to the new ad I just posted. Remember the dating service I told you about, the one for tall singles?"

"Yeah, well, that sounds promising. Good for you. Let me know what settles to the bottom and what rises to the top after you've sifted through those." Pete got up to get her coffee and settled onto the comfy leather couch. Turtle jumped up and morphed into a tight ball next to her. It was colder this morning than it had been recently, so Pete cinched her bathrobe more tightly around her. Sheila assured her she would give her an update as soon as she'd read through them, and pressed her for more information.

"Well, we talked a lot, and Fiona has this way of getting me to share more about myself than I usually do. It's like I can't say no to those big eyes, and I also get kind of hypnotized when I watch her lips move. Embarrassing to say out loud. I end up feeling interviewed, but not in a bad way. She just needs to peel back layers, but she's also willing to expose herself to me. She's just magnetic, Sheila. You'll see when you meet her. And yes, the sex is crazy good. We had a marathon session into the wee hours of Saturday morning that included heavy equipment and some light bondage, then we passed out at 8:00 without even having a proper dinner."

"Heavy equipment? Do tell."

"Well, she must have packed half the contents of her nightstand in her backpack when I wasn't looking, because it was toy land…" She blew on her hot drink and took the first sip.

"This one's going to keep your attention, huh, Pete? You two already played a little tie me up and love me? Really?"

"Mm-hmm. She tied me to the railing of my loft with a silk scarf."

"Shit, girl, if you two are having these kinds of adventures four days in, what will you be into down the road? Okay—I'm truly inspired. I mean it."

☆☆☆

Fiona took the steps to Calvin's floor two at a time and rapped on the door. "It's me." It opened, and her friend stood there in his pajama bottoms looking very tired. They hugged hello, and Fiona started walking toward the guest bedroom, but he stopped her with a gentle tug on her arm.

"He wants me to tell you. He's calmer now, but he said he wants me to explain about the dream before he sees you. When I asked him why, he just became more adamant, so I told him I would."

"Okay," Fiona said. Concern prevented her eyes from blinking, and her mouth formed that tight line all worried parents get. She tossed her backpack on a chair and then sat on the L-shaped couch. Calvin seemed to know by the look of her that she hadn't had any caffeine yet and put a cup of it in her hand. "Thanks, you're a prince. So—what happened?"

Calvin knew she liked details, so he gave some background on their time together before getting to Mack's night terrors. "We had a great day. The exhibit was cool, and held Mack's interest. I pretended not to know him when he informed a staff member that a stegosaurus fact on a placard was incorrect."

"That's my boy." Fiona sighed. The coffee was strong, and she needed it. She had spent herself in Pete's bed and felt as though someone had removed her batteries.

"We made dinner together here: Mack's mac and cheese. We played with Legos, read a book, and then he fell asleep around 8:30. Everything was pretty normal until he screamed and woke me up at four."

"Four? No wonder you look like shit."

"Hey—you look like bigger shit. You know, if you don't sleep you'll die, and if you die, you can't have any more sex. Plus, I look like shit because I had a very busy day yesterday before our little angel even arrived..."

"Actually, you're too pretty to look like shit. You just look tired. So tell me, what happened?"

Calvin explained in detail how he'd heard Mack scream and ran to his room to find him balled up on the floor in the corner, hiding his head. He was crying by the time Calvin got in there, sobbing so violently that it took him a while to catch his breath before he could describe the nightmare. "Mack dreamed that both of you were walking down the sidewalk near your house, holding hands and singing, when a silver car careened down the street really fast and then ran half its wheels up over the curb and came straight at you. You used your body to shield him and took the full impact while he got knocked sideways. Mack saw you crushed and bleeding everywhere and tried to get up from the street, but couldn't move. He could only make out a dark outline behind the wheel; he couldn't see the face of the driver who managed to get the car back in the street without hitting anything else, and then aimed again at Mack. At that point, he screamed himself awake."

"Wow. Shit—that would terrify me too. Poor little guy. You were able to calm him down but not convince him to stay longer, huh?"

"He kept saying he wanted to go home. I feel so bad for him. I haven't seen him quite this upset in a long time."

"Well, thanks for handling it. I'll go in there." She squeezed his shoulder before she went to her boy. She opened the door slowly and saw him fully dressed, sitting on the bed next to his backpack, staring down at his feet. "Mackles, sweetie? Mommy's here." He lifted his head, and some of the tension drained from his face as he looked at her. He didn't get up, so she sat beside him and draped her arms around his shoulders. He melted into her, burying his head in her sweater.

"I'm sorry, Mom," came out of him before he cried against her.

"Oh, baby," she soothed as she held him closely, "you have nothing to be sorry for. Just cry if you want. I'm right here."

His emotions came salty and jagged until the wool he'd hidden his face in was damp. Fiona tried not to cry in response to his pain, but her body betrayed her, and a few tears made their way down her cheek. When Mack stopped, she scooped him up, grabbed his bag, and then turned to see Calvin leaning against the doorframe. He opened his strong arms to them, and the three were knit together in the quiet of another rainy day.

It was only after Fiona got Mack home, coaxed him to eat some breakfast, and put on a movie for the two of them that she texted her sweetie with an update. *We're home, he's better now, but still shaken. Call you at bedtime? xo*

As the music of the opening credits faded and the dialogue of the animated picture began, Fiona's phone vibrated.

*Glad to hear it. Yes, of course. Xoxo*

☆☆☆

After Pete got off the phone with Sheila, she walked Turtle in the light rain and then made herself an enormous breakfast to quiet her roaring stomach. She showered and then straightened up a bit. Turtle's eyes followed her as she paced around the open floor plan. She paused and looked up through the enormous windows at the dramatic sky. Within the many panes, she saw a large bouffant of a cloud that was suddenly backlit by sun. The rain ceased, and she decided to toss the mystery she was almost done reading in her bag, grab Turtle, and take a two-mile walk to a local dog-friendly cafe.

The powerful aroma of coffee made her feel better the instant she walked through the door of Spike's Place. As wonderful as it smelled, she knew better than to have more caffeine when she was feeling anxious, so she settled Turtle at a small table in the corner and ordered some ginger tea. It was noon, and the place was fairly crowded with a classic Cambridge assortment of students, retirees, and people who loved to read or use their laptops in a coffee shop. Turtle made love-eyes at a woman who sat next to them. Remarking on how cute he was, she petted his curly head, which delighted the dog so much he stood up and leaned into her leg. Pete thanked her and expressed how glad she was that dogs were allowed in before opening her book and gluing her eyes to the page. Her smiling neighbor took the hint graciously, stopped talking, and then fastened her eyes to her magazine.

*Tanya's heart nearly pounded out of her chest as she tried the last key on the keychain, and it turned the lock. She'd been afraid she wouldn't be able to get in, and now she was scared of what lay on the other side of the door.* It wasn't the writing that hooked Pete; it was the puzzle of the plot. Like the sculptures and collages she made, the mysteries she read were assembled out of incidental, seemingly random bits that all made sense when looked at from the right angle or from the last page in the novel.

"Tanya!" bellowed a burly man who walked in. The woman who'd petted Turtle stood up, went over to him, and gave him a hearty embrace.

"Steve, it's so good to see you. I'm glad I got your message before I left my apartment so I could bring you your spare set."

"Me too. I haven't locked myself out in a long time. At least this time I was fully dressed. Remember that other time?"

Tanya laughed. The two of them sat at her table, and Pete was distracted not just by the coincidence, but by the size of this man. His long legs spilled out of the chair, and when he put his elbows on the table, it was dwarfed by the heft of his arms. Pete guessed he was about six foot six, a full eight inches taller than the average man. When she caught herself staring at him, she focused again on the book and continued reading at her usual fast pace.

*Her father's study had been a favorite part of her childhood but was now a sad place. It was a tomb, not for her father's body, but for his mind. He died before he could complete his studies, and Tanya's suspicions about his suicide being a homicide—*

"Did you hear about the homicide in our hometown? It's a bizarre one. Some guy ran his own brother down with a Jeep. My mom was going on and on about it on our weekly Sunday phone call this morning," Tanya informed her companion.

"No—I didn't. That's pretty black comedy for Portsmouth. Geez. Was he mentally ill or just a homicidal maniac?"

She provided more details, but Pete tried to block out her words and focus on the book. She needed it to be her distraction right now, and this strangely synced-up conversation was an impediment. It was as if Pete were stuck in an echo and couldn't move away from the source of the reverberation. At one point, she decided to change tables, but there were none available. Despite the fact that some words on the pages came out of Tanya and Steve's mouths, she managed to finish the chapter just as she drank her last sip of tea.

She glanced around the noisy place, and her eyes landed on the vintage Bruins wall clock, which told her something over its innocuous yellow "B," something she didn't want to know. Shadows crept into her vision, and suddenly the world seemed too dark and too bright at the same time. It was still noon. Maybe the clock had stopped? She fished her cell phone out of her jacket pocket, and it only confirmed that the black-and-yellow face hadn't lied. She had to get out of there.

Having hiked home much faster than she'd walked there, Pete had broken out in a light sweat by the time she made it inside her loft. Knowing his person was agitated, Turtle stayed close and kept his gaze on her. She removed her boots and jacket and paced around, grabbing a hand towel out of the bathroom so she could blot her face and wipe the back of her neck. Running a hand up and down the back of her head, she stood looking at her workbench. No matter what time it was, it was time to start a new sculpture.

☆☆☆

It took longer than usual to get Mack settled for the night because he was afraid he'd have another nightmare, but Fiona was patient, adding a few extra stuffed animals to the menagerie that lived in his bed. It moved her when she saw him pulling the comforter up closer around the chins of his assorted dogs, bears, and other furry companions. How the same boy who used adult vocabulary to explain sophisticated concepts also tucked in his stuffed toys was beyond her. She was just relieved when she saw him act like a regular kid. These moments made her believe the intellectual gap between her and her child wouldn't widen so much one day that she couldn't reach across anymore, or remind him of these simpler times.

Mack had asked her to stay in the room with him until he was sound asleep, but she stayed by his side long after, watching him and thinking. As she smoothed his hair lovingly and saw his widow's peak, she was reminded of his father, one Mr. George Nikolaidis, whom she'd befriended when she did some volunteer work at a nursing home eight years ago. She knew George was crazy smart from a very young age, like Mack, but now found herself wondering if he had nightmares as a little boy too. There were so many questions she wished she could ask him, but now he could only speak to her through memory.

When Mack's breathing was smooth and slow and his eyelids fluttered with what she hoped were sweet dreams, Fiona got up to call her lover. She ached to hear the soothing, rich voice she'd fallen for that first day.

Pete was still at her workbench when the phone rang.

"Hi, babe," Fiona said.

"Fiona, hi. How you doing? How's the little guy?"

"You sound tired, babe, am I wearing you out?" Fiona teased.

"Not yet, but you can keep trying. Maybe I am a bit fatigued. I've been working on a new sculpture since the early afternoon. Tell me, how is Mack? Asleep, I hope?"

"Yes, it took a while. We watched movies he's seen already all afternoon—I think he found it comforting. He didn't want to talk about the nightmare, so I didn't push it. Basically, I got run down by a madman in a silver car which then turned and aimed for him, but he woke up before that, thank goodness. The blood really freaked him out."

"Shit. That would scare me, and I'm a grown-up! Well, most of the time..."

Fiona giggled and was happy to have a reason to laugh at the end of a long day. "I think he's okay. I'll just keep an eye on him. He can get really upset about things, almost in an obsessive way, but has never been this freaked out by a nightmare." While Fiona had Pete on speaker, she undressed completely and got into bed. She wanted to be naked while she listened to Pete. Fiona was a free spirit who frequently felt fettered by clothing in general; she was more at home in her own skin than in any garment. "You know, his dad had an amazing and overactive brain like Mack's..."

"Yeah? What was his dad like? You can keep talking; I'm just going to make myself comfortable on the couch."

Fiona shared the story of Mack's father with her. She'd quit her job as a flight attendant and just gotten into paralegal work when she saw a flyer looking for volunteers. She had always enjoyed the company of older people. Some of her best times as a kid were spent in the company of her grandparents when the family would drive south to Connecticut to visit them. Unlike most young children, Fiona hadn't minded the long, meandering, autobiographical stories or the slow pace of seniors. So it was no surprise to her that she had enjoyed her Sunday visits to Saint Bartholomew's Senior Care Home. Her job had been to spend time with the residents who didn't have visitors: read out loud to them, help them walk or wheel them through the grounds—those sorts of things. When she'd first met George, she had to do a double take. Sitting up in his bed reading without glasses, alert, and sporting a full head of salt-and-pepper hair, he had looked too young to live there. He had been sixty-nine but, between a series of strokes and two broken hips from a motorcycle accident a few years earlier, hadn't retained enough mobility to live independently.

Working at Saint Bart's, Fiona had experienced stereotypically dirty old men who seemed to be in a second adolescence; their brains let their bodies grab and grope women as they pleased. She'd also drawn the attention of polite, charming old men who weren't overtly lusting after young women, but concealed their salacity beneath greasy charm. But George had been neither. He had been an extremely smart and well-spoken man who looked like an aging movie star. Their first conversation had been about the Hemingway book he was reading when she walked in. Fiona had been forced to read it in high school, and that experience left her wondering why anyone would choose to read Hemingway at all. At the time, she'd concluded it must be a "boy book." So when she'd asked him if he was enjoying *A Farewell to Arms*, he had answered enthusiastically and shared some information about it, which intrigued her more than the novel itself. He'd explained how, in early editions, the words "shit," "fuck," and "cocksucker" were replaced with dashes, and how there were at least two copies of the first edition in which Hemingway reinserted the censored text by hand. This exchange was a pleasant surprise for Fiona, and their easy connection made her take a closer look at the gentleman in room 21-A.

That had been the first of many conversations. Over the months, the two had become friends and confidants, a fact which had thrilled Fiona for many reasons, one being that, as a volunteer, she was supposed to spread herself around and not get too involved with the residents. Fiona was in her comfort zone, breaking rules. It was during this chapter of her life that her biological clock had suddenly showed its face to her and ticked loudly. When she'd mentioned this to George, she found herself articulating her desire to have a child so passionately that it took her by storm. She'd explained that she wanted to get started now, at almost twenty-nine, and didn't want to wait for the right partner. So Mr. Nikolaidis had proposed they break a really big rule together and make a baby. Fiona had been startled at first, and afraid of how it might change their friendship, but as the idea sank in, dreams of motherhood began to take root. Why not George? Unlike some form she could read at a sperm bank, he had been real, honest, and right there in front of her, with an amiable temperament and genes for intelligence, good looks, and height. She would not merely know what ethnic ingredients were being added to her Italian and Irish—Greek, Scottish, and Cherokee—but also have names, faces, and stories to share with their child.

Fiona had mulled the proposal over carefully and started tracking her ovulation. He'd said he wanted to be her donor, and she knew he hadn't made the suggestion just to have sex with her. She'd given in to her dreams and his generosity and officially said yes. Their first attempt had involved a collection cup and a turkey baster, but, despite Fiona's carefully researched plan, had not resulted in pregnancy. The disappointment had made her feel small compared to her enormous desire to be a mother; she then did more research and vowed not to fail again. One snowy January day, she convinced George to make love with her, and they did so furtively, with tender purpose, and conceived their baby boy.

"Crap," Fiona said, a bit self-consciously, "I didn't mean to go on and on like that."

"I'm glad you did, Fi. You can't always do the investigating, sometimes you have to open the book and let me just read the pages, you know? Pretty interesting. I admit it... I'm struggling a bit with—" She paused to reach for just the right words. "—with this particular chapter, but at the same time I'm glad to learn about the other half of the Mack equation. So, when did George pass away?

"When Mack was barely two, but they got to see each other a lot before then. I wish he were still here. I just have to make him as alive as I can for Mack with stories and pictures. And, babe, I get your discomfort. It's understandable, but I hope you know you can say anything you want to me and ask me as many questions as you need to. You know, you'd think the forty-year age gap would have made us feel awkward, but maybe our connection as friends got us to a different place than that..." She decided not to share any more details on the subject.

"Does Mack know everything?"

"Yes, I've always been honest with him. I think because he's so intelligent, he gets it. You know, that it was an unconventional way to bring a baby into this world? But you know what? My family doesn't even know the real story—well, just Anthony. I mean, they adore Mack, and there's a lot of love to go around because so far he's the only grandchild, the only nephew, but as far as my parents and other siblings know, Mack was the result of a one-night stand with a British investment banker whose name I couldn't recall and whose contact info I never got before he left town... That's the mythology I invented for them, and Mack knows to play along. Gosh, that sounds sooooo wrong as I say it out loud..."

"I don't know," Pete offered supportively. "It's your right to keep some of your life private from your family. I'm sure you have good reasons."

"Yeah, well, actually, making up a story about Mack's father was easier all around. George's age would never have sat well with my mother, because she was sexually abused by her grandfather when she wasn't quite a teenager. She didn't even tell me any of that until I was in my early twenties. Long before that, however, I had picked up on the fact that older men seemed to creep her out. Shit. I guess I just thought she would pass judgment and say things she couldn't take back. I didn't want her awful contact with an old man to even brush against my pure and positive experience with George. I mean, he gave me Mack. My little boy. But I am asking my kid to lie for me, and I feel conflicted about that for sure. Family sure is fucked, huh?"

"Super fucked. Sounds like Mack was made in love, and I can see he's being raised with love. That's more than a lotta kids can say."

Fiona turned her head and let it sink more into the pillow as she listened to Pete. Exhaustion was claiming her now from head to toe; each limb felt twice as heavy as it had been when she'd fallen asleep in Pete's arms the night before.

"Thanks for saying that, Pete; I don't feel judged by you." The register of her voice was lower now from weariness, but she went on a little more. "I have a shoebox George put together for Mack before he died. It has photographs, some video footage of him talking about his life and giving Mack advice, and some letters he wrote to him for when he's older. He was a really good man. I've heard Mack explain about his dad when asked by other kids. He says his dad was an older man who has passed away. Honestly, having Mack was the smartest thing I did in my twenties. I've got some stories about some less than wise decisions I made when I was younger..." She yawned.

"We all have them. I'll listen to any kind of story you've got." Pete yawned too, and then asked, "When will I see you again? I'm pretty busy this week, but I know I'll need a fix before the weekend."

"Hmmm, me too, Pete. Me too. Let's talk tomorrow and figure it out then. I'm too faded to even remember what's on my work calendar right now," Fiona said.

"Sounds good. Have sweet dreams, okay?"

"They will be if you're in them. Naked." This made Pete giggle. They said good-bye, and Fiona switched off the light on her nightstand.

☆☆☆

Before turning in, Pete checked her emails, because she couldn't recall if her new painting gig started at 8:00 tomorrow or 8:30. She resisted four messages from Sheila with *wait until you read this* in the subject line before locating the information she needed. It was 8:30 that she would begin painting a kitchen for a nice elderly man in Somerville.

She opened Sheila's first email, which included copied and pasted highlights from the least likely candidate of the seventeen respondents; it was a real can of snakes. He didn't include a photograph but went on in great detail about how he was a better-looking version of Abraham Lincoln. He also outlined how intelligent he was, which, as far as Sheila was concerned, never needed to be explained; it would just ring on its own like a bell in the wind. The second was from a guy named Strider who took a real social risk by not only mentioning he had a large penis, but also explaining how he had named it Mr. Happy. This actually made Pete laugh out loud. The third and fourth included highlights from the same man, a guy named Damon who could really write. Pete was taken with how much of his personality came across in the way he crafted his words. Sheila liked his response so much she immediately wrote back, which delighted Damon enough to send an email twice as long as the first. Sheila was asking Pete's opinion about whether she should keep writing for a few days and then speak on the phone, or just go for it. She also wondered if he was too good to be true. Pete wrote her an email saying that she was overthinking it, and to just let it all unfold.

The final chapter of the mystery she was reading remained, and for Pete it was like the last square of a really good chocolate bar waiting in its wrapper. She soon found herself ensconced in blankets, reading happily. The book surprised her in the end, which was a rare delight for a perceptive reader like Pete. The weariness that had been weighing her down all day finally claimed her, and she turned out the light.

Not long afterwards, she reached for the lamp again after waking suddenly. Pete was roused from a bad dream that featured her lying on an operating table in an otherwise empty room that had a mirrored ceiling in which she could see her abdomen cut open and her organs exposed. She couldn't feel pain, but the feeling of terror was very real, because she couldn't move and had no idea why she was there.

☆☆☆

The next evening, when Pete spoke to Sheila on the phone, she mentioned it, because her friend loved to analyze dreams. Sheila listened attentively, but couldn't quite put her finger on it, so she asked Pete to hold on while she got out her dream dictionary.

"To dream that your abdomen is exposed represents issues you have with trust and feelings of vulnerability. You are expressing your primal emotions and instincts," she read.

"Hmm," Pete said warily, "not sure what to make of that."

"Well, friend, dreams are amazing to think about, and dream dictionaries are cool things, but please don't trip. I know bad dreams can sometimes haunt you. Get you obsessing. But I also know that talking with Dr. P can help. When do you see her again? Wednesday?"

"Tuesday."

"Well, tell her about it, and let's talk after then. I also want to know what she says about your experience with the clock in the waiting room."

"Okay, Sheils," Pete assured her. "Don't worry about me—I've been really good lately. Things have been good; my head has been a little quieter than usual."

"Even with your spicy new redheaded sex goddess? That plotline in your life is anything but quiet," she said lovingly.

"Yeah, actually," Pete reflected, "maybe Fiona is wearing my body out so well that my mind doesn't have enough energy to scrutinize itself. But enough about me—any more emails bouncing back and forth between you and Damon? Exchange pictures yet?"

"Yes, a few more emails. Great emails, actually, about my dogs and my work and his work. He is a social worker at a nonprofit that helps at-risk youth. Pete, this guy seems fucking amazing, actually. No pictures yet, because neither of us has offered one or asked for one. I'm sooooo curious, but also a little afraid. What if he's a troll or thinks I'm a troll?"

Pete laughed before cutting in. "Neither of you is a troll. Send that picture of you and the dogs from your last birthday. Just attach it to your next email. You look really great there. Trust me."

☆☆☆

The waiting room of Cambridge Holistic Health and Wellness Center looked different to Pete somehow, since she'd met the fabulous Fiona here last week. Rather than avoid the confusing clock, she confronted it head-on and noted the time it told was the same as on her cell phone: 3:55. The clock was behaving, and Pete noticed the receptionist was new. Instead of Gum Snapper, there was now Clark Kent, who called out softly to the room of waiting patients, "Petra Orvatch?" She looked up and decided he had such a kind face that she wouldn't correct him with her usual, *It's Pete, actually*. She wanted strangers to call her Pete. She didn't mind when people close to her occasionally used her given name. Maybe she should have changed it legally as Sheila suggested so long ago, but then again a man's name on her medical forms could also lead to confusion—damned if you do, damned if you don't. "Dr. Percy will see you now."

"Thanks," she returned as she passed his desk and entered the room she'd become so familiar with over the past three years. The walls were absent of the typical abstract art or landscapes she had seen in other doctors' offices, and instead had only framed credentials and one bold drawing crudely signed by the child artist. The conspicuous absence of a desk had taken Pete aback at first, but when Dr. P explained that furniture could be an unwanted barrier, it made more sense. The doc sat in an old leather recliner next to a small round table with her laptop on it. Patients had a choice of seating: a garish yellow vinyl beanbag, a traditional armchair, or a rocking chair. During their first session, Dr. P had offered her the choice along with a joke about the beanbag being for your inner child, the armchair for those wanting stability, and the rocker for the anxious or restless.

"Pete! Missed you last week. Come in and let's get caught up." Her voice went with the rest of her; it was high and clear, like you might expect from a short, wiry woman. Pete sat in the rocker today and immediately took advantage of the chance to move, hoping the back-and-forth motion would help her decide whether to lead with the clock incident or with the story of Fiona. Unexpectedly, her mind landed on something that hadn't occurred to her earlier: was Fiona one of Dr. P's patients too? They hadn't asked each other about their appointments that day; they had been swept up in their carnal attraction, and the subject hadn't come up. Worry ricocheted in her mind as she debated whether or not to change Fiona's name, but then her words decided for her as they tumbled out.

"Yeah, wish I could say the same, Dr. P, but I actually had another kind of appointment with this amazing woman I met in the waiting room. I've got to tell you about Fiona."

"Wow, okay, I'm intrigued," she responded. Jing-Wei Percy was not only unconventional, but at times rather informal with her patients. "Do tell! I never know what goes on out there because I'm always in here!" Her voice was coiled with laughter ready to spring. Pete started to feel less anxious as Dr. P's warmth and humor worked their magic on her. Off and on over the past sixteen years, she had seen a total of five practitioners for help; some were therapists and some psychiatrists. Dr. P was both, and, so far, had helped her feel calm in her own mind more than anyone else had, except Grandma Sweets, of course.

Pete appreciated how Dr. P understood that Pete's visions made sense in her grandmother's world; but outside of that safe and special place, they were much harder to sort out. Pete had explained how when her father died, parts of her went numb, and until her grandma came to live with them shortly after that tragedy, she had felt alienated in the family unit that now only offered her a brother who seemed to be her exact opposite and a mother who misunderstood or hurt her on a regular basis. When religion seeped into the cracks of her mother's fragile new identity as a widow, Jessica Orvatch had embraced it like the drowning reach for life preservers. She had tried forcing the faith on both her children, and Pete resisted throughout her adolescence, but was dipped in Catholicism just long enough to absorb some guilt and shame. Pete and Dr. Percy had giggled about this crazy notion that had doomed women since it was first propagated; the idea that a woman could give birth, yet remain pure, is an impossible standard for women to measure themselves against.

At just ten, Pete had gone head to head with her mom on this virgin mother thing. Earlier in the fifth grade, she had been taught about reproduction, and the summer before that had surreptitiously read *The Joy of Sex* cover to cover with her friend, Allison, who liberated it from her mother's secret hiding place, so she felt well-armed against her mother's assertions. There was no winning with her, though. Pete had explained to Dr. P that her mother always ended the intellectual discourse before it could really begin and insulted her, banished her to her room, or worse. She would occasionally pull one ear up roughly or slap her full force in the face to get her attention. When her mother had really disliked any opinions that came out of her children's mouths, she forced them to drink a ladle full of vinegar. Pete had told Dr. P how the abuse seemed to have soured Rudolph's independence permanently because he became a virtual automaton, but she just got angry from the bitter taste left in her mouth.

This physical abuse was one of the first things Pete had shared with Dr. Percy. From the safety of the beanbag chair, Pete had also poured out a short history of her visions, her erratic and sometimes destructive behaviors, all the different meds she'd tried, went off, tried again, and ultimately stopped taking two years prior to meeting the doctor.

In childhood, Pete knew she was different from most other kids, or was at the very least less "normal." She'd shared with Dr. P how once, at recess, a particularly cruel girl in another class had overheard Pete addressing a bird in a tree as "sister crow." This was a habit she had learned from her grandmother, who considered all animals her family. That brat and her posse called her "sister stupid" for the rest of the year.

By the end of elementary school, she had been dubbed "the weird girl." She had felt compelled to tell her doctor how, at the beginning of junior high, she'd had a premonition about her math teacher that came true. One afternoon, instead of doing homework, she suddenly felt a weight on her chest as the notion that Ms. Flowers was going to be in a car crash cast a dark shadow in her mind. She didn't say anything about it to anyone, not even Grandma Sweets, because she'd assumed it was just a random thought. The next day at school, she had a substitute teacher for her first-period math class, and before morning break, all the students and teachers were gathered in the auditorium, where the principal announced that Ms. Flowers had been in a serious car accident, was in a coma, and might not make it. Pete almost threw up when she heard this, and from that point forward, told her grandmother about any dark thoughts or forebodings she had. She'd even written them down in a secret journal. When her teacher died four days later, young Pete felt responsible and had trouble sleeping for several weeks.

In high school, she started seeing auras, and sometimes shadows she later called "dark spirits" around people she'd seen in passing. Grandma Sweets assured her that this was the gift of seeing, and not to worry. She used to gently warn her, "Be careful how you talk about what you see, and even more careful about what you do when you see more than others see."

Like with other clients of Dr. P, it was during college that Pete began to confuse reality with fantasy. Her strange visions, premonitions, confusion about time, and vivid dreams continued throughout her adult life. As she got further into her twenties, she had developed mood swings and sometimes became extremely argumentative. Her psychiatrist at the time diagnosed her as having bipolar disorder, and even though Pete openly acknowledged her struggles, she resisted this label. She preferred to think of herself as having the type of vision that doesn't fit neatly into the world.

Pete had told Dr. P losing her grandmother was incredibly hard, but that before she left the earth, she saw Pete's conflicts and suggested things like healing circles, praying, employing the teachings of the medicine wheel, and going to sweat lodges. Losing Grandma Sweets sent Pete into a tailspin, and if it weren't for meeting Sheila shortly after her passing, she might have become completely unglued.

It was when her erratic behaviors caused her to lose a job at a health food store that she first turned to western medicine to help manage her issues. While some of the meds calmed her, others made her more anxious or caused other undesirable side effects. The last one she was on, diazepam, caused her to hallucinate. Pete attributed the incident at Petworld, when she had seen a human face on a fish, to that drug. But she knew this was revisionist history, because she hadn't taken that medication for several months before that day, and had already gone through withdrawal. It was virtually impossible for Pete to have an accurate perception of her problems, because the line between fact and fiction was a blur to her; when her brain coiled so tightly she felt it might spring and snap, she lost sight of her true self, and had to rely on other people's reactions to her behavior for some indication of who she was. After making a scene at the pet store, she decided to seek out different ways to fit into a more socially acceptable version of reality.

Dr. Percy had acknowledged that Pete's baffling ability to predict events and know things about strangers was mysterious, inexplicable, and outside the realm of mental health diagnoses. She referred to Pete lovingly as her "magical enigma." She was a doctor who focused on managing behavior rather than overseeing a diagnosis. When Pete pressed her for one, Dr. P had said, "Schizoaffective tendencies with claircognizance and clairvoyance." When Pete had heard this, she preferred to focus on the part about seeing and knowing things without explanation. Pete hadn't yet been ready to tell her doctor about the voices she sometimes heard in her head, and had been hopeful when Dr. Percy introduced her to cognitive behavioral therapy, working with her to develop plans to meet goals. She was the only health practitioner who made Pete feel seen, and not merely analyzed. She encouraged her to keep a journal that tracked her moods and visions, and she did so faithfully. Sheila was Pete's check-in person because their friendship was old and deep, a reservoir of love and loyalty.

After Dr. P listened to Pete talk about Fiona and Mack for a good portion of their fifty minutes together, she said, "Well, it certainly seems like you trust each other already. Maybe it's your time to enjoy a relationship again?"

"I do trust her, and when I'm with her I don't switch parts of myself off," Pete responded. "And I really like her son. He's not like any other child I've met." She then told the doctor about the dying man she'd seen when the three of them went walking after pizza and explained how shocked she was that Mack saw it too, and how Fiona didn't react negatively or even ask questions later.

"So, she just accepted what you said?" asked Dr. Percy.

"Yeah, she did." Pete knew she only had about fifteen more minutes left to relate the clock incident, so she steered the conversation that way.

Dr. P must have noticed the rocking chair go faster as Pete shared the details of the incident.

"Did you write it all down?"

"Yes, and I told Sheila about it. She seemed more worried than I was," Pete said. "I think because I haven't had a problem with time in so long she was hoping I was all done with those. Guess not." Pete rocked back as far as she could and kept the old chair there for a moment as she looked up and studied the flowering orchid on top of a high bookshelf. Its blooms were delicate and fire-colored, making Pete think of Fiona.

"Well, that's why she's your check-in person." Dr. P went on to say that, while Pete should not freak out, she should pay close attention to any distortion of time, note all the details in her journal, and together they would continue to look for some pattern or figure out what triggered them. Their appointment was just about over, and Dr. Percy stood up to stretch while she spoke. "Oh, and Pete, Fiona isn't one of my patients, in case you were wondering."

"There you go reading my mind again!" Pete said with a smile.

"Isn't that what your health insurance pays me to do?" she joked. The two women hugged as they did at the end of every session.

On the drive home, it happened. Since Pete hadn't experienced it in several months, she was hoping it wouldn't occur again, but it did; the gender-ambiguous voice came like thunder in her brain, like fire in her private hell. "Dr. Percy can't fix you, Petra. No doctor can. What you have is not an illness or a gift. It's a curse! You're doomed to live your whole life with a head full of visions, voices, noise, and things you can never explain to anyone without seeming like a madwoman. You're cursed!" Then it stopped just as abruptly as it began, leaving her with head pain and an achiness around her eyes. She hadn't told Sheila or Dr. Percy about the voice. Telling about it would make it real, so she only told Turtle, who listened with love as dogs always do, offering comfort rather than passing judgment.

☆☆☆

Calvin was at Fiona's door right at 6:00, like he said he would be. She'd asked him to come over and help her move some furniture, promising him homemade meatloaf for dinner. Fiona let him in, and Mack appeared in the entry to greet him. Mack was wearing a pink shirt, orange pants, and a bright green sweater. One foot was bare, the other in a black sock with bright yellow lightning bolts on it.

"Hey, little man," Calvin said as he squeezed Mack's shoulder. He hugged Fiona and whispered in her ear, "Not a day you dressed him, huh? He's the king of clash." This made her grin, and she had to suppress a laugh. Calvin draped his jacket over the nearest chair, took his shoes off, and the three of them sat in the living room. "So, this is the monster we're moving?" he asked as he patted the couch they were on.

"Yup. And it's way heavier than it looks because it's a sofa bed, and we can't drag it or I'll mess up my landlord's hardwoods," Fiona answered. "I also want that trunk moved to Mack's room, but I really don't want to empty it out, so we're gonna hafta muscle it up and out." The antique she pointed to was in the art corner near the drafting table, and had been given to her by her Grandpa McCauley when she first left Maine.

"Oh yeah, me and Uncle Calvin watched a movie out here once when you were out late, Mom. Remember the movie, Cal? It was scary but silly scary?" Mack got up abruptly and removed the cushion beneath him until he saw the mattress inside. Then he put the cushion back and awaited a response.

"I do, Mack, I do. We've had lots of boys' nights right here in this very spot."

"Yup," he said, getting down from the couch and going back to the kitchen table to continue a popsicle stick building project. The meatloaf had been in the oven for a while, and Fiona was in no hurry to move things around, so the two of them stayed put and talked.

"So, Mr. Campbell, how are you this fine September evening?" She turned so that her back was against the arm of the sofa, bent her knees, hugged them to her chest, and faced him.

"No complaints," he said, "just feeling restless."

"What do you mean?"

"Well, maybe not restless—more just kind of off. Or uncomfortable, I don't know." He paused and ran his hand down his face from forehead to chin. He looked through the kitchen doorway at Mack, who was completely engrossed, but still he lowered his voice before continuing. "One of my clients came into the restaurant."

"Shit, really? To see you?"

"No—he had no idea I worked there; I don't tell any of them anything about me. This guy is a client I've been meeting with a few times a month for the past three months or so, and there he was pulling out the chair for his wife, and it was just awkward."

"Did they sit in your section? You had to wait on them?" Fiona's eyes got bigger as she asked.

"Yes. He stopped short just in time to prevent his double take from leading to some manufactured explanation, but his wife caught our eye contact. I wonder if she questioned him about it later. About me. I mean I was just my usual charming waiter self, but I was definitely distracted."

"I'll bet," Fiona sympathized. "Are you sure that was his wife?"

"Well, she had a wedding ring on," Calvin answered.

"Does he wear one?" Fiona inquired.

"Let me think," Calvin replied. "Um, no actually, he doesn't."

"So maybe that's not his wife," Fiona theorized. "Maybe she's cheating on someone to be with him and maybe he is married or maybe he isn't. Either way, we know he likes dick."

Calvin slouched down, letting the couch absorb him more fully before emitting a sigh. "Man, who knows? All I know is I didn't like seeing a trick in my workplace." He stared at his feet and closed his eyes.

"Cal," Fiona ventured softly, "maybe this intersection is telling you something. I know the money pays for your amazing condo, but what price are you paying to do this work? I've seen you get more and more discouraged by it over the past few years, and I'm just saying think about it. Maybe think about making a change."

The house smelled like dinner, Mack started singing to himself while he built, and Calvin opened his arrestingly pale blue eyes to meet hers.

"Maybe so, Fi. Wanna move stuff before dinner or after?"

She saw he was done with the topic, so she suggested they go into the kitchen to see how Mack's construction was progressing. Mack explained that after the glue dried he would paint and then hang the sculpture from his bedroom ceiling. It looked like a cube version of a figure eight. Calvin asked him what colors he had in mind, which led to a detailed explanation from the boy. Calvin teased him, warning him gently that his sculpture could end up looking a lot like the outfit he had on.

Mack screwed up his face, but didn't miss a beat, saying, "Pink and orange are in the red family, and green is red's color complement. I'm in perfect harmony."

"Can't argue with perfection," Calvin returned, and then carefully moved Mack's fragile creation to the end of the table so the three of them could eat family style. Their lively volley continued as they ate.

☆☆☆

After dinner, they moved furniture, and the living room looked more open than it had before. Calvin stayed long enough to tuck Mack into bed and then said good-bye to Fiona. The chilled air was in stark contrast to the house full of love and laughter that had just warmed him. He turned the radio up and drove the long way home.

☆☆☆

The two women had been apart just about as long as they could stand it, and arranged to be together Thursday night. Pete worked late and stopped home briefly to walk Turtle and shower, then left him by himself until her return early in the morning. Mack was already asleep by the time she arrived. Though she missed seeing the boy, she was thrilled to the core by what was waiting for her. Not wanting the doorbell to wake Mack, Fiona told Pete the front door would be unlocked, instructing her to let herself in. Once inside, she saw that the entry was lit by one candle, illuminating a small handwritten note saying, *Blow me out.*

She slipped off her boots and left them there, extinguished the flame with her breath, and headed toward another candle on a small table in the hall leading to the bedrooms. A second note informed her to blow this one out and proceed to the bedroom. Mack's door was closed, and Fiona's was open only an inch or so, allowing a scant amount of flickering light to leak out. Pete's senses were heightened by the darkness. She could hear the soft rhythm of her lover's footsteps on the floor and smell lavender mixed with a hint of vanilla. As she slowly pushed the door open, it was pulled from the inside so she could enter. Fiona stayed hidden behind the door and said nothing. There were candles on the windowsills, nightstand, and dresser.

When she emerged from the shadows, Fiona put to shame any goddess ever painted or sculpted. Her hair was tousled, and all she wore was a blissful expression and a full-length, pale gossamer gown so sheer that it revealed far more than it concealed. Their eyes met and spoke while their words remained unsaid. Fiona was the very definition of breathtaking; Pete's respiration faltered as her eyes moved over her body. It was cold enough in the room that Fiona's nipples pointed upwards in gorgeous defiance of age and gravity. The flimsy fabric clung to her flat stomach, hung more loosely around her hips, and then adhered sensuously to her long, well-toned legs.

"It's been ages," Fiona said as she moved closer to Pete.

"Oh Fiona," gasped Pete, "my beautiful, beautiful Fiona." They embraced and shared a kiss. They were helpless under the spell of their own chemistry and soon became dizzy. They stayed upright as they continued kissing, swaying slightly. Fiona had one hand on the back of Pete's head where her hair was damp from her recent shower and slipped the other inside her open jacket to remove it. Pete's shirt was shed, and the straight lines of clothing gave way to the delicate curves and balanced proportions she knew Fiona delighted in.

"Oh my exquisite Petra," Fiona said breathily, "whoever made you, made you right. Let's get the rest of these clothes off so I can look at you."

Pete stood where she was and finished undressing as she was told to until all she had on was candlelight. Fiona wanted to see her better, so she held both her hands, swung Pete's work-strong arms out slowly, and pulled back, the two linked in a graceful, frozen dance move. Her eyes went from Pete's beautiful wide cheekbones down her long neck to her breasts. Her palette was much darker than Fiona's: rosy brown areolas, golden skin, and hair dark as ink. Fiona's eyes lingered for a moment at the appendectomy scar on her right side, and then she touched her there gently. The cool air made her nipples stand at attention, but the goose bumps came from Fiona's sweet caress.

There in the quiet glow, they made love slowly, treasuring each other's tenderness. Fiona pressed her index finger to Pete's lips at one point to shush her when their passion made her forget the sleeping child down the hall. The flickering candles marked time as melted wax spilled over and pooled. The lovers were swollen with ardor and ready to burst. Movements from their two bodies became one rhythm, inhales and exhales replaced by louder throaty sounds. Fiona had to cup her hand over Pete's mouth to muffle her when she climaxed beneath her. Their eyes locked as Fiona's orgasm dovetailed her own. Pete's view rendered itself indelibly in her mind: Fiona with shoulders lifted, head tipped back, her luxuriant hair framing her face with her lips parted just slightly as she gasped with pleasure.

Pete couldn't hold the words back and set them free. "I love you, Fiona."

There was just one beat before her response came.

"I love you too, baby. I really do." She lay down against Pete now, cheek against cheek. Pete felt the distinct trickle of Fiona's tears, which made her cry a little too as they lay there in the silence together.

A while later, Fiona got up to use the bathroom, and, on her way back, blew out all the candles except the one next to the bed. Pete was awake with a peaceful expression on her face. Fiona slid under the covers and spoke softly. "I saw snow."

"Huh?" Pete questioned. "Snow?"

"In my head," she clarified, "when I came. I see things when we make love; I've never hallucinated with a lover like I do when we make love."

Pete felt slightly uncomfortable, so she applied some humor. "Uh-oh," she joked, "did my warning label mention that particular side effect?"

"Silly girl. Seriously, it's wonderful. The first time we made love, there was this huge blue sky in my head, not a New England sky, more like Montana—more enormous than you think a sky could be. And tonight it was snow. Big, fat flakes swirling fast, kinda like what happens when you shake a snow globe. I can still sorta see, or maybe feel, it."

Pete took her words in and didn't use humor to retreat from their meaning this time. "Wow, Fiona... I'm glad, I mean—I love that I can make you feel that good," she said earnestly, "and I love that we made snow in September..." She ran her fingers through Fiona's hair and breathed her in.

"Do you ever have visions?"

"During sex, you mean? Well, no—not quite like you described." Pete paused to consider the question more fully. "I mean, for me it's more like hot orange and blue under my eyelids when I come... But I do see things in my head other times. Things that don't make sense to most people."

"I know you do. You and Mack seem to see things mere mortals like myself can't. Want to tell me more about that?"

Pete felt so secure in Fiona's arms that she opened the gates wide and poured out her story. She told her about the visions, the premonitions, her wild behaviors, and the medications. Pete explained how Grandma Sweets named it the gift of seeing and even revealed how time had been a trickster the day they met.

Pete leafed through pages of memory as she spoke and found herself talking about what happened at Petworld. She had very clearly seen the face of a human on a fish in a large aquarium and demanded a young employee investigate the matter. She described how he had tugged nervously at his blue-and-yellow Petworld vest and scanned the store repeatedly, looking for help with this bizarre customer. Pete had taken a few steps toward the massive tank and put her face close to the glass. She tracked different fish and followed them silently with both index fingers at the same time. Seeing how nervous the employee named Vince was, she told him authoritatively that the goddamned fish with a face should make him nervous because it was a bad omen. She'd informed him how in Japan, they are known to cause tsunamis. That human-faced fish was a disaster just waiting to happen. Though her erratic behavior had alarmed him, her persistence wore him down, and he retrieved a long-handled net from behind the counter. Pete had begun scanning all the fish in the tank. She moved systematically, almost robotically, searching for the offending animal. This flashback ended when Pete revealed to Fiona she had reluctantly admitted to the clerk that she must have seen a reflection of a customer's face on the large black fish, which had frightened her. She then bolted out of the store and was rattled for hours.

Fiona heard about Dr. Percy and the nineteen journals Pete had filled over the past twenty-five years. Pete had not shared this with a lover since Robin. She talked longer than she meant to before stopping. The last candle blinked like it was about to go to sleep as Fiona responded.

"Thanks for telling me all this, love. I hope your intention wasn't to scare me off. I've fallen in, and I don't want out. Your experiences just make you more compelling to me, Pete. I like you, and I'll take all that comes with you because you've turned me inside out. You make me want to show you the things I've been so invested in hiding from the light all these years." She stroked Pete's shoulder, and covered it with the blanket.

"You mean you've got demons too?"

"We all do, honey. Yes. Hey—" She suddenly sounded wide awake. "I have an idea." She turned and sat upright, facing Pete, then put both her hands behind her back playfully. "Pick a hand—any hand!" The corners of Pete's mouth pulled up into a smile. Fiona got theatrical, altering her voice for dramatic effect, and announced, "In each hand is a different demon from the life of Fiona Angeli. Choose which handful of mystery you want revealed to you..."

Pete realized what she was doing. Fiona didn't want to leave her exposed, out in the open, alone. She was willing to stand beside her and share, so they could be vulnerable together. Pete grinned, pointing to her left side. "That one!"

"Oh," Fiona said, "that's a juicy little fistful if ever there was one." She lay back down so both of their heads were on one pillow and looked at the ceiling while she spoke. Pete turned a bit and watched her face, but they didn't make eye contact until Fiona was done talking. She listened without interruption, though questions threatened to spring from her tongue many times. Fiona declared she was a recovered sex addict and explained that on the day they met she had her monthly appointment with her therapist. She jokingly called it an oil change, assuring Pete it was for "basic maintenance," not a major repair. She'd been able to stick to her recovery plan for the last two years or so.

She stuck to the headlines, telling Pete she assumed no one wanted to read the fine print. Fiona said that in her years as a flight attendant, she had sex with more people than she could count. She highlighted the small miracles: no pregnancies and only one straightforward and curable sexually transmitted disease, four negative HIV tests, three years of really helpful therapy, and the overwhelming desire to avoid returning to these all-consuming behaviors. She went on to say that motherhood was the best incentive she ever had to peel back the layers from an obsession that made her feel so bad and so good at the same time.

When she was done talking, she turned to Pete, and their faces were so close Pete saw her in a slight blur. Pete noticed her eyes were moist and put a hand to her face lovingly, letting her thumb stroke Fiona's lips ever so lightly. They both closed their eyes in a silent pause before Pete responded. "That *was* a juicy fistful, Fiona... I believe who we are is where we've been. And we're all works in progress; our imperfections are lessons, and sometimes they're even beautiful." Fiona pulled her face away from Pete's just enough to focus on her clearly, and they stared into each other's eyes as Pete continued. "We're all tinted with some degree of madness, and it makes us more fragile, more interesting. We both have struggles, and all we can do is the best we can do, right?"

"Yeah. Well said. Since I've been working toward recovery, I feel cleaner and more honest. Saner. More present in the parts of my life the addiction overshadowed." She bit her lower lip, lowered her gaze for a moment, then looked Pete in the eye again. "So, I'm not too dirty of a girlie for you, Pete?"

"Dirty?" she repeated with a smile. "Yeah—I think you're just dirty enough for me. Shameful? No. You've got your history, and I've got mine. I've done things that better judgment should have prevented me from doing. I'm grateful you told me all that. Grateful we met." This time no tears came from Fiona's eyes. Instead, she just shut them, sighed, and cuddled as close to Pete as she possibly could. "We've both been going to the same place for the past few years; I'm surprised we didn't bump into each other in that waiting room sooner," Pete marveled.

"I know. Unbelievable." Fiona yawned. "I usually see my therapist the first Thursday of the month, but she had a conflict for September, so you and I collided on a Wednesday. Sometimes conflicts are the sweetest things..."

The little white candle that had so faithfully lit their conversation was now losing fire. The stub of the wick finally drowned in wax, and the two women welcomed the darkness and fell asleep.

# CHAPTER FIVE: ABOUT FACE

*We were having no trouble so the devils got busy.*
*~ Russian Proverb*

Time slows down for two people falling in love; every moment together expands before it contracts. Though they were both independent by nature, Pete and Fiona attached as naturally as shadow follows an object in the sunshine.

One week became two, then three, four, and more; the women were spending a fair amount of time together. Pete wished she could see Fiona more often, but understood that, as a single mother, she had very little free time. Pete did manage to share Fiona and Mack with Sheila by the end of their third week, when the four of them went out for brunch and then to a dog park. Like most people, Sheila was captivated by Fiona's charms, and the two women hit it off. Mack loved how tall Sheila was, telling her she reminded him of a dilophosaurus.

Afterwards, Pete explained to Sheila about Fiona's sex addiction, saying she would have told her sooner, but wanted them to meet first. Sheila listened compassionately and made two sage comments. One was about how we can't change a lover's past stories, just write new ones together. The other was simply a gentle but firm warning to be careful, because addiction of any kind had a way of complicating people's lives.

Shortly after this, Fiona had Calvin and Pete over for dinner, and they shared a laughter-filled evening. Afterwards, Calvin encouraged Fiona to give this relationship a chance, because he really liked Pete.

The warm days of Indian summer were giving way to the cooler, crisper ones of October as New England dabbed apple cider behind her ears and donned a brilliantly colorful frock of autumn leaves.

Mack's eighth birthday was just around the corner, and he wanted help planning the festivities. On a Sunday, Fiona invited Liz, her friend and occasional sex partner, over, and she and Mack sat at the kitchen table writing down ideas for the party and making lists of things they would need to buy or do. Fiona was preparing chicken noodle soup and homemade bread for dinner.

"Babe, you wrote out all twenty-six invitations, right?" she asked him as she opened a can of corn.

"Yeah...I still don't like having to invite everybody. I don't like every kid in my class." He was disgruntled, but resigned, because he knew his mom wouldn't budge. She insisted he invite his whole class every year.

"Well, we can't be *friends* with everyone, but we can be *friendly*," Fiona advised. *We can't have sex with everyone, but we can be sexy,* suddenly flashed in her brain. She almost laughed out loud at her own thoughts. At her therapist's urging, Fiona had decided to drag herself to a Sex Addicts Anonymous meeting. She was having a lot of trouble keeping her demon on a leash lately and, even though she hadn't read the green book in a long time and had an atheist's allergy to the term "higher power," she knew she could derive strength from the chapters in other people's lives. Fiona knew their stories of both triumph and of failure would resonate more with her than the prescriptive twelve steps. She would wait until the Tuesday evening meeting in Lowell, a half hour away. On Tuesdays, Calvin could usually watch Mack, but if not, Fiona could ask Liz or hire a sitter.

"Four," Mack pronounced.

"Four what, sweetie?"

"That's how many kids in my class I like," he said broodingly, reinforcing his point.

*Step four: Make a searching and fearless moral inventory of ourselves,* ricocheted in Fiona's mind.

"Well, four is not enough for a party," Fiona said gently.

"When is Uncle Anthony coming?"

"He's trying to get away this month, but might not come until November. While it's possible that he will be at your party, I don't think it's very likely. I keep meaning to call him and check in," she answered.

"Four makes a group, but not quite a party, Mack. You can have way more fun with more kids here. You know how we talked about hide-and-seek? Well—that's better with a crowd. Think about it," Liz said as she draped her arm around his shoulders.

As Fiona watched them interact, she thought of Pete and how quickly she'd earned Mack's trust. It had taken him several months to warm up to Liz. For a brief moment, she imagined conquering her addiction and being with Pete indefinitely.

Liz and Mack stayed at the table talking, planning, and laughing, while Fiona took the bread out to cool and let the soup simmer. Since the two of them were busy, Fiona stole some time to lie on the couch to read an issue of *Popular Mechanics* that she was in the middle of.

A few hours later, they enjoyed dinner while watching *The Karate Kid*. Liz had told Mack she watched the movie when she was his age, and he was so interested in the plot he wanted to see it. They were all cuddling together beneath a big blanket on the couch, and by the end of the film, Mack was yawning and asking what time it was.

"Eight," his mom answered as she smoothed his hair back lovingly. *Step eight: Make a list of all persons we have harmed and become willing to make amends to them all.*

"I know it's not my bedtime yet, but I think I wanna go to bed now. I'm really sleepy from the movie. I liked it—it just made me think a lot, and now I'm done thinking," Mack declared as he disengaged himself from the women, yawning as he spoke.

His sleepiness was apparently contagious, because Liz yawned as she gave him a goodnight hug. While Fiona got him settled, Liz cleaned up a few things in the kitchen. Then the two women crawled into bed themselves and curled around each other, talking softly in candlelight.

At one point, Fiona cupped Liz's face in her hands and studied her. She was pretty, with dark eyes, an olive complexion, and medium-length, curly hair. Her skin was flawless, making her look younger than she was. Her nose was wide, and her lips were full. Fiona thought of Pete and how different she was from Liz. Being with Liz was easy; she made Fiona feel good. But Pete's touch gave her goose bumps.

When the two of them made love, images of Pete flashed in Fiona's mind, and she squeezed her eyes closed, trying to shut them out, trying to be present. She wanted to stay in the moment; she needed it to be just sex. The last thought Fiona had before drifting to sleep was that she hoped she would never have to make amends to anyone.

Moments later, Fiona's cell phone woke her when it vibrated on the nightstand. When she lifted her heavy lids and saw it was Calvin, she picked up and whispered, "Hello," hoping not to wake Liz.

"Fi? Shit, sorry, I thought you might still be up. I'm sorry I woke you." His voice was colored by edginess, and had an urgency that got Fiona's attention.

"What's wrong?"

"Well, I'm okay—it's just that something happened. With a client. Can I come over just for a little while and talk to you about it? I don't want to wake Mack, but I really..." He stopped, his voice taut like it might break. Fiona got up slowly, grabbed her robe, closed the door quietly behind her, then made her way to the living room.

"Honey, you sound shaken. Just come over. The door will be unlocked, and I'll be up waiting for you." He thanked her, and after they said their good-byes, Fiona turned the heat on, gathered her robe tightly around her, switched on the old lamp next to the couch and sat waiting for her troubled friend.

After about ten minutes, Fiona heard Calvin come in very quietly, and when she saw him in the entry light, she gasped.

"Calvin! What the—a client did this to you? What the fuck? Come in." She hugged him tightly before closing the door. The embrace must have hurt his ribs, as he winced. He looked as if he wanted to cry, but his dam held.

"I'm okay. It just..." He paused and licked his cut, swollen lip. "This trick went sideways."

She studied him, gently touching his chin and tilting it up so his face caught more light. The golden brown skin he got from his mother and the blue eyes he inherited from his father made his face strikingly handsome. She loved him and his kind countenance so much that it pained her to see him beat up. She assessed the damage, and her eyes began to water.

"Fi—please don't get upset. I'm all right. Can I just tell you about it?" She nodded, and they both walked to the living room and sat on the couch.

He pulled off his shoes and sank down into the cushions. "Mack won't wake up, will he? I don't want him to see me like this."

"He hasn't had a bad dream since the night he stayed with you. Don't stress about it. If he comes out here, just think of something to tell him. Oh, Liz is here too, but she's a really sound sleeper."

Fiona wore the pink flannel pajamas with cowboys on them that Calvin had once said made her look like a little girl.

"So, who looks worse, you or him?"

Calvin laughed awkwardly, and then quietly went on to explain how a new client, a very wealthy guy who was a referral, got violent with him. Calvin acknowledged that he'd been told to expect a little rough play, but the account he gave Fiona included a lot more than a few slaps. This man, Thomas, basically tried to overpower him to fuck him in the ass, and when Calvin reminded him that he didn't bottom, a fact which had been made clear to him when he booked Calvin's time, he got even more physical. When Calvin had resisted, his client snapped, throwing punches to his face and torso. Calvin was descriptive enough that the ugly scenes played in her head. When she noticed three of his knuckles were bruised, she had to ask what state the client was in when he left. When Calvin assured her he was breathing, she didn't exactly feel encouraged. Her eyes grew wide with concern, and, as she listened to him, she realized he was trying to reassure himself.

"I don't think he'll call the cops because that would reveal his own culpability. I mean, he assaulted *me*," Calvin said, tapping his chest for emphasis. "This guy's a creep, Fiona. He's got a dark side."

She knew she should just listen, but couldn't hold back her words.

"He more than assaulted you, Calvin. He tried to rape you! You work on the dark side! This work, this—you, you've got to get out of it, Calvin! I know you like the money and maybe sometimes you like the work itself, but I mean, it's *dangerous* work. This is a sign." The pitch of her voice elevated as she continued, determined to say it all. "I know what you're going to say; you're going to tell me that ninety-nine percent of the time things go right and one percent of the time tricks turn bad and it just comes with the territory. You'll tell me this guy was a fluke, a freak, and not to worry. Well I *am* worried, Calvin. You're family, and when you hurt, I feel it too. I—" She stopped herself when she noticed his baby blues were brimming with tears. She held him as the walls finally broke, and he sobbed into her robe. When he caught his breath, he acknowledged something he clearly hadn't been cognizant of until he said it out loud to her.

"I know I have to change my life, but I don't know how, and I'm afraid I can't figure it out, and even more scared of who I'll be if I don't figure it out."

"I'm here," she said. "I'm here to help you sort through your shit like you help me make sense of my life. Want to stay over?" She hated the thought of him being alone when he was so brittle.

"No, no," he sniffled, and even though he didn't appear to want to go home, he said, "you've got a full house, and I should go home."

"If you're worried about Mack seeing your face, we can figure something out," she offered. He shook his head, wiped his nose, and thanked her with a kiss on her forehead. When he got up to leave he looked shorter somehow, as if his recent experience had compressed him. Fiona saw more than weariness in the way he hung his shoulders as he walked out her front door; she recognized the gravity of his life on him and marveled at how emptiness could weigh so much.

☆☆☆

Pete's current painting gig was all the way out in Essex, which was about a fifty-minute drive. Despite a lengthy commute, Pete had been enjoying the job so far, because the client was particularly nice, and the work was challenging and profitable. She was refinishing some woodwork as well as painting the kitchen and dining room of a beautiful old house owned by an engaging woman in her sixties named Hollis Dunn. Like Pete, she had a first name which, on paper, often fooled the world into thinking she was a man.

Normally, a client who was home all day would be a burden for Pete, because she craved solitude. But Hollis was different; she spent most of her time in her art studio working on watercolors, and when she wasn't in there, she was offering Pete a drink or a snack, usually accompanied by a short story from her colorful life. She'd been part of the women's movement, and helped found a Boston organization called Bread and Roses, which was the first socialist women's organization in the US. She, along with many other activists, advocated for concerns like abortion and other reproductive rights, equal employment, laws against discrimination, childcare, and preventing violence against women.

"We needed a meeting place, but didn't have any cash, so we were basically squatters in an unoccupied building owned by Harvard. We offered free childcare and classes for women, but the university managed to force us out. This ended up being a good thing, because our plight moved people to donate a lot of money, and we bought the place on Pleasant Street in Cambridge in '72, which, as you probably know, is the longest running women's center in the country!"

Pete would keep painting as she listened, occasionally looking up from her work to make polite eye contact. She imagined a young Hollis working with other ardent feminists to improve the lives of women by empowering them. She could hear her making speeches with a voice not yet textured by time. She pictured her with long hair— not the short, tidy coiffure Hollis wore now. When Pete first came to meet her for the estimate, she'd thought Hollis was a lesbian, but then discovered framed photos of her with her late husband and their three children.

The ochre paint went on the kitchen walls as the short stories came off her tongue. They were interesting and not too meandering, and while Hollis had much to be proud of, she was always matter-of-fact and never self-aggrandizing. In the 1980s, she managed to hold a high-profile professorship in the women and gender studies department of Smith College while also having her children. Pete remembered a few experiences of her own at that school. She used to get really restless in college and drive the hundred miles to Northampton to explore the town and the campus on foot. Hoping for some romance, she would scope out the "Smithies," but if no adventure could be found, she would settle for enjoying the facilities while she posed as a Smith student. She especially loved the stately brick library with its gently sloping ceilings and amazing book collections.

Hollis had several bookcases in her home, even in the kitchen; reading was an interest they shared. As much as Pete liked and respected this client, she still needed material for her sculptures, and by the last day of the job, Pete had pilfered several small items. She took a little round pin that said, *Woman's place is in the world*; a yellowed, slender volume of poetry; a tiny pewter decorative spoon that was one of dozens haphazardly displayed in a glass-doored cabinet in the dining room; a blue-and-gold pen that said *Smith College*, and a minuscule deer carved out of wood that fell to the ground when she moved a small bookcase to paint behind it. The only way she could assuage her guilt was to immerse herself in the very activity that justified the years of thefts; she incorporated the items into a new collage she started that night, working obsessively until four in the morning.

"I like how this one is starting off," Sheila remarked about it the following evening. "It looks like a timeline for a really interesting woman." Pete had lined the eight compartments inside an old wooden crate with torn pages of poetry and placed the other objects that belonged to Hollis inside the cubes, along with other small articles removed from various clients' homes. Sheila stood at the workbench and traced her sizable hand along the rough wood. "You really ought to share these creations, Pete; you haven't had work in a show in years. In fact,

Prospect Street Gallery is looking for local artists who work in three-dimensional and mixed media; my coworker Ren told me about that."

Pete looked up from the salad she was making them for dinner and said flatly, "I don't know."

"What stops you from trying to get your work seen and even sold? Your pieces are beautiful and thought-provoking."

Pete focused more on cutting up a cucumber than she needed to. Her eyes were fixed, and she didn't say anything.

"Is it the guilt? Or the fear that something in one of your sculptures will be recognized? I mean, I know you kind of walk a dangerous line, since the thefts could jeopardize your livelihood and all." Sheila took a few long-legged strides over to the kitchen, obviously hoping proximity would engender a more substantial response. They were extremely close friends, and part of what they did for each other involved pushing on sensitive spots.

Pete tossed the cucumber in the bowl and replied, "No, well, yes—sort of. I mean, it's highly unlikely that would happen. I'm guessing that when clients notice these things are gone, enough time has lapsed that they don't connect the lost items with their house painter. I know it's fucked-up, and illegal, and a violation of trust—but I can't seem to stop. I try to take little things..." She went about setting the table.

Sheila picked up her wine glass, took a long sip, and remained straightforward with her. "But sweetie, you can't know what anything means to anybody. As you well know, objects have story. They're bookmarks for memory, guideposts to help us navigate our own past. For all you know, that little wooden deer has a lot of sentimental value to Hollis. I'm just saying."

Pete's expression remained neutral as she countered, "Intellectually, I know you are one hundred percent right. But, well—I try to judge the value of something by where it's located. Shit, but as I listen to myself talk, it just smells like bullshit." She gestured to Sheila to sit and served them heaping plates of ravioli.

"It's not exactly bullshit, Pete. You just do what you do, like anyone else does. We're all flawed. We all break some rules. Do you think you could stop stealing? I mean, lots of your stuff is from dumpsters, junk shops, and flea markets, so why not get all of it from those places?"

Pete chewed on her salad and the question. Dark circles from her marathon work session the night before highlighted the intense look in her eyes as she spoke. "I suppose I need to take objects from people for them to have a certain kind of power or mystique." She used them the way a writer might recycle overheard conversations into dialogue, or combine other people's experiences with inspiration to create the alloy known as fiction. She stole belongings for her art like a journalist might turn someone's secret inside out for the sake of a big story.

Sheila stayed on the topic but took another tack. "In a fucked way, maybe showing your pieces would honor the people you took all that stuff from. You know?"

Pete said "maybe" with her face, took a bite of ravioli, and then stopped eating, staring at Sheila before she spoke. "I know you're concerned about my stealing, and I love you for it, but at this time, I'm not going to stop. So can we talk about something else, please?"

"Okay, Pete. I'll let you slide for now, but don't think I won't bring it up again," she admonished gently. "And if you find yourself in the type of jam that allows you one phone call, you'd better call *me*. I mean, I know Fiona is your girl, but she's also a mommy, and mommies are always busy because they are in constant demand. I'm here for you 24/7, sweetie. Till the end of time." She finished with a light squeeze of Pete's hand.

"Sheila Rider, don't ever change. I'll take you just the way you are. Now, let's talk about *you*." Pete decided it was her turn to do the interviewing and asked if Sheila and Damon had made a date to meet, or if they were still enthralled merely to be pen pals.

It turned out they had both wanted to get together over a week ago, but their schedules kept clashing, and they did in fact have a date for this Saturday. Sheila was all too happy to tell Pete the little things she'd learned about Damon in his most recent email. Her enthusiasm brought some needed levity to the evening. Pete was astonished to hear they hadn't exchanged pictures yet and had made a mutual promise not to check each other out via social media; they both wanted to be surprised, but did describe themselves physically for each other. Damon was six foot five and powerfully built, and had a dark complexion. He'd left Alabama to attend college in Boston, fell in love with the northeast, and stayed.

Pete asked her friend how she'd described herself, and Sheila replied, "My usual description: six two and skinny, brown hair, blue eyes."

"That's *it*? You didn't say you're pretty with great skin and fabulous long hair? You gotta stop seeing yourself as that gangly stork of a teenager you were twenty-five years ago, honey."

Sheila laughed and then went on to say she might have added more details, but in any case, he was still interested. Saturday couldn't come soon enough for her; she just had to figure out what to wear. Pete was happy for her friend and hoped this would bloom into a lasting romance. They finished dinner, cleaned up together, and then sat on the couch with Turtle, drinking wine, talking, and laughing for almost two more hours.

After Sheila left, Pete went right back to her workbench with her wine glass and stared at her sculpture for a while. Her head was fuzzy from the alcohol, and when her eyes landed on the delicately sculpted deer, she thought she saw its mouth move. She emitted a soft laugh and said out loud, "What, so now the things I steal are going to talk to me? I better have some more wine then." Thinking she was talking to him, Turtle came over with his tail wagging, looking up at her lovingly. "Hey, boy." She bent to him and rubbed under his chin and behind his ears. "Who's a good boy, huh? Who's my sweet boy?" He licked her face and studied her after she pulled away. She drained the glass of zinfandel and faced the miniature.

"Do you even remember the first thing you took from someone's house, Pete? If you do, I will tell you my story," the curio offered. Pete sat on the stool, her mouth slightly open for a moment before she could shape some words.

"I do. It was an antique button I found in the corner of a room. It was a really old house in Newton, and the client's name was Bunny. Who could forget that? I painted the upstairs bedrooms and her office—that's where I saw the button. It was just so beautiful and forgotten." Her speech was slow because she was fairly intoxicated by now. "So—now it's time for you to keep your end of the deal, little guy." Her vision was getting blurred now, but she continued to look at the tiny animal and was pretty sure its mouth was still moving.

"Okay. Here's my story: I was carved from basswood by Hollis's grandfather and given to her on her ninth birthday. The two had seen a buck when walking through the woods on the family land in Vermont, and young Hollis was captivated by its beauty. Turns out, I was the last thing the talented Grandpa Dunn could carve because of a stroke he suffered soon after he created me; his hands never worked the same. I am one of only three keepsakes from her grandfather that she had left. She will search until she finds me. She's sharp as a knife and will put two and two together, Pete, so be prepared. That's my final word to you."

"What do *you* know? You're not really talking anyway. Shit. It's the wine. Or my brain. Or both. I'd better write this all down before I pass out." Pete got up and stumbled a little as she made her way back to the couch with her dog following closely. She opened the drawer of the coffee table, and took out a fountain pen and a large journal with *#20* written on the cover. Turtle kept a close watch on her as she yawned, sighed, and began to write.

☆☆☆

Fiona's boss, Sharon, was so pleased with the work she'd done on the Bradshaw case that she let her leave the office early Thursday, so Fiona had several hours to herself before she had to pick up Mack from school. The house was clean, there wasn't much laundry to do, the refrigerator was well stocked, and she couldn't think of an errand she had to run, so she decided to go clothes shopping for something sexy to wear on her next date out with Pete.

She got off the T at Back Bay Station and made her way past all the urban characters who peppered the sidewalk in the South End to a favorite vintage clothing store she went to a few times a year. Your Auntie's Attic was a fairly large place in a brick building that housed some other interesting shops. The store windows were artfully dressed to lure shoppers inside, and as Fiona entered, she picked up a trace of patchouli in the air. A tall, beautiful woman with light brown dreadlocks the same color as her skin greeted her from behind the counter. There were maybe a dozen shoppers inside, most of them women.

An off-white forties-style blouse with a delicate collar and peplum caught her eye, and as she reached up to remove it from the high rack for closer inspection, she lost her balance and accidentally bumped a nearby woman with her colossal canvas satchel. "Sorry, I'm dangerous with this bag," Fiona said amiably. As the words came out of her mouth, she noticed how exquisite the woman was.

"No worries," came back wrapped in a piquant Australian accent. "They pack the merchandise in here so tightly collision is inevitable." Her gaze went from Fiona to the blouse, and she spoke again. "You'd look great in that."

"Oh, thanks," Fiona said, studying her. She recognized a familiar predatory glint in her eyes and felt a magnetic pull that made her keep talking. "I'm Fiona." She extended her free hand.

"Yes, you are," the woman stated with confidence and charm. "I'm Abigail, and I have to say—you look really familiar to me..."

Fiona screwed her face up a bit, trying to recall if she'd ever met this dynamic woman before. As she searched her memory, she took her in from head to toe: from the neck up, she had blonde hair in a stylish short cut, fair skin with freckles, almond-shaped hazel eyes, an aquiline nose, and well-turned lips. The rest of her was lean and sinewy with subtle curves. They stood roughly the same height, and Fiona couldn't tell if Abigail was older or younger than she was. Then it hit her: she'd seen her at a Sex Addicts Anonymous meeting about a year ago.

"SAA," Fiona said quietly.

"Oh yes, right!" Abigail's face lit up as she asked, "How's that all going for you?" waited a beat, then added, "Pretty nosy, aren't I?" Fiona was completely captivated by her looks, her accent, and her boldness.

"Well, you're asking about something I shared freely with you and others at the meeting, so nosy might not be the word I'd choose to describe your question." She bit her lower lip as she searched for more to say, but Abigail beat her to it.

"Why don't we meet in the fitting room and you can tell me all about it?"

The little hairs on the back of Fiona's neck stood up. Blood rushed to her loins, and she parted her lips to answer the invitation, but no words came out.

Abigail grabbed a blouse from the rack without even looking at it, then cast her eyes toward the back of the store before leaning in and saying in a near whisper, "I'll go on ahead, then you come in a minute after. They have four different changing stalls—I doubt anyone will notice if one's occupied for a while. Come on, I'll help you try that on."

Time slowed way down, and the tiny empty spaces between any markers that can measure it dilated, causing this exchange to take up more space than time. The invitation compelled in the same way a dangerous cliff dares one to walk to its precipice.

Abigail was close enough that Fiona felt her breath on her neck and smelled her skin; she was keenly aware of her own transmogrification to a base, animalistic, and ravenous state. Her longing made her much like a werewolf under a full moon or a vampire thirsting for blood. She was swallowed up by her own desire and, like she'd done hundreds of times in her life, decided to go on a ride with a virtual stranger.

"Okay, go," finally came out of Fiona's mouth.

She waited about a minute and then took the blouse to the fitting room she'd watched Abigail go into and furtively slipped between the curtains. She saw her leaning against the back wall with her index finger pressed against her lips, making the universal sign to be quiet. Abigail pointed first to her left, then her right, indicating they had neighbors on both sides and had to be silent. Then, with the same finger, she beckoned Fiona to come closer. She did and hung both the blouse and her bag on a hook, then walked into Abigail's open arms and kissed her passionately.

Abigail ran a hand through Fiona's luxurious hair and moaned. Fiona had one hand on the woman's neck. With the other she explored under her skirt, delighted to discover that she wasn't wearing panties. As they kissed, Fiona probed and teased, knowing it would be harder for Abigail to mute her arousal. The risk of getting caught hadn't lost its potency for either of them, and they each vented some small, throaty sounds of pleasure as Fiona touched her for several minutes. Abigail was hard, wet, and nearly ready to detonate, so Fiona slowed her movements down to tantalize her. Pressure built, kisses went deeper, and then came the familiar spasm that made Fiona feel larger than life. After she felt Abigail climax, she noticed through a tiny gap in the curtains that two customers were waiting to try on clothes and gestured to her partner in crime that they should be leaving.

Abigail mouthed the words *that was hot, thanks,* and *good-bye* to her, parted the curtains, and left. Fiona heard her tell the people in line, "My friend is still trying something on."

She quickly removed her sweater to see if the blouse did indeed fit. Making eye contact with herself in the mirror, she noticed the crescent-shaped scar on her forehead because it showed more than usual under the fluorescent lights. She had been sixteen when she fell down the front steps of her school and smacked her head into the railing. Although the doctor had stitched her up as carefully as he could, he'd recommended plastic surgery to prevent scarring. Fiona had refused, telling her parents she didn't want to make a fuss. But her real reason was that she hoped a scar would make her less attractive to others, somehow ordinary, and more overlooked than stared at. Some people declared that her beauty was marred. Others reassured her it would disappear over time. Twenty years later, Fiona thought it had become imperceptible, but here beneath the glare there was no denying its permanence, which got her thinking about her behavior and wondering if she could really change. She hoped her addiction, too, would fade into a faint trace of a story.

Abigail was right: she did look great in the top, so she made her purchase and then headed home.

☆☆☆

The rest of the week before Mack's party, Pete threw herself into a sculpture she was making for him. Collage was her favorite medium, and she had expertise in that area, but she also loved to render and sculpt things realistically in clay, preferring to leave them earthen than to add color to them. Sheila had suggested it when Pete asked for input on Mack's gift, because she loved these types of pieces, counting among her most prized possessions a sculpture of her and her four dogs Pete had made in honor of her fortieth birthday. Wanting Fiona to be surprised too, Pete kept the project under wraps. Fiona had been somewhat remote lately, so Pete was glad to have the gift to work on at her place in the evenings, finding it easier to be away from her than near her when she was remote. But this distance worried Pete less when she and Fiona ended up having spontaneous phone sex three nights before Mack's party, and she was relieved when they made love the next night.

One evening when she was working on the sculpture, Sheila called. Pete put her on speaker so her hands remained free. It turned out that Damon was a prince of a guy, just as amazing in person as he was in emails and phone calls. The two hit it off, and Sheila described how they had two wonderful dates, the second of which ended in bed. She was on fire, her voice more animated than usual. Pete was thrilled for her friend and expressed that she wanted to meet him when the time was right. Sheila warned that she was having enough sex to make up for her half-year dry spell and that it might be a while before they emerged from their sex cocoon.

When Sheila stopped doing most of the talking and asked Pete how she was, she almost told her how the deer figurine talked to her, but decided against it. She didn't want to dampen her friend's bright spirits with worry, even though she knew she had to unburden herself for the sake of her mental health. It was not enough to shelter the story in her journal.

☆☆☆

When his eighth birthday finally arrived, Mack came into his mother's room first thing in the morning.

"T minus five hours, thirty-four minutes! Can I open my present from Grandma and Grandpa now? And Uncle Liam and Aunt Francesca?"

"Wait till I'm up and dressed; I want to see you open all that stuff. 'Kay?" Fiona said through a yawn. He nodded and left. She slowly got out of bed to begin the morning breakfast rituals.

Mack was running around the backyard, firing an imaginary gun, and Fiona opened the sliding glass door to say, "Hey, mister! You're in bare feet! Come in and get some shoes on if you're going to keep zooming around out there!"

"Dogs don't wear shoes, so why should I?" he answered back. It looked like Mack was trying to reason his way out of obeying his mother, so Fiona had to hold her ground. She had her hands on her hips, which Mack emulated.

Suddenly he ran from her, opened the door, and went flying to his room. Moments later, Mack returned with his snow boots on, announcing that his feet were more than adequately protected and that he'd like some birthday pancakes, please. He ran outside, but came in after only a few minutes and moved all of his mail from the side counter to the table, where he tore into it.

Fiona's parents had sent him a card saying they were very sorry to miss his birthday celebration this year because their close friends were getting married the same day as the party, but that they would come to see him soon. Their gift was a large, colorful illustrated book about robots, his current interest. He was delighted to discover they'd inserted five-dollar bills in the pages. He counted one hundred dollars and squealed with delight.

"The perks of being the only grandchild," Fiona editorialized, "for now, but don't count Uncle Liam out—he's getting really serious about his current girlfriend."

Said uncle gave him a New York Yankees jacket and, in his card, invited them to come stay in the Big Apple with him and Tara. From

Aunt Francesca, he got a microscope. She worked as a molecular biologist for a company in Philadelphia, and hoped she wasn't the only scientist in the family.

"Nothing from Uncle Anthony," Mack said flatly. "I guess he forgot."

"I doubt he forgot you, baby; maybe his gift will come late. Do you remember what I told you? That he and Dawn are getting divorced? Well, that's some heavy stuff, so he might be kind of off right now, but I know he'll come through for you," she offered. "When do you want *my* present? Now or after the party?"

"Well, now sounds fun, but it would be really nice to save your gift for after the party."

She admired his restraint and told him he had a lot of wisdom for eight. Over breakfast, Fiona informed Mack that he had chores to do before guests arrived at one; he had to put his laundry away and clean his room, which had gotten extremely disorganized. She got her phone and dialed her parents' number, then handed her son the phone, telling him to thank his grandparents before they went to the wedding. After a short chat, he gave his mother the phone and dashed outside.

Calvin showed up around 11. Although his face looked much better than the last time Fiona saw it, he was still scuffed up.

"Where's the Mackster?" he asked.

"He's outside running around shooting invisible bad guys," Fiona answered. "I'll go check on him." She gestured toward the coffeepot, telling him to have some, and then went outside to retrieve the boy.

Mack came in and rushed to greet Calvin with a big hug. Fiona was right behind him. "I'm glad you're here before everyone else, Cal. Hey—" He stopped himself when he got a good look at Calvin's face. "What happened to you?" His voice was full of concern and his face drooped into an expression of worry.

Calvin spun a fib about boxing class, which prompted Mack to remark on how neat that was and ask him to show him some moves. Calvin said he would and asked him if he was ready for his big day.

"Yes and no. Yes, in that it's my real actual birth date today, not just the Saturday closest to it—so I'm very ready to receive presents. No, because Mom said I have to clean my room. Want to help me?"

Fiona chimed in that first Calvin was going to help set up the tables, chairs, and games in the yard, so Mack left to go start cleaning his room.

Parties for Mack always made Fiona a little nervous because they usually underscored what she had been worried about for years: her son's struggles with making and keeping friends. In preschool, his social skills were on par with his peers, but once he got to elementary school, he had difficulties. His classmates either labeled him as weird and kept their distance, or tried to be friends with him but were ultimately alienated by his intellect and odd behavior. He'd always gotten along better with adults or older kids, so Fiona did what she could to help him make friends his own age, including hosting an annual party.

When they were out there and Fiona said she couldn't believe Calvin was off work again, he informed her about his employer's request that he not return to work until his face looked better; looking the way he did now, he might upset the customers.

She was infuriated and said that it was total BS and illegal. She advised him to show up for his next shift, and if his boss said anything, to simply ask him two things: *1. So, if a server here is victimized by a crime that leaves marks on his or her face, he or she is not allowed to work? 2. Are you aware that this is a violation of Massachusetts labor law?*

He nodded and said that was good advice. Fiona was surprised at times by her friend's passive acceptance of things. They got the yard set up, and then Calvin went to check on Mack's progress, leaving her to do food preparations.

Most parents were happy to drop off their children and have a few hours of kid-free time, but some preferred to stay and enjoy the setting. After a few guests arrived, Fiona got a text from Pete saying she had one of her migraines and couldn't make it, but would try to come over later. She asked her to tell Mack she would make it up to him.

It was unusually warm for the third week of October, so the children ate their pizza and salad outside on two huge folding tables Fiona had borrowed from a couple she was friendly with in the neighborhood. Jack and Izzy were happy to help in this way, and showed up at the party with a gift for Mack. Other guests included the friends Fiona made in birthing class: Nadia and her son, Pavel, and Lily and her daughter, Wylie. When the kids were all younger, they got the group together more often, but after Nadia and her family moved to Worcester and Lily had two more children, they didn't see each other more than a few times a year. Still, Mack rushed to greet Pavel and Wylie and quickly integrated them with his classmates.

The games Liz and Mack planned went well; Liz supervised a relay race of sorts called Balloon Sandwich, and Mack explained the rules of hide-and-seek to everyone.

It was easy to see that Calvin got a kick out of the kids; he enjoyed watching them get grubby from eating and running around. He liked talking to Fiona's friends, especially Izzy. She had a fantastic sense of humor and cracked him up when she generated comical narratives about what the kids were up to, pretending to be a sports commentator. She was doing this while they were taking whacks at the robot piñata Mack and Liz had made together. "And curly-haired boy winds up to take a swing. This announcer suspects he is peeking because his blindfold is askew. Ladies and gentlemen, if this rookie hits the way I think he will, he may just be the player to smash that sucker open!"

Mack's expression suddenly caught Liz's attention, and she saw what was coming right before Fiona did. He walked up to the boy in the blindfold and raised his voice saying, "You're cheating, Spencer. Stop!" Fiona immediately intervened, trying to ameliorate the situation, but Mack was insistent and yelled, "You're getting all shadowy just like you do sometimes in class, but you're not going to win *here*!" Then he grabbed the bat from the boy's hands. Liz started to head over to them, but Calvin was closer and got there first. He took the bat from Mack and handed it back to Spencer, who'd now removed his blindfold and was starting to cry.

"Here," Calvin said to him. "Hit it till it breaks, come on." While Calvin managed this, Fiona escorted Mack to an empty corner of the yard for a tête-à-tête. Nadia emerged from the kitchen with the cake, oblivious to the awkward situation that had just unfolded. Liz went to her and quietly explained what happened, and Nadia looked over at Fiona and her son, appeared to interpret their body language, then suggested they just go ahead and serve the cake. Spencer finally smashed the robot open, and most of the children rushed to scoop up the candy scattered all over the ground.

Nadia was lighting the candles because she saw Mack walking over. He whispered in her ear that his mom had ordered him to serve Spencer the first piece along with an apology.

She rubbed his back and told him that was a great idea, but that he should make a wish first.

He looked up at the faces all around him. Then he closed his eyes, paused, and blew out the eight candles. Nadia handed him the first piece, and he dutifully walked it over to Spencer who was still upset. "Sorry, Spencer," Mack managed. The boy showed no reaction; that infuriated Mack because he thought the cake would fix things. "Here," Mack insisted, raising the plate closer to the boy's face, "take it—it's good, I'm *sorry*."

Still Spencer just blinked at him, saying nothing, and Mack lost a very short battle with his own impulse control. He shoved the cake in the boy's face and then ran into the house.

Calvin marched in after him while Fiona attempted to do some damage control, apologizing to Spencer and everyone else. Nadia encouraged the kids to line up for cake, which most of them did. Lily went into the kitchen and came out with a wet towel, which she handed to Fiona so she could wipe the boy's face. A few of the kids stayed close in an attempt to comfort poor Spencer who, surprisingly, wasn't crying. He was licking icing off his lips and blinking under the weight of cake in his lashes.

"Oh, Spencer, we are so very sorry, honey; Mack has *never* acted like this. I'll clean you up and get you another piece. Mack will make this right with you, I promise." She looked around and saw a few of the parents had disgusted looks on their faces, and she wanted to disappear. She saw Liz and Nadia passing out cake and hoped that would turn the tide of the party.

"Ow," Spencer said, "that kinda hurts." Fiona then wiped his face more gently.

As she cleaned him up, she asked if he wanted to go home, and he surprised her again when he said no. After he got his cake, the party almost got back on track again, but the birthday boy was still absent. Calvin had been trying to convince him to be a man and go out and apologize to everyone, but Mack refused.

"You should be asking me more about Spencer's shadows," he asserted. Calvin tried to make sense of this, but was losing patience.

After the cake had been gobbled up, the handful of parents present started gathering up their children and goodie bags, and the party got smaller. Having given up on Mack, Calvin came out to find the crowd had thinned considerably.

Before long, it was five: time for kids to get picked up. Lily and Nadia said some helpful things to try to comfort Fiona about her son's behavior, but she still felt terrible about it. Lily suggested Pavel and Wylie go say good-bye, but Fiona said that wasn't necessary, because if Mack couldn't come back out here, then he didn't get a good-bye. There were farewell hugs, and then just Fiona, Calvin, and Liz were left to clean up.

They were all in the backyard and didn't hear the doorbell at first. Anthony was standing there with a duffel bag on his shoulder and a present under his arm.

# CHAPTER SIX: SHINY THINGS

*Brothers and sisters are as close as hands and feet.*
*~ Vietnamese Proverb*

"Anthony!" Fiona sang out as she threw her arms around him. He set down his things so he could hug her properly.

"I was gonna call but figured—ah, why not surprise them! Is the party over?"

"Yes, it's over, but that's for the best. It's so amazing that you're here! I gotta say, you look really good, considering what's going on in your life right now."

He was about to respond but saw Liz and Calvin coming toward the entry.

"Calvin! Long time no see, man!" he said with a big grin. The two men hugged, and then Anthony looked at Liz and said, "Hello, good to see you again." His voice was deep and warm, and its timbre was like Fiona's, though his Maine accent was much stronger. They all moved toward the living room, and Anthony asked, "Where's the birthday boy? Playing with his loot? Ma-ack?" he bellowed.

Fiona was about to explain the situation when Mack appeared in the doorway. His face was bright for the first time since the piñata incident, and he crashed into his uncle, hugging him tightly around the waist. Anthony messed up his hair affectionately and told him he was taller than the last time he saw him.

"That was just this summer, Uncle Anthony; logically I can't be *that* much taller," the boy said. Anthony commented that he was still the same kid, just eight now instead of seven. He handed him his present, and Mack looked up at his mother searchingly. "Um, Mom, Calvin, Liz—I'm sorry for what happened at the party. Uncle Anthony, I *don't* want to get into the details now, but let's just say I made a big scene and I'll have a lot of explaining to do when I see my classmates Monday. Ugh," he said, sounding deflated.

"Oh Mack, it can't be *that* bad," his uncle consoled.

"Yes, it can," he countered. Behind him Fiona, Calvin, and Liz all nodded to Anthony, trying to convey that it was, in fact, a debacle. "There's *your* present and gifts from these guys to open, but I'm not feeling that deserving right now..."

"Oh Mack, seems to me you know you were wrong, and need a plan to make it right. It's still your birthday today, and opening gifts is what we do on birthdays," Liz imparted helpfully.

Fiona took her brother's coat and bag and put them in Mack's room, then asked him if he was hungry. He told her he was always hungry. She laughed and went to warm up some leftover pizza. Mack started unwrapping his gift, and Fiona returned in time to see him reveal the packaging for a fancy collapsible fishing rod.

"The other part of the gift is waiting in Maine. I'm going to teach you to drive the boat, and we're going on a fishing trip," Anthony announced.

"Cool! Thanks," said the boy enthusiastically.

Calvin's gift was next, and Mack eagerly removed the wrapping to reveal a rocket toy. "Oh—I know these things! You stomp on them, and they can go two hundred feet in the air!"

"Actually, this model can go as high as four hundred feet," Calvin informed him.

"Thanks, Calvin. Let's play with it before it gets dark, okay?"

"Sure, but you're not all out of presents yet, my friend," he said. Fiona went to the pantry, where her gift was hidden, and brought it out.

"Here you go, son," she said as she set it on the large, low table.

The rectangular package was heavy, and it made rattling noises when he moved it. He'd figured out what it was before he undid the wrapping paper, announcing, "It's a toolbox." Eyes wide with curiosity, he looked through everything. Inside were screwdrivers, a hammer, two adjustable wrenches, a small antique hand drill, pliers, a level, a lightweight utility knife with a Post-it stuck to it that read *with supervision only*, a twelve-foot tape measure, and a small handsaw. In addition to these implements, the box contained safety goggles, nails, screws, duct tape, sandpaper, and glue.

"Wow. That's all I can say, Mom. Thanks! I can do *so* much with all this; it's an awesome toolbox!"

Fiona was so happy to see him this excited, she almost forgot about the party disaster. Her phone chimed in the kitchen, and she saw it said:

*Migraine is finally gone. Can I come over with Mack's gift? OK if I spend the night?*

Fiona knew Liz had to leave soon, so she texted back: *Yes! You coming now?*

Pete wrote back that she would be there in about a half hour. Fiona went back into the living room and was enjoying the scene when Liz appeared with her backpack, kissed Fiona on the cheek, and said goodbye to the guys, giving Mack a hug before she left.

"Pete's coming with a present for you, Mack!" Fiona announced. He smiled as he kept reading.

Anthony raised his eyebrows at her, and Calvin smiled and shook his head slightly. She smirked at her brother, and asked if he wanted some salad to go with the leftover pizza, and he said he did, asking if she had any beer.

When Pete arrived, Fiona greeted her at the door with a kiss, taking Mack's gift from her and setting it down gently. "Oh, I can see traces of that migraine in your face. Is your head okay now, baby?" Fiona asked.

Pete nodded and said she was more or less better.

"There's someone here I want you to meet," she told Pete as she bent to pet Turtle's head. He ran into the house, sniffing the floor as he headed toward the kitchen. She took Pete by the hand, led her in there, and introduced her to Anthony, who was scratching the dog behind the ears and cooing to him. He stood up and greeted her with a hug.

"Great little dog! What's his name?"

"Thanks. Turtle."

They took stock of each other for a moment. She saw Fiona's eyes set in a darker face that was both friendly and handsome. His black hair was wavier and coarser than his sister's. He was tall and thickly built, with a lot of presence. Two shiny things caught Pete's eye: his unaffected demeanor and the gold band still on his finger.

He saw an attractive woman with a golden tint to her skin, short dark hair, and hazel eyes set in a wide face. To him, she looked intelligent, kind, and somehow familiar.

"Great to meet you, Pete. I've heard good things about you," he said.

"Likewise, Anthony," Pete said.

"You know who she reminds me of, Fiona? It just hit me," he announced, pointing to Pete.

"Haven't a clue," she responded.

"Michelle Fournier!" he said with satisfaction. Pete asked who she was, and Fiona said it was a long story. "You don't see it, Fi? They could be sisters." Fiona informed him she was going to make a real dinner and not to fill up on pizza.

"So," Pete said, "which one of you is going to tell me who Michelle Fournier is?"

The Angelis chuckled. Anthony mumbled something about his mouth being too full, which prompted Fiona to tease him, saying that usually didn't stop him from talking. They went back and forth like this for a little while, which made Pete reflect on how she and her brother weren't close enough to have this banter. Rudolph lived only an hour and a half away, and she hadn't even seen him in almost a year.

After Anthony had put away a few bites, he told Pete about Michelle. She was the first girl Fiona had liked, and apparently the two of them had a very steamy summer between sophomore and junior year in high school. It had been the early nineties, so people were getting more tolerant of different lifestyles, but they kept their romance secret because their town was so damned small. Anthony had known about it, because he and his sister were confidants. He maintained that Pete definitely resembled her, but Fiona insisted Pete was more beautiful.

"Take my word for it," Anthony said after a swig of beer, "you bear a definite resemblance, and that's a compliment."

"Okay," Pete said with a smile, "I'll take your word for it. Where's the birthday boy?"

"Outside with Calvin, playing with the toy he gave him," Fiona answered. "Let's go."

Turtle barked when he went out and saw the rocket shoot through the air. True to its claims, the toy went so high up they could barely see it against the darkening sky. Fiona had told Pete about how Calvin had gotten into a terrible fight with a client, but she was still taken aback by the bruises on his beautiful face.

"Pete!" Mack yelled, then ran to her. "Are you okay?"

"I'm fine, buddy. I just had one of those bad headaches I get sometimes. I'm *really* sorry I missed your party." His face got serious when she said that.

"It's okay, Pete. You're here now. Come try the rocket; it's really fun!"

They each took a turn launching it and, luckily, the rocket didn't stray over the fence. The five of them played until twilight made the toy virtually invisible, then came inside.

"Last one, big guy," Pete said to Mack as she pointed to her gift. "It's fragile so be very careful."

He heeded her warning, unwrapping it gently. Inside the box, the piece was swathed in bubble wrap, which would later be sacrificed to the god of fun in a popping frenzy.

"Whoa!" came from him when he saw the delicate sculpture, which he instantly recognized as himself and Turtle. He studied every detail of it, running his fingers over the faces. "You *made* this?"

"Yeah—just for you. Like it?"

"No. I *love* it. Will you help me build a special shelf in my room for it? I got a toolbox from Mom, so we can use *my* tools! I don't want anything to happen to it, ever," he declared.

Pete told him she'd be happy to help him do that.

Calvin said he had to get going, but didn't say why. When saying good-bye to Anthony, he thanked him for not asking about his face. Anthony smiled and shrugged his shoulders, joking that it was his business, saying there was rarely a happy story about a bruised-up face.

Fiona recruited Anthony to help with dinner, and the two of them chatted away while Pete and Mack went through the toolbox and discussed all of the things Mack wanted to build.

After a delicious dinner, Mack and Anthony cleaned up the kitchen while Pete and Fiona kissed and conversed in her bedroom. Pete offered to go back to her place to give Fiona time with her brother who, despite his joviality, must have needed to talk to her. Fiona agreed with this assessment, saying that, even though he always lit up around Mack, she could see from his eyes that he needed to unburden himself. "I want to wake up with you, baby. The boys will be up doing things, so we can just sleep in and hide away for a while..."

"Well, when you put it that way, I feel too essential to leave," Pete said.

They stayed in the room cuddling for a bit, but then decided to come out before the birthday boy searched for them. The kitchen was clean, and the guys were talking about ice cream for dessert, Anthony patting his stomach, saying he shouldn't. Mack told him he had to have dessert because it was still his birthday. Afterwards, Anthony and Fiona decided to walk the dog, who was only too happy to join them. Mack had already started a list of objects he wanted to design and build, so he and Pete were seated on the floor around the table, sketching out a few ideas.

☆☆☆

It was still fairly warm for nighttime in October, so they needed only sweaters as they walked briskly through the neighborhood. Anthony did most of the talking, and Fiona listened attentively.

"I don't even wanna go back, you know? I mean, I just don't know if I can rebuild my life, living in the same town with Dawn and the guy she's going to marry."

"Geez—she's going to marry him right away?"

"As soon as the divorce papers are final. She pressured me to sign them right away, so they wouldn't have to wait too long." He went on to describe how hard it'd been to function; he didn't know how to *not* be a husband. He likened it to trying to walk when the ground has been removed. He said he was still in shock from it all and was left feeling like he had been in one marriage and she in another. He never would have figured her for a cheater and a liar. When she had asked for a divorce, she had told him she would always love him deeply, but wasn't in love with him and couldn't go through the motions anymore. She had thought she'd lose her lover, Troy, if she didn't choose him over Anthony. He proposed to her the minute he could.

"Shit," Fiona commented. "That's harsh. Well, your livelihood and most of the people you know are in Cundy's Harbor, but you could start over *here*."

"I don't know if I can go, Fi. Mom and Dad are getting older and need my help now more than ever. I can't just abandon them," he lamented.

"It's not abandonment after working for them for over twenty years; it's a change you need to make for you. Plus, they could retire, couldn't they?"

"You know the old man's not ready to retire. He'd go crazy without work. He'd have to spend leisure time with Mom, and I don't think either of them really wants to sit around and read the paper all day. They're just not there yet."

Fiona emitted a little laugh as she tried to picture their folks doing this because, at sixty-eight, they were anything but sedentary.

"You think *you'll* ever get married?" Anthony asked.

"Hmmm..." She paused before answering him. "Not sure. The thought of it both thrills and terrifies me. Can you *see* me married?"

"Well, yes, actually, I could, down the road. But, um, so how are you doing with your sex addiction? I'm guessing Pete knows about all of that?"

Fiona wasn't sure how much she wanted to reveal to him on his first night here, so she opted to answer only part of the question. "Yes, she knows about my demons, and I've met hers. We're both flawed, and we accept each other's imperfections. It's getting colder; want to head back?"

"Sure, Fi," he said as he kicked a rock down the sidewalk. "It's really good to be here."

She reached up, put her arm around his neck, and kissed him on the cheek. He caught up with the rock and kicked it again. This excited Turtle, who pranced alongside it happily.

When they returned, Mack showed them plans he'd drawn for a shelf, a treasure chest, and a tree house. "Very ambitious!" Anthony said. "You going to work your way up to the tree house? That looks pretty involved!"

"Well, all I know is, first I'm building the shelf for my special sculpture," he replied. Fiona noticed he still had traces of chocolate ice cream in the corners of his mouth and wanted to always remember how happy he looked in this moment.

"Wow, Mack, I know you're going to do great things with this toolbox," Fiona encouraged. "I also know it's still your birthday but it's getting late, even for a Saturday, so I think you should get ready for bed."

"I can't stay up later?" he questioned.

"Well, Uncle Anthony is going to tuck you in, and he's crashing in there with you, so you guys will probably stay up for a bit and have some boy chat," she speculated. Anthony said he would go put his pajamas on too, and then he and Mack left the room with Turtle following behind.

About an hour later, Anthony returned to the living room, where Fiona and Pete were talking and laughing.

"The good news is," Anthony began as he sat with them, "he has a plan for Monday at school. He's going to give Spencer a handwritten apology note that we wrote together. And—" He yawned, stretching his arms. "—since most of his classmates were at the party, he's going to ask the teacher if he can address the whole class and apologize. It'll take courage, but I think he can do it. We went over what he's going to say."

"Wow—great work, super uncle!" Fiona praised.

"The thing is—" He paused as worry appeared on his face. "When I asked him why he picked on that kid, he told me I wouldn't understand." He yawned again and rubbed his cheek, making a scratchy sound against his stubble. "I encouraged him to try me, but all he would say is that I don't see things the way he does. He asked for *you*, Pete." He looked at her. "He wants you to go in there."

"Okay, I'll go," Pete said, getting up from the couch.

"He's a complicated kid, Ant, you know that. He doesn't always make sense to me, but I just keep asking him questions and showing him love," Fiona offered as Anthony scratched his head. "You helped him, and that's what counts."

"I guess so."

☆☆☆

When Pete entered Mack's room, she saw him sitting on his bed with his arms around his bent knees, drawing them up under his chin, and Turtle snuggled up next to him.

"Hi, Pete," he said sheepishly, indicating for her to sit by patting the bed next to him.

"Hey, Mack," she said as she sat. "Sorry again that I missed your party. I get really bad headaches sometimes, and I just have to lie down in the dark and be quiet until the pain goes away. I only get them a few times a year."

"They sound awful," he said sympathetically.

"I'm okay; they don't too last long. But enough about me, let's talk about you. Want to tell me about what happened with Spencer today? I've only heard your mom's version of things." Pete instinctively looked at her dog instead of making eye contact with the boy, because she knew he was more likely to open up if he didn't have to look her in the eye.

"Well," he began, pausing to bite his lower lip, "you know how we both *see* things? And *know* stuff? Like the dying man and the baby with super mental powers?"

She studied him briefly, noticing how the shape of his top lip was identical to Fiona's, and then looked away before she chose her words carefully. "Yes, Mack, I know what you're saying. We both have very active imaginations and so we see a lot of things other people don't. And sometimes we may even know things others can't, but we can't expect most people to understand," she said tenderly. "Tell me more about Spencer."

"He had shadows around him and was going to do something bad. I couldn't see what exactly, but I knew he was planning something that he shouldn't do." He looked down at Turtle while he petted him around the ears. The dog flopped on his back, offering his belly for Mack to scratch, which he happily did.

"Okay, I think I understand what you're saying. Did you hear a voice in your head telling you about these shadows?" She worried the boy might have the same curse she did.

"No, I just saw them and knew he was going to do something bad," he answered in a matter-of-fact tone of voice.

"Okay, I know you were trying to prevent something bad from happening, but did you have to get confrontational with him?" She looked at him now, and he seemed frustrated.

"Well," he sighed, "I guess not. But I was trying to do good by preventing him from doing something bad. It was my party, and I felt responsible."

Pete wanted to push him a little more, but not so hard that he would stop talking or cry. "Mack, my grandmother was like us. You would have really liked her. When I first talked to her about shadows and visions, she gave me wonderful advice. She told me to be careful how I talk about what I see, and to be even more careful about what I do because of it. Make sense?" Sensing he might retreat from the conversation, she put her hand on his shoulder to keep him present.

"Yeah. It does."

"Do you think the next time you see shadows you could tell me, or your mom? Before you do anything?"

"Yeah, but what if neither of you is there? What if it happens to me at *school*?" His eyes were round with worry.

"Hmm, you make a good point. Do you think you could ask to call one of us? Tell the teacher you don't feel well and want to call home? It wouldn't really be a lie because it doesn't feel good to see those shadows, does it?"

"No." He shook his head, then rubbed his eyes. "When I see them, it's like having a nightmare with my eyes open."

"Sorry, sweetie." Pete draped her arm around his shoulder, and Turtle nestled between them. "I want to help you."

"You did, Pete. I knew *you* would understand about the shadows." He threw his arms around her neck for a hug and sighed. She gave him a goodnight kiss on the forehead, told him to get some rest, and left.

☆☆☆

"We had a good talk," Pete explained to Fiona and Anthony when she came back into the living room. "I think he's learned a few things from today."

"Well, crap, I'm really beat," Anthony proclaimed as he stood up. "I haven't been sleeping too well lately. I think I'll turn in. Plus, three's a crowd anyway, right, ladies?" He grinned.

Pete shook her head, saying he was not crowding them. Fiona joked that he hadn't been there long enough to crowd them yet.

The two bedrooms were separated by the bathroom and a large linen closet, so, because there was more than just a wall between them and the guys, Fiona and Pete felt comfortable enough to make love, albeit quietly. Fiona relished the challenge of coming silently, not an easy feat with Pete. Once, when Fiona told her what an adept lover she was, Pete responded with, "You're only as good as your partner." Fiona loved that she could learn about sex from Pete, because she so often felt like she knew it all already, or as if nothing sexual would be new to her.

After they made love, they laid their heads on one pillow and talked for a while in the darkness. They spoke about what happened at the party, and Pete knew so many details, it seemed like she had been there. Fiona figured Mack must have described things extremely well.

Then Pete made a remark that hung in Fiona's mind. She said that even though she and Mack had planned carefully for the party, they couldn't have planned for what happened.

Fiona almost said something to her about how it was her friend Liz who helped Mack plan the activities, but she was so exhausted from the day that she let it go. She was sorry Pete had missed the party, but also relieved in a way, because even though she'd instructed Liz to act like a friend and nothing more, she was afraid Pete would sense something between them. Then Pete told her about the conversation she'd just had with Mack.

Fiona stared at the ceiling, just listening, and then thanked her for everything she did for her son, for all that she was to him. What Pete couldn't see was that her eyes were tearing up a little, and what she didn't hear was the sound of a mother's heart aching.

☆☆☆

As Fiona predicted, Mack and Anthony were up early; before she and Pete even got out of bed they'd already taken Turtle for a walk, played with the rocket launcher, and made breakfast. In the kitchen, Fiona was happy to discover a pot of coffee and waffles for the both of them being kept warm in the oven. She saw Anthony, Mack, and Turtle in the yard and noticed the boy was wearing his pajamas, snow boots, and new Yankees jacket. Watching them interact, she wondered if Anthony would be a father one day. Dawn had never wanted children, and her brother always said it was fine with him; that they had more freedom without children. But divorce has a way of stirring up the sediment in a person's life, and at thirty-eight, he could still have a child if he wanted to. She grabbed her mug and went out in the yard to say a quick hello while Pete got out the butter and syrup.

The morning passed gently, then Pete had to leave at noon because she and Sheila had plans. Fiona had assumed they were doing something fun, but when she asked, the answer saddened her. Sheila's father had died from a heart attack a decade ago, when he was in his midsixties. A few years after being widowed, Mrs. Rider was diagnosed with Alzheimer's, which had gotten so bad, she'd moved to a facility in Attleboro just for people with dementia. Most Sundays, Sheila went to see her mom, and the last visit had been so difficult, she asked Pete to come with her next time for moral support. Pete said her good-byes to the Angelis and headed home to drop Turtle off before meeting Sheila at her place so they could drive together.

"I did some research after my last visit with Mom and feel better prepared now for however she may behave," Sheila said as she drove.

"Well, I remember you said the last visit started off like usual, but then she got agitated, right? I never heard the details," Pete said.

"Yeah. We hugged hello like we always do and were talking, but then her speech sped up, and she yelled at me. She'd never done that before, which is why it threw me for a loop. I froze. She was screaming obscenities and asking me why I'd come. That's why I wanted you with me today."

"Sure. Also, I haven't seen her in a long time."

"Yeah. I think she'll be happy to see you. I'm never quite sure how clearheaded she'll be, so I usually bring things with fragrances that can trigger a memory or evoke a feeling. You know? I have a lemon with me, because we used to love baking lemon bars together. I've also brought roses in the past because she grew them in her front yard for decades..." She ran out of words and was stranded in that painful place between silence and tears. Pete knew she didn't want to cry and reached out with a question.

"So, you found some information to help you today if she gets verbally aggressive again?"

"Yes." Sheila collected herself, willing her tears to remain on the inside. "The materials I read said not to get upset, or at least not to show it; to focus on the person's feelings, rather than the facts of what happened; to be positive and reassuring and speak slowly in a soft tone."

"That all makes sense."

"Oh, also it's good to limit distractions, and shift the focus to another activity."

"All good suggestions," Pete said.

"Yeah, I mean, it's common sense stuff that I'm sure I've read before, but last time I didn't know what to do so I wanted to be prepared. I'm afraid this is just how our visits are going to be from now on."

The drive took close to an hour, and Pete heard the latest on Damon: all great news. Her friend admitted she was falling in love, and though this frightened her, it also thrilled her. She likened it to skydiving, saying nothing really makes you "ready" for love; you just sort of have to jump out of the plane and hope for a thrilling ride that lands you safely.

"Well, you know, I only spent an hour with him when we all met for coffee, but I really like him," Pete declared.

Pete described the party fiasco: how Mack might just be as strange as she was, how she was getting to know Calvin better, and, of course, about Fiona's brother coming to town.

"So, you like him, then?" she asked Pete.

"Yeah, my first impression is a good one. I mean, the man got his heart broken by his unfaithful wife and can still be upbeat. I give him a lot of credit for that. He's also just a really nice guy. Mack adores him."

As Sheila pulled into the parking lot of the Attleboro Care Center, she gripped the steering wheel more tightly; her tension was palpable. Pete noticed and said, "Oh, also—Fiona wants to host a dinner party, and you and Damon are invited. Are you both free this Saturday or the Saturday after?"

"I think this Saturday is good. I'll check in with him and get back to you. That sounds fun." Her voice was flat. As they got out of the car, Sheila seemed to droop and said, "I wonder if I'll end up in a place like this..." It was barely audible, but Pete caught it. Then she wondered how her own intense ability to remember would hold up as she aged.

They entered the building together, where they each signed in and got visitors' badges. Pete put her arm up around Sheila's shoulders and gave her a loving squeeze. She remembered how dynamic Mrs. Rider was when she first met her so many years ago. Sheila's parents had always been happily married—she used to joke that she came from a family so normal it was boring. She had one sibling, a sister named Connie, who fell in love with an Australian guy, married him, and moved there. She came to the States once a year and, because she didn't see their mother regularly, the changes in her condition were shocking to her.

Outside the door of room twenty-six was a placard that read *Miriam Rider, Helen Goff*, and featured photos of each woman before their minds had been hijacked by disease. Helen was out, so it would be just the three of them. Miriam's height came across even when she was sitting up in bed, as she was now. Her hair, an enviably thick silver mane, had been cut and styled since Sheila's last visit, and when they walked in, she was drawing in a sketchbook. Residents there had very structured days, since deciding what to do or having nothing planned could cause them a great deal of stress, but Sundays were left fairly open for visiting.

"Mom," Sheila ventured, "hello! I brought Pete, since you haven't seen her in a long time."

To Pete, Mrs. Rider's eyes looked vacant, like cloudy panes through which one could see her constantly shifting mental landscape. Though her face looked blank, she instantly recognized Sheila and opened her arms for a hug. They held onto each other tightly until Sheila let go so her mother could greet Pete.

"Hello, Mrs. Rider, you're looking well," she said as she bent and hugged her.

"Yeah, Mom, your hair is especially fabulous today."

"What are you drawing? Can I see?" Pete asked her. Miriam turned the sketchbook around for them to see some appealing drawings of horses. "Very nice!" Pete complimented her. "I always have a lot of trouble drawing horses, but you've done a great job with their anatomy."

Miriam smiled and closed the book.

"It's pretty nice out. Up for taking a walk?" Sheila asked. She hadn't been able to coax her mother outside the last few times she came and was hoping to get her out into the sunshine today.

"I can't, Sheila, I have to cook dinner for your father right now," her mother said, moving her eyes around the room.

Sheila didn't miss a beat because the illness had been her teacher. "Actually, Mom, it's still early, so dinner can wait. Come on, let's go. We don't have many of these mild days left before winter comes."

Her mother blinked a few times, then nodded. Sheila went in her mother's closet to get her coat. Pete just smiled, hoping this would all work out.

They stayed for three hours, two of which were spent outside. They walked slowly through the nicely landscaped grounds, intermittently stopping to sit in the sunny spots. Sheila's mother drifted in and out of total awareness of her present surroundings, but for the most part was able to converse with them, especially when encouraged to tell stories of her youth. Pete had asked Sheila before they arrived if she wanted her mom all to herself for any part of the visit, and Sheila said no, that she had a hunch Pete's presence would help. Perhaps it did, because this visit was a hundred times better than the previous one; Sheila was able to glimpse her mother through the fog of Alzheimer's, which didn't always happen.

On the drive back to Cambridge, Sheila thanked Pete again for giving up her Sunday afternoon, and Pete told her thanks weren't necessary, that she would always be there for her. She told Sheila her mother was still there and encouraged her to try to enjoy her, to focus on what remained, not what was gone. "Your mom's version of reality is bent by Alzheimer's, and mine is skewed because my brain is so strange, but you manage to love us both, Sheils. You're amazing, and I don't know what I'd do without you."

"Well, I suppose I *am* more normal than you, huh?" She laughed. "But you know, who's to say the rest of us aren't missing pieces that you have? Your life certainly is more interesting than many people's, and you make mine more exciting. Hey—even if you marry Fiona and I marry Damon, let's always be like this, okay?"

"More than okay," Pete answered. "Much more than okay."

☆☆☆

"Come on, big brother, time to get that thing removed," Fiona said, pointing to Anthony's wedding band.

"Nah, it'll come off when I lose more weight. I've dropped five since Dawn moved out, and if I lose some more, this sucker should slide right off."

Fiona knew this plan had to do with his pain and identity crisis. She also knew it needed to come off. She looked him in the eyes, took his hand in hers, and responded, "That's one way to get the ring off, but delay will only cause you more pain, Ant. The sooner you get rid of it, and actually see your finger without it, the sooner you can move on and see yourself as single. This little shiny thing announces to the world that you're married; it's telling you and everyone else a lie. It's gotta go." Her serious tone of voice helped the words sink in, and he considered what she said before speaking.

"Well, when you put it that way. I guess it *should* come off now." His words were heavy, like his heart.

"I know of a jeweler near a park Mack likes to go to. It's gorgeous out. Let's go."

The three of them got into Fiona's hatchback and headed to the jewelers. Anthony sighed when the cutting tool made a cracking sound and the ring came off, revealing skin much paler than the rest of his browned, work-strong hands. Holding it between his thumb and index finger, he studied the broken circle, then handed it to Fiona, asking her to make it go away. She slipped it into her jacket pocket, and they left.

The nice weather brought lots of people out, so the park was crowded with families. The climbing structure was one of the biggest and best around, so it was crawling with kids. Mack found a space and scrambled onto it happily.

"I think he's much better since the party mishap; I hope he can handle himself at school tomorrow," Fiona said as she and Anthony sat on a bench in the sunshine. They watched Mack and the other children as they spoke.

"Well, it's all a learning experience, and no matter how it goes, the main thing is that he tried," he added.

"True. We learn by failure, huh?" she suggested.

He nodded. "Hmm." He exhaled and looked down at his boots briefly. "Then I must be learning a lot," he said with a tinge of self-deprecation.

"What do you mean?"

"My marriage failed," he said softly.

Mack waved to the two of them from the highest part of the structure, and they both waved back.

"It didn't fail. *You* certainly didn't fail. Dawn failed to keep her vows. I mean, shit—if you want someone else, at least have the courage to admit it to your partner." As she spoke, she tasted her own hypocrisy. Attempting to divert attention from her remark, she gave him some advice. "The best way to get over someone is to get under someone."

"Spoken like a true sex junkie," he said with a grin.

"Well, bro, in your case, I think it's good advice. I mean, you haven't been with any woman besides Dawn since you were what, twenty-five?"

"Twenty-four. Crap, you're right—that *is* a long time."

"Perhaps you can meet someone while you're down here; maybe even look online? I know you can't picture being with someone new, but at least be open to it. It might be the best cure for what ails you right now." He nodded and looked at the pale stripe of flesh on his ring finger. "Also, you might want to stick that finger in the sun or use spray tan on it," she said tenderly as she squeezed his hand.

"So, you never told me how you're *doing* with your sex addiction—I mean, are you able to be with just one person? Or do you only have open relationships? You seem really in love when you're with Pete. In fact, I've never seen you this gone. But Liz—she stayed over, huh?" He lowered his voice, since a mother had just sat on the other end of the long, green bench.

She half wanted to bullshit him, but knew he'd see through it; they knew each other too well. She decided to lead with the good news.

"I hate to admit it, but I am falling for Pete, which is new territory for me. I thought I was in love before, but now I know how it really feels. It feels bigger than me, and better. But I—" She paused, searching for the right words. "I don't know if I can ever change..." She scanned the park, looking for Mack, and saw he was now on the swings. "Liz stayed over. We're friends who have sex sometimes."

"Fi," Anthony began, "are you still having sex with random people?"

"Well, right after Pete and I got together, I hooked up with this couple, just once. But I mean, she and I were literally brand-new, so it's not like that was off-limits."

"I sense there is an 'and' or a 'but' coming," he said matter-of-factly, trying to keep judgment out of his voice. Fiona's big eyes rolled around, taking in the details of her surroundings.

"Yeah, well, you know me better than most, and yes, there is an 'and.' A little while ago, I got together with this woman. She was aggressive, and I was weak. Actually, we'd seen each other at an SAA meeting about a year ago, and she recognized me. It happened really fast, and I regretted it instantly," she added, knowing what he was about to ask.

"Did you tell her?" He tracked Mack, who was now running around, playing some tag game with a few younger kids.

"No. And I'll tell you why: I'm hoping that will be the last time I act like that. And since it very well could have been the last time, I didn't see the point in telling her, of hurting her like that." Her voice didn't have the conviction she'd hoped it would.

"Yeah, that's what you're telling yourself, Fi. I hear the hope, but the reality is you haven't stopped having sex with strangers. You need to either stop or tell her you haven't. Just my humble opinion. *Can* you stop? Isn't she incentive enough?"

Fiona squinted in the sun, then closed her eyes, inhaling slowly. "She's the best incentive, I mean besides Mack. He's become very attached to her, and I definitely don't want to screw up what the three of us have."

"You can't, Fi. Love, real true love, doesn't visit our lives too many times. You've got to muster all your strength and change your ways. I know it's hard—well, I've never been addicted to anything but I know how it feels to have to give up a big part of yourself." He put his arm around her shoulders, and she leaned into him. "Do you still go to meetings?"

"Not too often, just a few this year. I was planning to go last Tuesday, but something came up."

"Yeah, well, while I'm here, I can babysit Mack. Will you go to this Tuesday's meeting?"

"Yes. I will. Thanks," she said lovingly. "For always being brutally honest with me."

"It's one of the things we do for each other, right?"

She nodded and fought tears. "I love you too much to bullshit you or dance around the truth. You always call me on my shit, and I wouldn't want it any other way." They both looked over and saw Mack sailing down a slide wearing a huge smile on his face. He noticed them watching and ran up to them after he hit the sand.

"Too bad grown-ups don't do this! It's soooo fun!" He jumped onto his uncle, and they wrestled around on the bench.

Anthony tickled him, saying grown-ups had plenty of fun things to do.

"Yeah," Mack managed to get out between bursts of laughter, "but you gotta admit, most of what you have to do is not as fun as what kids get to do."

☆☆☆

Fiona did make it to an SAA meeting, but didn't feel comfortable enough to share the details of her current situation; she only shared her name, how long she'd been a sex addict, and her desire to recover. She had to go on autopilot to attend these meetings; she was truly conflicted about recovery. Fiona felt that craving sex was just in her nature, and sometimes she thought the odds of her being rehabilitated were akin to those of a vampire not craving blood.

Anthony spent the days exploring Boston by himself, and in the afternoons, he would pick up Mack from school. The two of them made the most of their time together, usually playing outside until it got dark. Fiona managed to get Friday off, and they made a big breakfast at home, then went to kick around Faneuil Hall like they used to in their teens when they'd drive down from Maine. They talked, shopped, and ate their way through a very pleasant afternoon. Fiona was working on her brother to stay longer and move down there. He said he could probably extend his visit, but wasn't sure about moving. When he turned his life inside out to try to see himself in a new light, he could only recognize himself as a married guy who knew about the fishing industry and restaurant management.

Fiona was fixated on planning her dinner party for Saturday. Anthony wanted her to serve lobsters, but since Sheila was a vegan, Fiona chose to make the whole meal vegan. The menu included spicy tofu lettuce wraps, oven-roasted okra, roasted potatoes, homemade vegan bread, and coconut pecan bites for dessert. She was still searching for the perfect vegan appetizers. When Anthony raised his eyebrows at the food selection, she promised him a lobster dinner out and encouraged him by saying vegan food was so light they would all get more inebriated.

Pete came over Friday night for pizza and a movie. Mack had been dying to see *Ghostbusters* after he heard his mom and uncle reminiscing about it. Pete promised the boy she'd get up early and take him to the hardware store to buy what he needed to build his shelf and treasure chest. They would get the shelf up and then start the chest.

On Saturday, Anthony said he wanted to help with the dinner preparations, so Fiona invited him to go to the health food store with her while Pete and Mack were at Home Depot. She instructed him to check out women while they were there, saying health food stores usually had a more fit clientele than regular supermarkets.

"Yeah, now that I ditched the wedding ring, I won't look like a sleazeball if I cruise the ladies, huh, sis?"

"Nope. The world is your oyster!"

"Mmmm, oysters," he said.

"Tofu wraps," she countered. "Here, let's split up," she instructed, tearing the shopping list in half and handing him the bottom part. "That way you'll really look unattached. Off with you!"

"All right, I'll go see what there is to see," he said before he turned and headed toward the baking supplies aisle.

Fiona watched him walk away and thought about how he said he felt lost not being married. She believed the divorce would actually help her brother find himself, and hoped he would come to feel the same way in time.

By the time they met up at the checkout line, he'd caught the eye of four different women, but only noticed one of them. "Fi!" he called, then lowered his voice when his sister approached him. "I actually flirted!"

"Really? Do tell, where is she?"

"Oh, I don't know. We were both in the beverages aisle, and I thought I saw her looking at me," he said modestly.

"Details, please. Did you talk to her?"

"Well, yeah—we just talked about the drink selection briefly. But she kept smiling at me, and even though I felt awkward, it made me feel good, Fiona. Like maybe I could date somebody." He smiled broadly, and his striking eyes lit his swarthy, handsome face. He looked hopeful and that made her happy.

"Okay, it's a start. No exchange of names I take it?"

"Nah. But it was something, right?" He wanted her approval.

"More than something; we got you out of cold storage. Come on, Don Juan, let's get out of here. I have mucho housework to do before I even start cooking," she said as she tugged on his jacket.

They got home just as Pete and Mack were pulling up in front of the house, and all got out at the same time. Turtle yipped from the backyard. Groceries and lumber got unloaded, Pete stole a kiss from Fiona in the kitchen, and Anthony helped Mack move the lumber into the backyard. The house got cleaned, the shelf got built and installed, and all of the pieces for the treasure chest were cut and sanded by 4:00.

Then it was time for them to get cleaned up and changed, since their friends were arriving at six. Fiona and Pete showered together while the guys took Turtle for a long walk. Fiona laid out an outfit for Mack, hoping he wouldn't protest about the matching colors. She opted to wear a dark green dress that Pete hadn't seen her in before. Pete was ironing her shirt while Fiona buzzed around the kitchen.

Calvin arrived a little early and was the first to comment on how tempting the pitcher of mango coconut margaritas Anthony had made earlier looked. "Wow, a drink this colorful has to be delicious!" he marveled.

"Have one, there's enough for a few pitchers. The whole meal is vegan, in honor of Miss Sheila!" Fiona triumphed.

"Really? Wow, cool! So we won't need to count carbs, huh? It smells great in here. And you look extra beautiful, Fiona, you really do."

"Well, thank you. You're looking pretty yourself," she offered.

"Thanks. Hey, you know the soup kitchen in Dorchester I work at? Guess who was there last Sunday?"

"Who?" The two of them set the table as they talked. Fiona had put a leaf in to accommodate the seven of them.

"Mayor Menino! I shook his hand. He's shorter in person than he looks on television. He came to serve food and throw a spotlight on the place, because we desperately need funding. You know, after spending time with him, I think he actually might be one of the good guys," Calvin said thoughtfully.

"Can an elected official be a good guy, you think?"

"I do, actually. He was breaking a sweat and being really warm to the patrons—that counts for something."

"You know," Fiona said, "you really come alive when you serve, Calvin. I think you need to change careers and get into some kind of human service work."

"Well, I'd like to, but I've got my mortgage to think about... I doubt I could swing it on a do-gooder salary, and I don't want to supplement my income doing you-know-what indefinitely," he said.

"What about getting a roommate? Your place is big enough and conveniently located for commuting; you could probably rent the guest room out for a good chunk of change."

"Hmm—I like the money part, but not the living with a stranger part. I had lots of housemates in my twenties," Calvin lamented.

"Well, but it could be great. Hey, I'm trying to get Anthony to move down here. He could live with you for a little while. Come on, have a margarita, I'm dying to see if you like them." She poured, placed a lime wedge onto the side of the glass, and then he sampled the frosty drink.

"Wow, now that's really something. Yum."

"I've got miso sweet potato bites and avocado tahini dip with homemade bread for appetizers. Try those."

"I'm your guinea pig, aren't I?" he joked as he popped a sweet potato bite into his mouth. "Another yum. You really went all out, Fi, great menu. I'm sure Sheila will appreciate it. I mean, how many dinner parties are all vegan?"

"I just hope Mack eats something. There's always leftover pizza for him, I suppose."

The table was set, the appetizers and drinks were out, there was an eclectic playlist of ambient music going, and she felt as ready as she could be.

"Uncle Calvin!" Mack screeched from around the corner. "Come see the shelf we built and the pieces for my treasure chest!" He'd made an adjustment to the outfit his mother wanted him to wear. Instead of his gray pants with his blue sweater, he'd chosen some bright red corduroys. Fiona thought it could be much worse and let it go.

"Okay, partner, show me," Calvin said. He popped another sweet potato bite in his mouth, set down his drink, and followed Mack to his room, where they found Anthony putting his shoes on.

Pete came into the kitchen wearing a vintage 1940s western shirt Fiona hadn't seen her in before. Suddenly, she thought of her blouse from the same era and the dressing room escapade with Abigail. She pushed the recollection out of her mind.

"Wow, Pete, you look extra sexy tonight. I love that shirt on you!"

"Thanks. I haven't worn it in a while. You're the one who looks sexy. Man, you look great in that color."

"Come here and give me a kiss," Fiona urged. They didn't hear Anthony walk in.

"Aw, you two. Smooching as usual," he said with a grin. His eyes landed on the exotic cocktail. "Time for drinks."

"Plenty to go around," Fiona said.

"I can't believe this whole feast is vegan—that's so cool of you, Fiona. You're an awesome girlfriend," Pete lauded. This remark made Fiona think more about her recent infidelity, and she felt a twinge of guilt along with a slight wave of nausea.

Just then, Turtle yipped, signaling that Sheila and Damon had arrived. The two women left the kitchen and greeted their guests at the front door. Damon filled the whole doorway as he passed through it. Pete introduced him to Fiona. Turtle took a real liking to Damon, who petted him in all the right places until his tail thumped violently against Damon's pant leg.

"You look familiar," he said as he shook Fiona's hand.

"Hmmm," Fiona responded, "I get that sometimes. Well, it's great to meet you. Welcome." Sheila gave Fiona a hug and told her she smelled great. "Thanks. It's the lavender in my hair."

"Oh, I've got to try that. And what smells so delicious?" she asked. Pete took their jackets and hung them in the hall closet.

"Well," Pete said proudly, "my girl Fi here made an entirely vegan feast for us. Everything—the drinks, appetizers, entrees, and dessert are all vegan. In your honor."

Sheila's face lit up, and she looked at Fiona appreciatively for a moment before speaking. "Really? You didn't have to do that just for me. Thanks!"

"It was my pleasure. It was a real culinary challenge, and I enjoy challenges. I hope you like the menu. Come on in and have a mango coconut margarita," Fiona said.

They went into the kitchen to fill their glasses and then sat in the living room. Sheila looked around at the warm gold walls, the framed art, and the plants, and complimented Fiona on her decor.

Mack, Calvin, and Anthony came in from the kitchen. Calvin and Sheila had already met each other when they'd gone to dinner with Fiona, Mack, and Pete a few weeks earlier. Fiona made the necessary introductions. When Damon stood up to shake their hands, Mack's eyes went up from his shoes to his head.

"How tall *are* you?" he asked.

"Six foot five," he answered with a smile. "Too tall."

"I thought Uncle Anthony was tall but you're *really* tall," he marveled. Fiona encouraged people to eat appetizers and pointed the bread out to Mack, knowing the avocado tahini dip and sweet potato bites were too exotic for his tastes. "Is that like juice for grown-ups?" he asked as he watched them drink the margaritas.

The room bubbled with laughter, and Calvin answered him. "Yes, Mack, well said. It is indeed juice for grown-ups."

"Can I taste some?" he asked, looking at his mother for approval.

"Maybe just a sip," Fiona said. "Here, babe, try some of mine."

The boy took a sip tentatively and immediately crinkled his nose in disgust. "Blech! I don't know why you guys like that stuff!" He dashed off to get a piece of bread from the table.

"These sweet potato things are amazing, Fiona. I want the recipe," Sheila said.

"Sure, I found it online, but I changed a few things around. I can send it to you," Fiona said.

They ate, drank, and talked. Damon must have been asking Anthony about himself, because Fiona heard him say, "Oh, I'm very sorry to hear that," to her brother. She knew that alcohol loosened his lips and hoped he wouldn't bring down the festive mood by talking too much about the divorce. Pete, Calvin, and Sheila were engrossed in a conversation about vegan food and its health benefits. Mack came back in and looked around. Fiona patted the empty space on the couch next to her, and he sat there. She rubbed his back while he ate bread. When his mouth was no longer full, he blurted out a question to the group.

"Hey—it's almost Halloween, what's everyone going to be? And what is everyone going to do? Because grown-ups can't trick-or-treat." He looked from face to face, and it was Calvin who answered first.

"Well, I'm probably going to spend time with my favorite kid—you! As for a costume, I haven't decided yet. Last year I went for silly, but this year I might want to wear something really scary. What do you think?"

"Scary sounds more fun," the boy replied. "What about you, Pete?"

"Hmmm," she considered, "I always make my costume, and I'm getting a late start, so I'll have to keep it simple. Maybe a vampire?"

"That would be cool! I have face paint if you need some," he said. Looking up at his mom, he asked, "Well, what about you, Mom? Not a witch again, you can't. You were a witch the last two years in a row!"

"What if I like being a witch?" she teased. She shot Pete a sexy look and mouthed the words, *You know I'm a sorceress,* to her. Sheila caught the exchange and smiled.

"No. Something new," he insisted. Anthony and Damon paused their side conversation and focused on the boy. "Well?"

"Yeah, Fiona," Anthony chimed in, "how about a reprise from your childhood? You could be Wonder Woman again."

"Only if you're going to give an encore performance as the Terminator," Fiona quipped. Mack giggled because he liked when his mom and uncle bantered like this.

"What about you, Mack?" Sheila asked. "What are *you* going to wear?"

His face brightened as if he'd been waiting to talk about his costume. "Well, like Pete, I'm going to make my costume. I've already started making it in my mind. I want to be a dinobot," he announced triumphantly.

"A *dinobot*?" Anthony asked. "You mean a dinosaur robot?"

"Exactly!"

Mack went on to explain how he planned to make his dinobot costume out of cardboard, old plastic containers, and random little shiny things he'd been saving for weeks. When it seemed to her Mack might go into too much detail, Fiona suggested they eat dinner.

The meal was a success, and the many compliments made Fiona blush a little. Much to her surprise, Mack tried a tofu wrap and liked it. Conversations flowed freely and talk was lively.

☆☆☆

When Calvin was talking with Damon about his neighborhood, Damon mentioned he wanted to buy a condo there, but was out-priced, and joked with him that the restaurant he worked at must be pretty fancy if he could afford that zip code. Even though Calvin knew Damon had no idea he was a sex worker, a wave of paranoia came over him. Later, in the bathroom, he looked at himself in the mirror and said, "You are more than a hustler. You just do that to make money. It's not who you are." Then he washed his face before he went back to the group.

When he returned, he noticed Mack was pestering Pete, trying to get her attention by talking incessantly about his Halloween costume when she was clearly trying to converse with the other adults. He decided to run interference and started asking Mack about his new microscope, which prompted the boy to talk excitedly about how various items look when they're magnified. They talked for a little while, then he dragged Calvin off to show him a few things under the lens.

☆☆☆

At one point, Pete and Sheila were in the kitchen getting more margaritas for everyone, and Sheila surprised her with a question. "So, am I too silly now that I'm all in love?"

"Huh, what do you mean?"

"Oh, well—you know how people can get sappy and lose their edge when they fall in love? I don't want to be some insipid girl with hearts in her eyes."

"I think I know what you're saying, and no, you're not too silly. You're really happy, and that makes me happy. Love is wonderful. And we're both in love at the same time. With two great people. Just enjoy it, Sheils; you'll never lose your edge," Pete said and hugged her.

Sheila thanked her and told her she was going to bring Damon to meet her mother next weekend and was a little nervous about it. Pete reminded her that what her mother did was out of her control and said no matter how the visit went, it would be a bonding experience for the two of them. Sheila thanked her for the insights and changed topics, saying she liked Anthony.

"He *really* looks like Fiona," Sheila commented. "They're both really hot. I mean, I can tell he's sad about his divorce, but he's still attractive. Some nice woman will come along and scoop him right up."

"Let's hope so," Pete said. "He strikes me as the type who needs to be partnered."

Calvin was in the living room again, minus his sidekick. Mack had asked Calvin to say goodnight to everybody for him. Without a child in their presence, the adults were a bit more colorful with their language and range of topics.

Damon talked with Anthony about his own divorce twelve years ago and how dating a lot right afterwards helped him heal. Pete knew from what Sheila had told her about this that by "dated" he meant "had sex with." Damon was a very charismatic man and had no shortage of women coming after him when he was single. Sheila had told Pete his past didn't threaten her at all; in fact, being with all those women made him an excellent lover.

As Pete and Sheila were about to leave the kitchen, Fiona came in to get dessert. The three women chatted and laughed.

☆☆☆

In the living room, Damon was playing tug of war with Turtle, who'd brought him one of his toys. When Damon left to use the bathroom, Anthony lowered his voice and said to Calvin, "So, I hope Fi doesn't screw things up with Pete." He'd downed five margaritas and was speaking freely.

Perplexed, Calvin knitted his brows. "Huh? What do you mean?"

"You know, her sex addiction. The thing with that woman in the dressing room. I know she talks to you about all that."

"Yes, we talk about her struggles with her addiction, but I don't know what you're referring to specifically, and since she hasn't spoken to me about it, I don't feel comfortable discussing it with you."

"Oh, sorry, Calvin. I get you. It's the tequila loosening my tongue. She'll talk with you about it, I'm sure. I just—well, I like Pete and I want it to work out for the two of them because it's easier to go through life with someone by your side, you know?"

Calvin nodded, even though he didn't know what it felt like to have a partner, only a lover. He suddenly felt sad, not just about this fact, but because Fiona hadn't told him about whatever Anthony was talking about. But then, since the fight with his client Thomas, he'd been a little preoccupied with his own shit. Also, he hadn't specifically asked her about her sex addiction in a long time. He would ask her about it the next time they hung out, and he was sure she'd tell him whatever was going on. He was relieved to see the women return with dessert in hand. Damon came back with Turtle at his side.

Dessert was every bit as delicious as the meal. Pete entertained them with a hilarious story about a recent neat-freak client who had slipcovers on all of her furniture and made Pete put baggies on her shoes while she worked.

"I didn't know people used slipcovers anymore," Sheila remarked. "I mean, aren't those things really flammable?"

☆☆☆

Calvin got restless and was the first to leave; he intended to go cruise the Fens looking for sex. Shortly after that, Anthony said he wanted to get some air and took Turtle for a walk. He left because he wanted to call Dawn and needed privacy. He hadn't spoken to her in weeks and was just drunk enough to give it a shot. He dialed most of the number, then stopped. He wanted to cry but wouldn't let himself.

When he and the dog returned, Sheila and Damon were getting ready to leave. The men shook hands, and the women hugged, and then it was just the three of them.

"I'll clean up," Anthony offered. "Why don't you two just relax."

"I don't mind cleaning," Pete responded, "but let's give your sister a break."

"Thanks guys, I'm gonna go check on Mack, since I didn't say goodnight to him," Fiona said.

When Fiona opened Mack's door, she found him sound asleep with a faint trace of a smile on his lips. The light spilled softly onto his face, and she sat and looked at him for a little while, smoothing his hair away from his forehead. His face was changing; he no longer looked like a little boy. It was true what people always said: kids grow up way too fast. Turtle came in and jumped into the bed to take his usual place beside the boy. Fiona rubbed the dog's head, kissed Mack's forehead, pulled the door mostly shut, and left.

☆☆☆

On the way home, Damon finally remembered where he'd seen Fiona before and said, "Shit," when the realization hit him.

"What?" Sheila asked.

He told her he'd seen Fiona in a porno from maybe twelve years ago.

"Are you sure? I mean, that's a long time ago—she probably looks different now," Sheila suggested.

"Nope. Not that different. It's her, honey. I know." He shifted in his seat and slouched down a bit before sighing. "She's not someone you forget."

"Shit," Sheila said. "I'm not sure Pete knows about this. I don't know if I should tell her..."

"Babe, lovers don't need to know everything about each other's past; I wouldn't say anything."

She put her hand on his thigh and caressed it softly. Scenes from the porn flashed in his mind, giving him an erection that Sheila thought was for her.

# CHAPTER SEVEN: FROM SHAME TO GRACE

*It is easy to assume a habit; but when you try to cast it off,*
*it will take skin and all.*
*~ Josh Billings*

It was a cold, cloudy Sunday in Boston, and everybody slept in, even Turtle, who waited an extra hour for his usual early-morning excursion to the backyard to do his business. Fiona was tired from hosting the dinner party and dreamed of a lazy day with just Pete, but realized she would have to share her when Mack knocked on their door, crawled onto the bed, and asked Pete if they could build the treasure chest today. Fiona squeezed Pete's thigh under the blankets to let her know she should feel free to say no.

"Sure, Mack. After breakfast, okay?"

"Yay!" He bounced off the bed to leave.

"Please close the door behind you and let Turtle out, okay, sweetie?" Fiona requested. He nodded and left. Fiona wrapped her arms around Pete and sighed. "Why can't we stay in bed all day and make the rest of the world go away?"

"Ah," Pete said softly, "that sounds perfect. A whole day in bed with you..."

"We could even eat our meals in bed and just not leave the room—only to use the bathroom," Fiona added. "We need a getaway. Let's find some overlapping time off when Calvin can take Mack. We could go to the cape, or to Vermont; anywhere where all there is, is you, me, and beautiful scenery."

"That would be amazing," Pete said.

They stayed wrapped up in each other for a while before getting up and starting their day. When they came into the kitchen, they saw Mack already had his toolbox out. Fiona told him he had to eat breakfast and help clean up afterwards and that he couldn't do woodworking in his pajamas. He protested mildly, saying pajamas were just regular clothes we happen to sleep in.

By the time Anthony woke up wearing a hangover, the treasure chest was nearly half-assembled. He stumbled into the kitchen, his eyes on the coffeepot.

"Someone slip you a bad ice cube last night?" Fiona teased.

"Ha-ha. Yeah, I didn't need to drink those last two margaritas. They were just so tasty and smooth... I didn't act like a total jackass, did I? I mean, I remember most of the night." He sat and drank from his mug like it contained an antidote.

"You weren't a jackass at all. A wee bit lively, maybe, but in an okay way. Want some food to wash that coffee down with? I can make you some eggs," she offered.

"Nah." He wrinkled his nose at the thought.

"Well, you should eat something, maybe toast?"

"Thanks, but I really have no appetite. I'll eat when I get hungry. I think I just want some fresh air. Maybe I'll take a walk. Hey," he said, looking out the sliding glass door, "what are those two up to? Building something?"

"Yeah, it's so cute," Fiona answered. "He was in our room first thing this morning asking Pete to help him build his treasure chest, and there they are."

The boy was tapping screws into one piece of wood they were joining to another. The chest would be over two feet long and a foot deep when it was finished, and the design Mack had come up with looked like a modern interpretation of a pirate's chest. The two of them worked in harmony, seeming not to mind that it was a cold, sunless day.

"They're good together," he said and looked at Fiona. In her mind, she heard what he didn't say. *So don't screw it up with sex.* She looked at them for a while, then cleaned the kitchen.

Anthony finished his first cup and poured himself another, which he took outside. Fiona watched him ask Mack all about what they were doing. The boy beamed. Clearly, he was delighted to have Pete and Anthony's attention, and Fiona loved seeing them all together. This was family at its best. She hoped her brother would seriously consider moving here.

When Anthony came in, he told Fiona he was going to drive to the Arnold Arboretum and take a long walk. She asked him if he wanted company, and he told her he wasn't great company for anyone right now, that he just wanted to be alone outdoors. Fiona told him she'd see him later, sensitive to the need to give him his own space.

☆☆☆

When Anthony got back, he said hello to everyone then went to take a shower. Fiona suggested they all go out for that lobster dinner he wanted. Mack approved of the idea, saying that since they'd just built a pirate's chest, it seemed fitting to go to a seafood place.

The chest turned out really well. They got it all put together and stained it, and next weekend they would apply polyurethane and add the hinges, hasp, and lock. Fiona was proud of her little boy and grateful to Pete for helping him so much. He was already talking about the tree house he'd designed. In fact, he couldn't stop talking about it on the way to the restaurant.

"I think the tallest tree in our yard is big enough to support the structure I designed, Pete. I want it to be big enough to hold four people. Hey—what happens when the tree grows? Won't it move the tree house? How do people build structures in trees?"

"Don't forget, sweetie, we have to check with our landlord to get permission to build a tree house. I mean, we might want to keep it out of a tree in case we move and want to take it with us. And then there's the cost of the lumber. We'll have to check our budget and see what we can afford," Fiona advised.

"We're *moving*?" he asked, sounding concerned.

"No, honey—I said *if* we move." Lately she'd been thinking about Pete moving in with them one day, and knew they could use more space than her place had.

☆☆☆

They rolled into the parking lot of the Boston Lobster House and headed in. When they saw all the people waiting for a table, Fiona was glad she'd made a reservation. The hostess seated them in a booth in front of a large window overlooking the harbor; the view was splendid. Mack said he wanted to look at the lobsters in the tank they'd passed on the way in, and since Pete had to slide out of the booth to let him out, she went with him.

He put his face close to the large glass tank and observed the prisoners.

"Why do they have rubber bands on their claws?"

"So they don't harm each other," Pete answered. She loved his insatiable curiosity. "It also makes it easier for someone to pick them up without getting pinched. Did you know there are left- and right-handed lobsters?"

"What? No way!" His eyes got bigger as he took in the anatomical details of the prehistoric-looking creatures.

"It's true," Pete insisted. "Some have their large claw on the right, and some have it on the left. It's called their crusher claw. Your mom and Uncle Anthony know all about it."

He immediately searched for evidence of this and squealed with delight when he located the one southpaw crustacean in the tank. "I don't like how they're just waiting to die," he said sadly.

"I know, Mack, I hear you. But that's the business of food. We kill things to eat them. You've learned about the food chain, right?"

He nodded as he eyed one lobster in particular, who was moving very slowly; the boy's expression was unmistakably sympathetic.

*These poor beasts are cursed, just like you.* The voice in her head came so unexpectedly that Pete flinched. She closed her eyes, rubbed her temples, and took a deep breath before exhaling and opening them.

"What was *that?*" Mack asked, startled. "I thought I heard something."

Pete's mind raced, and she was deluged with worry; she treasured the affinity between them, but rejected the notion that he might suffer mentally like she did. Or worse, that her demons were somehow colonizing his amazing brain.

"I didn't hear anything," she lied. "Hey, let's get back to your family so we can order. Come on." She draped her arm around his shoulder and steered him away from the spectacle behind the glass. When they returned to the booth, Fiona and Anthony were laughing about something.

"Hey, I just noticed you shaved!" Fiona remarked to her brother, who had been pretty scruffy for the last few days. "I assumed you were growing a beard..."

"Nah, just being lazy; then I started wondering who that guy in the mirror was, so I knew it was time to shave," he joked as he opened a menu.

A perky, ponytailed server in a red vest came and took their drink order: beers for the grown-ups and a root beer for Mack. Pete immediately dubbed her Perky Red Vest in her mind.

"When will *I* have to shave?" Mack asked his uncle.

"Oh, probably not for six or seven years maybe," he answered as he felt the boy's cheek with the back of his hand. "No sign of stubble yet."

"Are you going to move here, Uncle Anthony?" The question caught him off guard. "Mom said you were thinking about it."

"Oh she did, did she?" he asked, shooting her a sideways glance and smiling.

"I might have suggested that," she admitted.

"We *really* want you to live here," Mack said before taking a huge gulp of soda.

"Well, I'm thinking about it, but please don't be upset with me if I don't relocate, okay? I've lived in Maine my whole life, so moving isn't a small decision, you understand, Mack?" The boy nodded. "I'd love to live closer to you all, believe me, and if I can make it work that would be great. But if I don't move, I'm only two hours away."

Perky Red Vest came and took their food order, smiling the whole time. Pete marveled at those people, the ones she called "smiletalkers." Their faces defaulted to a grin whenever they spoke, which Pete found disconcerting in general and especially disturbing when they talked about sad things. She noticed a lot of television newscasters were smiletalkers, and when delivering tragic news, they tried to straighten their mouths into a more serious expression, but always their lips pulled back into an automatic grin like a puppet's.

Dinner was the tasty, crunchy, buttery feast Anthony had been craving. Mack demolished his fish tacos and then had dessert. The adults were too stuffed with lobster to have dessert, but Mack didn't seem to mind being the only one to eat cake. When Perky Red Vest brought the check, she didn't know who to hand it to, so Fiona asked for it.

"No, come on. My treat," Anthony protested.

"But I wanted to treat you tonight. You're my guest," Fiona countered.

"Exactly—I've been a guest for a while now, and it's my turn to treat. Give me that," he said as he grabbed the bill.

☆☆☆

On the way home, they saw a billboard advertising the Boston Derby Dames and their big roller derby tournament coming up. Anthony got excited and exclaimed, "Oh, I forgot all about that; I have to go. The Wicked Sistahs might really win it this year! Plus Dangerous D is just so damned hot," he blurted like a teenager.

"You still like roller derby?" his sister asked.

"Hell, yeah," he affirmed. "Best sport to watch. Have you ever seen them? The Wicked Sistahs? And Dangerous D? She's their top scorer. Hey, want to go with me? It's this coming Friday."

"Isn't that Halloween?" Mack asked.

"No, sweetie, Halloween is the day before. On Thursday."

"Oh. What's roller derby again? I've heard of it but I don't remember exactly what it is."

Anthony sat up straighter and spoke enthusiastically, explaining to Mack that it was a fast-paced sport played on roller skates, that it started in the 1930s, was televised a lot in the sixties and seventies, and was having a revival. He went on to say that he liked it because it was really fast-paced and the women were amazing athletes.

Fiona couldn't resist chiming in. "And he thinks they're good to look at."

"Well, they are, admit it, Fi."

"They are, totally," Pete agreed. "My mom has a friend who played in the late sixties. She was pretty well-known in the roller derby world, actually; she was on the Brooklyn Red Devils. I remember she was really tall and fit; I think she was kind of a hero to my mom—a life unlived sort of thing. Her name was Dolores Del Motta, but her roller derby name was Big Red because she was six feet tall with red hair."

"That's pretty cool, Pete; is your mom still in touch with her?" Anthony asked.

"I think they're Facebook friends. I'd love to go check out the tournament," Pete said. "Are you game, Fiona?"

"Sure! We've got to see this Dangerous D woman big bro is so crushed out on," she teased. "It sounds like fun."

"Great! I'll get us tickets," Anthony offered.

"Well, wait till I make sure Mack can stay with Calvin. Mackles, sweetie, you want to spend the night at Uncle Calvin's while Mommy and Pete and Uncle Anthony go see roller derby?"

"Sure," he said, "as long as you're sure it's not Halloween. Because Halloween is important."

"I know, honey; it's the night after Halloween," Fiona responded, "and I bet you two can find a Halloween movie to watch."

"Yeah," Mack said brightly before asking, "Pete, what does *life unlived* mean? I've been trying to figure it out since you said it, and it doesn't make sense."

Pete was happy to clarify the term for him. She told him it simply meant when an adult wonders what her life might have been like if she had made different choices and lived a different life. He still wasn't quite getting it so she described how it referred to the concept that people could have lived different lives if they'd made different decisions. She told him we all live the life we live because of the choices we make.

As Fiona listened to her lover patiently explain this to him, she felt her gut tighten as she thought of her own choices and how they could jeopardize her relationship with Pete. She didn't want to lose her, and vowed to herself then and there that she would speak up at the next SAA meeting. She also needed to find a new sponsor, since the one she'd had for the last two years had moved to California.

Once Mack understood what Pete was saying, he changed the topic to Halloween. He was talking in great detail about his dinobot costume and how he had to finish making it soon, and then he asked them if they were coming to the haunted house at his school. They assured him they would be there. Then he asked if they would all take him trick-or-treating and wear costumes. None of them liked Halloween as much as the boy did, but they all promised to dress up. Pete would be a vampire, Fiona a witch in spite of her son's protests, and Anthony was as of yet undecided.

"You should be Frankenstein!" Mack blurted. "You're big and tall like him. I have green face paint you can use," he offered.

Anthony let out a little laugh and mussed up his nephew's hair.

After work on Monday, Pete stopped at a costume shop and got what she needed to be a convincing vampire. On Wednesday, Fiona dug out her witch costume and decided to put a new spin on it to surprise Mack: she would use face paint to make herself look ghoulish. She asked her brother if he'd gotten his costume together yet and was surprised to hear that he was all set.

"Are you kidding? I hope I never disappoint your son. I'm going to be the biggest, scariest Frankenstein at his school."

On Halloween, Fiona got out of work early to make it to school for the festivities. Pete quit early for the day too and went home to transform herself into a blood-sucking count before arriving on campus. She put a small black cape on Turtle so he would match her.

Mack was ecstatic when he saw his family arrive. "Whoa! Uncle Anthony—you look exactly like Frankenstein! You're even walking like he does. Creepy! And Mom, great face paint!" Turtle ran up to him and licked his face. "Guess what? I won the costume contest for the third grade! Most creative use of recyclables," he announced proudly. They all congratulated him.

"I am Count Petrov, and this is my sidekick dogpire, Turtle," Pete said in a Transylvanian accent. Mack laughed and told her that dogs were allowed on campus as long as they were on a leash.

"Well thanks, Mr. Dinobot. Show us this haunted house," Pete said.

The boy proudly gave them a tour of his whole school and then escorted them to the gymnasium, where the third, fourth, and fifth graders had assembled an impressive haunted house. There were lots of other parents there, and children hopped around like fleas. Mack couldn't move too quickly because his costume was cumbersome. He'd used recycled plastic containers, cardboard boxes, aluminum foil, and a lot of green paint to transform himself.

Anthony noticed that even when his sister had on scary makeup people checked her out. He saw somebody's dad stare at her for a really long time. It had been like that since Fiona was about thirteen; she oozed sex appeal and had the constant attention of admirers, whether she wanted it or not. He wondered how many of these parents cheated on their spouses.

As he was ruminating on this, a beautiful woman caught his eye. She was bending to tie her small daughter's shoe, and Anthony couldn't help but notice her good looks. When she stood up, they practically bumped into each other. She was a tall blonde dressed as a fairy princess.

"Oops! Sorry, Frankenstein!" she said playfully.

"Excuse me, Princess," he said as he extended his hand. "Hi. When I'm not Frankenstein, I'm Anthony."

"I'm Rachel," she returned, "and this is my daughter, Stella." The little girl looked up at him from behind her cat mask and meowed. "She will only meow today; she's like a hardcore method actress." He laughed. "Which one of these little darlings is yours?"

"The third grade dinobot over there, Mack, is my nephew. I'm down from Maine visiting, and he talked me into being Frankenstein," Anthony answered cheerfully. Just then, Mack realized his uncle had stopped following and hollered.

"Uncle Anthony! I mean—Frankenstein! Come on!"

Anthony waved to him but hesitated before leaving. "Well, gotta go. Happy Halloween!" He heard Stella meow loudly as he walked away and laughed to himself.

Halloween music played and various scary things popped out as they made their way through the massive haunted house. Fiona actually got startled when she walked into a giant rubber spider web she hadn't noticed. Pete caught her in a dark corner and bit her neck.

"Will you do that again later, Count Petrov?"

"Of course. You know I vant to sink my teeth in your pretty neck," Pete said. Then she noticed Turtle was trying to eat some of the spaghetti that posed as guts in a bowl with eyeballs. "Oops! No boy, come." He obediently stopped and padded after her with his little cape bouncing.

All in all, the haunted house was a great time. Mack had a blast, but was ready to go trick-or-treating. This year, he was going with two other boys in his class, and Fiona had agreed to chaperone. Having Anthony and Pete along made it more fun for her than usual. They laughed and reminisced about Halloweens past. Mack came home tired and happy with a bulging bag of candy. They all changed and got on the couch to watch *The Addams Family* while they ate dinner. Anthony was in a better mood, because tomorrow night he'd be watching roller derby.

Life was looking up.

☆☆☆

Fiona drove her hatchback to the Aleppo Shriners Auditorium in Wilmington, which was forty minutes away. She teased her brother about his thing for Dangerous D on the way there, asking him all about her: what she looked like, how old she was, how long she'd been in roller derby, and what he would say if he got the chance to talk to her tonight.

"Um..." He paused and thought before answering. "Well, I don't know, because I'm assuming I won't get to talk to her. I mean, they're busy the whole time, and after the match, fans swarm the players, so it's not like I'll have an opportunity to have a real conversation."

"But what if we sit close and she sees your baby blues, becomes smitten, and just *has* to talk to you. What would you tell her?" Fiona probed.

"Oh, okay—I see how it is. I would tell her I'm a huge fan, and then I don't know what else I'd say."

"Do you know if she's single?"

"She got divorced last year so, yes, I think she is single. But you know that I just have a crush on her and am happy to admire her from afar, right?"

Fiona chuckled.

They pulled into the bustling parking lot and saw a huge banner reading *Boston Derby Dames* draped over the outside of the massive building. The crowd was colorful and diverse. There were rockabilly couples decked out in pompadours and vintage clothing from the fifties, lots of tattooed people, gay couples, teenagers, families, and a few of what looked to be former derby players wearing their old uniforms. They got there early enough to score seats in the front, which Anthony was thrilled about. He brought his camera so he could capture Dangerous D on film.

The women went off to get beers while Anthony held their seats. Some of the players were skating slowly through the crowd, and Pete and Fiona enjoyed checking them out.

"Wow, these are some big, strong girlies!" Fiona declared.

"Indeed. Amazons on wheels!" Pete remarked. The home team was decked out in red and gold, and the opposing team from Oregon wore green and black.

"When's the last time you were on roller skates?" Fiona asked as they waited in line.

"Shit, I guess the eighties! How about you?"

"Well, does rollerblading on the Esplanade count? Mack and I have done that, but honestly, I don't think I've worn roller skates since I was a little girl." Suddenly Fiona experienced a wave of panic, because she thought she saw the couple she'd had sex with in a van that day in Brookline, but then realized it wasn't them. With her body count, it wasn't terribly unusual for Fiona to run into a former sex partner. She hoped that wouldn't happen tonight.

Pete ordered the beers while Fiona inspected the crowd. A cute young lesbian couple caught her eye because they were being very affectionate with each other. Noticing their wedding bands, Fiona recalled Anthony's questions about her getting married. She looked down at Pete's left hand and imagined a wedding band on it, then glanced at her own and did the same, making her ring finger feel hot. She was lost in fantasy for a moment and didn't hear Pete the first time, so she had to repeat the question.

"Would Anthony want an IPA or a pilsner?"

"Oh, sorry. IPA," she answered.

They made their way through the boisterous crowd and headed back to their spots on the bench where Anthony sat grinning like a fool. He was happy, and that made Fiona happy. *Fuck Dawn. He'll have a second chance at love, and I'm sure he will find someone loyal who will return all the love he gives, someone with a heart as big as his.* He had his camera out already, even though the match didn't start for twenty minutes.

"I spotted Dangerous D," he said cheerfully. "She's over there warming up." He pointed her out and took a big swig of beer. "She's so fucking hot." The women looked over, checked her out, and nodded in agreement.

"Yup, she's easy on the eyes all right," Fiona said.

"Oh yeah," Pete agreed, "hottie alert."

"It's fun to check out girls with you two. I could get used to this. I *should* just move down here. I mean, why the hell not? I'll figure out my housing and job stuff. The main thing is I'd have you guys and Mack and Calvin and my old friends who moved here after we graduated from high school That's more than plenty of people have when they move somewhere new and start over, right?"

"Oh Anthony," Fiona said as she squeezed his arm, "you know I want you here. It would be amazing. You've been in Maine all your life—it's time for a change! Mom and Dad can make do without you. Hell, maybe it would get them thinking about retirement if they didn't have you to rely on. I think you should make it happen. You know you can stay with us as long as you need to."

"This is exciting," Pete chimed in. "Mack will be thrilled."

As they waited for the match to start, they chatted happily about what Anthony's life here might be like. He was talking about how he wanted to settle down with someone again, and Fiona was cautioning him, advising him to date a lot first, to sample what's out there. She'd always encouraged him to be more adventurous when it came to women. He'd always said that he wasn't like her; he didn't need to have lots of sexual encounters. He needed love.

"I've got to hit the restroom before it starts," Fiona told them. She gave her beer to Anthony to hold and made her way down the bleachers.

Weaving through the crowd, she scanned the scene because she'd always loved to people-watch; it was one of the many things she and Pete had in common. Her eyes landed on a tall, muscular woman whose Fat City Roller Girls uniform said *VAL7*. The C on her arm told Fiona she was the team captain. She was right in Fiona's path, but didn't move out of the way when she saw Fiona walking toward her. Instead, she stared at her, smiled, and spoke to her.

"Hello, Red," she said flirtatiously. Fiona smiled, saying hello in response, and then their shoulders brushed as she moved past her. This woman was throwing off some real heat, and Fiona tried to shake off the attraction but she felt the familiar tingle up her spine that preceded carnality. She kept walking toward the bathroom and didn't look back.

When Fiona returned, the clock counted down, the match began, and the announcer's voice echoed through the huge place.

"We have the Wicked Sistahs taking on the Fat City Roller Girls. Wicked is second in the bracket, Fat City is third, and these two teams both really want the win, so we expect quite a battle out there tonight. All right and that's the whistle; we've got Fat City on the line and both jammers up against two walls of defense now, trying to find their way through. Maya Papaya is going for the middle; she heads for the outside. Good defense to start from both teams. Now on the jammer line we see Wicked's Dangerous D, who is by far the most influential jammer in the Massachusetts league."

Anthony sat up straighter and filmed the game intermittently as his favorite player dominated the track. Nonstop action made the time pass quickly. He was cheering loudly for the Wicked Sistahs, who were ahead by twenty-one with a score of ninety-three at the half.

Fiona went to the restroom again, and Pete and Anthony discussed the match. The players were skating through the crowd, and Fiona got a good look at some of them as she meandered through the throng.

VAL7 saw Fiona and skated alongside her. "Hey, Red," she said boldly. "Good to see you again. Tell me you're rooting for my team."

"Sorry to disappoint you, but I'd be lying if I said that," Fiona returned.

"I can live with that. I'm Valerie," she said, extending her hand. "My derby name is Val Halla. What's your name?"

"Fiona," she said. They were still holding hands. "It's nice to meet you, but I have to hit the ladies' room."

"That's where I'm headed," she said, smiling. As Fiona walked, Valerie managed to skate around her. She was lean and powerfully built, with dirty-blonde hair in a ponytail and golden-brown eyes. Fiona enjoyed her shameless pursuit, absorbing the attention like a sponge soaks up water. This woman exuded sex appeal. When they got to the restroom, there was a long line. Valerie was close behind her, and they made small talk.

Fiona's turn for the bathroom came up when a woman exited the designated disabled stall. Much to her surprise, Valerie skated into it with her and closed the door. "Thought it would save time if we went together," she said.

"That's not why you came in here with me, and you know it. You thought you'd hit on me in here."

"Well, yeah, so...why don't you pee and then come over here."

Surprising herself, Fiona pulled her jeans down and used the toilet. Valerie watched her wipe, seemingly delighted to discover she was a real redhead. Fiona pulled up her underwear and jeans before walking over to Valerie. They kissed up against the tiled wall. Their chemistry was so potent, it made Fiona feel off-balance. At one point, she thought about stopping, but was too aroused to turn back; her lust was in the driver's seat now, and she was going along for the ride. Pete would never know. It would be the last time. She would go to a meeting next week, pour her heart out, find a new sponsor, and get over this addiction once and for all, not because she necessarily wanted to, but because she should.

They kissed passionately, and Valerie whispered in her ear that she didn't have much time before working her big hand into Fiona's damp panties. Fiona tugged the athlete's tights down and touched her, thrilled by how slick and warm she felt. Valerie was skilled and knew how to excite her quickly; she massaged her clit with her thumb while working a few fingers in and out, faster and faster. They kissed the whole time and were so hot it didn't take long for them to come; first Fiona, then Valerie.

They rearranged their clothes hastily. Fiona opened the door to see Pete in line at the bathroom doorway. There was no escape. Pete saw her exit the stall with Valerie behind her, and both of their faces were flushed, leaving no mystery as to why they were in there together. Pete's face fell; Fiona could almost see her heart break. Fiona walked up to her and opened her mouth to speak, but Pete looked down at the floor angrily, then went into the next available stall.

"Shit," Fiona said.

Valerie heard her. "Girlfriend?"

"Yeah. Fuck. I can't believe this..."

"Sorry, I have to get back." She squeezed her shoulder and skated off.

Fiona waited outside the door so she could have a conversation with Pete. A few minutes later she came out. When Fiona saw her mouth in a tight line, she knew things wouldn't go well. She searched for the right words, and all that came out was an apology.

"Babe, I'm so sorry. It just happened. It didn't mean anything, it—"

Pete cut her off. "It means something to me, Fiona. It means I can't trust you." Her eyes were hard with pain as she spoke. "I have to get out of here. I need space. And time to think. I'll get my stuff and take a bus home—you two stay and watch the match."

"No, Pete, don't go. Please," Fiona pleaded.

"I'm leaving," Pete said before she turned and walked away.

Fiona had to fight tears as she stood there. She felt as if the sides of her world were caving in on her. She struggled a bit to breathe, as if remorse were choking her, and leaned against the wall, which held her upright despite the weight of regret. She wanted to rewind time so she could make a better choice. But there was no way to undo what she'd just done. She was broken inside. After a few minutes, she walked back to her brother, who wore a dumbfounded expression.

"Pete said she had to go, grabbed her coat, hugged me, and left," Anthony said. "What the hell happened?"

Fiona couldn't look him in the eye; she thought if she did she would cry, and she hated crying in public. "I fucked up. Big time," she managed.

"Oh, Fi, you didn't..."

"I did. In the bathroom with a player from Fat City. Pete saw us come out of the same stall. I can't believe I did it."

"Look," he said softly, "there are a lot of things I could say to you, but I don't think it would be anything you haven't already said to yourself. You gotta go after her. Let's go. I don't mind leaving now."

"No," Fiona said. "Thanks, but she said she needed space and time, and if there's any chance in hell of her forgiving me, I can't get in the way of what she needs. Let her go. Let's stay and watch the rest of the match. I can't go home now. Shit—what am I gonna tell Mack?" Her eyes were big, wet marbles.

Anthony hugged her, thinking of what he could say to comfort her. "Hey, don't worry about Mack right now. Figure that out later. Just breathe. It happened. You just have to go forward. Give her space like she asked for and maybe she'll reach out. I know she really loves you, Fi. She'll come around."

"I don't know," she said, her voice devoid of hope. "You didn't see the hurt in her eyes. I really fucked up this time, Anthony. Why did I *do* that? Why did I have sex with that woman?"

"You know why. You have a problem. You're working on it. All you can do is try to change, Fi; you're an addict, and maybe this is rock bottom. I just hope you don't lose Pete, because I think you two could really go the distance. She must have known the risks when you told her about your sex addiction," he said, trying to console her.

"I don't know, Anthony. I don't know."

The match started up again, but Fiona felt like she wasn't really there, as if she were watching herself in a dream.

Much to Anthony's delight, the Wicked Sistahs won, and he even got to high-five Dangerous D as she skated through the crowd, every bit as sexy up close and sweaty as she was in photos.

They were quiet on the ride home. He didn't know what to say, and she didn't want to talk, so she turned the radio on and tried not to cry as she drove.

☆☆☆

All of Pete's things were gone when they arrived at the house. She'd even washed out the dog bowls Fiona had bought for her visits that were in the kitchen and set them in the dish drainer to dry. On the kitchen counter was the house key Fiona had given her not long ago; the sight of it pushed her to the brink of tears again. She imagined the heartbreak she would cause if she had to tell Mack that Pete and Turtle were out of his life.

Anthony came in and saw her there, sad and frozen. "You gonna be okay? Anything I can do to help?"

"You're doing it. Just make sure I get my sorry ass to that meeting Tuesday; don't let me make any excuses."

"Okay. You know, where there's love, anything is possible, Fiona. She adores you and Mack, and you love her. Just be humble and honest and open to anything she has to say to you. She's hurting now, so just give her that space she asked for. It's late. You should go to bed."

"No. I'm wired. I can't stop thinking about what I did and why I do the stupid shit I do. I mean, I've never fallen this hard for anyone before. The stakes were extremely high, and I blew it."

"No point in beating yourself up. It's done. And you don't know that your relationship is over," he said tenderly.

"You're right. Thanks." She pulled away. "I think I'll watch something mindless on television. That might put me to sleep."

"Want company? I could make us a snack, and we could sit out in the living room."

"Yeah, actually, I'd like that."

"I'll make cinnamon toast," he said and went into the kitchen.

They stayed up for nearly two hours watching *Star Trek* episodes until they couldn't keep their eyes open. When Fiona laid her head on her pillow, the tears came. She sobbed so hard that she almost couldn't catch her breath.

☆☆☆

By Tuesday, Fiona still hadn't heard from Pete: no calls, emails, or text messages. She'd resisted the urge to contact her, but it was getting harder. She was hoping to find a new sponsor at the meeting tonight; she knew she needed help to tame the monster within.

Anthony and Mack were going to have a pizza-and-games night while she was out. When Mack asked about Pete and Turtle, Fiona told him Pete was really busy this week but that he'd see her on the weekend. She prayed it was true. She didn't feel like she deserved another chance, but desperately wanted one.

As she pulled into the parking lot of the Pawtucket Congregational Church in Lowell, she felt that old familiar dread rise up in her; being at a Sex Addicts Anonymous meeting meant she had a real and undeniable problem, one that she couldn't get a handle on by herself. She would have to unpack her history, explain her current situation, and open up about her destructive behaviors. Hearing the words come out of her mouth would be difficult; it always was.

The church was an impressive old brick pile complete with spire. She disliked that these meetings were in churches, probably because religion made her very uncomfortable. The way Fiona saw it, religion was the single most destructive force in the world. The only way she could endure hearing the term "higher power" so much in SAA was to substitute the phrase "my best self" in her mind. She appreciated that the program had value despite its religious underpinnings. She also accepted her odd-girl-out status, since most people believed in a god of some sort. She remembered that one of her first late-night conversations with Pete was about religion, and how they both thought it was an assault on intellect and creativity. They'd lain on their backs and watched the flickering shadows the candles made on the ceiling as they talked. She recalled feeling that night that not only had she met her match sexually, but she'd also found a woman with a keen and hungry mind, the kind of brain that could keep her interested for a long time. Her heart ached for Pete. The past three days were the longest they'd gone without speaking since they met nearly two months ago. She felt tiny drops of rain on her face as she went slowly up the steps and into the church.

All churches smelled the same to Fiona; they were a musty blend of incense, dust, and people's breath trapped in the wooden surfaces of the walls, pews, and floors. She went to the basement and saw there were already quite a few people at the meeting. She took one of only three available seats left in the circle and sat on the hard, wooden folding chair. She set down her bag, removed her coat, draped it over the back of the chair, and got up to get coffee.

The meeting was going to start in six minutes. She drank the bitter brew and scanned the crowd. Like most SAA meetings she'd been to, this one was attended by more men than women; Fiona was one of only three women out of the fourteen people there. The facilitator was someone Fiona recognized from a few meetings she'd been to a long time ago. She couldn't recall his name, but did remember that he was funny, which made the meetings more endurable. Some of the faces looked familiar to her, but most did not. She sipped her drink and looked down at her feet.

She heard her phone vibrate in her bag and reached for it. It was a text from Anthony saying: *U better talk at this meeting. U know I'm gonna grill you when u get home. Mack is killing me at checkers. xo bro*

A surge of gratitude for her brother welled up inside her. If it was over between her and Pete, at least she'd have Anthony around; they could lean on each other while they each rebuilt their lives. She texted back: *I promise I will be an open book. Watch out for Mack's triple jumps—he's notorious for those! xo*

Since she had a few more minutes to kill, she checked her email, hoping against hope that she'd have a message from Pete. As she suspected, there was no word from her. If she didn't hear from her by Friday, she was going to call or email her—she had to. The silence was making her crazy.

There was a short, supportive email from Calvin in which he'd included a quote from one of his favorite poets, Anne Sexton: *Put your ear down close to your soul and listen hard.* He was always there for her. She'd called him the Saturday after the roller derby incident and told him she needed a walkabout. When she was really upset, she liked to walk and talk with him. These walks were more like hikes because they lasted several hours. That day they ended up walking over seven miles to Jamaica Plain and back. She'd done most of the talking, and Calvin had been extremely supportive but tough on her too, saying he was disappointed by her behavior because she sabotaged something really great in her life. He also had told her he was hurt that she didn't tell him about the Abigail incident her brother referred to at the dinner party. She had acknowledged what he said and knew it came from a place of love. She wrote him back a quick thank-you email, and then it was time for the meeting to start.

"Welcome to SAA, everyone. I'm Louis, your facilitator for the evening. If you're not ready to laugh, cry, or spill your guts, leave now."

Ripples of laughter went through the room, followed by a group greeting of *Hello, Louis.*

"And you regulars know this, but for the handful of new people I see here tonight, the coffee is not for amateurs, it's strictly for those with iron stomachs.

"I'll start the spilling, and I'll try to keep it fresh for those of you who know my story well. I'm a sex addict and have been for thirty-seven years, ever since I found my dad's *Playboy* collection and masturbated to those pictures every chance I got. In my youth, I cheated on every girlfriend I had and even had sex with my best friend's girlfriend, which cost me my best friend. When I found a woman foolish enough to marry me, I screwed that up by cheating and having sex with prostitutes. That cost me full-time access to my own kid. I was forty before I could admit to myself that I was a sex addict. Part of the problem was that, when I described my behaviors to friends, they didn't see the dilemma; they told me I was lucky to 'dip my wick' that often. Then I talked with a female friend, who instantly saw the destructiveness of my ways and referred me to SAA. I got help, got sober, and even met a woman crazy enough to take a gamble and marry me. The gamble paid off; we've been happily married for ten years. She understands I'm an addict and will always have my struggles, but she accepts the chaff with the wheat."

He paused for a moment and swept his eyes around the room to look at each person's face. "Your stories are different, but the themes are the same; that's why you're all here. No matter where you are with your addiction, you're in the right place. You've got support here in each other. Some of you have sponsors and some of you don't. I highly recommend getting one. It's hard to go it alone. If you need help finding one, I can help you. I've got lists full of people who would be happy to take you on.

"So now that I've warmed up the room for the next person, I encourage you to share your stories. There's no judgment here, only compassion. Who would like to go next?"

He raised his silver eyebrows and scanned the faces of the attendees hopefully. Body language never lied: those who didn't want to speak suddenly inspected their shoes; those who were thinking about speaking next looked around at each other but avoided prolonged eye contact with any one person. The few who felt brave enough to talk now looked Louis in the eye, and it was one of these people to whom he extended an invitation. "You, in the blue sweater, why don't you share?"

The man he addressed sat up straighter in his chair and cleared his throat before he spoke. "Okay... I'm Paul."

Everyone then said *Hello, Paul.*

"I usually go to meetings in Waltham, but today it was easier for me to get here after work, so here I am. Anyway, I guess I'll give a little background. I've been a sex addict really ever since I can remember. I couldn't keep my hands off myself, which earned me the nickname Li'l Tugger from my big brothers." Some laughed at this and others suppressed their laughter. "It's okay, go ahead and laugh. It's funny," he encouraged. "We have to be able to laugh at ourselves or everything will get too serious, and if it gets too serious we can get overwhelmed or paralyzed." He smoothed his thinning red hair back, adjusted his glasses, and cleared his throat again.

Fiona sat up straighter too, partly because the chair was uncomfortable and partly because she wanted to be as attentive as she could.

"When I was twelve, I got into pornography pretty heavily. Even though my mom punished me severely every time she caught me looking, I could never stop. It was like what was enough for most people was never sufficient for me. It wasn't enough to have sexual relationships with five different women at the same time; I had to have group sex, and that got really crazy. I had my first threesome at seventeen and realized I was bisexual, which doubled the pool of potential sex partners, and man, I can't even count how many people I fucked or got fucked by. It's all a blur.

"And when I had trouble finding sex partners, I went to prostitutes, both men and women. I even worked as a prostitute for a while but I stopped, because doing it for money took the fun out of it for me.

"I wasn't able to commit to one person, and I saw my friends settling down, getting married, having kids, and there I was, still stuck in the same place. I became depressed and even suicidal. When I started seeing a therapist, he recommended I come to an SAA meeting. That was seven years ago. I've been mostly sober the past five years, but every now and then I slip up, and I know some of you know what I'm talking about." He paused to sip his drink and continued. "You think it'll be your last time, or somehow it doesn't count. But it isn't the last time, and it does count. I come to meetings to keep myself together, and right now I have the best incentive not to act out: I'm in a monogamous relationship with someone I really care about. So far, so good. These meetings really help. That's it, I guess; I've talked enough tonight." He drank some more coffee, then leaned back in his chair.

"Thank you, Paul," Louis said. "Anyone else want to share? We have lots of time."

He scanned the crowd, and Fiona was about to talk, but a young woman seated across from her spoke first. She was maybe twenty-five and had blonde hair in a bi-level haircut with the tips dyed bright purple. She had a melancholy demeanor, and the deep voice that came from her didn't go with her small, wiry frame.

"I'm Bianca, and this is only, like, my fourth or fifth meeting, and I've never said much at meetings before, so I'm nervous."

She paused and looked up while the crowd said *Hello, Bianca.*

She smiled weakly, then began. "I've known I have a problem with sex for maybe ten years, but I didn't know it was addiction until this year. It sounds silly, but I actually watched a documentary one night, just randomly, on Netflix, about sex addiction, and I was like—that's me. I lost my virginity at twelve, and it was like some sort of demon in me woke up. I couldn't get enough sex. And I had sex with anybody who wanted to have sex with me, which was such a bad idea. I did it to feel better about myself, and it usually made me feel worse. In fact, it made me feel so bad I started cutting. On my legs, where no one could see.

"My parents were clueless; they worked all the time, and my brother and me were like accessories or something. I swear, they paid more attention to the dog than us. So, the documentary gave me the idea to come to a meeting and get help, so here I am. I'm doing something to support my sobriety: for every day I don't have sex, I put a ten-dollar bill in a jar, and when it's stuffed full I'm going to treat myself to something." She looked around the room. Fiona smiled at her when their eyes met. "I really don't know what else to say. That's kinda my story. Thanks."

She looked down at the floor self-consciously until Louis spoke.

"Great, Bianca, thanks so much for finding the courage to share. Keep coming to meetings and keep putting money in that jar!" She nodded. "Next?" He glanced around the room, and when he looked at Fiona, she nodded slightly, indicating to him that she was ready to speak.

"Hi, I'm Fiona," she began.

*Hi, Fiona* chorused the group.

"And I'm a sex addict. I got started very early, and at this point I've lost count of how many sex partners I've had. Let's just say it's way too many... I was doing pretty well until recently. That's why I'm here, actually."

She paused and looked around at her fellow addicts. "I really screwed up. I've been in this happy relationship with an amazing woman for the past two months. We fell hard and fast for each other, and everything was going great. I told her about my history, my problems with promiscuity, and she was understanding and compassionate. The only thing I left out was the porno I was in a long time ago... I thought that might be too much information. We're really in love. And she's great with my son. I have an eight-year-old boy named Mack. I mean, he's incentive enough to get my shit together, and now the stakes are even higher, because my girlfriend has become a big part of his life. I'd be letting down two people instead of one." She stopped to drink some of her dark, bitter brew, which tasted even worse than before because it was cold now.

"So, I hooked up with this couple the day after I was first with her and never said anything about it because we'd just met and I didn't want to scare her away. Then it was just her until I had a quick thing with a woman I'd met before. I thought about telling my girlfriend about it, but I didn't. I just hoped it would be my last time. But it wasn't. And just last Friday night I had a brief, meaningless encounter with a woman in a bathroom, and my girlfriend caught me. That was that. She told me she needed space and time and left, and I haven't heard from her since. I really hope it's not over because—" She stopped herself to keep her emotions in check. "Because I can see a future with her; I want a future with her. I'm not sure *I* would give her a second chance, but I'm hoping *she* does. I just love her so much. I've got to get control over my life. I can't act out again. I just can't..." Her words trailed off because she didn't know what else to say. She shook her head, disapproving of herself.

"Thanks, Fiona," said Louis. "Who would like to share now?"

Several more people opened themselves up to the group before the meeting ended. One guy totally inspired her because he'd been really out of control and acting out until he got into a relationship and pulled it together. If he could do it, so could she.

After the meeting, she and a few other people approached Louis to see about getting a sponsor. He gave her several names and email addresses and told her he hoped to see her at another meeting.

What started as a sprinkle was now an all-out downpour. The roads were slick, and Fiona had her windshield wipers on the fastest speed. At red lights, she listened to their steady squeaky thump across the glass. She tried to listen to her soul and heard herself crying. She sobbed most of the way home.

☆☆☆

When she returned home, Anthony was sprawled out on the couch reading, and Mack was in bed. He could tell she'd been crying, so he sat up and opened his arms to her. She sat next to him, leaned in and cried a little more.

"You talked, huh?"

She nodded.

"I'm proud of you, Fiona. I can't imagine how it feels to expose yourself like that, but at least the meetings remind you you're not alone, right?"

"Yeah. People's stories are pretty intense. Some of them were inspiring, though." She wiped her nose. "How was your night with the little guy?"

"He kicked my ass at checkers, then we read a sci-fi book together. We had a great time. I'm gonna miss him when I leave," Anthony said.

"You don't have to miss him because you're moving here," she replied with a smile. "I'm kinda wiped out. Think I'll crawl into bed with a book."

"You okay? The meeting was okay?"

"Yeah—I have a few leads for sponsors. I'll email them tomorrow. Goodnight." She kissed him on the forehead and got up to check on her son before going to bed. The last thing she did was shoot Calvin a text message to see if he was free for dinner tomorrow night. He wrote back saying he'd make her dinner and to come at 6:30. She was relieved she would see him soon.

☆☆☆

When Calvin opened his door, Fiona was greeted with the aroma of his cooking and a big hug.

"Wine?"

"No, thanks, I didn't sleep well last night, and I'm tired so wine would just wipe me out," she said.

"Beer?"

"No—just water will be fine. It smells amazing in here!"

"I know you like my chicken-and-broccoli casserole so I made it just for you. Should be ready in fifteen minutes. How are you holding up?" He poured her a glass of water and they sat in the living room.

"I'm sad but I haven't gone to pieces. And you know what? You were great to listen to me go on for hours on Saturday, but tonight doesn't have to be lopsided. I don't want it to be all about my problems. How are *you*?" she asked.

He studied her for a moment before answering. Her eyes were puffy from crying, and she didn't have any of her usual sparkle.

"I'm good, actually. I had two days off in a row and have been putting together my resume. I'd like you to look at it before you go, and tell me what you think."

"Good for you, Calvin. I'm proud of you." She squeezed his shoulder.

"I'm looking for a position at a nonprofit, preferably one that serves homeless people. I'm ready for a change, Fi."

"What about your mortgage?" she asked with concern.

"Well, I have a few ideas." He sat up straighter on the couch and had a very focused look in his eyes. She liked it. "One is to keep a few shifts a week at the restaurant. Another is to get a housemate, like you said. Or—if I had to, sell this place," he said.

"But you love your condo. Don't sell. Keeping a few shifts at La Fleur Bleue is a better idea, even though that means working a lot. Or go with the housemate idea. You *can't* sell. This is your home. You know, Anthony's almost sure he's moving down here. He'd be a great temporary housemate, Cal." She drank some water and ran her hand through her hair.

"Maybe. I'll figure things out."

"Well, Anthony would be easy to live with. He's neat, knows how to give people space, and has plenty of money in the bank, so you could charge him whatever for the room. And he cares about you."

"Yeah, maybe. First I just have to get a job. Because you know what?"

"What?"

"I haven't had a client in two weeks, and I'm hoping to not ever have another. I can't. It's so unhealthy. I feel like if I do it anymore I'll be erased, you know?"

Fiona started tearing up as his words sank in. "Yes, I do. I've been waiting a long time for you to say that. Good for you, honey." She couldn't help herself; she started crying. He opened his arms to her, and she fell into him. She loved him so much, and she loved that he didn't ask her why she was crying. "Me too," she said softly. "I'm not going to let myself be erased by my addiction. Even if Pete leaves me, I shouldn't keep having random sex anymore. I can't." She pulled away and looked at him.

"She's not going to leave you, you'll see, Fi. She's hurting for sure, but she loves you too much to bail. I'm telling you. Don't give up."

She wiped her eyes with the back of her hand before speaking. "So, do you really think it's possible for us to reinvent ourselves?"

"Yes," he affirmed. "If we give it our all, yes, I do."

# CHAPTER EIGHT: TIP OF THE ICEBERG

*Sometimes, when one person is missing,*
*the whole world seems depopulated.*
*~ Lamartine*

After Pete got her things out of Fiona's place and came home, she was paralyzed and just sat on her couch with her coat on, petting Turtle absently. She wasn't sure how much time went by before she got up and mechanically put things in their place. Her loft seemed empty because her heart felt vacant. She paced around, not knowing what to do. It was almost ten, and she didn't feel tired enough to sleep.

Sheila was no doubt with Damon, but Pete needed to reach out so she sent a text: *sorry 2 bug u if u r with your man, but things went really wrong with Fiona tonight and I need 2 talk.*

Sheila called her back a few minutes later because, as it turned out, she and Damon had just split.

"What?" Pete asked incredulously. "But you two seemed so happy! What happened?"

"Well, we were spending lots of time together, and I thought things were going great, but then he said he didn't think he was ready for a serious relationship after all." Her voice was heavy as she continued. "He said he just realized he needed some more time and space for himself. Remember how he just ended a serious relationship a year and a half ago?"

"Yeah," Pete said.

"I guess he's not ready to partner again. We talked for hours, and it just kept coming back to that: that he couldn't give me what I wanted in a relationship. I'm still kinda stunned, Pete. I've just been going over and over it in my head, and I can't decide if he knew how he felt from the start but didn't break it off right away because he liked the sex, or if he's being sincere. It's really bothering me, because if I can't trust my instincts, what can I trust?"

"You're asking someone who blurs reality and fantasy on a regular basis? Wish I could respond to that, but I've just about given up on my intuition. Maybe you should just assume he is being sincere, Sheils. He probably is, and in any case, it's less wear and tear on you to go with that. I'm so sorry. Please don't give up on dating. Just keep putting it out there."

"Thanks, I will keep searching for true love; I just may have to lick my wounds for a while. Okay, so what happened with Fiona?"

As Pete told her the whole story, the evening's events stung her all over again, and her wounds deepened.

Stunned and sad, Sheila asked if she wanted her to come over.

Pete said she was touched at the offer but no, she would probably stay up late and work on a collage to take her mind off things.

"What are you going to do?" Sheila asked.

"I don't know; I just know I need time, like I told her. I have to figure things out. I know I love her. And I love Mack. Shit. I would miss that kid so much...but I don't know if I can take more of this kind of hurt, you know?"

"Yes, I do know, sweetie. Just stay in the present and focus on how you're feeling, and try to see the lessons in all of it. I believe the universe wouldn't have sent you a beautiful, wonderful, troubled sex addict if you couldn't handle it. She's flawed. And so are you, but you're also both strong. I hope you two can stay together, Pete," Sheila said tenderly.

"Yeah, well thanks for listening."

"Any time. Hey, what are you doing tomorrow? Want to commiserate and spend the day together? Maybe go to the Salem Witch Museum? We've been saying we wanted to go there for a long time. It'd be fun."

"Hmmm—it's tempting," Pete responded, "but I won't be the best company."

"So? Me neither, that's why we're perfect companions. And how cheerful do you have to be at a witch museum anyway? Come on, it might lift our spirits," Sheila said persuasively.

"Okay. You convinced me."

"You won't regret it. You shouldn't be alone at that workbench with your thoughts fermenting. I'll call you in the morning. See you tomorrow. Let's get bagels and coffee on the way out of town."

"Sounds good. Thanks, Sheila."

"Love you, Pete," she said sweetly.

"Right back atcha. And Sheils, I'm *really* sorry about Damon."

Sheila sighed, telling her she'd bounce back, and then they said their good-byes.

Pete decided to have a glass of wine and work on a collage. She put Depeche Mode on the stereo and turned it up loud. The lyrics spoke to her, with the singer's talk of slowly losing himself over and over. She went to the piece she'd been working on. It was made entirely of toys and made her think of Mack. She fought tears. Fiona's face flashed in her mind, and she could hear her voice haunting her, telling her she loved her.

"If you love me, why did you *hurt* me?" she said aloud.

Turtle walked over and studied her face. He wagged his tail a few times then stopped, still staring at her, trying to read her emotional state. She reached down and rubbed his head. "It might be just me and you again, boy, just me and you..."

She pulled the arms and legs off a small action figure and worked them into the piece so that they appeared to be coming out of other toys. She couldn't stop thinking about Fiona's infidelity; she tried to discern why it mattered so much to her, and all she came up with was loyalty. The older she got, the more she valued this trait in the people who inhabited her life. Intellectually, she knew she should have seen it coming; sex addicts crave sex, and even though the two of them had a strong erotic connection, being with Pete alone couldn't satisfy Fiona's need to engage in anonymous sex. Pete was angry with herself for being so thrown by it when, logically, it was a likely event. She felt a familiar crowding in her mind as she obsessed about it all.

She stared at the collage for a while and then left the workbench. She sat on the couch and reached for the remote. Unable to focus on art, she decided to watch a movie. Wanting to escape, she poured another glass of merlot and searched for something depressing. *Million Dollar Baby* would be perfect. She pushed play, pulled a blanket around her and Turtle, then settled in for the drama.

By the time the film ended, her eyelids were heavy, and her mind was quieter. The movie made her cry, and that release felt good. After she turned off the television, the quiet stunned her a bit so she sat motionless until she rose to go to bed.

☆☆☆

When Sheila arrived the next morning, she gave Pete a python hug. "You look tired. Did you sleep last night?"

"Yeah, not well, but I did sleep. You look pretty good considering." She studied her friend. "You holding up okay?"

"I'll be okay. He sent me an email this morning that explained things a little better. It made me feel slightly less brokenhearted." She bent down, picked Turtle up, and kissed his head. "You ready to go?"

Pete grabbed her bag, and they left. Like many early-November days in New England, today was damp and sunless. The pale gray sky promised rain. Pete liked the weather; it went with her mood.

Sheila said it was perfect museum weather and talked energetically about the Salem witch trials. "I remember learning about it in school, don't you?"

"Yeah, but the details escape me right now," Pete said.

"Not me, I find it all too fascinating to forget. I remember something like twenty people were executed. Eventually, the colony admitted the trials were a mistake and compensated the families of those convicted. As if you could compensate someone for loss of life."

"Yeah, really," Pete said flatly.

"I hate seeing you this heartbroken, Petra." Sheila gripped the steering wheel more tightly than she needed to.

"Not sure if my heart is actually broken, like as in can't be repaired, but it's at the very least cracked. I mean, I figured being in a relationship with a sex addict could get complicated, but things with us were going so well I guess I just got comfortable; I almost forgot about her problem. That's why it was so shocking to see her with that woman."

"I can imagine," Sheila said sympathetically.

"You know, I hate to even say it out loud," Pete began, "but honestly, I wonder if there have been others..."

"Oh shit," Sheila blurted, "I hadn't even thought of that. Crap. Well, my advice is to just try to push *that* thought off to the side. Just worry about what you know happened. It sounds like it was really random with that roller derby player."

"Yeah. I almost wish I hadn't caught her. Then I wouldn't know, and nothing would have changed between us."

"I hear you. I don't think you should give up on her, Pete. I've never seen you this in love, and I've known you a long time. But only you can figure out what to do. Maybe just give it some time; I'm sure she's willing to wait."

"Yeah. I hate not hearing her voice. Being out of touch," Pete lamented.

"I know, it must be hard."

When they arrived in Salem, the rain stopped, and as they drove up to the museum, they saw the imposing statue of Salem's founder, Roger Conant. For eleven dollars, they could lose themselves in history and legend for a few hours. The exhibits were engaging, giving museum visitors a lot to think about. They read about how the witchcraft craze was strong in Europe long before the 1600s; tens of thousands of people, mostly women, were killed.

The Salem witch hunt started when a reverend's nine-year-old daughter and eleven-year-old niece started having fits. They screamed, threw things, uttered strange sounds, and contorted their bodies into unusual positions. Three women were blamed for afflicting them, including a Caribbean slave named Tituba, who confessed that "the Devil came to me and bid me serve him." She described elaborate images of black dogs, red cats, yellow birds, and a "black man" who wanted her to sign his book. She admitted that she signed the book and said there were several other witches looking to destroy the Puritans. All three women were put in jail.

"I've told you that four times in my life I was asked if I was a witch, right?" Pete asked.

"Yes, that sounds familiar. Well, you're kind of mysterious. Maybe that's why people asked you that," Sheila offered.

"Maybe so..."

As they headed to a different exhibit, they saw a woman who resembled Fiona, and Pete stopped in her tracks. Sheila squeezed her shoulder as if to say *don't stare*. She was taller than Fiona and looked to be maybe five years older, but her face shape and coloring were very similar. Pete studied her briefly, then made herself look away. She hadn't even been thinking about Fiona until she saw this doppelganger.

After the museum, they got lunch at a vegetarian cafe and then drove back. The rain started up again, heavier this time. They discussed the exhibits and the history behind them, but then Pete needed to talk some more about her situation.

"So I was doing fine until I saw that woman who looked like her. I was enjoying the exhibits and not thinking about the whole mess, but then it got all stirred up again," she said with weariness in her voice.

"I know. She really did resemble her."

"So—what would you do if you were me?"

"Hmmm. I guess, like you, I would need space. If I were you, I wouldn't walk away. But I would lay down some conditions," Sheila advised.

"Conditions?"

"Yes, tell her how you need things to be. For starters, I'd say she has to get a sponsor and go to meetings regularly. You can help support her with that by babysitting Mack. I would also tell her no more stepping out on you. Either she is one hundred percent faithful and committed or you're done. Tell her you won't tolerate any more of her sexual encounters with people."

"Would you ask her if there's been anyone else besides the roller derby girl? Or would you let that lie?" Pete asked.

"Not sure. I guess if you're prepared for the worst kind of answer, you could confront her about it but if not, I'd leave it alone."

"Yeah, I see what you're saying. For all I know, she could have been with lots of people since we got together, but my intuition tells me otherwise. I think I'm disinclined to ask her about it right now. Thanks for the good advice, Sheils," Pete said.

They talked about Damon some more, and Sheila said the sex was so great she was afraid she wouldn't ever have better.

"Ever is a long time," Pete said.

When they got back to Cambridge, the rain had stopped, and the skies were considerably brighter than they had been earlier. Pete took Turtle for a long, brisk walk. She was so lost in thought about Fiona she didn't realize how much time had passed or how far she'd walked until she noticed she was just a few blocks from Fiona's house. Part of her wanted to show up at her door, to forgive and forget and fall into her arms again. But the rest of her turned and headed back, getting home just before dark.

She made herself chicken stir fry for supper and read while she ate. She'd just started another mystery by her favorite author and was thoroughly enjoying it. She was so engrossed that she didn't hear her phone until the third ring. She wondered if it was Fiona, and if so, would she answer it?

The screen showed a number that looked familiar, but she couldn't quite place it. It turned out to be a prospective client she'd given an estimate to saying he'd love to go ahead with the job and asking how soon she could start. Pete was relieved. She'd thought she wouldn't have work for the coming week and dreaded the downtime in light of her troubles. When things were bad, she preferred to work. She would rather have a job than rattle around her place with too much time to dwell on things. She would start Monday at 8:00 and expected this particular job to last about a week and a half. Pete had a big job lined up for after Thanksgiving, so this was perfect, because she could still get some time off this month to rest her body and make art.

On Sunday, Pete got a call from a friend she hadn't seen in a long time. Stephanie was a client of hers a few years ago, and they really hit it off, so they started socializing. They didn't see each other that often, because Stephanie was frequently out of town for her job as a travel nurse. It was great to hear from her; she was one of those people who was always upbeat and fun to be around.

"It's been ages, Pete!"

"I know. Too long," Pete agreed.

"What are you doing with yourself today?"

"No special plans, was just going to work on a collage, why?"

"I happen to have two tickets to see Neko Case, and I know you love her. I just won them on the radio. I can't believe it, after all the times I've called radio stations and just gotten a busy signal. I finally won something! Want to go with me? It's an early show—starts at 4:00, and I thought we could get lunch first."

"Well, it sounds great," Pete responded, "but I should warn you, I might not be the best company today, Steph."

"That's okay, Pete, you know I'm perky enough for the both of us," she said with a giggle.

"That's actually true," Pete said. "Well, as long as you can accept me at less than my best, yeah! I'd love to go."

"Fantastic! We should definitely take the T, because parking around there is impossible. I know a great Thai spot right near the Downtown Crossing station."

Pete said that sounded perfect, and they decided to meet there at 2:00 so they could have a nice, long lunch before the show. When she got off the phone, Pete realized how much she was looking forward to seeing Stephanie and how the timing of her invitation was a stroke of good luck.

"Well, Turtle, I'm all yours until one, but then I have to go bye-byes. Want to go for walkies?" The dog answered with his tail, and Pete smiled for the first time since Friday.

☆☆☆

Her friend had guessed it was girl trouble that had Pete down and wasn't surprised to hear about Fiona. It turned out that Stephanie had dated a guy four years ago who was a recovering sex addict, and his version of acting out was way more out of control than Fiona's. Hearing about Stephanie's ex almost made Pete grateful things weren't worse with Fiona. But then an image of the *Titanic* flashed in her mind along with the question that wouldn't let go of her: *What if what I caught her doing was only the tip of the iceberg?*

She shook it off and answered some of Stephanie's questions. *Yes*, she was in love with her, and *yes*, she could see a future with her. *Yes*, she was willing to work at it.

Steph's conclusion on the matter was that unless any more incriminating information came to light, she should cautiously proceed and let Fiona know more behavior like that would mean the end.

The concert was wonderful; it actually lifted Pete's spirits a bit. It was the lyrics of a song that were most important to her. Some poetry of her own was starting to take shape in her mind, so she grabbed her journal and wrote.

*I could never have too much love, it's true. If I could only get it back to the sweet places I've heard of, a dream worth repeating. Beautiful like you in the morning, beautiful like you in the evening...*

When Pete woke up at 6:00 on Monday, she immediately recalled a bizarre dream featuring her mother and Fiona. The setting was a large, all-white room: white ceiling, walls, and floor with no windows. A much younger Jessica Orvatch—she was maybe thirty-five—stood about ten feet away from Fiona. Staring without speaking, the women slowly walked toward each other. When they were very close, less than a foot apart, Fiona kissed her on the mouth. Pete's mother returned the kiss, then stopped abruptly and slapped her in the face, hard. Then everything that was white turned black, and the dream ended.

Pete felt unsettled and shook her head in disbelief; it was a disturbing dream, and she would have to run it by Sheila. She shook her head again, got out of bed, and went to work.

Pete's new client was man in his late fifties named Joseph, and he was a pretty interesting guy. Twenty years ago, he'd invented a small part used in airplane engines, and had been living on the money from it ever since. Pete wasn't sure how well off he was, but he didn't appear to have particularly expensive tastes. He owned a nice house, but it wasn't very large. He drove a modest SUV and wore old clothes. When she first met him for the estimate, she was surprised at how much stuff he had in his home; he jokingly referred to himself as a junior hoarder. Pete decided he wasn't a true hoarder because, for one, a hoarder would never paint because that would require moving stuff. Also, Joseph's house wasn't messy or dirty in any way—it was just very full.

Pete hadn't known anyone still wore pocket protectors until she met him. In his shirt pockets were assorted pens, pencils, a small pocketknife, and a calculator. When she arrived to start work, she was surprised at how much stuff he'd moved out of her way. Unbeknownst to her, he had a spare bedroom that was virtually empty, so he'd put a lot of his things in there. The clutter was mostly books and magazines, but there were also some antique tools and various-sized cardboard boxes. He welcomed her by offering coffee, which she accepted gratefully. When she'd first met Joseph, her hunch about him was that he'd be an easy-going, low-maintenance client, and so far, so good.

As a tradeswoman who brought clean fresh color into people's homes, she'd heard and experienced a broad range of things over the years. There was the widow whose first line to Pete when she arrived for an estimate was "Well, my husband's been dead for eight years. It's time to paint." There was the client who had just left her job because her multiple sclerosis was getting worse. She was so bored and hungry for company, she shadowed Pete, talking at her all day as she worked.

Sometimes the houses did the talking, like the Jamaica Plain fixer-upper she painted for a young couple who'd gotten the house below market value. They didn't like the dark colors and wanted to, as the husband put it, "Change the energy with fresh paint before we move in." The first day on that job, Pete experienced an intangible but ominous feeling, which distracted her from her work. The second day, she brought Turtle to keep her company, and he picked up on something too. Instead of sniffing all around and then settling on his bed with a chew toy for the duration of the shift like he usually did, at this house he never stopped sniffing and even whined in a few specific locations. Pete brought Turtle every day because she didn't want to be alone there, and just tried to power through the job and get it done. Before she was done, Pete heard from a neighbor that some sort of a high priestess had lived there and performed many freakish rituals, including animal sacrifice, which she transacted in the bathtub. That was why the price was right.

House painting seemed like a straightforward job, but Pete knew that being in someone's home could be anything but simple.

Her Monday was off to a good start; she was so busy setting up and beginning the prep work that she didn't think of Fiona until her phone vibrated with a text message from Sheila: *how u doing today sweetie?*

Since her hands weren't dirty yet, she texted back: *ok, actually. not thinking about hard stuff. just want to work. nice quirky client. how u? doing ok?*

A message came right back: *basically. work is a distraction from my sadness. call later if you want to grab dinner or a drink. xo.*

Pete replied with: *ok tx.*

Pete's plan was to start with the dining room, then paint the living room and hallway. She removed the outlet covers and switch plates and laid drop cloths, sipping coffee between tasks. The weather was moody; gray skies and wind but no precipitation. Rain was a painter's enemy, because it stole light and slowed down drying times.

There were a few boxes marked "fragile" in her way, so she asked Joseph to move them. He grabbed the one on top and smiled, saying, "After you're done painting, I plan to go through this stuff and purge. The trouble is, every little thing holds a memory, and I don't want to forget. My father went senile, and he never kept stuff—not cards or letters or mementos—so he had very few reminders of the life he lived. My sister and I tried to tell him stories from his past to help him plug back into his own life, but nothing worked as well as an object. He had a sterling-silver tie bar he got from his grandfather on his eighteenth birthday. He could hold that thing and tell a detailed story about Grandpa Joe, but he just didn't have enough keepsakes to coax that many memories. That's what got me thinking it was better to hold onto stuff than sell it at a garage sale." He paused, seeming a little self-conscious. "And yet I go on."

"No, I hear you. I mean, objects hold stories for sure. I save stuff; I actually make sculptures and collages out of random relics. I think it's important to keep things, but only the important things," Pete responded.

"Yeah," Joseph said, setting the box back down. "Like this tiara." He pulled a tarnished diadem out of the box and held it up for Pete to see.

"Your mother won a beauty pageant? So did my girlfriend's mother!" Pete said, feeling a wave of sorrow wash over her.

"Yes, Miss New York, 1948!"

"Miss Connecticut, '68. It was her fifteen minutes of fame."

"My mother had to be talked into it by friends; she was really modest. See why I can't get rid of this thing?" Handling it gingerly, he put it back in the box. Something else caught his eye. He pulled out a medal on a red-white-and-blue ribbon and studied it fondly.

"Math award?" Pete asked. The words came out before she had time to stop them.

"Huh?" Joseph asked, astonished. "Yes, actually. It is. Won it in eighth grade, but how did you know... Just a good guess?"

Pete looked up from a crack in the wall she'd been spackling and read his face. She took a gamble. "Actually, more than a guess. I see things in my head sometimes. I hope that doesn't freak you out—I can't help it. I could have just lied and told you it was a lucky guess, but that didn't feel right. My grandmother called it a gift, but it sometimes feels like a burden...now it's my turn to go on," Pete said sheepishly. Joseph smiled back, which was a relief to her.

"Wow, okay. I get it. My sister is a little like that. Ever since she was a kid, she's occasionally had these dreams that can predict something that'll happen in the future. Not major events, just random things like the neighbor's cat dying. Do you have those too?" He was curious, but his tone of voice told Pete he was trying not to be nosy or pry. He was just an inquisitive sort of person.

"Sometimes, but more often I just see things or know things, if that makes sense," Pete replied. She went to her toolbox to get a larger spackling knife, hoping the conversation would end soon and she could just dive into her work undisturbed.

"Hmmm." Joseph sounded sympathetic. "Yes, it does. Well, I'll grab these boxes and leave you to it. I'm thinking a forty-five-year-old math medal is not exactly essential. Let me know if you want more coffee. There's plenty." With that, he took the boxes and left.

As Pete spackled another crack in the plaster wall, she wondered what things she would take from Joseph, and hoped they wouldn't be important.

☆☆☆

After work, Pete didn't feel like having leftover stir fry for dinner or eating alone, so she called Sheila, and they made plans to try a new Japanese noodle place in Somerville. The food was delicious; they enjoyed themselves while they dined and talked. Sheila told Pete about a new employee at the shelter who was great with the very shy and skittish dogs. She had a way about her that made the dogs calm down and trust her. Sheila believed some people just had that gift. Pete told her about Joseph's pocket protectors, and they both laughed. As Pete watched her friend crack up, she noticed just how good it felt to laugh.

"Sheils," she began, "I think we're going to be all right. Yeah, it sucks that you and Damon didn't work out and that my *objet d'amour* is a sex freak, but ultimately, none of that can change who we are. We're still us, and we're still laughing."

"We are, aren't we?" Sheila was smiling broadly now. Pete noticed some new crow's feet around her eyes, which made her think about how long they'd known each other and how fast time moved. "Hey, if it doesn't rain on Saturday, want to meet for brunch at House O' Waffles and do a dog hike afterwards?" She took a big bite of noodles and drank some sake.

"Okay, yeah. Not sure what the weekend holds yet, but that sounds good," Pete responded.

"You can let me know last minute, it's all good." Sheila pushed a long, brown strand of hair behind her ear. Despite Pete's protests, Sheila got the check, insisting she wanted to treat because of her recent raise.

On the drive home, Pete thought about Fiona and how attached to her she was after only a few months, then tried to imagine how close they would be after knowing each other as long as she'd known Sheila. She guessed it might feel like they shared one skin.

☆☆☆

Fiona woke up to a sunny Wednesday morning with a feeling of dread in the pit of her stomach. She'd thought of Pete continuously since she last saw her. She was trying not to obsess, but it was difficult; she became almost superstitious about it, believing if she stopped thinking about her, it would somehow hurt their chances for reconciliation. She had to make herself stop checking email every hour, because she thought that was desperate and unhealthy.

At the SAA meeting the night before, as she listened to her fellow addicts' narratives about excess, betrayal, and despair, she couldn't help but think she wasn't as bad off as many of them. She felt like she had a good shot at changing her behaviors this time. She didn't like herself for comparing like this, but she found it encouraging.

Helen, her new sponsor, was buoying her spirits with her regular check-ins via text messages. She had an unusual sense of humor Fiona found refreshing. She was forty-three, married, and hadn't acted out for the last five years. Her sex addiction had almost ended Helen's marriage, but with the help of the program and her sponsor, she'd learned to control her destructive behaviors. They'd attended last night's meeting together, and Fiona felt safer emotionally with her there. Like Fiona, she was a self-described devout atheist, and when the term "higher power" reared its ugly head at the meeting, they made eye contact and smirked ever so slightly. Fiona told Helen about Pete, and she was very supportive; when asked what she thought about Fiona contacting Pete if she hadn't heard anything by Friday, she said that seemed perfectly reasonable.

Fiona rose and went through her morning routines mechanically, feeling removed from her surroundings. Anthony was up and out already. He'd joined the YMCA and was working out every day in an effort to lose his paunch. She was happy he'd decided to extend his stay and even happier that he didn't seem to feel guilty about it. When their mother was saying on speakerphone that he was needed back at work sooner rather than later, Fiona'd chimed in with the fact that Anthony hadn't taken a real vacation in over three years, which put an end to her guilt trip.

Mack was in a particularly good mood, which heartened Fiona. He was chattering away about his latest obsession: fish. It had started with the science unit his class did on the oceans a week ago, and now it was in full bloom. He'd already checked out five fish books from the library and watched one documentary. His favorite fish was the Asian sheepshead wrasse from the Labridae family that was typically found in China, North Korea, South Korea, and Japan. Wrasses had jutting, thick lips and a unique jaw structure, with protruding "foreheads" and "chins."

"Doesn't it look like a person, Mom? It has a weird, chubby face like a man," he commented at breakfast as he leafed through a book all about this species of fish. She sat next to him and studied the large color photographs. She felt his eyes on her face instead of the book. When she looked at him, she saw he had a serious expression. "Mom, are you sad today?"

"Huh? Oh no, honey, I'm fine," she answered evasively. "I just don't feel like going to work today. You know how you don't want to go to school sometimes?"

"Yeah. Do you *have* to go?"

"Yes, Mack, I do."

"You'll be happier when it's the weekend and we see Pete," he said encouragingly.

She nodded, then got up to pour herself some more morning courage. When her back was to him, she let her eyes water but did not cry. She couldn't let him see her cry. She asked him some questions about the Asian sheepshead wrasse, which he answered enthusiastically.

She left Anthony a note on the kitchen table, reminding him that Mack was staying at school later than usual today for chess club and thanking him for all his help.

When she got to work, she still felt like she was on autopilot so she had another cup of coffee, hoping it would help her feel less checked out.

Sharon Nagel was a great boss: kind, supportive, and funny. But she expected only the best from her paralegals, and Fiona didn't want her to see her off her game. She had a handful of client interviews to do today, some documents to draft, and some research for a custody case.

The day went by quickly, and just before 5:00 she got a text from Calvin: *I have some interesting news. Want to grab dinner somewhere tonight?* She texted Anthony to make sure he was available to make dinner for himself and Mack, and he wrote back that he was fine with that.

They met at Big Boy Burgers at 6:30. Calvin gave her a long hug, and they looked for a table that might be quiet, or at the very least not too close to other tables. Since the restaurant was new and had gotten a great write-up in *The Boston Globe*, it was buzzing with diners wanting to check it out. They saw a table for two in the corner and grabbed it.

"I'm starving," Calvin said. "I didn't really have time for a proper lunch today. I'm gonna get the double cheeseburger."

"Yeah, I didn't eat much for lunch today either. I just haven't been hungry lately," Fiona said.

"You have to eat whether you're hungry or not. No word from your lady, I take it?"

"Nope. I think it's going to take a while, Calvin. I really hurt her."

"Well, I know things suck right now, but I have a good feeling about it," he said optimistically.

"Truly? You're not just saying that to bolster my spirits?"

"Yes. I do genuinely have a strong hunch you'll stay together. Right now, things are hard, and it might even get darker before the dawn, but you'll see. You two were meant to be together."

His words comforted her. "I think I'm better with her than without her. And I'll fight for this relationship if I have to. I love her so much. When we're together and she leaves it's like..." She paused to search for the right words. "Like she takes some of my skin with her."

Calvin reached across the table and squeezed her hand, looking into her eyes, not saying anything. The calmness of his gaze soothed her, and she let herself believe, like he did, that things were not over between her and Pete.

Their server approached the table and asked if they were ready to order. He was very cheerful, and Fiona wondered if that was a job requirement or if it was just his personality. When he left, Calvin unpacked his news.

"So, you know how I had a second job interview today at Horizons Center?"

"Yeah, I've been wondering how that went," Fiona replied.

"It went well but weird. You know why? Because it was my second interview, they had a few members of their board of directors there and guess who one of them was?" His eyes went big under arched brows before he continued. "Thomas."

It didn't register at first. Fiona couldn't think of a Thomas in his life, and then it hit her. "Thomas, the guy you beat up because he tried to rape you Thomas?" she asked, incredulous.

"Yes. Him. I couldn't believe it! I mean, talk about a small world—that's just extraordinary. When he walked in, I was just stunned. My mouth opened a little but nothing came out. He was just as shocked as I was, but then somehow we both managed to act normal, and I don't think anyone noticed. I just stayed focused on the questions, and I think I did pretty well. When I shook hands with everyone before I left, he gave me a good handshake and looked me in the eye as if to call a truce, which made me feel uncomfortable."

"A truce? Are you sure? How do you know he won't sabotage your chances for the job, invent a reason to disqualify you?"

"Well, I suppose I don't know that. I just sense it. I mean, yeah, he has a dark side for sure, but he's also trying to help homeless people. I'd never have guessed that. All I could tell from being in his home was that he was wealthy. Apparently, he also gives a shit about his fellow human beings," Calvin said.

"Wow. Talk about a bizarre coincidence. I don't know how you stayed so calm after what he did to you," Fiona remarked.

"Well, I stopped him from doing real damage. And I couldn't lose it at this interview. I need a job. I need to be more than I have been. Lots of people see sex workers as disposable, and I was starting to see myself that way too. They said they would let me know by early next week. *I* would hire me!"

"I would hire you too, babe. And Thomas did damage you; you just haven't allowed yourself to admit that."

She could tell he didn't want to talk about the incident anymore, so she asked him if he had any other job leads, and he told her about a few, then they got back on the subject of her riven love life. "So, like I said, if I don't hear from her by Friday, I'm going to reach out. When I think about what I'm going to say to her, it's all jumbled, and I want to be clear. What do *you* think I should say?"

It pained him to see the sad, searching look in her eyes. He loved her like a sister, and when she hurt, he felt it too. "I would tell her you're sorry and that you know you hurt her. I'd let her know that you're committed to going to meetings, you have a new sponsor, and you're determined to conquer your addiction. I'd ask for another chance but tell her you don't think you deserve it. Be humble," he advised.

"Humble. Yes. That's good advice. I am humbled at how alone I feel without her. I let her all the way in, deeper than I thought I could let someone in, and if we aren't together anymore, I'll be left with an open wound that won't heal for a long, long time. God, I wish she'd call me or write to me."

"Be patient, sweetie," he counseled.

☆☆☆

When Pete got home from work Friday, she walked Turtle, put on some water for pasta, then took a quick shower. When she got out, the water was boiling, so she put in the rotini and made a small salad while it cooked. She heated up the sauce, and the aroma of it made her even hungrier than she already was. When dinner was ready, she thought about watching TV while she ate but got out her laptop instead. She saw an email from her client, Hollis Dunn, and opened it. Pete wondered if she wanted more work done; there was plenty to paint in that big old house. The email was short and to the point. When Pete finished reading it she just kept staring at the screen.

*Hello, Pete, I want you to know that I've been getting a lot of compliments on the woodwork you refinished for me, and the painting. I love my new ochre kitchen so much—what a difference paint makes! The other reason for this email is because there are a few things I haven't been able to find since you worked at the house. Please write or call at your earliest convenience. Hollis.*

"Shit," she said aloud. Turtle looked at her with concern in his big brown eyes. "Shit," she said again. Suddenly she wasn't hungry. She looked down at her dog. "I'm in trouble now, boy. I guess it was only a matter of time before my bad habits caught up with me."

When she looked back up at the screen, she saw that her inbox had just received an email from Fiona. She took a deep breath before opening it, then read.

*My Dear Pete,*

*I know you asked for time and I don't want to deny you that, it's just that it's excruciating not hearing from you, so I thought I'd reach out. I hope you won't feel an email is less personal than a phone call, but when I thought about calling you, I was worried it would seem confrontational so I opted to write instead. I'm so deeply sorry for my actions and for the pain they've caused you. I know I can't take back what I did, or undo the damage to our relationship, but if I could, I would. I never meant to hurt you. I thought my addiction was under control but, obviously, it's not. I've got a new sponsor and am committed to going to meetings regularly. It's time to change. When I try to put myself in your shoes, I find myself feeling like it would be so much easier to walk away than to stay. Also, I'm not sure I could forgive me if I were you, so I'm not asking you for absolution. I'm asking you to take a gamble and give me one more chance. I love you more deeply than I thought I could love anyone. You came into my life and Mack's life and made everything sweeter. I don't want to lose you, but if you're done with me, I would understand. Please get in touch with me soon. Not hearing your voice, or seeing your beautiful face, or feeling your touch is like not being all the way alive.*

*With all my heart,*
*Fiona.*

She read it again, and her eyes started to water. She got up from the table, leaving her untouched plate of food, and lay on the couch, where she curled into a fetal position and cried. Turtle jumped up and licked her face. She wrapped her arms around him and sobbed into his rough fur.

# CHAPTER NINE: SHIFTING WEIGHT

*The reality of the other person lies not in what he reveals to you, but what he cannot reveal to you. Therefore, if you would understand him, listen not to what he says, but rather to what he does not say.*
*~ Kahlil Gibran*

"Thanks for seeing me earlier in the week, Dr. P; I really need to talk to you. Things are a mess," Pete said as she sat in the rocking chair.

"Well, I'm glad I had an opening in my schedule. So, talk to me," Dr. Percy said gently.

Pete stared at the floor, trying to decide how to begin. She needed to talk about how her relationship was in jeopardy, but did not want to tell the doctor about the voice in her head.

"Well, things with Fiona and me were going really well, and then she slipped up. Remember I told you she was a sex addict?"

"Of course."

"Well, we were at a roller derby tournament, and I caught her coming out of the disabled stall of the restroom with one of the players. They had sex in there, and she apologized, but I just left and haven't seen her since. It's killing me because I really love her. And her son. I miss them, and I haven't seen them in over a week," she lamented, running her hand through her hair, which she was growing out because she wanted to change her appearance. Pete thought if she changed how she looked, it might help her feel better somehow.

"You haven't had any contact with Fiona, then?"

"Well, she emailed me Friday. She acknowledged how she hurt me, apologized, and told me she has a sponsor and is committed to going to SAA meetings, to conquering her addiction. She asked for a second chance. It was a very humble email. It made me cry. But I haven't written her back because I'm confused." Pete rocked back and forth as she spoke.

"What are you confused about? How you feel?"

"Actually no, I know how I feel. I'm in love with her, and I'm in deep. I can really see a future with both of them, because when we're together it feels like family. I'm confused about what to do because she's an addict and I'm not sure I can handle the pain that comes with loving an addict. I hate thinking about her having sex with anyone else. It just breaks me..." She looked back down at the floor. She knew it wasn't her therapist's job to tell her what to do, but she desperately wanted that.

"She is an addict, this is true. And being in a relationship with her is complicated; it might always bring you some amount of grief. But would walking away hurt you more? Which path looks less painful?" She gazed in Pete's direction, waiting for her to look up so she could make eye contact with her, read her. When she did raise her head, Dr. Percy's expression acknowledged the distress and tension in her face.

"I don't want to walk away. Fiona's amazing. She's this beautiful, intelligent, strong, funny, compassionate woman with one bad trait. I don't want to be without her, but I never want to feel this way again," Pete stated firmly.

"Well," Dr. Percy began, "you come to me for help with your problems, which are not insignificant, and she sees a therapist, has a sponsor, and goes to meetings. Seems to me you're both trying to be healthy. Maybe you can both keep on supporting each other, helping each other work through problems. You said she's comfortable with your eccentricities, right?"

"So far. But she doesn't know about all of it. I'm like an onion; you peel back a layer and you get more layers. You know that better than anyone, except maybe Sheila. Fiona doesn't know I take things."

"Ah, that. Still doing that, huh?"

"Yes—and that's what my other problem is about. One of my recent clients emailed me about some missing items. I didn't write back. She's a nice lady, and I'm hoping she won't press charges. I've got to get back to her. It's been three days, and I need to make it right."

"Can she prove you took the missing things? And if she can, do you have a plan for how to make things right?"

"Well, maybe not, but if she pushed it, who's more credible: an articulate, middle-aged woman who had this stuff before I painted, or a house painter? I don't really have a plan. I'll apologize and return the items, of course. Except that one of them is ruined. It was an old book of poetry, and I pulled out the pages, tore them up, and glued them inside a wooden crate. Maybe I could try to find another like it."

"What if you apologize, return the items, and offer to do some work for her free of charge. Do you think she'd be receptive to that?"

For the first time this session, Pete's expression was somewhat hopeful. "Maybe. It's a good suggestion. I'll write to her with that offer when I get home. Shit, I hope she doesn't report me—do you think she will?"

"I can't say, Pete, but you need to stop taking things from clients' homes. Consider this a sign. It was only a matter of time until you got caught, and now that you have been, you've got to change your behavior," Dr. Percy insisted.

"I know you're right, but it's hard to stop. I can't imagine getting excited about only making sculptures and collages with stuff I bought at flea markets. It's not the same."

"No, it won't be the same, but it will be morally right, Pete. You have to stop; you know it's more than a habit. Kleptomania is an impulse control disorder."

"I know. And I've read that people who steal like I do often have another mental problem, like bipolar disorder. It's just that I crave objects with stories; it's a real need. And when I see little things in people's houses all the time, things I want to put into my pieces, I take them and instantly feel better. I'll do my best to stop; that's all I can do, right?"

"That's all anyone can do." Pete knew she was referring to Fiona. "Pete, are you going to respond to Fiona's email?"

"Well, yeah. But I want to talk to her in person. I need to see her, to look into her eyes. I'll call her tonight to set up a time to meet."

"What will you say to her? How will you respond to what she wrote to you?"

"Well, I don't really know. I just think I'll know what to say when I see her. Does that make sense?" She looked at Dr. Percy searchingly.

"Yes, it does. Just arrange a time to meet and play the rest by ear, follow your gut. At the end of the day, we're animals and need to be true to our instincts. I know you've said you feel out of touch with your instincts, but I know you have them. We all do."

They discussed her relationship with Fiona for several more minutes, and Dr. Percy suggested that, if she stayed involved with Fiona, she join a support group for people in relationships with sex addicts. She told her about a group called COSA, Codependents of Sex Addicts, and urged her to look into it.

Pete knew she had to tell her about the talking deer sculpture and dreaded it. She took a deep breath and told the story, trying to make it sound like she was more inebriated than she actually had been, because it was easier to attribute the illusion to her drunkenness than to her mental problems or gift of seeing. Dr. Percy listened and then asked her if she'd written about it in her journal and relayed the event to Sheila. She said yes to the first question and no to the second, explaining that she didn't want to worry her friend, especially now, when she was dealing with her own heartache. Dr. Percy admonished her, reminding her that her recovery plan required her to tell Sheila about things like this. She also reiterated that if Pete wanted to avoid using medications to stabilize her, she had to adhere to the plan for her behavioral therapy.

Pete acknowledged that Dr. P was right and promised to tell Sheila about it. When they hugged good-bye, Dr. Percy wished her luck with Fiona and the client who'd asked her about the missing items. When Pete left, her load didn't feel any lighter than when she'd arrived, but it did feel like the weight had shifted somehow.

☆☆☆

Since Anthony was leaving on the weekend, Fiona had Calvin over for a good-bye dinner on his only night off from the restaurant, Monday night. She was feeling very down about the lack of response from Pete but made her best effort to be cheerful. She was going to make fish, because she had a craving for it, but thought that might make Mack talk even more about fish than he had been lately, so she decided to cook steaks instead. Hoping to cheer her up, Calvin brought over her favorite ice cream: mint chocolate chip.

"Hey, man, you're looking good. Haircut? Lose a little weight?" Calvin said to Anthony when he saw him.

"Thanks! Both, actually," Anthony replied. "Just five pounds."

Calvin asked Fiona if she needed help, and she said no, telling him to go in the living room and visit with the boys. Mack had a fish book open on the coffee table. Try as he might to change the subject, Anthony had accepted the fact that Mack was stuck on fish this evening. The boy knew the family business was fishing, but it was like it had just now fully sunk in, and Mack had dozens of questions for Anthony. Calvin tried to interject a few things, but it was pointless, so he ruffled Mack's hair affectionately and went into the kitchen to keep Fiona company.

"Major fish fixation in there. How you holding up?"

"I'm okay. I kind of have to go on autopilot to get through the day, though, you know?" She wanted to take the focus off her, so she asked him a question. "So, no word about the job?"

"No," he said, sounding discouraged. "I probably won't get it."

She handed him a beer and grabbed one for herself. "But they said early this week, right? It's still early. I bet you'll hear something tomorrow."

"Well, I don't know about that, but I do know I'm trying not to dwell on it; I'm sending resumes out in all directions," he said as he stole a carrot out of the salad.

"I'm proud of you, Calvin, for trying to change your life," she said lovingly.

"Well, so are you! You have a sponsor, and you're going to meetings."

"And potentially losing the woman I love," Fiona inserted, hoping she didn't sound too self-pitying.

"She's not gone, Fi, you'll see. Just hold onto hope." He walked over to her and gave her a big hug. She wanted to weep, but didn't; she could do that later, when she was alone.

Dinner was delicious, and the three adults worked as a team to steer the conversation away from the topic of fish. When Mack finally dropped it, he talked about the tree house, which led to the subject of Pete. Fiona had told him a white lie; when he asked why they didn't see Pete on the weekend, Fiona said she had to go out of town on business. He bought it, but he didn't stop talking about her. Anthony and Calvin could see the pain in Fiona's face when Mack went on about how Pete was going to help him build it, and Anthony changed the subject.

"So Mack, when do you want to go fishing? You have to break in that fancy fishing rod you got for your birthday, huh, buddy?"

"Yes, I suppose I do. What kinds of fish can we try to catch?" With that, he was back onto fish, which was better than talk of Pete.

After dinner, they had ice cream and cookies, and then the boy reluctantly went to bed. Calvin asked Anthony about his plans to move there. Anthony said he was ninety percent sure he would relocate. He would be returning to Maine on Sunday and wasn't looking forward to telling his folks.

"That's the hardest part for me," Anthony explained. "Also, Dawn wants to see me."

"Why?" Calvin asked. "Divorce details?"

"Worse," Fiona said, "she left him a voicemail this past weekend saying she might have made a mistake."

"Shit," Calvin said, "what's up with that? Have you spoken to her?"

"No," Anthony answered. "I emailed her and told her we'd speak when I got back. I don't want to get into anything on the phone or through email. I want us to talk in person."

"So, you think her relationship blew up and she wants to get back with you?" Calvin inquired.

"Maybe," Anthony said, "but it doesn't matter. She can't undo what's been done. I admit, when I got her message it threw me. I mean, it's not like you can just stop loving someone after all those years together, but something in me shifted when I found out she was cheating on me," he stated emphatically. Worried he'd upset Fiona, he looked over at her. Her expression was blank. "I'm not saying couples can't recover from infidelity; I'm saying her infidelity underscored what was wrong in our marriage."

Calvin obviously suspected Fiona was thinking about Pete and offered some unsolicited advice. "Fi, if you don't hear from her in a day or two, call her. You don't have anything to lose. It'll just show her you're serious about reconciling."

"I mean no disrespect, Calvin," Anthony began, "but I completely disagree. She asked for time and space, and you've got to give her that."

"Well, shit," Fiona said, "you both make good points. I don't know what the fuck to do... Maybe I'll wait until after my meeting Tuesday. If I still haven't heard from her by then, I'll reach out by phone. I could also ask my sponsor what she thinks—she's a really smart woman."

Fiona changed the subject and talked about the possibility of Calvin and Anthony being temporary housemates. They talked for another hour or so, and then Fiona told them she was really tired and was going to bed but encouraged Calvin to stay and hang with Anthony, since they wouldn't see each other for a while. She hugged them goodnight and went to the kitchen to clean up.

"No, Fi, I'm going to clean up. You go to bed and get some rest," Anthony said.

She thanked him and went to check on Mack before going to her room. As she looked at him sleeping, she imagined how awful it would be to have to tell him Pete wouldn't be coming over anymore, and her eyes watered. She kissed him on the forehead and tucked the blankets around him.

She crawled into bed, feeling too weary to sleep. She stared at a small crack in the ceiling, trying to empty her mind, but thoughts kept coming fast and jumbled. She closed her eyes and found herself reflecting on how she'd gotten to where she was.

The faces of old lovers popped into her mind one after the other until she got upset, angry about the choices she'd made. She'd started much younger than her friends did and regretted it all. She worried she would never be normal sexually; never know how it feels to want just one lover. She turned her head and looked at the pillow beside hers, thinking of Pete and missing her more than she knew she could miss someone. She wanted sleep but tears came instead. Just then, her phone vibrated on her nightstand. It was Pete. She wiped her eyes with the back of her hand and grabbed the phone.

"Pete?" she said, sniffling.

"Fiona. Did I wake you?"

"No, no, I'm awake; I'm so glad you called." She sat up. "Pete, I'm so sorry. Deeply sorry, I—" Pete cut her off.

"I know, Fi, you said that. Thanks for the email. It was very humble, and I appreciate what you wrote. You don't need to keep apologizing. It happened, and now it's part of our story," Pete said dispassionately. "Also, I don't want to get into things on the phone. I'd rather we talk in person."

"Oh, okay, I agree. When are you able to get together?"

"Well, either a weekday evening or some time on the weekend, I suppose," Pete answered.

"When is the soonest you can meet?" Fiona asked eagerly.

"Um, I guess Wednesday. You free then?"

"Yes, sure," Fiona said, uncertain of what Pete had in mind.

"Is Anthony still staying with you? Can he watch Mack that night?"

"Yes, I'm sure he can. Where—um, did you want to eat a meal or meet after dinner? What did you have in mind?"

"How about an after-dinner drink at Flanagan's? At eight? Is that okay?"

Fiona was disappointed they wouldn't be at Pete's place, but kept that disappointment out of her voice when she responded. "Sure, that sounds good."

"Okay, well, it's late—I'll let you get to bed," Pete said softly.

"Pete, thank you for calling. Really. Goodnight."

"Goodnight, Fi."

Fiona set her phone down and let out a big sigh. She jumped out of bed, put on her old brown robe, and went out into the living room, where Anthony and Calvin sat talking. They looked at her with concern in their faces. "She called! Just now. Pete called!" She sat right between them and leaned on Calvin, who put his arm around her shoulder.

"That's great, Fi," Anthony said, "I mean, is it great? Was it good? Was it an okay talk?"

She told them how their brief conversation went and that she felt cautiously optimistic, nearly certain Pete didn't have "break-up tone" in her voice. She asked her brother if he was free Wednesday to stay with Mack, and he told her he was. They were both happy for her and expressed their hopes that it would all work out.

"I'm telling you, Fi," Calvin asserted, "I see you two together."

☆☆☆

Pete's phone rang Tuesday evening, and when she saw the 351 area code, she knew it was Hollis calling about the email she'd sent. She didn't want to pick up, but didn't want to put off the conversation either, so she took a deep breath and answered.

"Hello?"

"Pete, it's Hollis."

"Oh hi, thanks for calling," Pete said, trying to sound polite. Not knowing what else to say, she waited for Hollis to speak.

"I got your email, and I appreciate you being so honest, not just about taking the items but about why. I revere artists, but I do not respect thieves. Seems you are both."

*Fair enough.* Pete waited for the other shoe to drop.

"As for your offer to do some work free of charge, I can't accept that."

"Well, Hollis, I appreciate you saying that, but you may feel otherwise when I tell you that I can't return one of the things I took from you," Pete said cautiously.

"Which one? Not my little deer I hope."

"No, I'm afraid I tore the pages out of that little book of poetry and glued them inside a crate. But I'll try my best to find another copy."

"What book? What's the title?" Hollis asked.

"Um, I didn't save the cover, but I think it was called something like *Ode to Mother Nature, A Collection of Poems.*"

"Ah," Hollis sighed, "that book. I didn't even notice it was gone! I've had it forever; got it at a garage sale. I don't care about that book, Pete. But you have the pin, the spoon, and my deer?"

"Yes. I can bring them to you tomorrow if that's all right. Are you—?" She paused, wondering if the question would insult her in any way. "Are you going to report me to the police? I'd understand if you did. I feel terrible about what I did."

"No, I won't make a fuss, provided you return my things and promise never to steal again. Can you do that?"

Pete felt like a small child being scolded. "Yes, I can bring these to you at your earliest convenience and yes, I can promise not to steal anymore," she said, thinking there was no guarantee she would stop. "Can I ask you about the little deer? It's a beautiful piece, and it seems very old."

"Well," Hollis replied, "if you must know, it is. My grandpa made it for my ninth birthday. It was the last miniature he carved, because soon after that he suffered a stroke. We were very close, and the deer reminds me of him. He was a great man. Oh, just talking about it makes me more upset that I don't have it here with me now."

"I see," Pete said with a lump in her throat. For as long as she could remember, she had received information without knowing how or why. What she knew about strangers defied logic, and having all those stories from their lives inside her head crowded her thoughts, overwhelmed her. She wished she could control it and have these experiences only when she wanted to, but it didn't work that way. It didn't always feel like a gift of seeing to her. It was an invisible burden; a third eye she wanted to put out.

"Can you bring me my things tomorrow? Around noon?"

"Of course, Hollis," Pete promised. "Is there anything else I can do? To make it up to you?" She was earnest. She needed to set things right.

"No, truthfully I don't want to have anything to do with you after tomorrow. And you know how I gave your card to my neighbor who wanted all that work done? Well, I had to tell her not to call you. I told her you stole from me."

"I see," Pete said. "I understand. See you tomorrow." Then she heard a click that told her Hollis didn't even want to say good-bye.

Even though it wasn't an easy conversation, when Pete got off the phone, she did feel a sense of relief. She would lose a few hours of work at Joseph's place, but she would gain peace of mind. Her stomach rumbled for supper, but she wanted to extricate Hollis's possessions first.

She took the old crate off the shelf and set it on her workbench. First she removed the spoon, which had just been glued to one of the poetry-lined compartments. Then she pulled the button out, which was easy because she had just stuck its pin into the soft wood. Lastly, she retrieved the amazing talking deer from the tiny bird's nest she'd set it in. She stared at the beautiful object, waiting for it to speak again, but it remained mute. Hollis hadn't mentioned her old college pen, so Pete decided to keep it. A pen could easily be misplaced, and she thought it would make things worse if she admitted she'd stolen an additional item.

Pete wanted to do more than merely return these things. She got the idea to give her a book since she had taken one. After searching her large bookcase for a few minutes, she found the appropriate volume. Years ago, she and Sheila had gone to a book reading by Gloria Steinem and each gotten an autographed copy. She didn't want to part with it, but knowing Sheila had one was comforting. Pete put it in a small box along with the stolen goods. She knew she needed to make a peace offering more than Hollis needed or wanted one.

She could no longer deny herself food and went to the kitchen to prepare dinner. Turtle followed her, knowing it was his suppertime too. The wall clock in the kitchen said 6:10. Pete prepared his food first and then decided on grilled cheese and tomato soup for herself.

She thought about Fiona, wondering what it would be like tomorrow night when they met up. Would seeing her be what she needed to crystallize her decision about the relationship? Her anger about the betrayal was like tea; it got stronger as it steeped. Pete was also curious about what Fiona was thinking and feeling. Did she expect them to stay together? To break apart? The part of her email that said, *Not hearing your voice, or seeing your beautiful face, or feeling your touch is like not being all the way alive,* had struck a chord with Pete, because she felt the same way. Without a daily dose of Fiona, her world just wasn't as vibrant.

After dinner, she was still dwelling on it all, but those thoughts came to an abrupt halt when she saw the clock. It still said 6:10. Hoping the battery had died, she looked at her cell phone but it had the same time. *Not again*, she thought. *I don't need this shit right now. I've got enough going on.* She decided to call Sheila after dinner and tell her about this and the talking deer. As she cleaned up the kitchen, she felt as if she were being studied by someone, like a specimen being observed in an experiment. Intellectually she knew she and Turtle were the only ones in the place, but psychologically she felt otherwise. Her stomach clenched as she wondered if the voice would invade again.

Sheila sounded out of breath when she answered her phone and explained to Pete she had just taken the dogs for a vigorous walk that ended as more of a jog. Pete asked her if she had the time and energy to help her sort through her burdens, and she responded with a yes, inviting her to come over and see the dogs for a change of scenery. "Bring Turtle, he can see the pack!"

Pete liked the idea of going out, since she felt weird energy in her place, and told her she'd be there in twenty minutes.

Turtle squealed with excitement when he realized where they were going and happily let himself be sniffed by all four of Sheila's dogs: Fred, Romeo, Mimi, and Mr. Dibbs. Fred was Turtle's favorite, and the two quickly broke from the pack and started romping in the living room.

Pete hung her coat and Turtle's leash on the hooks by the door and gave her friend a hug. "How's my bestie? Any better?" Pete asked.

"Too tired to focus on my drama; we were short a staff member so we all had to do extra work. Dibbs!" she scolded. "Leave Turtle alone!"

Mr. Dibbs was humping Turtle, who clearly wasn't enjoying it but was not protesting. Pete laughed.

"Dibbs is the same as ever, huh?" She bent to greet Mimi, a sweet little Chihuahua mix who was pawing her leg for attention. The dog licked her nose affectionately, and Romeo was right behind her waiting for his turn. Pete hadn't seen the dogs in a while and was happy to be with them. She marveled at how neat Sheila's place always was, what with four dogs living there. Also, it never smelled like dog. She claimed it was because she bathed them regularly and vacuumed frequently.

"So, sit down. Want a drink? Beer? Wine? Whiskey? Tea?"

"Do you have any of that almond tea I like? A hot drink sounds good," Pete answered.

"I know—it's so cold tonight! Winter is just about here. I think I'll have some too."

Pete sat on the couch, and Mimi was on her lap in seconds. Turtle and Fred were playing tug-of-war with an old dog toy, and Romeo was licking her hand. "I think those two really missed each other!" Pete remarked about Turtle and Fred.

"No doubt. Speaking of missing, did you respond to Fiona's email yet?"

"Yeah, I called her. We're meeting after dinner tomorrow. At a bar."

"Good! That sounds like progress. Do you know what you're going to say?"

"Not exactly," Pete explained. "I think I'll figure it out when I see her. I need to see her before I make any decisions. You know?"

Sheila said she understood and then brought up the burdens Pete had mentioned on the phone, asking why she'd used the plural. Sheila wanted to know what else was troubling her. So Pete started at the beginning with Hollis' stolen objects and then spilled the story of the talking deer. Sheila's eyes got big. The kettle let out its shrill whistle, and she got up to pour the tea. Her mouth was a tight line of worry.

"You should have told me about it when it happened. Did you write it down, at least?" Sheila asked.

"Yes. And you're right, I should have. Dr. P gave me some shit for that too," she admitted. Then she started to tell her friend about Hollis, but Sheila wanted to respond to the deer story first.

"So, how drunk *were* you?" she inquired. Mr. Dibbs was trying to hump Turtle again, but Sheila snapped her fingers, and he stopped.

"Well, I'd had three glasses of wine so I was pretty buzzed. Kind of drunk but not 'full-on don't know what the hell I'm doing' drunk," Pete answered.

"And," she asked with worry in her voice, "when was the last time something that doesn't talk talked to you?"

"Well, you remember that time I heard Turtle talking in my head, about the lead poisoning?" Sheila nodded and sipped her tea. "Well, it was kind of like that, but different. Its mouth moved like it was really talking."

"Shit, Pete, maybe you should consider meds again?"

Pete shook her head. "No, you haven't heard the strangest part yet. Turns out the deer's story was true."

"What the fuck? How do you know that?" Sheila sounded baffled.

"Well, my other burden besides my cheating girlfriend and my hallucination is that I got caught stealing," she admitted.

"What? Oh Pete. I knew it was a matter of time. Not that I'm saying I told you so…"

"But you did tell me, and you were right. I'm lucky Hollis didn't report me. When I asked her about the deer, it turns out everything I imagined it said was *true*! Once again, I somehow knew things about a stranger—my damned gift of seeing." She drank some tea and waited for Sheila to respond.

"Oh my fucking God, Pete," Sheila began. "They should study you. I mean, seriously. Your brain is pretty amazing. How do you deal with all of this knowing? I know you have me and Dr. P to talk to but it—it's just intense. Your gift is such an onus, and that weight takes a toll on you. You're not feeling self-destructive, are you?"

Pete hated that Sheila worried. "It *is* intense, but no, I haven't wanted to hurt myself for a very long time," she assured her.

"And as for getting caught, I think it was a blessing. Luckily for you, the client who busted you is a nice, understanding person. I think this is a sign from the universe that you've got to show your art. You need to put your work in a gallery. Put all that thieving and crafting on display. It's time," Sheila proclaimed.

"Maybe you're right," Pete replied.

"What about your promise? Can you stop taking things?"

"I can try."

"Yes, you can. If Fiona can stop her destructive behaviors, you can stop yours," she preached. "Wow, you do have burdens."

"That's not all," Pete started. "Time stopped in my kitchen tonight. That's why I called you."

"Shit, Pete. Maybe Dr. P and me and the journals aren't enough."

"No, Sheila, I'm okay. I'm doing okay. I don't want to go on meds again. They just make me numb. I'm so much better than I was before, I am. I'm fine. I've been different ever since I can remember, and that's not going to change. I'm not the only one in the world who is psychic. Or psychotic," Pete declared.

"You're not psychotic," Sheila assured her.

"Actually, technically I am. Psychosis means a mental disorder characterized by delusions or hallucinations that indicate impaired contact with reality. That's me, your psychotic best friend." She laughed.

"Are you *sure* you're okay? Is there something else you need?"

"Yeah, I need Fiona back," Pete said. "I need my life to be sweet again."

"Well, you can work on that tomorrow. She loves you, you love her. Sure, your relationship has problems, but pain is a possible side effect of love. That's just the way it works."

They stopped talking for a moment and just watched the dogs play as they drank their tea. Pete did not want to be the topic of conversation anymore, so she asked Sheila about her mother.

The two of them talked about family for a while, and Sheila told her about a strange dream she'd had earlier in the week.

About an hour after Pete finished her tea, she thanked her for listening, leashed up Turtle, and said good-bye. On the drive, she thought about seeing Fiona the following night, and it made her feel warm all over. Maybe this warmth would comfort her if she still felt like she was being watched when she got home. Maybe it would soothe her troubled mind that was so cluttered with other people's stories.

☆☆☆

It was a cloudy Wednesday, and as Pete worked at Joseph's, she kept thinking about Sheila's suggestion that she show her art. To Pete, it seemed only fair to share the creations she made with other people's things; in an odd way, it honored the items because it gave them a new story.

She decided to seize the moment before she talked herself out of it, and call the gallery Sheila had told her about on her lunch break. She hadn't had the best luck with galleries in the past and knew getting into a show wasn't easy. Initially, she'd walked into galleries with her portfolio; the manager of the first was rude, so Pete left before she said something harsh. The next tactfully suggested she call gallery owners to schedule an appointment, saying no one gets lucky with the old-school door-to-door approach. The most recent time she got into a group show, she'd been dating a friend of the gallery owner.

The morning passed quickly. Joseph was out running errands when Pete ate her sandwich in his kitchen. She looked up the gallery number and called. The owner, Kent, was extremely friendly and suggested she bring her portfolio by that day, since he'd be there until 6:00. He only had two spots left in the upcoming show, and was specifically looking for collages and three-dimensional work. She made an appointment for 5:00 because that would give her time to go home, get cleaned up, and grab her portfolio. She wasn't meeting Fiona until 8:00, so she had plenty of time.

Joseph was out most of the day, so Pete had solitude and silence, which could be dangerous because the noise in her mind might become more audible than she wanted it to be. She tried listening to NPR, but found that she wasn't really paying attention to the stories. They just became noise. She turned the radio off and let the hum in her head take shape. She was reflecting on how her kitchen clock had stopped last night and found herself remembering the first time she had a strange experience with time.

☆☆☆

In eighth-grade science class, they were studying time and her teacher Mr. Brooks had defined it as "the space between two events." Even though this made sense to her, it wasn't satisfying. Later that evening, she got the huge dictionary down from the bookshelf and searched for a different definition. She found: *indefinite and continuous duration regarded as that in which events succeed one another*.

As she sat on the floor of her room pondering this, Grandma Sweets came in, parked herself next to her, and asked what she was doing. When Pete explained, her grandmother nodded in understanding.

"Ah, time. Time is a trickster, Petra. *Everything dies in time: Time ripens the creatures, and time rots them.* This is from the *Mahabharata*, the longest epic poem ever written. Have you studied India yet in school?"

"A little. In sixth grade, we studied ancient India, and I remember learning about Hinduism in seventh grade. I was just curious about time because my science teacher's definition seems incomplete." Looking at the fine wrinkles around her grandmother's dark eyes, Pete thought they were beautiful.

"What did he tell you, sweetie?"

"That time was the space between two events."

"That *is* incomplete. I mean, first of all, why is it the space between just two events? Events are infinite. And does he mean the measured space between two observable events? Then there's the difference between time and how time is marked. An hour on a clock is not time;

it's how we measure it. My ancestors used the sun to mark time and lived their lives approximating time, not measuring it like bakers measure flour. Our experience of time is affected by who we are. We all operate to different beats. Did you know that?"

"No. Time is complicated!"

"Yes and no. My grandfather was a restless and impulsive man; for him, time moved faster than it did for other people. My grandmother was relaxed; I think time lasted longer for her. Albert Einstein said, 'Put your hand on a hot stove for a minute, and it seems like an hour. Sit with a pretty girl for an hour, and it seems like a minute. That's relativity.' It's all relative, Petra. Just like all living things are connected to something larger than any one living thing, time is connected to things that can't be measured. And why would anyone think time is linear? That it only goes forward. This is not so."

"What do you mean, Grandma?" Pete swiveled and faced her more directly, then awaited explanation.

"You haven't experienced anything strange yet, with time?"

"No. But I swear, my boring classes last twice as long as the fun ones," Petra joked.

"Yes, our perception of time affects our experience of it for sure. You know how you knew about poor Ms. Flowers last year? This information came to you because of the gift of seeing. Well, sometimes people who have this gift fall into cracks."

"Cracks?" Petra interrupted her grandmother because this was starting to sound very strange to her.

"The cracks in between," her grandmother said, as if that were enough information.

"The cracks in *between*? In between *what*?" she asked, not understanding.

"It's hard to explain with words. It will make more sense when you experience it for yourself. But I will try to make you understand it." Grandma Sweets paused, closing her eyes while she searched for the best way to describe it. "If you think of time as an enormous, living, breathing thing, as big as the universe itself, that has powers, then imagine what time can do to people. Time stops sometimes, and even goes backward. Trust me on this, Petra. Chances are you will fall into the cracks, but don't be scared. There's magic in those places, the kind of divine stuff that doesn't happen to most people. You're not most people, you know that." She stood up and asked her if she wanted to help make dinner. Young Petra had more questions, but could tell that her grandmother was done talking about time.

Later that week, she had trouble falling asleep. She sat up and read for a while; this usually made her sleepy, but not tonight. She switched off the light and stared at the digital display of her clock radio. She noticed the time, 11:34, said "'hell" upside down, then thought about all the words that could be spelled with the numbers going backwards or forwards. Several glowing red words flashed in her mind; then she tried to make simple phrases with the words. Before long, her eyelids grew heavy, and she fell asleep.

She had a vivid dream with colors more bright than they normally were. In the first sequence, she was walking barefoot across what she thought was a desert, but when she dialed the scene in more closely, she saw she was actually treading across flat, golden stones. Between them were dark cracks of varying sizes. Her pace went from a brisk walk to a jog and then a full-on sprint. She ran and ran and then stumbled on a particularly wide crevice and fell in, feet first.

Down and down she fell, so fast that her hair was blown back by the force of the air as her body cut through it. All she could hear was the whooshing sound of her movement and her heartbeat pounding in her ears. Gradually, her speed decreased, and she landed on a soft, spongy surface. It was very dark, but there was some type of light source, because as her eyes adjusted to the dimness, she could make out what looked like cave walls. She stuck her hand out and felt cold stone. She saw it was lighter up ahead, so she kept her hand on the wall and dragged her fingertips over the rough surface as she walked. She began to hear a low hum that got louder as she approached the light source, until finally she saw what was creating the glow.

When the stone wall stopped and she emerged from the tunnel, she found herself out under the night sky, which was heavy with twinkling stars. Way up high were the sun and the full moon side-by-side. They were very close together and vibrating, creating the hum. Pete's breathing slowed down, and she felt very calm. Suddenly a giant red digital clock display glimmered against the indigo night, flashing 11:34.

She woke up with a gasp, rubbed her face, and looked at the clock on her nightstand. It said 11:34. That was impossible! Time must have passed since she first noticed the words in the numbers. She turned on the light, got up, and went to look at her wristwatch, which was on the dresser. It, too, said 11:34. She sat in bed, hugged her knees to her chest, and stared at the ceiling. She wanted to go down the hall and wake her grandmother up, but she didn't want to disturb her. Instead she lay down, turned off the light, and stared at the unchanging readout on her clock radio until she could no longer keep her eyes open.

☆☆☆

Fiona was going on her third outfit; she couldn't decide what to wear to her meeting with Pete tonight. She'd gotten it in her mind that what she wore was extremely important and that her outfit had to convey just the right message to Pete. After deciding against a dress, she put on the jeans and boots she was wearing the day they met, hoping to trigger a fond memory, but was now unsure of what top to wear. She put on a forest-green sweater but wondered if the neckline was too low. She went out to the living room to ask her brother.

Mack was lost in deep thought as he did his science homework at the coffee table, and Anthony had his nose in a history book.

"Ant? Can I get your opinion?" He looked up from his book and smiled. "How's this outfit?"

"Great, you look great," he answered.

"No, I mean—what does it say?" She mouthed the words, *Fuck me? Or love me?*

"Um." He paused, trying to say something that would calm her nerves. "Both. Yes, both."

"Hmm, not sure what to do with that."

"Fi, you're overthinking it. If you feel comfortable, wear it. Tonight's all about being yourself," he said.

"Where are you going, Mom?" Mack asked.

"To meet a friend, honey. Sorry to bother you when you're doing your homework."

She quickly went back to her room, aware of the time. She had about fifteen minutes before she had to leave. Looking in the mirror, she assessed her appearance and hoped Pete would see her in a good light. *The last time she saw me I broke her heart*, she reflected. *I can't do that again.* Her ringing cell phone split her thoughts. It was Calvin.

She picked up, saying, "I love you, darlin', but I only have about five minutes or I'll be late to meet my lady."

"Uh, okay. All I need is five minutes. I didn't get the job."

"Oh sweetie, I'm so sorry to hear it. And sorry about how I answered the phone. That was obnoxious."

"No, it wasn't. It was honest."

"Did they say why? I guess potential employers don't really offer up that information, huh?"

"No. I don't think I have enough experience for the position, and they didn't want to take a gamble on me. Oh well, it was just one job I applied for. I only started looking a little while ago. There are other jobs out there. Know what's really whacked?"

"What?"

"Thomas wrote to me! It felt invasive to see his name in my inbox, but I was too curious not to open it. He said he got my email address from my resume and wanted to suggest other places for me to send my resume to! Bizarre, right?"

"Whoa," Fiona responded as she hunted through her dresser for a different sweater, "that's just creepy. I'm sorry that happened. Did you delete it immediately, or was his advice worth reading?"

"I need all the information I can get, so I kept the list of organizations. It gets weirder. At the end of the email he acknowledged the assault, saying he was on new medication at the time. He didn't say what he was taking it for, just that the meds were bad for him, especially in combination with alcohol."

"Was he trying to apologize? To make excuses?" she asked angrily.

"How the hell should I know? I don't really care, and he's way off the mark if he thinks I do. Most people apologize to make themselves feel better."

"I hear that. You'll probably never hear from him again."

"Let's hope. Well, I should let you go. Good luck tonight, Fi. Just be yourself. Love you," he said supportively.

"Love you too," she said. "Bye."

She tugged the sweater down around her hips and inspected herself in the mirror. She thought she looked nice and hoped Pete would think so too.

☆☆☆

Pete's emotions were a blend of exultant and anxious; she was excited her work had been selected for the art show, but afraid something would go wrong when she saw Fiona. Her hair was growing out at odd angles, but she'd managed to subdue it into a style. She was wearing an outfit she thought made her look good, hoping it wouldn't look like she'd tried.

Pete found street parking right in front of the entrance to Flanagan's and arrived earlier than she thought she would, so she was able to get a booth for them. She knew it was better to meet in public because this way there was less of a risk of them tumbling into bed. Pete didn't want them to try to solve their problems with sex.

This Irish pub had been in Cambridge since the 1920s. Pete loved the old woodwork and various Celtic flags that hung from the ceiling; she moved her eyes around, taking in all the details. Then she stared at the door and held her breath, but the sight of Fiona walking in took it away from her. She wasn't just beautiful; she gave the word another dimension. Pete stood up so Fiona could find her more easily in the dimly lit place.

Fiona approached and opened her arms for an embrace, and as they fell into each other, Pete thought she heard her emit a small satisfied sound. She felt so good to Pete, it made her ache. They pulled apart and sat down.

Pete felt apprehensive about jumping right into heavy conversation, so she led with her recent good news. "I just met with a gallery owner about getting into a group show, and I'm in!" Pete said with a smile. "I still can't believe it; I thought for sure my work wouldn't be selected, because getting gallery representation isn't easy. The show opens on the 22nd, the Friday before Thanksgiving."

"Fantastic! Congratulations! How many pieces will you have on display?"

Their server walked up and asked if they wanted to order food. They said no and ordered two beers, then resumed their conversation.

"Well, I'll have a fair amount of room, about twelve feet on a wall, and I also get table space. I should be able to fit all my current stuff. Sheila screamed when I told her on the way over here; I'm really glad she pushed me."

"Me too. Your art is sublime," Fiona said before licking her lips.

Pete's eyes went to Fiona's mouth, and her thoughts turned to kissing her. "Well, thanks, but I don't know if I'd go that far. Kent, the gallery owner, liked it a lot. Now I have the difficult task of pricing the pieces. He suggested a price range but his numbers seem too high to me," she said modestly.

"Don't undervalue your work, Pete. People buy art because it speaks to them, because they want it in their home, and because they can afford it. Go with Kent's suggestions and see what happens." Their server appeared with their drinks, and Fiona looked around at the place. "I haven't been here in a while. All this dark wood reminds me of the first place we went together. Remember the coconut curry mussels?"

"How could I forget? Sexiest meal I ever had," Pete said in fond remembrance. "I couldn't believe you talked to me, let alone shared a meal and invited me home."

"I wanted you," Fiona stated.

"You've wanted a lot of people, and you've had most of them. Was I any different—I mean, at first? Did you know we would add up to more than just sex or was I another conquest that grew into more?"

Fiona considered her words carefully before responding. "I was intensely attracted to you; I was drawn to your looks, your voice, the words you used, all of you. When we first kissed, it wasn't just my body that responded." She leaned in closer and lowered her voice. "My heart reacted too. There were emotions between us right away so, yes, you were different than my other encounters, right from the start." She reached her hand across the table, palm up.

Pete stared down at it and then held it. "I've missed the feel of your hand," Pete said. "I've missed a lot about you. Every day we've been apart at least a dozen things happen that I tell you about in my mind. They pile up in a corner of my brain and make me wish you were there to hear about them. You've become part of me, Fiona. You're under my skin and in my bones." Pete was still looking at her hand, and when she looked up she saw Fiona's eyes were starting to water. "That's why you can make me feel so good or so terrible. But I don't hate you for what you did; I just hate how it makes me feel."

"I know, baby, I know. You're part of me too, Pete. And part of Mack. He's missed you as much as I have; he talks about you all the time. We both love you. And we both need you. It scares me to admit that I need you, Pete. I've always been independent to a fault, but I don't feel as good when you're not around; I don't notice as many of the little things that make life interesting, and I miss your stories and your inexplicable experiences. Meeting you woke up my sense of wonder; you made me believe in the amazing magical parts of life that defy explanation. You make me see snow and fire in my head when you touch me..." Her words trailed off; she didn't know what to say, so she took a long drink of her beer and waited for Pete's response.

"Yes, we have crazy chemistry, Fiona. You make me feel like I did in my twenties; I was wilder then than I am now. You coax out my sense of adventure. Like the time in that dressing room. That was risky. I think people heard us." Pete was smirking as she replayed the event in her mind.

☆☆☆

Fiona's head suddenly felt hot, and her chest got tight; she didn't know what Pete was talking about. She drank more beer, thinking of how to respond, but Pete spoke before she could.

"I can still smell all those vintage clothes. I felt so naughty when you finger-fucked me in there. I'm pretty sure the people waiting could see through those curtains." She let go of Fiona's hand to drink her beer.

Fiona stared at her blankly. Her thoughts were swirling rapidly, but looking at Pete, she felt as if she were in slow motion. *Did Pete follow me to Your Auntie's Attic that Thursday and see me with Abigail? Was she stalking me? Was this some kind of a test?* She brought herself back from the brink of panic and decided to play along. "Yeah. Sex in dressing rooms is not for beginners, huh, baby?"

"Exactly. Hey, you haven't worn that blouse you bought that day in a while. I really like it on you. That peplum is so Joan Crawford." She paused, and her expression changed from nostalgic to serious. "If only sex was our solution instead of our problem."

Fiona's head was still spinning as she tried to stay present while she figured out how Pete could know about that. She tried to connect the dots but couldn't, and was starting to feel crazy. She knew Pete saw things. *Is it possible Pete saw this in her mind? Does her gift of seeing allow her to know what's going on in other people's lives? Or is she just fantasizing; is it all an eerie coincidence?* Fiona was struggling, but before she could find her footing, Pete pulled the ground out from beneath her.

"I have problems with your behavior, Fiona. I can't go through anything like that again," Pete asserted.

"I know, baby. I understand. I'm trying my best to kick this fucking addiction once and for all. I mean it. I have a sponsor now. Her name is Helen, and she's really smart. I think I'll do it this time, Pete."

"You have to, Fiona," Pete replied softly, "for you and for Mack."

"And for you, Pete," she promised. "I can do this for you."

Pete looked down briefly before responding. "I didn't realize how big my trust issues were until you betrayed me. Now that I know, I don't know how we go forward. There's no way I can know you won't hurt me like that again," she said haltingly.

"There's no guarantee lovers won't hurt each other; being in love is partly a leap of faith. But with me it's more than a leap." Fiona paused, and stared at Pete. "It's like jumping off a cliff with your eyes wide open." Pete didn't respond, so Fiona began to plead. "Pete, what do you need from me? For us to stay together on this wild ride called life. What do you need? Ask me for anything."

"I need you to let me be angry...and maybe just let me go." She looked down, finished her beer, and stood up. Fiona's eyes were moist as she watched Pete take out a five-dollar bill and put it next to her empty glass. Their eyes met briefly and exchanged worlds of hurt, and then Pete turned to leave.

"Pete, wait," Fiona urged. "We never made love in a dressing room. I'm not sure why you have this memory; maybe you're confused. I was just sort of going along with it when you brought it up, but I had to say something because it's just so odd."

Pete's face was blank at first, but then her expression twisted into one of hurt and anger. "You're wrong, Fiona. You were there."

That was all Pete said before she left. Fiona hung her head in an effort to keep the tears in, and when she was sure she could walk out of there without crying, she exited the pub.

# CHAPTER TEN: UNMOORED

*Love is a force greater than most obstacles.*
*~ Sheila Rider*

Fiona cried on the drive home. Her head actually hurt from trying to figure out what had just happened. She couldn't see clearly and desperately needed it all to make sense.

When she got home, Anthony was in the hallway and walked toward her. "He was just asking for you. He went to bed early and woke up from a nightmare a little while ago," he told her. "I comforted him as best I could, but he can't seem to fall back asleep.

"Uncle Anthony?" Mack called out from his room. "Mom?"

"Coming, baby," she called. Then said to Anthony, "He hasn't had a bad dream in a while. Poor guy."

"Poor *you*. You've been crying," he said and gave her a hug. "That bad, huh?"

"I'll tell you all about it..." She went into her son's room and saw him in his robot pajamas, sitting up with the light on. She walked over, sat on the bed, and threw her arms around him. "Want to tell me about this bad dream your uncle says you had?" She stroked his hair as he spoke.

"It was terrible, Mom. Me, you, and Pete were walking through a really pretty forest, like we were going on a hike. Only Turtle wasn't with us, which didn't make sense. But dreams don't have to make sense. Everything was fine until the earth started shaking, I guess like it does during an earthquake. Big cracks started forming in the ground, and I almost fell into one, but Pete grabbed me. We ran; we were trying to get away from the cracks, but they were everywhere. Then Pete fell into one and completely disappeared. We heard her scream, and then I woke up. Why do I have bad dreams, Mom? I *hate* them!" he lamented, almost in tears.

"I don't know, Mack. Most people have bad dreams sometimes. Kids seem to have them more than adults." She felt like she wasn't doing a good job of consoling him. "The main thing is that it was just a bad dream, and you, me, and Pete are safe. Do you think you can fall back asleep?"

"Will you stay with me until I do?"

"Of course. Now just lie back, close your eyes, and pretend you're at the beach watching the waves roll in and lap against the shore. You can smell the salt in the air and hear the waves crashing; they sound peaceful, and they make you feel calm." She spoke as softly as she could and watched his face start to relax. "You're lying on a blanket in the sun, and you're covered in sunscreen so you can't burn; you can only feel the good, warm rays of the sun on your back as you start to drift to sleep." She stopped when she saw his breathing slow down, and he was no longer awake. She stayed with him for several minutes, then left.

Anthony was stretched out on the couch reading when she went in to tell him Mack was slumbering peacefully. He sat up and waited for her to tell him about her evening, his eyebrows arched with concern.

"It was bad with Pete. Bad and *bizarre*," Fiona said, staring at a tuft of white dog fur on the carpet. Anthony waited patiently for her to elaborate.

"It started off okay—she told me about getting in a show at a gallery—but then things got strange." She thought about the most concise way to explain what happened and then did.

Anthony's eyes grew wider as he listened to her. He scratched his head, both literally and figuratively, trying to figure out how Pete could think she'd had sex with Fiona in that dressing room, or how she could know that Fiona did with another woman. He shook his head and blew air between his lips.

"Wow, Fi. This just went from sad to weird. I don't know what to say. I'm not sure *what* I think about all this." He ran his hand through his thick, wavy hair and sighed.

"I know, right? I went over and over it in my head, and there's no way she could have followed me and seen us. I've come to the conclusion that it's more likely Pete *is* clairvoyant. She *does* see things. I mean, some of the stories she told me from when she was growing up defy all explanation, Anthony."

"Well," he reasoned, "if that's true, then does she really think she was in that dressing room with you, or did she see you in her mind with that woman and this was her way of letting you know she knows? Her way of fucking with you."

"Oh." Fiona thought about it. "I don't know. Any way we slice this, it's ten kinds of crazy. If she knew I did it, why didn't she get mad at me *then*? Maybe she sees things and they get mixed up into her memories, and that's why she thought it was us in there. I played along at first, but after she told me how angry she was about what I did with the roller derby player, and that she might be done with our relationship, I felt like I had to tell her we were never in Your Auntie's Attic together, to set the record straight. It's all so twisted. I just want her back." She started to cry again.

"Oh, Fi, is it really over?"

"I don't know. I just know I'm not done with us."

Anthony wrapped his big arm around her shoulders and held her. "Well, you gave her space and then reached out. She responded because she wanted to see you. I know things are as clear as mud right now, but if you want her back, then fight, Fi. Fight for the relationship."

☆☆☆

"Ice cream delivery," Pete announced as Sheila opened the door. Her dogs swarmed, greeting Pete enthusiastically. As always, she said hello to Fred first, then acknowledged Mimi, Romeo, and Mr. Dibbs. After she'd left the pub, Pete had phoned Sheila to ask if she could stop by. Pete was glad her friend would help her make sense of what had just happened. Knowing that Sheila was hurting too, she didn't want to be needy and was determined to have a two-sided conversation. Sheila was such a generous listener; Pete wanted to give that back to her.

"Thanks for bringing the yumminess," Sheila said as she hugged her. She looked at Pete's face. "You look sad."

"Oh." Pete removed her jacket and put it over the back of a chair. "I'll tell you about it, but first tell me how *you* are." Sheila went to get spoons, and then they sat in the living room with the pack.

"Well," Sheila began, "I'm still sad, but I can feel myself starting to level off. I'm sure that, eventually, I'll feel neutral about it, and then I can think about dating again." Sitting there in her flannel pajamas with cartoons of dogs on them, digging her spoon into the ice cream, Sheila looked like a big kid to Pete.

"Have you heard anything else from him?" Pete asked, not wanting to mention his name.

"No, and I don't think I will. I think we're done. When I do look at dating sites again, I think I'll avoid the one I met him on. In case he's there. I just—I want to look elsewhere, you know?" She put a particularly large bite in her mouth and savored it.

"Makes sense to me." Pete took small bites of her strawberry ice cream because she wasn't that hungry.

"What about *you*? I know you were seeing Fiona tonight. From your face I'd say it didn't go well."

Pete sighed and told her all about it, and how her parting remarks about them not getting it on in a fitting room were particularly confusing. Sheila was so stunned by it all, she lodged the spoon firmly in the melting creamy goodness and stopped eating.

"Well, I'm not sure what to make of all that. Pete, I'm worried. Fiona is a sex addict, and I'm sure that all addicts lie to themselves and others to some degree, but lying about this doesn't make sense to me; if she says you two didn't do that, you didn't. I think..." She paused, trying to be diplomatic. "I think you've spun that memory out of the magic dust in your mind. You're confused. Like with the clocks, only different. You know?"

"No, Sheils, I don't. I can see us there in my mind. Look, I know I get disoriented, but *most* of the time I know what's real and what's not, and *this* was real." They stared at each other, and Sheila knew she had to push a little harder.

"Pete, both of you can't be right. When do you see Dr. Percy again? Maybe you can see her sooner? I think this is not good, sweetie." She put her hand on Pete's shoulder lovingly, but Pete was stiff.

"I don't know if I *want* to see her anymore. I mean, why do I need to tell her about all this stuff? All she does is remind me to write in my journals and check in with you! Maybe I should just embrace my strange gifts more and analyze them less." She had a hardness in her eyes. Pete guessed that this made Sheila uneasy and addressed it. "I'm sorry, Sheils. It's got to be hard to be my friend. I'm such a freak." She cast her gaze down at the floor, and Fred put his nose to hers; he clearly knew she was down.

"You're not a freak. You're special, Pete, and I wouldn't trade you for anyone else. I just think maybe you can't handle your gifts without help, you know what I mean?" She started eating her ice cream again. Pete was relieved to see the situation hadn't taken her appetite away.

"I hear you. I do. But I know I can figure things out without a shrink. I've already had to unravel dozens and dozens of confusing experiences. Did I ever tell you about the food poisoning incident at my high school?" She was starting to enjoy her ice cream more now and took a big bite. When she was all done, she would let Fred lick the spoon.

"No," Sheila answered.

"Didn't think so. Mind if I tell you about it? It might help you make sense of this shit."

"Sure, go ahead." Sheila shifted on the couch, making herself more comfortable.

Pete began unfolding a story from her sophomore year of high school. "So, one time the school cafeteria somehow served contaminated greens in a salad, and the next day, about fifty kids called in sick. They all had the same symptoms of food poisoning. I was fine until I heard about it. I immediately felt nauseated and then vomited. While I was waiting in the nurse's office, my friend, Susan, walked by and saw me. She came in to see what was wrong with me, and I was able to get out a few words about my food poisoning. She and I sat together at lunch most days, and she told me that I hadn't eaten the salad the day before. She asked me if I remembered I'd brought a lunch from home. I remembered things differently than she did. The nurse sent me home, and I was as sick as the others for several days.

Sheila listened attentively, then waited for the punch line, hoping to have clarity.

"So, do you see how these things work for me?" Pete asked her.

"Not exactly; can you spell it out for me? It was a long day at work, and I'm starting to fade. Sorry."

"Don't be sorry," Pete said. "This shit is not easy. My mind and body conspire to confuse me. Whether I ate the bad salad or not, I believed I did and got sick from it. So, whether it's my reality or someone else's, I still *feel* what happened; I still have the memories." She ate one more, big bite of her ice cream, and then offered the spoon to Fred when Mr. Dibbs wasn't paying attention.

"Oh, I see what you're saying. So, you remember things the way you remember them because you feel the sensations strongly, with your body. Are you comfortable with colliding realities?"

"Hmm." Pete thought about the question. "I think that's what I've been trying to do since I was a kid: get comfortable with my reality versus what everyone else calls reality. I mean, when you think about it, the notion that there is one static reality we all participate in is kind of like the idea that there is only one universe. You know?" She got up to put the rest of her ice cream in the freezer, and Sheila pondered what she'd just said as she finished her pint. Pete came back in the room and saw her holding the empty container out for Mimi to lick.

"A little bit won't kill them. They love the cream," she said. "I'm thinking about all this, and I'm starting to get my head around it, but what about the question of your relationship? Do you want to end it? Or are you open to trying to work things out?"

"I know I love her. I just don't know if I can trust her." Pete's tone was softer now, more vulnerable.

"Hmm," Sheila began. "Have you ever loved anyone the way you love her?"

"Well...no. I thought I knew how it felt to be in love before I met her, but after we connected, I realized that what was between us was more profound than anything I'd experienced before. Looking at life with her by my side, everything is pulled into sharper focus. With Fiona, I can lose control or take it; I can lead or follow. She makes me laugh, and she makes me think. Making love with her is the closest I've ever felt to flying." She sighed and then stopped talking. Sheila broke the silence.

"Well, my friend, I know she betrayed you and that left a scar. But I also know she's working hard to make sure that never happens again. Honestly, if you walk away, you'll have to accept the fact that big, fat, crazy love doesn't always knock on our door more than once in a lifetime, and you may never feel like that about anyone ever again. And at the end of the day, I believe love is a force greater than most obstacles."

Pete took a moment to consider the wisdom of her friend's words and then responded. "Spoken like a true romantic. You always make sense, Sheila; that's why I need you to sift through the broken bits and pieces of my life and help me figure out what to do," she said gratefully.

"Well, Petra, no one can tell you what to do or how to feel; I just call it like I see it."

"Thanks, Sheils. I'll keep you posted. At least I have the art show to focus on, huh?"

"Yes, you sure do. That's so great. I'm proud of you."

"And I'm *grateful* for you." Pete thanked her again for being such a solid friend, and they said their good-byes.

☆☆☆

All day at work on Thursday, Sheila kept thinking about Pete and Fiona; the more she mulled it over, the more she believed they belonged together. At lunch, she looked up the phone number for the law firm where Fiona worked and called her.

"Sheila? Hi. How are you?" Fiona asked when the call was transferred to her.

"Hi, Fiona. Have I caught you at a bad time? Do you have a few minutes?"

"Yes, I'm on lunch so I've got time. Is everything all right? Is Pete okay?"

"Oh, yes. I didn't mean to scare you by calling. She's okay. Listen, I don't want to come across as a meddler, but I just wondered if we could meet and talk. Is that something you'd be open to?"

"Sure. That's fine; I like talking to you, Sheila," Fiona assured her. They made a plan to meet at a cafe that evening and then said good-bye.

☆☆☆

Throughout the rest of her workday, Fiona kept thinking about the call; the hope she felt at first on realizing that her lover's best friend wanted to intervene had been replaced with doubt and fear. *What if Pete is sending Sheila to officially break it off?* That didn't seem like Pete's style, so she talked herself out of that scenario and tried to focus on her work.

Anthony stayed with Mack while Fiona went to meet Sheila at a place called the International Cafe. It was a very popular spot, partly because of the good coffee and food, and partly because it stayed open late. People could congregate there until 11 every night of the week. She saw Sheila seated at a table by the windows and walked over. They said hello and embraced.

"Thanks for meeting me, Fiona. I appreciate it. Have you ever been here?"

"Not in a while. I like this place. It's kind of homey. Must be all the *tchotchkes*." The cafe's decor was eclectic; old kitchen implements hung on the walls like art, and there were several stuffed chairs and small couches where people made themselves comfortable. Most of the people around them were either reading books or on laptops.

"I'm getting their almond chai latte and a slice of apple pie. You ate dinner, right? If you didn't, they have real food too," Sheila said. She was a little uncomfortable, and Fiona picked up on it because she was speaking more quickly than she usually did. They went to the counter and ordered their drinks. Fiona didn't want anything to eat. Since she and Pete had been on the outs, her appetite just wasn't there.

"I was sorry to hear about you and Damon; Pete told me."

"Oh, thanks," Sheila sighed. "I'm starting to get over it, but it's been hard."

"I can imagine. Sounds like you two were just in different places. I'm sure there's someone out there who wants what you want, Sheila." She didn't say anything more on the topic for fear she'd sound like a cheerleader. Their drinks and the pie arrived, and the aroma of almond must have made Sheila feel calmer, as she launched into what she wanted to say.

"Fiona, I don't want to overstep any boundaries; it's just that Pete is not only my best friend, she's my family, and, well, she's an odd duck." She blew on her frothy drink to cool it down.

"Oh, I know. Odd doesn't even begin to cover it, really. She's kind of magical," Fiona replied.

"Pete loves how you just accept her the way she is. I appreciate that about you too. I feel like we both see her for who she is."

"Well, in case you haven't noticed, my son marches to the beat of a different drummer as well. Maybe raising him somehow prepared me for understanding, or at least accepting, Pete's stuff. I don't always understand it," she admitted.

"Me neither. That's kind of why I'm jumping in here. I think because of her issues with reality, I feel the need to get involved."

Fiona nodded, then took a sip of her hot chocolate.

"First off, I want to thank you for meeting me. I know you must have a heavy heart. I also want to say that I'm a supporter of you and Pete. I want your relationship to continue." Fiona felt a wave of relief, but waited for the other shoe to drop. "But I am also angry about what you did. I know I'm not in the relationship, but I can't help but feel like Pete's watchdog. I mean, as you know, I'm her check-in person for her behavioral therapy plan. I don't want to come off as condescending or harsh. I just want to say that what you did was damaging. Honestly, I got mad about it before Pete did. She's angry *now*." She paused and ate a bite of her dessert.

"Oh, I know she's angry. And I can understand why you feel the way you do." She looked down at her drink, wishing this would be over soon.

"I guess I just wanted to say this to your face, and not just talk about you to Pete. You can't fuck up like that again. If you want to stay with Pete, you have to get your demon on-leash and never break her heart like that again." Sheila hesitated, unsure if she'd gone too far. Fiona's response surprised her.

"I know I can't be unfaithful to her, and I would love nothing more than to have my shit under control, to not act on my compulsions. I'm mad at myself too, and I respect you for speaking your mind. I'm not saying I'm comfortable right now; part of me feels like crying and the rest of me wants to scream at you." She smiled, hoping to break some of the tension. Sheila's expression began to mellow.

"Well, thank you. Thanks for hearing me and not getting defensive. As hard as all this must be to listen to, I hope you really know that I'm a fan of you two. I give Pete my honest opinions about your relationship when she asks; I told her that real love is a rare visitor. I know this to be true." She took another bite of pie and washed it down with a long drink of her latte.

Fiona took her in; Sheila looked fragile to her, like a hurt bird. She felt the sudden urge to be very tender toward her.

"Thank you, Sheila, for being real and raw with me, for speaking your truth. Pete's lucky to have you in her corner. If she and I can't go the distance, I want to tell you that it's been great getting to know you," she said with conviction.

Sheila reached out and took Fiona's hand in hers and squeezed. Both women wanted to cry, but didn't. Instead, they finished their drinks as they talked about Pete's upcoming art show and then went their separate ways.

☆☆☆

Fiona woke up just after four in the morning on Sunday extremely aroused from an erotic dream she'd had about Pete. She did what she always did when she woke up from a sex dream; she started touching herself. But she couldn't fantasize about Pete, not now when they were in limbo; she was numb to her own touch and stopped. She turned to bury her face into the pillow, sobbed, and eventually fell back to sleep.

A few hours later, she woke up, got dressed, and found Anthony and Mack in the kitchen making a special breakfast. Her brother was returning to Maine that morning, and he wanted to have one last family meal together.

"Hey, sis! We're making banana pancakes," he said cheerfully.

"Yum," she said, walking over to Mack and giving him a hug. She poured herself some coffee and asked Anthony how he was feeling about going back.

"Mixed. I'm excited to move here and make a fresh start," he said.

"I can't *wait* for you to live in Boston, Uncle Anthony!" Mack blurted.

"But I worry about how the folks will react. I mean, I've been their right-hand man for twenty years." Then he lowered his voice to a whisper and leaned into his sister's ear to say, "And I'm worried about you." Mack didn't see when she mouthed the response *I'll be okay*, because he was flipping pancakes.

"Last one's done!" Mack sang out. "Come on, let's eat!" Anthony got the rest of the pancakes out of the oven where they were being kept warm, and Mack put the maple syrup and butter on the table. He insisted that his mom just sit; he wanted to wait on her.

"Good job, Mack," Anthony praised.

They all sat and ate; Mack stuffed his cheeks like he usually did.

"Sweetie, these are delicious!" Fiona said appreciatively.

"I know, they really are," he said with a mouthful. "So, after breakfast, Uncle Anthony has to go back home. I'm gonna miss him a lot."

"I'll miss you guys too, but I'll be here in a few months. We can visit in the meantime."

As Fiona looked at them both, she saw a resemblance between them, and that made her happy. She hoped Mack would grow up to be as strong and kind as her brother.

"Well, the other thing I was going to say is that I *really* miss Pete. We haven't seen her and Turtle in forever. Is she done working that long job yet?"

Anthony and Fiona made eye contact before she responded.

"No, honey, I think she's busy today too, but I'll call her and see when she's free."

"I want to talk to her too. About the tree house," he said.

"Okay, Mack," Fiona said, chewing her pancake slowly because she felt too upset to swallow. She made herself snap out of it because she knew mothers of young children couldn't fall apart in front of them; they had to appear unbreakable.

As they ate breakfast, Anthony talked about things they could do together in Cundy's Harbor. They could take a cruise out to Bailey Island, maybe break in that new fishing pole, and of course Grandpa would want to take them out on one of the boats.

After breakfast, Fiona told Mack to get dressed, and while he did, she and Anthony cleaned up the kitchen.

"I'm really gonna miss you, you know, and not just because of all the childcare," she told him.

He smiled. "Hey, can you get Calvin to commit to watching Mack on Tuesday nights so you can make your meetings?"

"Sure, and if he can't, I've got some babysitters I can call. Don't worry, I'm not going to stop going. Even if Pete dumps my ass," she said as she wiped the counter.

"I have faith in you, Fi. So does your sponsor. And Pete is not going to dump you. I've seen the look in her eyes when she's with you."

"I hope you're right. Mack would be crushed. But really, Anthony, it's been a great couple of weeks."

"Yes, it has."

They talked some more, and then Mack appeared in the kitchen with a piece of paper in his hand.

"Uncle Anthony, I wanted you to have this." He handed him a drawing he'd made. It was a fairly detailed pencil drawing of his uncle with a big smile on his face, wearing a Boston Red Sox shirt and standing in front of Fenway Park. "It's from your future here with us. See how happy you are?"

Anthony looked like he might cry. "Wow! Thanks, Mack! You're quite the artist. This is very detailed. You even have the two little red socks facing the right direction." Anthony told him he'd hang it up on his refrigerator so he could see it all the time.

Soon afterwards, Fiona and Mack walked Anthony out to his car and took turns hugging him. Anthony picked the boy up, looked into his eyes and said, "It's not good-bye, it's see you later! There's a difference. Hey—when I move down here, you're gonna see me so much you'll get tired of me." He put him down and tickled him.

Mack sniffled and put his arm around his mother's waist while the two of them watched Anthony drive away.

☆☆☆

Saturday and Sunday were hard for Pete. She'd gotten used to spending the weekends with Fiona and Mack, and she longed for their company. She suspected Turtle missed being with them too, because he seemed less perky than usual, so she called Sheila in the morning to ask when she thought she'd be back from visiting with her mother, and if she wanted to take the dogs on a hike. Sheila said if there were a few daylight hours left when she returned, she'd call.

Pete took Turtle for a walk around the neighborhood, then set about pricing her pieces for the show. As she did, she thought about the impending holiday, which made her think about her family. She hadn't spoken with her mother in a few weeks, and hadn't talked to her brother in over a month. She guessed they wanted her to come to Springfield for Thanksgiving. Some years she spent the day with them, and other years she spent it with Sheila. She found herself half hoping she could be with Fiona and Mack, but then her anger woke up, so she made herself focus more on her upcoming show. She made a list of prices for all the pieces, then looked at the unfinished collage on her workbench. She hadn't believed she'd finish it in time for the show, but as she fixed her gaze on it, she thought maybe she could.

It was a square wooden box, about two feet wide and three feet high, filled with dozens of tiny objects, including buttons, keys, little pieces of rusted metal, and a few small children's toys she had taken from clients' houses. Some of the keys and buttons she'd had since childhood. Grandma Sweets knew Pete liked them, so one day she gave her a big cookie tin filled with them. Some had accumulated in her junk drawer over the years, and others she'd found at garage sales. Young Petra was delighted and immediately started sorting them.

"Oh, Grandma," Pete said aloud, "I wish you were still here. I think you'd like this art I make with the random bits of people's lives. I guess I'm telling stories with objects. I miss *your* stories..." Turtle had walked over to her and was standing by her side with his ears pricked and his head cocked, like he always did when she talked to herself. It was like he was listening for his name and waiting to be of service. She bent down, petted him behind the ears, reached her hand under his chest, and pulled him close for a hug. His tail thumped happily. "You miss Fiona and Mack too, huh, boy? I'm trying not to think about them, but it's hard."

She worked for about two hours, adding some shiny metal pieces and old matchboxes to the mélange. She couldn't decide if it was finished or not, so she took a break, planning to come back to it later. Even though she was excited about the art show, she also felt odd sharing things with the public that she made for such personal reasons. She decided to make some lunch and write in her journal about everything she was feeling. She sat on the couch, taking bites of her turkey sandwich between her bursts of writing.

*Making art helps me make sense of all the stuff I collect. It lets me sort out all the things swirling in my head too. My brain takes pictures and stores them whether I need the information or not. I can still see my first-grade classroom in detail. I wish I could shut it off, tune it out, or power it down—but I've never been able to. My mind only calms down when I'm making art, making love, or playing with my dog. Sometimes it's louder than a four-lane highway in there and I wonder if it will just get louder and louder until it explodes. Pop! Here lies Petra Orvatch, whose head blew up because it was too full.*

*Even though I'm used to this brain, I often wish I had a different one. Inexplicably knowing things about strangers' lives, seeing things happen before they happen, remembering too much—all of it weighs me down. Grandma Sweets always called it a gift, and said it was only a burden if I compared myself to others too much and tried to be more like them. She said I would never be like them and that I should try to use my gifts to help myself and help others. She told me there was no point in fighting it. I should try to quiet the noise in my mind when it gets overwhelming, yes, but I should never expect my perceptions to be like other people's.*

*Grandma used to say, "A dozen people, a dozen realities. A hundred people, a hundred realities. You can walk in someone else's shoes, but it's better to try to climb into his skin and walk around in it."*

*It wasn't until I read* To Kill a Mockingbird *in eighth grade that I realized she'd borrowed that advice from one of her favorite characters of all time: Atticus Finch. I loved that book. Atticus reminded me a little of my father and I could relate to Scout because neither of us were girlie girls. I'm just going on about unconnected things; it seems I can't focus. I should just pick a topic and stick to it.*

*Fiona.*

*That's my topic. My beautiful, heartbreaking Fiona Angeli. I've never met anyone like her before; I never got so close to a lover so fast. I didn't even know my heart could dilate so much that I could let someone in so completely. Falling in love means allowing yourself to be helpless. Love is a kind of craziness, really. You have to trust someone as much as you trust yourself and most people hurt you in the end. Fiona hurt me deeply. All in about seven minutes. I'm guessing she spent about that long having sex with the roller derby player.*

*Was it worth it, Fiona? Was getting her off or letting her get you off really worth all this pain? I know you can't unring a bell, but I know you want that evening to do-over. If I hadn't caught you, would you have told me? Have there been others? Were you fingering someone else in that dressing room? If not me, who? And how many others have there been? Before me? During our relationship? How many will there be after me?*

*Oh, I know it's an onus to be that beautiful; people behave differently towards those who dazzle, people want to consume beauty, to own it. I've tried to imagine how it feels to be you, but I can't. What's it like to be a beacon? A lightning rod? A sorceress who makes dicks hard and pussies wet? What's it like to have people be nice to you just because they like how you look? It can't all be burdensome. You must enjoy some of the attention you get. Though I must admit, Fiona, when I first met you I expected you to be more vain, to be a woman who took advantage of her looks, and I haven't seen you behave that way. If you do get off on being gorgeous, you must do it privately.*

*Shit, you're hot. I crave you so much it hurts. I miss kissing you, touching you, savoring your sweet and your salt. I yearn to see the parts of yourself you conceal; the pieces you only share with me. I long to see those special glimpses: flashes of flesh in the night, your face blurry because it's so close to mine. Wishing, wanting, desiring, needing you. Fiona.*

She stopped writing because her eyes were brimming with tears. One briny drop hit the paper and made the ink smear, an artifact from a sad segment of her life. Watching the paper absorb it, she saw that it left a watery black halo around the "o" and "n" in Fiona. She wiped her tears away with the backs of her hands and blinked the room into focus. Pete hoped she was done because she hated crying; she always had. It caused her temples to throb and made her feel like she might drown in emotion.

She got up and cleaned the kitchen and was pacing around her place thinking about the collage on her workbench when the phone rang. It was Sheila, saying she'd be back in Cambridge in about two hours and would love to go for a dog hike. Pete was relieved because she needed to move.

They met at Noanet Woodlands in Dover, which was a beautiful place to hike because Noanet Peak offered amazing views of the Boston skyline. Dogs were allowed off leash on the more than seventeen miles of trails. The preserve, which used to be Native American hunting grounds, also featured an old mill site that Pete liked to photograph. They talked about Sheila's mother, work, Damon, and Fiona. It was a partly sunny day with mild temperatures, and they hiked vigorously, which the five dogs enjoyed immensely. When they got to the top, they took in the panorama, then Sheila suggested they meditate; she wanted them to offer a little prayer to the universe about what they each wanted in their lives.

Pete thought it was a good idea. While the dogs sniffed the ground and the air and scurried through the brush, the women stood still, breathing deeply as their unspoken words churned hope in their minds and hearts.

Though she felt better after getting outdoors and spending time with her friend, when she laid her head down on her pillow later that night, it felt heavy. It was almost 9:00, much earlier than she normally went to bed, but Pete just wanted the day to be over, so she closed her eyes and willed sleep to come quickly. After a minute or two, the phone rang, and when she reached for it, she saw it was Fiona. She thought about not picking it up while it rang but then grabbed it.

"Pete! I *miss* you," Mack declared.

"Hi, Mack, how nice to hear your voice," Pete replied, catching herself smiling for the first time in hours.

What she didn't know was that Mack had just had a meltdown of sorts; he'd thrown a tantrum about missing Pete and convinced his mother that it had been too long since he saw Pete or even talked with her. Fiona had to admit to herself it must have seemed odd to her son that Pete was so busy she couldn't even talk with them on the phone.

"When are you coming over? I want to show you my latest tree house design. Oh, and you've got to see the treasure chest now that it's all done and filled with treasures. Does Turtle miss me? I miss him," he said, breathing into the phone like kids do.

"Soon, Mack. I will be over soon, and I would love to see your designs and your treasure chest and anything else you want to show me. And yes, Turtle misses you." She closed her eyes, trying to picture his face.

"Well, okay. Um, I'm not much of a phone person so I guess I'll say goodnight and pass the phone to my mom, okay?"

Pete opened her eyes and stared up at the rafters. "Sure, big guy, goodnight. I love you," she said.

"Night. Love you too."

"Hi, Pete." Fiona's voice was sultrier than Pete remembered.

"Hi."

"You sound sleepy. Did we wake you?"

"No, I'm just lying down in bed, but I wasn't sleeping. Just sort of resting."

"I hope you don't mind the call. I know the last time we saw each other you were angry, and you probably still are; it's just that he's been asking about you so much, and then he begged me to call you..."

"It's okay. It was good to hear his voice. Made me miss him more, though," Pete admitted.

"Well." Fiona sounded almost coy now. "That could be remedied. I was wondering if we could come to your art opening this Friday." Her speech sped up as she continued. "I mean, I totally understand if you don't want me there, but it would be so great for Mack to see your work, to see that side of you. And it's well before his bedtime. What do you think?"

Pete had mixed feelings about it, but didn't want to give her a maybe. "Well, okay. But I'd like to see you first, for us to meet privately before we see each other in a public setting. Is that okay?"

Fiona was surprised by this, and found herself getting excited at the thought of seeing Pete sooner than Friday. "Yes." She didn't want to sound too eager. "Of course. Anthony went back to Maine so I suppose I could get a sitter or—"

Pete cut her off. "I can come over. That way I could see you both. We can talk after Mack goes to bed. Would that be all right?"

"Sure. Would it be too much to suggest I make us dinner?" Fiona regretted saying it the minute it came out of her mouth.

"Um, that's a nice offer, but I'm going to pass. Is it okay if I come around 7:00? When your dinner is over? That way I can have some time with Mack."

"Sure." She tried to keep her disappointment out of her voice. "That's fine. When?"

"Thursday?"

"Thursday it is," Fiona said.

"Okay." Pete didn't know what else to say, then Fiona ended the silence.

"All right, well, get some rest, and I'll see you Thursday. And thanks, Pete. Thanks very much."

"Okay. Goodnight." Pete stared blankly at her loft curtains, then looked at pictures of Mack and Fiona on her phone until she felt as if she might cry again. She powered it down, turned off the light, and waited for sleep to quiet her mind.

☆☆☆

When Fiona tucked Mack in for the night, he kept talking about Pete and the tree house. Fiona said she understood he was excited but that it was time to wind it down for the night, to shut his brain off and sleep.

"Your brain doesn't shut off when you sleep, Mom. That's a silly thing to say," he said. "It does lots of things when you're sleeping, you know that!"

"Yes, Professor MacProfessor, I do. You know what I meant. Now go to sleep." She kissed him on the cheek and switched his light off.

She decided to fold some laundry, then get in bed with a movie to try to focus on something besides Pete. As she was searching the laundry basket for a missing blue sock, her phone rang. Hoping it was Pete, she grabbed it off the coffee table and saw that it was Anthony.

He asked her how she was doing, and she told him about the latest developments between her and Pete. He told her that sounded hopeful, then asked her if she was ready to hear his account of how it went with Mom and Dad, saying she was in for a pleasant surprise. She sat on the couch and stopped folding, telling him to fire away.

He told her how they invited him over for dinner, and the first thing they did was compliment him on losing a little weight. They said they'd missed his work, that Taylor, who'd filled in during his absence, wasn't as detail-oriented as he was. They asked him about Fiona, Mack, and his time in Boston. Their mother was particularly concerned about how he was feeling about the divorce. She said she'd seen Dawn around town, and she didn't look too good, kind of tired and stressed out. She speculated that it was over between her and Troy, and warned Anthony not to go back to her if she started working that angle. He assured both of them that his life would not go backward.

When he told them he had some big news to share, they said they did too and encouraged him to go first. He just came right out and told him that he didn't think he could really be happy after the divorce if he stayed in Maine; he thought he could better reinvent himself in Boston and was moving there. He described for Fiona how relieved he felt when they said they understood why he wanted to relocate and told him they were supportive of the move. They even joked about how now they could visit two of their children and their grandchild in the same place. Their father, Anthony Sr., was particularly glad Mack would have a male role model close by. Their mother promised they would visit often and said it would be even easier now.

When he asked why that was, their father explained that they'd just sold the business and were going to retire. Apparently, a young couple from New York hit it big when they sold their tech start-up and wanted to start a family in some beautiful coastal location. They made an offer the Angelis couldn't refuse. They were so excited to finally have time to visit their children more and go abroad; they were going to see places they'd always dreamed of traveling to.

Fiona tried not to interrupt, but couldn't help blurting out a few wows. He told her there was more great news; they were giving him a sum of money as a sort of severance package and thank-you for all of his years of service: $100,000. They'd also started a trust for Mack's education, and were going to give Liam and Francesca some money too, because the way they saw it, the whole family had sacrificed for the business. With their retirement funds, investments, and the money from the sale, they expected to live comfortably for the rest of their lives. Their mother joked that if they both lived past ninety-five, they might run out of money.

"Isn't it just astounding news, Fi? I'm still sort of in shock. I can't even picture them not working!"

"But apparently they can. Good for them! Wow. Amazing. So now you can move down here in good conscience. It's almost like the universe conspired to help you get out of Cundy's Harbor," Fiona said.

"Indeed," he agreed.

☆☆☆

Anthony felt edgy and out of place in his house, which seemed big and empty without Dawn and her things. After he'd unpacked, straightened up, and put some laundry on, he put Mack's portrait of him up on the refrigerator, and looked at it. *I do look happy in my future. I like that.*

He got a beer and sat in his comfortable old leather recliner. It was scuffed and had a small tear in the seat. Dawn had nagged him to get rid of it, and though he was generally compliant regarding her wishes, he'd refused to part with it, saying it was the most comfortable chair he ever had. It must have been designed with a tall person in mind, because it fit his frame perfectly. He looked out the window and imagined what his life might be like in a few months' time.

He was fairly sure he could get Dawn to agree to sell the house, and his share of the income from that, along with the money his parents had given him, would be enough for him to get a modest house in the Boston area and tide him over while he was between jobs. He'd look for work in the restaurant industry, or maybe even try to get a teaching credential. He'd always had it in the back of his mind to be a biology teacher; when he graduated high school, his plan was to work in the family business for a few years and then go to college to become a teacher. Maybe it wasn't too late; people switched careers in their late thirties all the time.

Then he wondered when he would start dating again and tried to predict how that would feel. The idea both scared and excited him. Fiona was right; he hadn't been with anyone but Dawn since he was twenty-four, and he should experience other women. He looked forward to having sex again, but was even more thrilled about the prospect of falling in love again.

He suddenly felt like writing. He read poetry more than he wrote it, but he occasionally put words to paper. Anthony had been writing poems since junior high school, but had only shared that side of himself with Fiona and, later, with Dawn. He got up to get his notebook and another beer, then returned to the chair he would never get rid of and wrote a poem about how it would feel to find new love.

*our love is like the ocean itself;*
*so vast and deep it has to be measured in miles and fathoms.*
*we are unmoored;*
*our voyage has just begun.*
*new ports are in the offing.*

## CHAPTER ELEVEN: FOUND OBJECTS

*The truth is, everyone is going to hurt you.*
*You just got to find the ones worth suffering for.*
*~ Bob Marley*

Pete slept poorly Sunday night, and even though she woke up tired, she was looking forward to being on the job site; physical work always made her feel better. Even though it was just 8:00 in the morning, Joseph was already shaved and dressed, with pocket protector in place. This time, in addition to his customary pens, pencils, pocketknife, and calculator, he had a magnifying glass in his collection. Pete had to scratch her head at that one. They exchanged greetings, and he offered her a cup of coffee, which she accepted gratefully. She needed extra caffeine this morning.

Around 11 o'clock, Joseph went out to run an errand. The sun had come out, and it was shaping up into a classic cold, crisp, Massachusetts autumn day. One of Joseph's boxes was blocking her access to part of the baseboard, so she moved it. It was surprisingly light; Pete assumed it would be heavy because it was large. As she set it down in the dining room, something shiny inside caught her eye. She took it out and saw it was an antique Christmas tree ornament: a silver dog with a red collar. The coating had flaked off a little near the nose and paws, but other than that it was in good shape. She had no idea how old it was, but it reminded her of some of the ornaments her mother had inherited from her parents. She held the delicate object in the palm of her hand, enjoying how it caught the sunlight coming in through the window. Pete liked it a great deal and was seized with the desire to take it. She looked to see what else was in the box and saw it was filled with more ornaments that were wrapped in yellowed newspaper.

*Was this little dog his favorite? Did it come with a special story like the one the wooden deer told me?* Pete thought of Fiona and how hard she was working to stop her destructive behaviors. Then Sheila popped into her mind, telling her again to stop stealing. She imagined Mack at her opening, asking her where she got all that stuff from, and felt her gut tighten as she reminded herself she hadn't even told Fiona the truth about the objects. Holding the silver dog close to her face, she stared at its little black eyes and said, "Don't worry. You can stay with your old friends." Then she nestled it back among the others, where it rested safely against the brittle papers.

☆☆☆

Fiona was having trouble concentrating at work Monday morning. She kept thinking of Pete and wondering how their time Thursday would go. She was also missing Anthony; it had been hard to say good-bye to her brother. The day was dragging by; it was only 11, and the last time she looked at the clock it was quarter of. Her sorrow, along with the slow pace of the workday, weighed her down; she felt misery land on her shoulder and dig its talons into her like a vulture.

She decided to call Calvin; maybe his company would lift her sagging spirits. "Cal, feel like grabbing lunch downtown with me? I can take an hour and a half today, because Friday I worked through my lunch break."

"Okay. Where?"

"How about that same falafel place we ate at the last time you met me for lunch. Remember it?"

"Oh yeah, I liked that place. What time?"

"Twelve thirty?"

"See you then. Bye, Fi!"

He was five minutes late and explained that parking was really tough. He gave her a long hug and then said, "You look really sad, Fi. What can I do to cheer you up?"

"You're already doing it. You're here. Just looking at you makes me feel better."

"Any new developments on the Pete front?"

"Well, I called her last night. Mack threw a shit fit because he really wanted to talk to her. Then I got on the phone and asked if we could come to her opening this Friday. She said yes, but wanted to meet with me first. So she's coming over after dinner Thursday. I'm nervous, Cal."

"Of course you are. I mean, the last time you two saw each other, it was rough, so it makes sense that you'd be anxious. Just be real, that's all you can do. Be yourself."

"Being myself got me into this mess," she lamented. "Why the fuck did I have to be a sex addict? Couldn't I have just been an alcoholic? That would be more straightforward." He looked up from the menu, staring at her blankly. "I'm kidding. I can beat it, right?" She searched his eyes, hoping to find comfort there.

"Definitely! You're bigger than your addiction, Fiona. Just don't give up on yourself. You can change your life at any point. I'm proof of that," he said triumphantly.

"Oh shit—you had a job interview last week, I almost forgot. How did it go?"

"Really well, actually," he answered, and then took a sip of water. "It was at one of the places Thomas suggested I send my resume to. It's a center for homeless youth in Dorchester, about a mile from the soup kitchen. They have an opening for an assistant program coordinator, and the salary is actually halfway decent for a nonprofit. The hiring committee was really impressed with all of my volunteer work. Did you know I've been volunteering for twenty-eight years now? I didn't even realize that until I was answering questions in the interview and found myself describing my experience at the veterans hospital when I was six. I'm really hoping to get a second interview; they said they would contact me by the end of the week, so cross your fingers!"

A cheerful server arrived to take their order. Fiona realized she was only slightly hungry; she ordered a salad.

"Still not eating much these days?"

"Nope."

"Well, don't lose weight—you're perfect the way you are." He smiled, hoping to make her smile, but her mouth remained a straight line. "Hey, it's a good sign that she said you could come to her opening. And the fact that she wants to see you first seems positive too."

"Maybe."

He could see she needed a topic change, so he told her more about the position he'd interviewed for. Then Fiona talked about the Bradshaw case, which was dragging on. When her lunch break was nearly over, he walked her the few blocks back to the office, and she thanked him for making her blue Monday considerably less blue. He gave her a kiss on the cheek and told her he loved her.

☆☆☆

As Fiona sat through her SAA meeting, listening to her fellow addicts' tales of triumph and woe, it occurred to her that, although going to meetings was proof of her commitment to changing her behavior, it wasn't enough. She had to do more. She'd never understood why people used the phrase "madly in love" until she fell for Pete. The ocean of feeling she had for her did make her feel a little crazy, and their separation was, in fact, maddening. She didn't speak up at the meeting, not just because she didn't feel like opening her veins and pouring out her pain, but also because she was distracted by her own musings.

On the drive home, she thought more about her addiction and how she could show herself and Pete that she could conquer it. She needed to prove to herself she was getting better, that she was worthy of Pete's love. An idea occurred to her, and even though her instincts told her it was crazy, the notion quickly took root.

After Mack was asleep, she went online to look up sex clubs; she intended to run the gauntlet by going to one and resisting sex. It would be her very last trip to a sex club. If she could do that, it would mean she was making progress with her addiction. The one she'd gone to earlier this year had closed, and the locations and schedules of these places changed frequently, so she had to do some research. She found one called Bliss, which had a bisexual night on Wednesdays they called Hump Night. After reading some positive reviews of the place, she emailed Calvin and asked if Mack could sleep over at his place tomorrow night. She intended to tell him about the sex club, but since she knew he would try to talk her out of it, she decided she would tell him after the fact; she told a white lie about needing a night to herself to drink some wine and cry.

She went to her closet and took a carton down from the top shelf; it was her Pandora's box of fetish wear, and once the lid was off, there was no turning back. Most of the garments were black leather, but she had one latex jumpsuit that was indigo; she thought of it as her blue cat suit. Fiona took off her clothes and tried it on for size. She became aroused the instant she felt the slick, cool material against her skin. After she slipped into it, she inspected herself in the mirror; it didn't fit as tightly as it had the last time she wore it because she'd lost some weight recently, but it still looked good. The last time she had it on, she'd had sex with seven different people in one night. She felt like a "sex superhero" in it; when she donned the erotic costume, she was the exact embodiment of her sex addiction itself. She thought she heard Mack get up to use the bathroom, so she took it off hastily and put it back in the box. She put on her pajamas and got into bed with a favorite book she was rereading in the hope that the novel would take her mind off her woes.

It turned out that Calvin was off Wednesday night, so he picked Mack up at 6:00. Mack was excited to have a sleepover on a school night, and Fiona made him promise he'd be asleep by 9:30 at the latest. After they left, she put on her slinky blue suit and knee-high boots. She wore a pair of jeans and a button-down shirt over them. The doors at Bliss opened at 8:00, so at 8:15 she downed a large glass of red wine to take the edge off and then left. She wondered about the crowd a Wednesday night event would attract, since weekend nights were the most popular at sex clubs.

Parking was easy enough to find in the South Boston warehouse district. When Fiona entered the place, the familiar smell of lube and come hit her nostrils. The man who took her money was enormous; he had muscles everywhere that bulged under his shirt and pants. With his shaved head and waxed handlebar mustache, he looked like a nineteenth-century circus strongman. He told her she could go inside only after she read the rules, which were posted in large red print on a sign screwed to the wall.

They stated: *no cell phones, cameras or recording devices; do not turn off lights; no touching without permission; no loud talking, laughing, or rude behavior; no solicitation of any type; no alcohol, drugs, or sleeping allowed; condoms are required for penetration but not for oral sex; clean up after yourself.*

Fiona guessed that people drank or did their drugs before they arrived, because most couldn't face a sex club sober.

She parted the heavy, dark blue drapes and entered the lobby, which had lockers and changing areas, a few couches and chairs, and a condom and lube dispenser. Fiona had already caught the eye of a middle-aged man who sat on one of the couches. He smiled at her, but she just nodded in response. He was not someone who would tempt her; she was far more attracted to women than she was to men, so she had to find a man extremely appealing to have sex with him. She removed her coat and street clothes and put them in a locker, then put the key down her boot. She unzipped her jumpsuit to reveal a little cleavage and began to prowl.

The lighting was dimmer once she left that area, but she could make out small playrooms with their doors ajar and sections of the club that were curtained off. She saw men sticking their heads through the draperies with their hands on their cocks, so she knew there must be some action going on. She approached but didn't stand too close to any of the voyeurs, then parted the velvet so she could see what was holding their interest. On a purple vinyl couch were two men sitting on either side of a woman; they were all naked and kissing each other. The woman had dark brown skin, buzzed hair, and a slender, beautiful body. One of the men was also lean, with a dancer's build, and the other was stocky and bearded. Their pale skin contrasted dramatically with the woman's deep brown complexion. The bearded man was fondling the woman's breasts while she stroked his penis. The other man was kissing her and touching himself. While this scenario held promise, the pace of the action was not arousing to Fiona, so she moved on.

As she walked toward one of the playrooms, she sensed she was being followed. When she turned around, she saw a beautiful young woman in a chainmail bra, tight leather pants, and high-heeled boots. She had shiny, straight black hair, dark eyes, golden skin, and high, prominent cheekbones. Fiona was definitely attracted to her, so she forced herself to engage.

"Hello," Fiona said softly.

"Hello yourself. I haven't seen you here before. What's your name?"

"Constance," she replied, using her favorite pseudonym.

"I'm Jiwoo," the woman said, licking her lips and looking Fiona up and down; she was a hungry cat sizing up her prey. "Were you heading to that playroom?" She gestured toward the open door with red light spilling out.

"Yes, I was. Have you been in there?"

"No, let's go together," Jiwoo suggested.

As they walked, Fiona noticed the club was starting to get more crowded. There was a nice balance of women and men; usually there were more men out on the bisexual nights. Fiona went in first, with Jiwoo following closely behind. The walls, lights, and furnishings were all red. It took her eyes a moment to adjust, and when they did, what she saw intrigued her.

She and Jiwoo were in the company of four other watchers. A naked woman was tied to the posts of a bed in the center of the room and a woman dressed in dominatrix attire stood over her, tickling her body with a feather, which made the bound woman twist and shudder. The woman in charge circled around the bed with slow, deliberate strides as she teased her submissive with the prop, dragging it from her foot up across her leg, over her belly and up around her nipples, then down again past her navel and between her legs. She had no pubic hair, so her sensitivity to the feather play was acute, and the woman in black tickled her clit repeatedly, making her captive moan with pleasure.

Suddenly, Jiwoo stepped directly behind Fiona and cupped her breasts; she was so startled, she inhaled sharply. She hadn't considered the finer points of what she would and would not allow. Her goal was to avoid having sex, but did that mean she shouldn't let people arouse her? Wouldn't it take even more fortitude to resist if she allowed herself to be turned on? She decided not to pull away, and Jiwoo pinched her nipples and kissed and bit her neck, giving Fiona goose bumps.

She closed her eyes, trying to decide her next move. When she opened them she noticed that the woman tied to the table was getting wet from the feather play and that two of the men in the room were jerking off. A man and woman in the corner were making out and starting to remove each other's fetish wear.

Jiwoo was getting bolder now; she tugged Fiona's zipper down and moved her hands inside to touch her breasts. The woman with the feather was fingering her partner while she kissed her, and one of the masturbators shot his load. Fiona flashed on the club rule that said to clean up after yourself, wondering if anyone ever wiped up their come, and felt sorry for the people who had to clean this place at the end of the night. Her thoughts were racing as Jiwoo caressed her breasts and squeezed her nipples. Fiona turned to face her, and they kissed for a while, but then she stopped, questioning her decision to cross this line.

"Sorry," Fiona managed, "I can't." She pulled her zipper up and made a hasty exit. She was turned on and still had forty-eight minutes to go, because she had set a goal of lasting at least an hour.

Hoping Jiwoo wouldn't follow her, she quickly ducked into another playroom. This one was nearly full to capacity and didn't have a main attraction. There were cushions on the floor, and people were seated and lying down, groping each other. Couples leaned against the walls, kissing, touching, and fucking. One man was on his knees, giving a guy a blowjob, while a woman watched with fascination. A guy was fucking a woman in the ass and making out with another woman; this made an already aroused Fiona even more hot. She stood very near them, and a man walked behind her, brushing his erection against her ass, adding to her arousal. She turned to face him and liked what she saw: he was tall, muscular, and had an intelligent face. Fiona thought he looked like the type of guy who wore glasses but had decided to leave them in his locker. He wasn't wearing anything except sandals and smiled at her.

"Hello," he said.

She found it hard to keep her gaze at eye level when she had already seen his perfectly shaped cock.

"Hey," she returned, staring into his eyes. Then she surprised herself as she broke a rule and grabbed his penis. She leaned in, kissed him, and then wondered if anyone here asked permission before touching. He kissed her back, and someone bumped into him, which knocked him off balance, causing him to fall against her. She let go of him and used both arms to catch him. His erection was now right against her pussy, and when he regained his balance, they kept kissing passionately, which stimulated Fiona immensely. They made out and moved against each other for several minutes. Fiona had to avoid going to the point of no return; his cock felt so good on her, she was afraid she would come right through her cat suit. She pulled away abruptly, flashed him an apologetic smile, weaved her way through the crowd, and left the room quickly.

She felt pleased with herself for walking away from two people who turned her on and was determined to find more and endure the hour. She didn't feel great about leaving him in the lurch, but guessed that someone so hot would soon find another person to play with.

Out of the corner of her eye, she saw Jiwoo, so she changed direction and walked toward another curtained-off area with several spectators gathered around it. Behind the heavy fabric were two sex swings mounted from the high ceiling. One had two men fucking in it, and the other held a woman who was fucking another woman with a strap-on.

The stakes were higher now, because this scene made Fiona recall memories of exciting sex toy play between her and Pete. Pete was amazing when she wore a harness; she was such an intuitive and skilled lover.

The spectators were turned on too; Fiona saw several men and women masturbating, couples fucking or sucking, and a few threesomes forming. Because she saw quite a few people who looked good to her, she didn't know which direction to turn. She pulled the other end of her zipper open, closed her eyes, and started touching herself. When she opened her eyes, she saw an attractive woman standing right in front of her. She was wearing nothing but nipple clamps and, like Fiona, was fingering herself.

Instead of hellos, they greeted each other with a kiss. She was a little taller than Fiona and appeared to be about the same age, but it was always hard to tell someone's age in the dark. She had short, straight dark hair, an olive complexion, and reminded Fiona a little of Pete. She was a good kisser, and they both got more and more excited as they kissed and pleasured themselves.

Fiona wasn't sure how much time passed before she realized that she couldn't give herself an orgasm or kiss this woman while she came; that would be sex. She'd been getting so aroused, she lost track of her own boundaries, but now it was time to turn back.

She stopped touching herself and backed away from her partner, who asked, "*Qué estás haciendo?*"

Fiona darted in between the curtains and returned to the main space, not looking back. She zipped herself up and looked for the bathroom. Thankfully, there was no one else in there; she was getting crowd fatigue. As she washed her hands, she wondered how much longer she had to stay; it felt to her like she'd been there almost an hour.

When she came out, it was even more crowded than it had been just a few minutes ago. It amazed her that there were this many horny swingers in Boston who would go out on a weeknight. She saw a large clock high up on one of the walls that said 9:25. *Only ten minutes to go. If I can just resist one more temptation, I've done it!*

Fiona's eyes landed on a man and a woman dressed in matching black latex suits who were holding hands as they strolled amidst the debauchery. The man had shaggy red hair and was androgynous-looking. The woman was a thin, pale blonde with a pleasing angular face. They looked like they'd just arrived, because their eyes were big with curiosity and their hair wasn't mussed. Fiona wanted to spend her final moments of this self-imposed trial with these two, so she sidled up to them, eyes wide, intentions clear. The man noticed her first and smiled, clearly approving of her. His companion eyed her up and down, then extended her hand.

"I'm Enora, and you're too beautiful to be all on your own here," she said in an Irish accent.

"Thank you," Fiona returned. "I'm Constance, and you are—?" She looked up at the man.

"Hoyt. Pleasure to meet you. It's our first time here. You?" He too had an Irish lilt, and Fiona found them utterly charming; she'd always had a weakness for Irish accents.

"Me too," Fiona answered, taking his hand and placing it on her zipper. He pulled it down slowly and put a hand inside, which instantly made her nipples hard. Enora leaned in and cupped one of Fiona's breasts. Then Fiona started kissing her, and Hoyt got hard watching the women's lips touch. He rubbed their backs and inserted himself between them so he could kiss Fiona too. Enora suggested they find an empty couch.

They managed to find one that didn't seem sticky, and they all sat down and resumed making out. Hoyt was partly on top of Fiona now, and she felt his erection against her; this made her throb and crave penetration.

*I just have to last ten more minutes and get out of here,* she told herself, *and go home. Then I will have won this contest. I can do this.* Then she had a thought: a strategy for surviving this last sexual embroilment.

"I'd like to watch; you're both so beautiful. Why don't you put on a show for me?"

Hoyt smiled and pulled Enora's zipper down, then began kissing her nipples. She lay flat on the couch, and Hoyt unzipped her all the way, then did the same for himself and pulled his cock out. Both of them were so pale they practically glowed in the dim blue lighting of the club. Fiona stood over them while they fucked vigorously.

She and Enora made eye contact, so Fiona thought she should give her something more to watch. She loosened her suit so that her breasts were in full view and started masturbating, which delighted her Irish acquaintance. Fiona was careful not to bring herself too near climax, so she slowed it down a bit. Hoyt's eyes were closed, as if he'd gone inside his own head while making love to Enora, but she never took her eyes off Fiona. Hoyt moaned as his lover's breathing came harder and faster, and they came, first her and him right after. Fiona enjoyed the show, and when her eyes found the clock, it said 9:37. She'd done it.

"Thanks, you two. That was hot, but I've got to go," she said. As she turned to leave, Enora touched her arm.

"But we want to play with you, Constance."

Hoyt looked at her and nodded in agreement.

"Next time, perhaps," she said, knowing there would never be a next time. She went to the lockers and got dressed. As soon as Fiona got home, she peeled off her clothes and showered, washing the club off her, letting the experience go down the drain.

☆☆☆

Fiona woke up Thursday morning with her chest tight from anxiety and stared at the ceiling for a while before silencing the alarm clock. Scenes from the night before played in her mind, causing her to panic. She'd meant only to test herself, to prove she was getting better, but now worried she'd crossed a dangerous line.

This thought had occurred to her before she went to the club, but she'd pushed it aside. She'd briefly kissed and touched people, allowed them to fondle her breasts, watch her masturbate, and rub against her for short periods of time, but nothing more. She tried to convince herself she did the right thing by telling herself that it was, in fact, harder to resist having full-on sex because she took things as far as she did. If she'd only watched and not participated, would that have been enough of a trial? If she'd merely been a passive voyeur at the club, that would have been similar to watching porn. Her reasoning went round and round like an animal chasing its tail, and she could not get peace of mind.

Haunted by guilt, she wasn't sure what to do. She hadn't intended to tell anyone about her outing except for Calvin and her therapist, but she decided she ought to let her sponsor know what she'd done. Helen probably wouldn't pick up her phone this early in the day, but even leaving a message would help, so when she got her voicemail, that was what she did. She asked Helen to call back as soon as she could. She also considered moving her therapy appointment up rather than waiting for her usual time.

Before she left to pick up Mack from Calvin's and take him to school, Fiona got out her box of fetish wear and searched through it, removing everything except a few items she'd worn with Pete. Then she picked up her blue cat suit from the floor and threw the whole pile in the trash can outside. She took a deep breath and told herself her intentions had been good, what happened couldn't be undone, and she had resisted giving in completely to her dark side.

☆☆☆

As Pete painted the window frames in Joseph's living room, her mind replayed some of the conversations she'd had recently. Her first of the day was with her client; they were talking about art, and Pete mentioned her opening. Joseph said he enjoyed art shows and asked if she would mind if he attended. He wanted to bring a friend of his who particularly liked pieces made with found objects. Pete thanked him for showing interest and gave him the gallery name and address. As she thought about it now, she wondered if it would make her feel strange to have a client attend a show full of art made from objects stolen from other clients.

*Maybe he won't go,* she reasoned, *or maybe if he does, it won't bother me.*

She reflected on her brief but touching phone chat with Mack. Hearing him tell her he loved her tempered her anger; hearing his voice reminded her she was in a relationship with not one but two people. Her conversation with Fiona had been short and surprising; Pete hadn't expected her to attend the opening.

*Shit.* Pete realized she had an age-old dilemma. *What am I going to wear?*

She texted Sheila to see if she had any interest in going clothes shopping after work and maybe grabbing a quick dinner. She could stop work a little early, and on Thursdays, Sheila got off work at 3:30. Pete didn't have to be at Fiona's until 7:00, so they could spend a few hours shopping and eating dinner together.

Sheila texted back: *sounds good. I could use some new blouses.*

They made a plan to meet at Harvard Square, which had many choices for clothes shopping and food. If they didn't find anything in those stores, they could travel the short distance to Central Square, where there were used clothing stores. They had no luck at the first few stores, and Sheila made a comment about all the new fashions being generic.

"You're right; let's go vintage," Pete said, and they headed to Central Square.

In addition to a fairly large Goodwill, there were a few used clothing stores with items from the forties to the nineties. It was in one of the little boutiques that Sheila found a blue suede jacket that actually had sleeves long enough for her and fell in love with it.

"It's a little pricey," she commented, "but I really want it!"

"Well what the hell, you just got a raise, and you just broke up with someone. I think you're entitled to treat yourself; just go for it," Pete encouraged.

Sheila said she'd think about it while they shopped a little more.

Pete was looking for a stylish shirt to wear; she had a few cool women's blouses in her hand when a beautiful burnt-orange, men's western-style shirt caught her eye. It looked fairly old, maybe from the late fifties or early sixties. "I'm gonna try some stuff on, Sheils."

"Ooh," she remarked, "I love that color!"

Pete saw two people waiting by the fitting rooms and took her place behind them. There were three stalls, so she didn't have to wait long. She parted the heavy gold curtains, and the familiar smell of old clothes hit her hard. She guessed the small space trapped the odor more. It was a blend of mothballs, old wool, dry cleaning chemicals, mustiness, and sweat. She didn't like it, but didn't mind it either.

She tried on the blouses; one didn't fit right, and the other was a bad color for her skin tone. The minute she slipped her arm into the western shirt, she knew it would be perfect, and it was. She liked how she looked in it and stepped back from the mirror for a better view.

As she turned and looked over her shoulder, she had a flashback of being in that dressing room with Fiona. She could see her there, see both of them pressed against the wall while Fiona touched her. She became aroused as she relived it, then found herself wondering if it had really happened. She couldn't reconcile how she remembered it so distinctly, and Fiona denied it so strongly. She moved closer to the mirror and looked at herself closely.

"Well, Orvatch, what're you gonna do tonight, huh? Probably see her and thaw on the spot. She's so fucking gorgeous it almost hurts; that's the truth. And the kid, he owns a big piece of your heart. Shit. Well, stay strong and stay true to yourself; that's all you can do." She'd been having these little tête-à-têtes with herself in mirrors since she was a little girl. One time, her mother had caught her and demanded to know what she was doing and why. She gave her the third degree, looking at her as if she were an exotic insect that had landed on her arm. Young Petra had told her she was just trying to decide something by talking to herself in the mirror. Her mother then shook her head and walked away.

She bought the orange shirt, Sheila splurged on the suede jacket, and they decided to eat pizza for dinner. Pete teased her about soy cheese, saying it didn't really melt, that it just sort of sweated. Sheila laughed and defended her beloved soy cheese. She asked Pete how she was feeling about seeing Fiona and Mack that night.

"I'm angry, sad, and slightly hopeful. I don't know that we'll figure much out tonight; I just know that I want be with them in private before I see them in a crowded setting."

"Yeah, maybe don't try to fix what's broken tonight. Just enjoy Mack."

"I've really missed him. If it's over, I'm breaking up with him too, and I don't want him out of my life, Sheila. I really don't."

"I hear you, Pete. He's part of the equation, for sure."

☆☆☆

Pete arrived at Fiona's with Turtle a few minutes after 7:00, a gift for Mack tucked under her arm: a beautifully illustrated book about building. Fiona was only able to hug her hello for a few seconds before Mack tackled them.

"Pete! Turtle! I missed you!"

The dog was so excited to see both of them, he didn't know whom to greet first. He jumped on Fiona's leg, and she bent to let him kiss her face; then he went to the boy, who squealed with delight.

"Missed you too, Mack, a lot," Pete said as she gave him a squeeze. "I brought you a present, here," she added, handing it to him. "I know you've already made a design for the tree house, but I think you should read through this book before we build. You'll like it; it has really detailed illustrations."

He flipped through it, skimming and smiling.

"Thanks, Pete. It's cool. Wanna see my design? I'll go get it."

"Let her at least get her coat off!" his mother urged.

Pete laughed, then removed her coat and tossed it over the chair. Turtle followed Mack into his room, and Fiona asked Pete if she wanted anything to drink.

"Beer, if you have it, thanks," Pete said.

"I always have beer, although I don't need to buy as much since Anthony left."

Suddenly Pete thought about how her absence combined with Anthony's departure must be affecting them, especially Mack, and she felt bad. Fiona came back with two bottles, and they sat on the couch. Pete was conscious of the gap between them.

"How's he doing? Is he still going to move here?"

Fiona told her about the sale of the business and his big gift from their parents. Then Mack returned with a few papers in his hand.

"I really missed seeing you, Pete. It felt different around here. You're weird like me, and you always understand me. It's good to have someone around who always understands you," he said as he sat down.

Fiona locked eyes with Pete, and they had one of their wordless conversations.

This was what family felt like, Pete thought. *This could be my family.*

Fiona was quiet as the two of them talked excitedly about the building plans. He informed her they had a budget of $300 and that it counted as his Christmas gift. Pete told him that should just about do it, because she had several plywood sheets, some other lumber, screws, and paint she'd been saving for a project and would be happy to donate to the cause. Pete was also willing to use her own money for the project if need be. The "how" of the project shifted to the "when" and Mack couldn't wait to start.

"I'm off all of next week for Thanksgiving; are you, Pete?" Mack asked eagerly.

"Well, actually, I expect to be done with my current job by the end of Monday, and then I guess I am off the rest of the week," Pete responded.

Fiona looked at her. Pete realized she was trying to tell her with her eyes that she shouldn't feel obligated to spend the holiday week with him. "Pete might have plans, honey, for Thanksgiving," she said to Mack.

The boy looked confused. "Why wouldn't you spend it with us?" he demanded.

"I think next week will work, actually," Pete said, putting her arm around his shoulder. While Mack was looking down at the design, Fiona stared at Pete and mouthed the words *thank you*.

Pete mouthed back *you're welcome*, and was seized by the impulse to kiss her. Mack snapped her out of it.

"Cool! I want to show you something else, Pete." He handed her the paper under the design. It was a school assignment he'd written about fish. "I got an A+ on my report, Pete! You can't get any higher than an A+!"

"No, you can't!" She read it carefully while he watched her and then commented on how well written it was. Then she looked at him and teased him, saying he'd grown a lot in the last two weeks.

"That's illogical, Pete. I couldn't have grown that much in such a short period of time!"

"Oh, he is growing," Fiona insisted. "He outgrew his robot pajamas!"

"I did," Mack admitted. "The sleeves got really short so Mom put them in the donation pile. I want fish pajamas now, but we're having a hard time finding a pair. We found ones with cartoon fish, but I want either real pictures or realistic drawings of fish on them. No little kid stuff."

While watching him talk, Pete noticed he'd lost a tooth. "You lost a tooth while I was gone too? See? You're growing like crazy, Mack!"

They laughed, and then he told them he was going to his room to get some fish books he'd been wanting to show her. As usual, Turtle followed him to his room. Pete took a long drink from her beer, unsure of what to say to Fiona.

"It means a lot to me that you're going to help him build his tree house, Pete. Thanks so much, really. And I'm glad our landlord said it was okay to build something into the tree. That really surprised me. Turns out he had one when he was a boy and wanted Mack to experience that. I'm lucky to have such a nice landlord."

"That was very cool of him. I'm looking forward to it. It'll be a great experience for the both of us."

Fiona pushed some hair back behind her ear, put her lips to the bottle, and took a sip of beer. Pete kept looking at her lips, thinking about kissing her, and wanted Mack to come back soon.

"He lights up when he's around you," Fiona said, shifting on the couch. "So do I. The Angelis are under your spell." She gazed into Pete's eyes just long enough to make her feel awkward.

"I couldn't decide which one to bring, so I brought them all," Mack said, as he returned with a stack of books.

"Anyone want a snack?" Fiona asked. "I was thinking about making popcorn."

Mack nodded, and so did Pete. Fiona got up and headed to the kitchen.

When she returned with a big bowl of the warm, buttery goodness, Mack was reading aloud to Pete from one of the books. The three of them sat there eating and looking at the photographs and captions. He told them about his upcoming field trip to the aquarium, which Pete thought sounded very exciting.

At 8:00, Fiona told him it was time to get his pajamas on and brush his teeth, and then he could stay up a half hour more but that was it. He tried to negotiate for more time, but his mother wouldn't budge, insisting he go to bed at the usual time because it was a school night. He gave in and left, with his furry sidekick close behind.

"He chooses his own clothes now, all the time," Fiona announced.

Pete chuckled. "Well, I knew he picked out today's outfit, because I can't imagine you would put pink, red, and orange together."

"Hell no," Fiona said, and then drained the last of her beer. "Want another?"

"Sure," Pete said, taking her shoes off so she could make herself more comfortable on the couch.

She found herself watching Fiona's ass as she walked into the kitchen. She felt conflicted; she longed for Fiona, but believed she would most likely hurt her again. If only she could shut off her brain and let her body make decisions; that would be more fun than making rational decisions.

Fiona came back with the beers. "Pete, I'm really glad you said it was okay for Mack and I to come to your opening. Thanks."

"Well, you've been supportive of my art and that means a lot to me." She took a deep breath. "There's something I want to tell you."

"Okay." Fiona suddenly seemed nervous. She took a long drink.

"Well, it's not anything horrible, or something that affects our relationship. It's just some of my own bullshit I feel the need to 'fess up to," Pete began. Fiona waited patiently for her to continue. "Remember when you asked me where I got all the interesting old stuff that I use for my collages?"

Fiona nodded.

"And I told you junk shops, flea markets, dumpsters, places like that?"

"Uh-huh."

"Well, that's true, but it's only part of the story. I steal. I take little things from my clients: stuff I think they won't notice. Taking the objects makes me part of their story, and the things become part of my story because I stole them... I just find it more interesting to work with things I've taken. I've been doing it since I started house painting. Sheila and my therapist have been urging me to stop, and I'm really trying to. In fact, just the other day I wanted to take this antique Christmas ornament—but didn't. I thought I should tell you the truth before the opening. I don't know why I didn't tell you sooner; I guess I was embarrassed..." She looked at Fiona, trying to read her face and predict her reaction.

"Thanks for telling me. I think I get it. I mean, I understand why stolen stuff would have more mojo. Have you ever been caught? Or is that something you worry about?"

"Well, I've taken probably over a hundred things, and only one client has accused me of it. Not long ago, actually. I admitted to the theft and explained to her why I did it, then offered to paint something for free, but she just wanted the items back. I don't think she wanted me to be in her house again; I took something really special, and it stung her." Pete hung her head and waited for Fiona to say more.

"I'm glad you're trying to stop, Pete," she said tenderly. "And this might sound odd, but in a way I'm relieved that I'm not the only one in this relationship with a compulsion."

Pete lifted her head, stared into Fiona's impossibly large eyes, and started laughing. Fiona laughed too, and they both leaned their heads back against the couch, giggling and looking up at the ceiling together like two cloud watchers who'd just seen the same amusing shape in the sky.

"Did you miss me?" Mack blurted as he literally plopped down on top of them, wearing new pajamas that were bright green.

"Of course we did, but can you turn down those pajamas? They're hurting my eyes," Pete teased.

"Ha-ha," Mack said sarcastically. "Hey, wanna hear some fish jokes?"

"Sure," Pete responded, "fire away!"

"What did the fish say when he posted bail?"

Pete looked at Fiona who shook her head, smiling at the corniness of it. "I've heard his fish jokes already," she said.

"I give up!" Pete declared.

"I'm off the hook!"

Pete laughed, not because the joke was funny, but because Mack was so damned cute.

"Why don't fish like basketball?"

"Dunno," Pete said.

"Because they're afraid of the net! Wanna hear one more?"

"Of course!"

"Why did the vegan go deep-sea fishing?"

Pete shook her head, waiting for the punch line.

"Just for the halibut! Get it?"

"Ooh, that's a good one, I'll have to tell it to Sheila," Pete said.

They talked some more about the tree house, and Mack promised to look at the book before next week.

Then Fiona told him he had five more minutes, and he asked if Pete could tuck him in, and if Turtle could sleep with him. Fiona and Pete exchanged glances; naturally he would assume Pete was staying over. Pete figured the dog could stay with him until she left and told him yes.

☆☆☆

When Pete agreed to let Turtle sleep with Mack, Fiona got hopeful for a second, but then realized that, just because the dog was going in his room, it didn't mean Pete was spending the night.

Fiona returned to the kitchen where she'd left her cell phone on the kitchen counter; she had a voicemail from Helen, which she promptly listened to.

"Hi, Fiona. Got your message and well, I have to say, that was a pretty wild way to measure your progress. If you'd asked me what I thought before you went, I would have advised you against it, but what's done is done. If you feel a sense of accomplishment because you didn't have sex with the people you approached, then I suppose you got something positive out of the experience. Focus on the good and not the guilt. There's no point in second-guessing yourself or regretting it. Just go forward. I'm around if you want to talk. Take care."

Helen's words were a slight comfort to her. She wondered how Calvin would react, suspecting his response might make her feel better about it all than she did now.

When Pete came out of Mack's room, Fiona was on the couch staring into space, thinking of what she could possibly say to Pete to convince her to stay, not just for the night. She wanted Pete to stay in the relationship.

"I think Turtle really missed cuddling with him; they're all curled up together," Pete said as she sat down. "I've missed him too. He's a good kid."

"He adores you, Pete; you understand him in ways that I can't."

She was sitting just two feet away from Pete, within arm's reach. Pete looked as if she wanted to wrap her arms around her but was determined not to.

"Pete, what do you need from me? For us to be together again? What do you want? Ask me for anything." An intensity shone from her eyes; she was showing her vulnerability, entreating Pete to return to her embrace.

"I need a promise," Pete replied. "A vow from you that you'll never betray me like that again, Fiona. And if you do, I'm gone. I couldn't take it. I'd break. Can you make me that promise? I want to trust you again. I also want to support you. Maybe I didn't do enough to help you with your addiction, maybe *I* let *you* down. Dr. Percy told me about a support group called COSA, Codependents of Sex Addicts. Maybe it would help me understand you and your addiction."

Fiona's eyes brimmed with tears now so she closed them, inhaling deeply before she responded. "Oh Pete. You've done more than anyone else ever did; you never judged me or made me feel like I was a bad person because I've had too much sex with too many people. And your love is loyal and true." She sniffled and clasped both her hands around both of Pete's as she spoke. "More than anything else, I want to be able to make that promise to you and keep it. But I'm just not there yet; I can promise to go to meetings regularly, keep working on my addiction, and not keep anything from you. Do you understand; can you accept this?" Pete's eyes were moist now too. Fiona was being brutally honest; she had laid herself bare.

It was hard to say who leaned in for the kiss; maybe it was the gravitational pull all lovers have that caused them to collide. They kissed, first lips on lips, then tongue to tongue. Feeling like parts of her that had been dormant were suddenly wide awake, Fiona leaned in hungrily, kissing Pete passionately. They held each other as they made out.

The top of Pete's head began to melt; she had only taken one sip of Fiona and was already intoxicated. Pete pulled away suddenly, and Fiona just looked at her, confused as to why she stopped.

"We shouldn't, Fiona. It's not that I don't want you; I do. I just think we need to figure things out before we get intimate. And I'm still angry; I don't want to make love when I'm angry. Don't you think we need more time to work it all out?"

"I suppose. But I want you too, Pete. It's so much more than sex with you; it's more than I knew I could feel. If you want to stop, I accept that. I just don't understand it." She cast her eyes downward in sorrow, then looked up at Pete.

She ran her fingers through Pete's hair, then caressed her face. They held hands and looked into each other's eyes for a bittersweet moment. Then Pete said she was going to collect Turtle and go. The dog didn't want to leave the boy; Pete had to pull him out of their cozy nest. She leashed him up, put on her coat, and gave Fiona one last hug before leaving.

☆☆☆

All the next day at work, Fiona was feeling excited but anxious about the opening that evening. She managed to leave work early, then picked up Mack from school and got home with a few hours to spare before they had to go to the gallery. She showered and changed; the hot water did not have the calming effect on her she was hoping for. She decided to lose herself in a magazine for a while.

For a science unit on waste and ecology, all the third-graders in Mack's school had been given the homework to take notes on how much trash and recycling their families produced in a week. Fiona was completely absorbed in reading when Mack told her what he was going outside to inspect; she only half heard him and nodded. When she'd nearly finished the article, Mack ran in with something in his hand, blurting excitedly.

"Mom, Mom! I found a superhero suit in our trash, look!"

The sight of her blue cat suit in his hand elicited an immediate dark feeling in her. It was something she'd never expected to see again, let alone see in her child's hands.

"Isn't it cool?" He held it against his body, the legs draped past his feet on the floor. "I think it's definitely a girl superhero costume... Is it yours, Mom?" He squinted at her excitedly. "Do you have a secret identity besides being a mom and a paralegal?"

Fiona considered the question as she got up from the couch and took it gently from his hands. She didn't want it touching him; it was an unholy connection between all that was bad about her and all that was good in her. How she longed to be superhuman in her son's eyes, and to be decent in her own eyes. She felt tarnished, like she'd never be truly shiny.

"Ah that," she started, making it up as she went along. "That's something I bought for Halloween a long time ago. Before you were born even! I was cleaning out my closet the other day and tossed it."

"But you always send things to Goodwill. I saw some other clothes in the trash too. Why not donate them instead of toss them? Our landfills are already running out of space, in fact, scientists estimate that by the year 2050, we won't—"

She interrupted him. She had to. "If you look close, you can see it's stained and has a small rip in a seam. No one wants this old thing, or any of the stuff I put in the trash." She balled up the garment forcefully, like she was angry at it, and then told him it was time for him to comb his hair and get ready to go.

"Well, I guess I'm done with my homework... Mom, you don't need a fancy suit to be a superhero. You're *my* superhero." He kissed her on the cheek and left the room.

She closed her eyes and inhaled slowly, then exhaled, opening her eyes. She wanted to cry, but instead went out to the side yard, fished out all of the fetish wear from the trash, put it into a plastic bag, and shoved it into her car. She closed the hatch and tried to put it all out of her mind.

# CHAPTER TWELVE: SKY, SEA, AND SHORE

*Have patience with everything that remains unsolved in your heart.*
*...live in the question.*
*~ Rainer Maria Rilke*

On Friday, Pete left the job site a little early so she would have plenty of time to get ready for her opening. She gave Joseph the good news: she would be all done by the end of Monday. That would give her the rest of the week off to build the tree house with Mack. Pete walked Turtle, showered, and then got dressed.

As she put on her black bra, she recalled the first time Fiona took it off her. Snapping her new shirt on, she thought about how much Fiona loved shirts with snaps because she could just yank them open. Pete slipped into her vintage tan wool trousers and then tugged her cowboy boots on. If Fiona didn't wear heels, they would be the same height tonight.

Even though she was hungry, she was too excited to eat anything before leaving; she would just pick on the snacks there. It was a chilly evening, so she put on a vest and her leather jacket, then inspected herself in the full-length mirror one more time, turned off all the lights, locked up, and left.

Sheila was there already; Pete saw her talking to one of the other artists and walked over. Sheila practically screamed when she saw her.

"Pete!" she exclaimed. "Your work looks wonderful in here. I'm so excited for you."

"Thanks," she returned as she hugged her, then said into her ear, "I needed a push; you made all this happen, Sheils."

Pete wondered when Fiona and Mack would show up and felt a little nervous, so she excused herself and got a glass of wine. When she came back to Sheila, she noticed a red dot next to the placard for one of her wall collages; she'd sold a piece already.

Suddenly, she heard the little wooden deer mocking her. She closed her eyes for a moment, trying to silence the voice, and then opened them.

"How'd it go with Red last night?" Sheila inquired.

"Well, it was great to see Mack. And we talked a little; nothing got resolved. We kissed, and she wanted me to stay over, but I left. I'm not there yet."

"Wow, so, are you feeling any less angry?"

"No. I'm still angry, and I still want her," Pete said, shrugging.

Kent came over to congratulate her on her first sale and she introduced him to Sheila. Then he encouraged them to come meet all of the other artists in the show, which they did.

About ten minutes later, Fiona and Mack arrived. She was stunning in her trench coat and an olive-green dress, and the boy had on his best button-down shirt and a sweater vest.

"Hey, handsome," Pete said to him as they walked over.

Fiona hugged her and Sheila hello, and then commented on how crowded it was.

"Hi, Pete! Mom put me in charge of pictures, so smile!" He put the camera close to her face and took a picture.

Fiona leaned in and whispered in her ear. "I thought he might get bored so I gave him a job to do; he'll probably take a few hundred pictures." Her breath on her ear aroused Pete. As Fiona pulled away, she looked her up and down. "You look great, Pete." Then she looked around the gallery and said, "So does your work!" Mack was already standing in front of Pete's area, taking pictures.

"One of my pieces sold already," Pete informed her. She scanned the gallery. "I wonder who bought it..."

"That's great! Cha-ching! Does the gallery get half?"

"Most galleries do, but Kent only takes forty percent," Pete replied.

Just then, Joseph walked over, a middle-aged woman at his side. He'd dressed up a little bit and wasn't wearing his pocket protector. Pete was happy to see him and even happier she hadn't stolen from him.

"Joseph, thanks for coming," Pete said, shaking his hand.

"My pleasure. This is my friend, Rita. Rita, this is Pete."

"Nice to meet you," Rita said. As Pete introduced them to Fiona and Sheila, she wondered if they were dating or just friends.

"My stuff is over there." She pointed to the far wall and saw another red dot.

The triangular piece made of silverware, old book covers, and knick-knacks, including the tiny toy gun from some action figure belonging to the boy in Brookline, had sold. Through the crowd she could see the gun was pointing right at her, and then it fired: *bang*! Pete touched her hand to her vest, where she'd felt a small sting. She noticed Rita was looking at her and scratched her chest to make her behavior seem normal. She shook it off and took a long sip of her wine.

The gallery was filling up, and the sounds of people talking about the art filled the air. Joseph and his guest meandered through the crowd to get a closer look at all the art. When Pete was talking to another artist, she saw her friend, Stephanie, walk in and waved her over.

"Pete! Wow! This is great, congratulations!" she said cheerfully as they hugged.

"Thanks for coming, Steph!"

"Well, I got your email, and luckily I wasn't scheduled to be out of town. Hey—" she lowered her voice. "—you gotta introduce me to your lady. How're things?"

"Up in the air, but not ugly," Pete answered.

Sheila came over to say hello; the two of them had met a few times. Then Pete introduced her to Fiona.

Moments later, when Fiona was out of earshot, Stephanie told Pete she was a total hottie and said again how much she hoped things worked out between the two of them. Pete smiled and thanked her.

It was a great evening; a definite highlight in her life. Amy, an old friend of hers from college she hadn't seen in a long time, showed up with her partner, Kathy.

When the third red dot appeared on Pete's wall, she felt her anxiety rise. Her mind sank its teeth into the notion that all the stolen objects would start talking. She excused herself from her conversation with them and looked for Sheila. When she found her, she whispered to her about what was going on.

"You're imagining things because you're feeling guilty about making money off stuff you stole. But Pete," she said, looking her in the eye, "the objects aren't talking or firing tiny bullets at you. That's your fear taking shape. You stole little things and made art out of them; what's done is done. You gotta let it go. Your pieces are selling because people love them, and because you're a good artist. The stolen stuff is just part of the story. The rest is you and your vision. Plus, you've stopped stealing, right?"

Pete nodded, looking at Joseph, who was studying some fabric collages on the wall adjacent to Pete's area.

"Also, you've got to talk to Fiona about this. I mean, not right now, but you should start sharing these episodes with her."

Pete looked at her blankly.

"I'm not saying don't talk to me when you're freaking out; you can always talk to me. I'm just suggesting you let her into your dark places a little more, like she lets you into hers. You know?" Pete still didn't have words. "So, are you okay?"

Pete looked up at her tall and wonderful friend, then searched the crowd until her eyes landed on Fiona, who smiled at her and winked. "I am. I'm okay now," she said. "Thanks."

Fiona, Amy, and Kathy were all talking to the artist who made the fabric collages, and Pete and Sheila headed over to join them. Pete noticed Mack was still near her pieces and had an odd expression on his face, so she told Sheila to go ahead and checked in with him.

"Mack? You okay? You look upset." She squatted down so she was at his eye level.

"It's just weird," he said softly.

"What's weird?"

"I've been taking pictures since I got here, but when I just zoomed in to get a close up of one of your pieces, I heard talking. In my head," he explained.

Pete tried not to look as alarmed as she was. "What do you mean, exactly? The little objects were talking? What were they saying?" Pete had her hand on his shoulder.

"Just three of them talked to me. One said what year it was made: 1958. Another told me it was from Waltham, and the third was just mumbling. I've seen weird stuff before, but I never heard stuff till now." He looked upset, and she was determined to help him.

Just then the voice that was neither male nor female started singing in her head, threatening to drown Mack out as he spoke. *Knowledge can make you rich as a king but the price of knowing things can cost you the crown.* She blinked in an attempt to mute the cruel tune and listened attentively while Mack described how he felt. *The gift of seeing can blind you, and then you're lost, never to be found.* Pete felt a chill on her back and, out of the corner of her left eye, saw a shadowy form that appeared to be a disembodied, androgynous, bald head with its mouth open, grotesquely singing the third line of the ditty. *He's like you, a helpless pawn in an ancient game of genetic roulette.* The chill remained, but Pete's eyes felt hot as she stared at Mack, struggling to focus on what he was saying, trying desperately to shut out the taunting melody and comfort him. She thought the noise had ceased, but then came the last of the lyrics. *You can't silence the noise or lift the curse; generations have tried but none have succeeded yet.*

Pete stood up, her hand still on Mack's shoulder, and in her field of vision saw the electric flashes of light that can accompany dizziness. She lost her balance a bit, and Mack's eyes got wider with concern until Pete managed to smile and shake her head, indicating she was fine.

"Did you just hear something too, Pete? You know stuff, so you must hear stuff. You do, I know you do." Emanating compassion, he looked up at her with more wisdom than any eight-year-old could be expected to possess. She forced her mouth into a half smile and shook her head.

"Let's not talk about me now, Mack; let's talk about you. This is what I think: you're extremely intelligent, and you have a very active imagination. I believe what happened is that you were looking closely through the lens and started wondering about the objects and your imagination kicked in. That's why you imagined them talking to you. They didn't really talk; that's impossible. Think about it. Does what I'm saying make sense to you?"

He considered her words carefully, and his expression started to relax. "I guess so. I guess you're right. Pete? Can you not tell Mom about this, please? I don't want her to worry."

"I can't promise you that, Mack. I think moms should know when their children are upset. Why don't you wait until tomorrow and tell her about it yourself? If you can't, I can help you. Okay?"

"Yeah, I guess so. Can you hold the camera? I took a lot of pictures, and I don't want to take any more," he said.

"Sure," she answered, taking it from him and then standing up. She took his hand in hers. "Let's go see your mom and my friends."

They walked over to the group, hand in hand, and Pete reflected on the irony of the troubled helping the troubled. She worried about Mack, and wished her grandmother were here to help him.

☆☆☆

Saturday afternoon, Fiona got a call from Calvin telling her he'd been offered the position of assistant program coordinator. He asked if she and Mack wanted to have a celebratory dinner with him that night. She accepted, teasing him about being so respectable now, and cheering him for courageously transforming his life.

He responded by saying, "You're doing the same thing, Fiona, and we'll be celebrating your triumph too."

They decided to meet at a favorite Italian restaurant of theirs, because Mack could get his pizza and the adults could enjoy grown-up food like chicken parmigiana and salad. Fiona and Mack arrived slightly early so they got a table for three.

"What exactly are we celebrating again?" Mack chirped as he fidgeted with the salt shaker.

"We're celebrating because Uncle Calvin got a job he really wanted. He'll tell you about it," Fiona answered as she scanned the crowd.

She noticed a man who was staring at her despite being out with a female companion. She suddenly wondered if she would get less attention if she buzzed her hair off. Many times over the years she'd thought of doing it, but the truth was, she liked her hair; she enjoyed running her hands through it and wearing it up or down. She looked away from him, hoping to discourage him.

"Look at the menu, Mackles; see if you want to have something besides pizza," she suggested.

"But I love pizza, I don't need to try something new."

"Mack, every food you love now was once new to you, even pizza. I'm just saying it's good for you to try new things."

He shrugged and sprinkled a little bit of salt on the table, then tried to balance the bottom edge of the saltshaker on the crystals; this was a trick he had seen Pete do but hadn't been able to imitate.

"Don't dump any more salt out, honey. Remember, Pete said it only takes a few crystals to balance the salt shaker."

"Yeah, yeah, I know, Mom... I can't do it; it's too hard," he said in frustration.

Fiona saw Calvin walk in and waved so he could find her more easily. Her admirer was still eyeing her from a few tables away; Fiona hoped Calvin would block his view when they sat down.

"Hey, family," Calvin said as he approached the table, "great to see you both." He gave Fiona a kiss on the cheek and Mack a fake punch in the shoulder.

"Hi, Uncle Calvin," the boy said. "I can't do this trick. It's too hard."

"Ah, yes, that's a toughie." He sat down, and when he was all the way into the booth, Mack gave an order.

"Don't anyone touch or bump the table; I can't have any vibrations if I'm going to succeed at this!"

"Yes, sir!" Calvin responded, putting his hands up to show Mack he wouldn't dare interfere with his efforts.

"Congrats, Mr. Assistant Program Coordinator!" Fiona said to her dear friend. "You got it! Are you excited? Did La Fleur Bleue take it okay when you said you wanted to cut your shifts down?"

"Yeah, they're cool with it. I made it clear to them that I couldn't work Tuesday nights, so no worries there. I'm going to keep three shifts to start and just try my best to cut back on expenses to make my new salary work. I'm definitely excited, but I'm also kind of nervous because there's so much I have to learn. I start the Monday after Thanksgiving!"

"Well, you're nervous because you want to do a good job, but they wouldn't have hired you unless they were confident in your abilities. You'll be great!"

"Got it! Mom, take a picture and send it to Pete!" He was beaming with satisfaction. She pulled out her phone, Mack lowered his head so he would be in the shot, and she took a few pictures while he made funny faces.

"What shall I text her from you, son?"

"Um..." He scrunched up his face in thought and then said, "Write: *finally did your trick. Wish you were here to see it.*"

Their server came, and the saltshaker fell over right as she approached. She hadn't bumped the table; it must have been the vibrations of her footsteps. Mack was all right with it since his feat had already been celebrated, documented, and shared with Pete.

"Calvin, Mack asked me about your new job, and I said you'd explain it to him," Fiona said.

"Well, Mack, as you know, I've been working as a waiter for a long time, and I decided I needed a change. You know the volunteer work I do, helping people?"

"Yeah. Mom says I'm going to do volunteer work soon," he answered.

"Right. It's an awesome thing to do. I've always loved helping people, so I got a job at an agency that's dedicated to supporting young homeless people. I'll be the assistant program coordinator, which means I take care of details and help in lots of different ways. I'm really excited about it." Fiona was happy to see Calvin so animated as he spoke.

After dinner, they all ordered dessert, and Mack spontaneously invited Calvin over to watch a movie. Calvin said that sounded like a great idea, and Fiona asked Mack if he was sure he could stay awake for a whole movie. Mack insisted he could, saying Saturday nights were for staying up late.

Despite his assurances, halfway through the animated movie Mack selected, he was sound asleep between them on the couch.

"Sorry," Fiona said softly.

"I'm not. It's good to be with you guys. Want to tell me about Pete's opening? About you and her? I wanted to go but I had to work last night."

"I know, and she knows that too," Fiona said. "Let me carry this guy off to bed first; I don't want him hearing any of this."

Calvin said he wanted to tuck him in, and she told him to go for it. When he returned, Fiona told him all about the opening, and where things were with her and Pete.

"So, you're kind of in limbo, huh?" His eyes were the shape of concern.

"Yes. It's hard, but it's better than things being over. I know she loves me; she just doesn't trust me right now. I have to earn that back."

"Hmm..." He thought about it. "Maybe so."

"I did something kind of crazy to try to prove to myself I was getting better. That I have a better grip on my sex addiction."

"You've got me curious..."

She told him about going to the sex club, mentioning the highlights but leaving out the nitty-gritty. His eyes got wide as he listened, and at one point he closed them. Fiona wasn't sure if he was imagining what she described, disapproving, or just concentrating, but when she was done, she was anxious about what his response would be.

He looked at her as he inhaled deeply and sighed. "Oh Fiona. My dear Fiona. I love you, you know that. And most of the time I understand you. But just when I think I know you as well as a friend could, you surprise me. I'm in no position to pass judgment on you, that's for sure, but I gotta say, that was kind of a crazy idea." He squeezed her shoulder affectionately as he continued. "The way I see it, in order to prove you could resist sex with strangers, you had sex with strangers."

"What do you mean? I didn't really have sex with anyone. No one touched my—" He cut her off.

"Don't get defensive, I'm not attacking you, sweetie. Just listen. Just because there wasn't any penetration, and no one touched your private parts, doesn't mean you didn't have sexual encounters. You know that. I mean, shit, sometimes clients paid me to just stand there naked while they touched themselves. That's sex. Other times me and a client would be fully clothed, just grinding against each other. That's sex. It's all sex, Fi."

She hung her head a little, starting to feel stupid and ashamed.

"But I totally get why you did it. You did it for love. You love Pete with all your heart, and you desperately want to be faithful to her, so you wanted to put yourself in a tempting situation to see if you could hold your own. And basically, you did. From what you just said, you got aroused but didn't take things further. To me, it's a case of good intentions, bad idea. But if you feel a sense of accomplishment, or even triumph, no one can take that away from you. That's yours."

"Well, it's not easy to hear you say that, but thanks for being honest with me... I threw away my fetish wear. I never want to go to a sex club again. I'm done with those days, I'm serious. I'm a mother, and I hope to be a good partner, and I just can't go backward." He gave her a hug, and she leaned into him, feeling like she might cry.

"Yeah," he said lovingly, "keep going forward."

☆☆☆

The opening was a transformative experience for Pete. It encouraged her to show and sell her art; it made her feel more like an artist and less like a house painter. She looked forward to seeing all the photographs Mack took; she was glad he'd documented the event because it was so important to her. She was inspired, and spent most of the weekend making art. She finished the piece on her workbench and started two others, one of which was a mobile.

As she worked, she blasted music and dreamed of doing more with her art. Perhaps she would create a website for her collages and sculptures and try to keep showing and selling. Though she was still confused and somewhat angry about her relationship with Fiona, her mind was clear when it came to art. She wanted to see Fiona and Mack before the tree house project began but was feeling awkward about calling.

Pete was working on her mobile Sunday morning when her phone rang. She wiped her hands, grabbed it, and saw it was Fiona. "Hey," Pete said.

"Good morning, is this Petra Orvatch, the famous artist?"

Pete laughed. "No, it's Pete, the house painter who dreams of being a successful artist. I was actually just working on a new piece, a mobile. How are you?"

"That sounds interesting. I'm doing okay. I was just calling because I have a kid here who has a few hundred pictures from your opening that he'd like to show you. I was wondering if you wanted to come over for dinner and pictures tonight. But be warned, he will most likely talk your ear off about the tree house. What do you say?"

Pete was conflicted because, although she craved being near them, she also wanted to avoid contact with Fiona until she knew what to do about their fractured relationship. She decided to say yes, because she was going to be over there building the tree house soon anyway, so she might as well go tonight.

"Okay. What time? And what should I bring?"

"Six. Just bring your dog," Fiona said.

"All right, see you then."

"Bye," Fiona said.

Pete set the phone down and had to admit she felt excited about going over there. She didn't expect their problems to get worked out; she would focus on Mack and just play it by ear with Fiona.

She sat on her stool and stared up at the mobile, which was hanging on a hook suspended from the ceiling. It was her first attempt at a kinetic sculpture since she'd made a simple mobile in elementary school. The crisscrossed rods were metal, each of them about three feet long, and from them hung wires to which she'd attached a few items. She'd made three-winged fish out of clay, and two large five-pointed stars. Now she was sculpting some hearts, but not the pretty, symmetrical ones. She was looking at *Gray's Anatomy* and making anatomically correct human hearts about four inches across. Pete wasn't sure what else she wanted to attach, but she was enjoying the challenge of creating something new. After spending the whole day at her workbench, she showered, changed, grabbed a nice bottle of red wine she'd been saving, and left.

Mack greeted her and Turtle at the door and said his mom was cooking.

"Dinner smells delicious!"

"Yeah, it's fried chicken, mashed potatoes, spinach, and corn. She said she had a craving for fried chicken. Hey, Turtle!" Dog and boy greeted each other exuberantly.

When Pete went into the kitchen, she saw Fiona in an apron. Her hair was up, but some of it had broken free of the bun she'd put it in, and she had some flour on the side of her face.

"I brought some wine," Pete said. "Dinner smells amazing!"

"Thanks, I don't make this very often, but I really love it. I hope you will too."

Fiona gave her a hug, and Pete defaulted to a kiss on the cheek, but her aim was off; her lips landed closer to her ear, giving Fiona shivers. Pete felt it too, and suddenly thought of cohesive attraction; she remembered learning in high school how molecules that were mutually attractive would stick together.

"Do you need help?" Pete asked.

"No, but you can open the wine and pour us some. I bet Mack wants you."

"Right," Pete said. She got the corkscrew, opened the bottle, poured two glasses, and handed one to Fiona.

"Pete?" Mack called from the living room.

The women smiled at each other, and Pete went to him. He was on the couch with Turtle, who was getting a good belly scratch.

Mack looked anxious as he spoke. "I didn't tell my mom about the voices I heard. I didn't know the best way to explain it. Can you help me tell her? Not at dinner, or right after, because we'll be looking at pictures. Maybe when I go to bed?"

"Of course, Mack." She put her hand on his head affectionately and decided to change the topic. "So, you ready for Project Tree House? Have you had a chance to look at that book?"

He told her he'd read through it and learned some things. They discussed their plans until Fiona came out and announced that dinner was ready.

"This is so yummy, Mom!" Mack proclaimed after he took his first bite of crunchy, juicy goodness. "You should make it more often."

"I'm glad you like it."

"It's delectable," Pete praised, suddenly thinking about Fiona's taste.

"Thanks, I'm so glad you think so," Fiona said before taking a slow sip of merlot.

At dinner, they talked about the art opening, Pete's new pieces, Fiona's latest case, and, of course, the tree house. When Mack asked if Pete was spending Thanksgiving with them, there was an awkward silence that was shattered when Turtle sneezed loudly, which made Mack laugh. Pete stared at Fiona, who jumped in, not wanting her to feel uncomfortable.

"I think she's spending it with her family, sweetie."

"But can't you share the day with us, maybe see your family in the morning and then come to Maine with us in the afternoon?" he asked before shoveling an enormous bite of mashed potatoes into his mouth. Pete was thinking of the best way to answer this when Fiona swooped in.

"They live in Springfield, honey, and it's not close by." She drank more wine as she tried to read Mack's expression.

"Mack, when we spend this week together building the tree house, that'll be better than eating turkey across the table from each other. I appreciate the invitation, and I'd like to meet your grandparents and see Anthony, but I'll be with my family. I guarantee you, our structure will be all done before you have to go back to school," Pete promised. "Unless it rains, but I don't think it's going to rain." She took a big bite of chicken and looked at Fiona, who was smiling at her.

"Okay," he said, and ate another ridiculously large bite of food. Fiona was reminded how quickly kids get over things, then wondered if she'd ever get over Pete.

After dinner, Mack went to get Fiona's laptop and brought it into the living room, then called to his mom and Pete, who were cleaning up after dinner. "Come and see the pictures!"

"Be right there!" Fiona yelled, then turned to Pete. "We haven't looked at any of them yet; he wanted to wait for you."

Pete smiled, and the two of them finished straightening up the kitchen without talking. It wasn't an awkward silence, but rather the comfortable kind lovers can share.

When they came into the living room, Mack was seated in the middle of the big, brown couch with the computer on his lap. He patted the cushions on both sides of him, inviting them to sit. Turtle jumped up and leaned against him.

"Come on, there are lots of pictures to see!"

They sat. Fiona put her arm around Mack's shoulders, and her hand touched Pete's arm. She didn't move away; she liked the contact.

The three of them looked at over two hundred photographs, some of which Mack commented on, explaining why he'd taken them. Pete narrated several shots, and Fiona commented on how good the photography was.

"I like taking pictures," Mack said. "It's fun to turn real life into rectangles."

After they'd looked at and talked about all the pictures, it was time for Mack to go to bed. He campaigned to stay up later, but was unsuccessful, pouting ever so slightly. When she told him Pete could tuck him in, he was more agreeable. As usual, Turtle followed, and once they were in Mack's room, he asked her if she could go tell his mother he wanted to talk to her about something.

"Sure thing, Mack, and don't be nervous. You'll see; you'll feel better when you tell your mother what happened." She gave him a hug, instructed Turtle to give him kisses, and then went to talk to Fiona, who was sitting on the couch, filling their wine glasses.

"You have a rather serious expression on your face," Fiona observed. "Is everything okay?"

"Yeah, it's just that Mack has something he wants to talk to you about."

"Oh," she said, getting up.

Pete started walking with her. "And he wants me there too," she said to Fiona, who had a worried expression on her face.

When Fiona walked in, Turtle looked up at her with love-eyes and thumped his tail. Pete sat on the bed and scratched behind the dog's ears.

"Hey, Mackster, what did you want to tell me?" she asked gently.

He pursed his lips, obviously trying to think of the best way to say it all. Pete wondered if she should help him, but decided to wait a minute before she said anything.

"Well, something happened at Pete's opening that was weird, and I told her about it, and she helped. But when I told her I didn't want to tell you, she said that I should. That moms would want to know that kind of stuff."

"What happened?" Fiona asked, her mind flooding with worry.

"I heard talking. In my head. Things were talking, and things can't talk. I was trying to take their picture, well, pictures of the sculptures they were in, and they talked to me." He stopped speaking because he was starting to feel uncomfortable.

"I'm not understanding, sweetie. Can you explain it a little more?"

He sighed, then inhaled before speaking. "I was taking pictures for Pete, and one of the little things told me the year it was made. Another said where it was from. Pete said because I'm smart, I have an overactive imagination, and that's why I thought I heard stuff. It made me feel better because I didn't like them talking in my head..." His eyes were big as he looked at his mother, awaiting her response.

"Well, I'm really glad you told me, Mack. Parents like to know about anything that upsets their children. And I think Pete is right. It's your imagination. Has anything like that ever happened before?"

"No."

"Will you tell me if anything similar happens again?"

"Okay," he said, then threw his arms around his mother. Pete put her hand on his head affectionately, and then left so they could have privacy if they wanted. Mack asked his mom to stay with him a while, and she did.

When she emerged from his room, Pete sat on the couch drinking wine. Fiona sat down, careful to leave some space between them.

"Are you worried about him?" she asked Fiona.

"Hmm," she began. "Not worried. A little concerned. I mean, I know he's an unusual kid. His brain is wired differently than mine, that's for sure. But I don't like that he was scared. I'm glad he had you to talk to. Do you think he needs help?"

"You mean therapy?" Pete asked.

"I guess, or something. It just seems like he feels burdened, and I want to take that weight off his shoulders, or at least be able to explain to him why he feels this way."

"I'm not sure, Fiona. I think you need to pay close attention to any behavior that seems odd and maybe, yeah, find someone he can talk to, someone who can figure him out." She drank more wine, enjoying the buzz it gave her.

"I'm so glad he has you," Fiona said, biting her lip.

"I'm grateful for him in my life, Fiona. It's the time of year we're supposed to take stock of our blessings, and he's top of the list." Fiona smiled and said nothing, which left space for Pete to say more. "I'm not just in a relationship with you; I'm in one with Mack too and—" She stopped because she was starting to get upset. "I don't want to lose that."

Fiona shifted a little, set down her nearly empty glass, and pulled out her bun, which made her hair fall down at crazy angles. She ran her hand through it as she thought about what she wanted to say. "So, are you saying if we break up, you still want to be part of Mack's life?"

"No," Pete replied, "well, yes. Oh, I don't know. I guess what I'm saying is I'm not sure what will happen with us, and I would be really sad if I didn't see Mack anymore... But I would understand if you told me I had to stop seeing you both." Pete closed her eyes and waited for a reply.

"Oh Pete, honestly, the idea that we are really over terrifies me. I can barely get past the thought that I might not see you anymore to think about what it would all mean to Mack. I can't tell you yes, that would be okay, but I can't tell you no either." She shrugged.

Pete let her words sink in before she spoke. "Okay," she said, "fair enough."

Then she turned to face Fiona, and they just looked at each other for a few seconds before kissing. Pete's better judgment began to give way, passion surging through her body as they made out.

After a few minutes, Fiona paused to talk to her.

"Are you still angry?"

"Yes," Pete answered.

"Are you angry right now?" She ran her hand up Pete's thigh.

"No."

"Good."

She nuzzled Pete's neck and bit her lightly, which drove Pete wild. The rational parts of Pete's brain gave in to her feral desire; she surrendered to the unknown, gave in to the unresolved, and yielded herself to the irresistible temptation known as Fiona. Before long, Fiona was on top of her and the couch could no longer accommodate their ardor.

☆☆☆

Fiona got up and extended her hand to Pete, saying, "Come on," and led her to the bedroom like she'd done so many times before.

They rolled around, but, as inflamed as they were, neither initiated sex, both of them a mixture of desirous and tentative.

She hadn't made love with Pete in weeks, and Fiona wanted her so badly it hurt; being so close to Pete and not having sex was ten times harder than her sex club test, but she found the will to stop because she didn't want to jeopardize their chances of staying together long-term. She knew Pete needed her anger to leave before she wanted to be vulnerable with her. She understood how Pete wanted to feel she could trust her again before they shared skin. Their faces were pressed together, and as Fiona gently kissed Pete's eyelids, she tasted a trace of salt, then pulled away to look at her.

"What is it, baby? Talk to me." She ran a hand through the slick black hair she loved so much, trying to soothe her lover.

"I'm afraid I'll scare you away. I know you're already worried about Mack, and I don't want you to be concerned about me too." She looked down.

"I haven't been chased off by your demons yet, have I? You can tell me anything, Pete."

Fiona kissed her forehead, and the walls started to come down. Pete spoke quickly out of nervousness, clearly wanting to get it over with. She told her about the voice she sometimes heard in her head and how it had sung to her and taken on a shadowy shape while Mack was explaining his experience at the gallery. She said she intended to talk with Sheila and her doctor about it and then asked Fiona if she thought she was crazy.

"No, I do not think you're crazy. Look, I believe anything is possible in this big-ass universe. If Grandma Sweets and her people believed in the gift of seeing, and that cultural conviction doesn't make sense to the rest of society, maybe the voice you described represents some kind of conflict. Or maybe it's actually a spirit trying to communicate with you; maybe you receive information most people can't and that makes you important. Meeting you confirmed my belief in inexplicable and magical events. I think—" She paused and stroked Pete's cheek tenderly, her eyes filling with briny emotion. "I think you should worry more about how to manage the overload you experience in your mind than what it is or what it means. You've been getting help for a long time, and you're better now than you have been in the past. You may never know exactly what it's all about, but you can learn to cope with it. I believe you can, Pete, just like I know I can deal with my problems. I wish we could both lay all of our burdens down, but maybe the best we can do right now is help each other shoulder them."

Pete soaked her words in and sniffled. She thanked Fiona with her eyes, and then their lips met; the magnitude of emotion registered by one kiss amazed them. Waves of pleasure began to wash away words and worry. Desire inundated them, and clothes were jettisoned for the journey their bodies had begun. Feelings quieted their minds, making words unnecessary. They were naked, lying on their sides facing each other as they kissed and bit each other's lips, necks, and earlobes. Drawn together by chemical signals, they exchanged transmissions of love-colored lust.

Pete had to touch her; for her, touching Fiona's slick pussy was like coming home. Fiona's intuition told her to receive before she gave, so she bent her knee up and loosened her hips to invite Pete further in. When Fiona wasn't moaning or breathing too heavily, they kissed deeply. Her mounting pleasure made Pete hard and swollen with longing.

Both women opened their eyes at the same time, holding each other there in that tender place, and Pete silently gave Fiona the permission she'd been waiting for. She recovered the treasure she'd thought was lost to her as emotions came with such intensity Fiona thought she might cry as she touched Pete. Lost in the rhythm lovers love to lose themselves in, they moved against each other, inside each other, until Fiona could no longer hold back her orgasm or her tears. Pete climaxed with her, and as their eyes locked, Pete cried too. She wrapped both arms around Fiona so tightly there was scarcely any space between them.

They inhaled then exhaled, breathing as one, and then Fiona whispered, "Please don't ever stop crying with me."

Pete woke up at 5:30. Reluctantly, she got out of bed and dressed quietly in the glow of the night-light. Fiona opened her eyes just as Pete was about to go.

Before Fiona could say anything, Pete knelt next to the bed and said, "I have to go now. I gotta do a couple of things before I go to work. Go back to sleep." Then she kissed her and went to collect Turtle from Mack's room.

As Pete drove home through the dark, Fiona fell back to sleep and had a dream about waltzing on a rooftop with Pete.

☆☆☆

Joseph was his usual pleasant self, offering Pete coffee when she arrived. He complimented her again on her artwork and then left her to finish up. The work went quickly, and Pete had Fiona on her mind most of the day. Flashbacks of their lovemaking made her shiver.

When she finished up, Joseph gave her the final check; they shook hands and then said their good-byes.

Because of the holiday, Pete's session with Dr. Percy had been scheduled for today, not their usual time. Pete was thinking of telling her she was going to stop their work together and was feeling nervous about it. She knew Dr. P would ask her what she planned to do to manage her issues, and because she didn't have a concrete answer, she would simply tell her she felt compelled to follow her instincts.

Cambridge Holistic Health and Wellness Center must have been doing all right, she thought, because they'd redecorated their waiting room in the last few weeks. Gone was the wallpaper, turquoise vinyl chairs, and cheap plastic wall clock that had cozened her nearly three months ago. The walls had been painted a soothing, earthy gray, and Pete couldn't help but notice the crooked color line where they met the white ceiling. The new chairs were burnt-orange, made of high quality leatherette, and more comfortable than their predecessors. Roughly in the same spot the old clock used to be hung a modern digital clock. As Pete looked at it, the liquid black rectangles that formed the seven-segment display numbers twitched, and 3:50 became 3:51. Something about the clock being digital rather than analog comforted Pete; her personal logic told her that meant it couldn't mess with her mind like the old one had.

Then she worried she was thinking about it too much and that gave it power over her, so she forced herself to take in other details of the makeover, like the plants and artwork. She guessed Dr. P had a hand in selecting the greenery and thought the room looked and felt much better, much healthier. She studied a photograph of a jungle, wondering where it was taken, then looked at Clark Kent, who was such an improvement over Gum Snapper. He'd grown a beard since the last time Pete was here, and she thought his nickname no longer suited him, because Superman shouldn't have a beard.

There were seven other people besides her in the waiting room: five women and two men. One of the women appeared to be severely depressed; her face looked like it had forgotten how to smile, its parts all weighed down by the invisible gravity of sorrow. Sad Mask was reading a magazine but looked to Pete like she was just flipping through it robotically, not reading or even seeing the pictures on the pages. The man across from Sad Mask was one of the hairiest people Pete had ever seen. He had long, black hair in a ponytail, bushy sideburns that connected to a thick, untrimmed beard, and eyebrows that joined in the middle. His sleeves were rolled up, revealing arms that had fur all the way around them, not just on the top part like most people. Wolfman's watchband was submerged in his pelt, with only the face of the watch showing above the miniature black forest.

When her eyes again landed on the clock, Pete saw it read 3:47, then felt a light sweat on the back of her neck. Not sure if time had in fact gone backward four minutes, she pulled her phone out of her pocket and saw that it too read 3:47.

*Not again*, Pete thought.

She closed her eyes and took several slow, deep breaths. When she opened them, there were three people waiting for their appointments, not seven. The clock said 5:01, and it was completely dark outside. She'd just lost over an hour and had no idea where it went. Her head started aching, her heart rate accelerated, and her thoughts began to race. She panicked, wondering if she was stuck in some time trap; maybe she would always have to exist with time that moved in more than one direction.

*What if*, she considered, *time spun so far backward that I ended up in early September again, eleven Wednesdays ago, the day I met Fiona. And what if one thing changed, if I did one thing differently, and that altered the trajectory of the whole day and I never met her. I don't want to go down a path that doesn't lead to Fiona.* She was perspiring more now; her face was moist, and her mouth went dry. She felt queasy, and her head pain intensified.

Pete closed her eyes again, fighting an urge to yell out. In her head, she heard herself scream, so she started coaching herself, trying to calm her thoughts. *It's all right, Pete, you'll get through this. You know how you are, how you've always been: your reality is just different from other people's. You see things and know stuff, and it can't all be explained. You're magical and important, like Fiona said. This time confusion will stop, and you will have your appointment with Dr. P and it will all make sense again. Fiona is real, and time shifts can't change that.*

She opened her eyes, and the clock on the wall said 3:59, and the last traces of daylight could be seen outside the windows again. Sad Mask was gone, but Wolfman was still there.

"Petra?" the receptionist called out softly. "You can go in now." He smiled, the new beard accentuating the kindness in his face.

"Thanks," Pete returned as she got up and walked to Dr. Percy's office. She wiped some moisture off her forehead with the back of her hand and went in.

"Pete!" Dr. P called out from her old leather chair. After Pete closed the door behind her, Dr. P stood up to give her a hug but paused, a concerned look on her face. "You feeling okay? You look pale."

"I'm okay now. Just had a wave of nausea in the waiting room. I'm fine."

They hugged, and then Pete settled into the rocking chair. Rather than tell Dr. P what she'd just experienced, Pete decided to start off with the art show. She kept an eye on the clock as she spoke, to make sure time wasn't shifting again, and also to be sure she left enough time in their hour together to talk about what had happened in the waiting room. Rocking her chair slowly the whole time, Pete told her about the tempting silver dog, how she didn't take it, and how she thought she could stop stealing from clients.

Dr. Percy praised her for getting her artwork in a show, and for not stealing. She told Pete that these behaviors demonstrated personal progress and good mental health.

She asked where things were with Fiona, and Pete described the steamy gray area they were now in and told her about the upcoming tree house project. Dr. P encouraged her to take her time figuring out the next steps and said she thought that no matter what happened between Pete and Fiona, spending time with Mack was a good thing to do right now.

Pete was on the verge of telling the doctor she was going to end their therapy sessions, but surprised herself when she started talking about what had just happened.

"Well, there's something else I have to tell you about, Dr. P." Pete inhaled before continuing. "The clock," she began, "the new digital clock on the wall, it—" She stopped and rubbed her face. She was so weary of her bizarre and disorienting experiences. "Time went backward and then back to the right time. It freaked me out. I had a little panic attack and had to talk myself through it." She stopped and looked at the doctor.

"Well, Pete, I'm sorry you experienced that. I wish these kinds of things didn't happen to you. If it's any comfort, I met a Polish psychiatrist at a conference last week, and she also has a patient who experiences what you do. She's conducting a scientific study on him in the hope of developing more helpful customized treatment. Like you, he was diagnosed as having bipolar disorder in the past. He has similar unusual behaviors and reports strange incidents with clocks. She's promised to share her findings with me."

"Hmm," Pete said. "I don't know if it comforts me or disturbs me to know that other people go through this..."

"Well, my dear," Dr. Percy said encouragingly, "what you can take comfort in are the positive developments in your life that you just told me about. You should cheer yourself for all of it, Pete."

Pete nodded, but couldn't get to a place where she felt celebratory. She wanted to rest her head on Fiona's shoulder and tell her about the clock. Time was up, so Dr. P said good-bye, and as they hugged, Pete felt relieved she hadn't told her she wanted to stop therapy.

She went home, cooked herself dinner, then sat on the couch with Turtle and wrote in her journal about what had happened. She also called Sheila, not only to check in about her upsetting experience, but also to see how she was handling the absence of Damon in her life. They talked for a long time, and she felt better afterward; she knew they would always be close, and that fact was a comfort amidst all the disturbances in her life.

Just before Pete went to bed, Fiona called her.

"Hey, babe. I just wanted to thank you for a very special evening."

"You don't have to thank me. It just sort of happened, huh?"

"Well," Fiona started, "I know, but it happened because your heart was open to it. I mean, I know it doesn't mean our problems are fixed or we're back together, but it means a lot to me."

"Me too, Fi."

"Mack can't wait to start construction; I haven't seen him this excited in a long time," Fiona said.

"I'm looking forward to it too." Pete yawned, realizing how tired she was.

"Well, I'll let you get to bed. Bye."

"Bye, Fiona."

☆☆☆

Since Calvin was free Tuesday, he offered to help Pete and Mack get lumber for the tree house. Pete was glad to have help with the large, bulky sheets of plywood they needed to buy. On the way to the store, Mack chirped away about how they would paint the structure after it was built and how he wanted to decorate it inside. Calvin and Pete listened as attentively as they could, occasionally smirking at each other over his head as he went on to describe in excruciating detail how he wanted it to look. His color ideas were wild, but the adults just listened without commenting on them.

"I've got work gloves for you in the truck, Mack, for handling the lumber. Let's go," Pete said.

At the store, Mack insisted on inspecting their shopping list twice before checking out. He wanted to be absolutely sure they had everything they needed. Then, when he was done, he asked about paint.

Pete told him they needed to think about their color scheme first and then come back for primer and paint. He was satisfied with this plan, and they made their way to the register.

After they paid, Calvin and Pete lifted the sheets of plywood into the back of the pickup, and Mack loaded the hardware and smaller pieces. On the way back to the house, they stopped for bagels so they'd have snacks while they worked. Mack was still talking excitedly about his ideas for paint colors.

"Well, big guy," Calvin began, "I'm not sure your mom would be so psyched about neon orange with lime-green trim and a baby-blue door. That's a lot of color, you know?"

Mack bit his lower lip in contemplation, opened his mouth to respond, but then closed it again.

"Look at the houses as we drive by," Pete suggested. "See the color combinations on them?" Mack did as she told him, observing that many houses were white or some shade of beige, and only a few were what he considered a real color, like the blue and green ones.

"So, you want our tree house to be just as boring as these houses? I don't."

Pete and Calvin made eye contact, and then Pete responded.

"No, no way, Mack. I just think we should choose colors you're going to like for a while, not outrageous ones. I know we'll find colors you like, but we will have to compromise to get there. You know what I'm saying?"

"Yeah," he mumbled, hanging his head.

"But you know what?" Pete asked. "You can make the inside whatever crazy colors you want it to be."

"Really?" he asked, his face brightening.

"Definitely!"

Mack smiled, and Pete noticed Calvin was smiling too. He winked at her over Mack's head and mouthed the words *good job*.

Later, after they'd brought the lumber into the backyard and set up the sawhorses, Calvin told her again how well she communicated with Mack. "Really, Pete. I suspect he's been craving the kind of understanding you demonstrate. He's a pretty unusual kid, but you seem to have him figured out. You're great with him; I'm so glad you're part of his life."

"Thanks, Calvin."

"I told Fiona not to blow it with you, and I know she's doing her very best not to. You're good for her."

"Pete! Come on!" Mack shouted from the kitchen. "Let's build!"

Calvin gave her and Mack good-bye hugs and left. When Pete went out to the yard, she saw Mack was all suited up in his safety goggles, tool belt, and work gloves. She pulled out her phone and took a picture to text to Fiona.

A few minutes later, when they were measuring and marking the wood, Pete felt her pocket vibrate, pulled out her phone, and saw a message from Fiona: *Love it! Tx for brightening up my morning. xo.*

Mack teased her, telling her to put her phone away, saying they had too much work to do. Turtle barked, as if in agreement.

And work they did: measuring, cutting, and assembling all day, stopping only for a bagel and later for lunch. By the time it got dark, they had the platform and the whole frame built. The structure was about seven feet off the ground, so they designed and constructed a wooden ladder and attached it to the massive red oak tree. Mack must have climbed up and down it twenty times before they put away their ladders and tools and covered the lumber with a tarp.

Pete told Mack to take a bath, then she sat in the kitchen, trying to figure out what to do with herself. She was sure Fiona would want her to stay for dinner and spend the night, but she didn't know if she should.

Just as she was mulling it over, Fiona texted, saying she was bringing home her favorite pizza as a thank-you dinner. Because of Thanksgiving, Fiona's regular SAA meeting was canceled. Pete decided to eat with them but go home afterwards.

When Fiona came home, Mack was in his pajamas and visibly tired from his workday. "Mom!" he yelled from the couch. Turtle got to her first, jumping and dancing for her attention. "We got a lot done. You gotta see it, it's so cool!"

"Okay, sweetie, that's great," she said, setting the pizza down so she could hug him.

She tossed her bag and coat onto the chair near the entry, came in, and gave Pete a hug too. Pete caught a whiff of lavender and wanted to bury her face in Fiona's hair.

"Hey, you. Hungry?"

"It smells great; we're *extra* hungry," Pete said as they walked into the kitchen. Mack had already turned the patio light on and gone into the backyard. He called for his mother to come. What she saw was no simple child's tree house; even in the dim light, she could see how beautifully designed it was.

"Wow! Impressive!" she exclaimed, taking it all in. "How did you do all this, just the two of you?" She was standing directly under the platform, awestruck, as she gazed upward.

"We cut the plywood into sheets small enough for us to handle and then—"

"Pete's really strong, Mom!" Mack interrupted. "Mostly I just held the ladder in place while she lifted the pieces up. We built the frame for the floor first."

"Mack, honey, Pete was talking. Try not to interrupt," his mother chided.

"Oh, sorry," he said, rubbing his eye.

"It's okay, Mack, I know you're excited," Pete said. "I'm hoping to be done with the construction and have the outside painted by the day after Thanksgiving. The hard part is done. It's totally sturdy too. We made the ladder extra safe by adding a railing, see?"

Pete showed her what she meant, and Fiona nodded in approval. Fiona held Mack's hand, and Pete took his other one, and the three of them walked slowly around the majestic tree.

"Mackles, how many people will it be able to hold?"

He spoke excitedly when he responded to her question, as if he'd just been waiting to explain it to her. "Well, the platform is built as close to the trunk as possible, but we left some space around the tree to allow for ten to fifteen years of growth. We made the platform level by cantilevering the beams and supporting them from below. We also added diagonal bracing." He paused, looking at Pete to make sure he was explaining it correctly.

She nodded at him, smiling.

"We used lag bolts, because they cause less damage to the tree than through bolts. Oh, and Pete talked to the tree! She apologized to it before drilling the first hole into the trunk. And we didn't use too many fasteners because it turns out that one large bolt is better than lots of screws or nails." He traced his hand along the trunk as he spoke and then finally answered her question. "We researched how to design it to hold a lotta weight safely; this tree house can hold four adults or a maximum of one thousand pounds. Pretty cool, huh?"

"Wow, Mack. I didn't know you guys went that deep into the engineering of it, but everything you say makes sense. I think you should take lots of pictures as you're building it and bring them into school for show-and-tell. Pavel and Wylie will really love playing in this thing. Let's invite them over when it's all done, okay?"

"Yeah," he answered.

"And maybe Jeffrey from your class could come over?"

"Sure, maybe." Mack shrugged and then changed the topic. "Pete said we had to choose a sensible color for the outside but that I could paint the inside any colors I wanted!"

"Sounds good, Mack. I'm just amazed at how great it's coming along. You and Pete are an awesome team. The pizza's getting cold and so am I; let's go eat!"

They paused by the patio for one last look and went inside.

At dinner, Pete asked Fiona about work, and she said things were quiet for the moment, because of the holiday. She asked Pete about her mobile, and Pete told her she was going to work on it some more that night. Trying to hide her disappointment, Fiona asked her more about the sculpture.

Shortly after dinner, Mack announced he was very tired and wanted to go to bed. Both Fiona and Pete tucked him in. He talked about the tree house before he fell asleep; the last thing he said was that he wanted to make sure no dark spirits were able to get into it.

Fiona stared at Pete, her eyes wide with worry.

"It's okay," Pete said softly before they left his room.

They sat on the couch with Turtle between them.

"I'm not sure I'm qualified to take on *dark spirits*; I think it's time to get help with Mack, don't you?" Fiona's eyes were filled with the kind of apprehension caused only by parenthood. Mothers liked to fix everything for their children, but Mack's issues would need more than an extra kiss or a Band-Aid.

"Probably so. I mean, I've been struggling with my own stuff lately and wondering if therapy is the best way to manage it, so I'm a little biased right now. But yeah, if the odd things he says and does concern you, it's time. Shit, my mother just made disparaging remarks or punished me for being different. I know you'll do much better for Mack," Pete said, taking one of Fiona's hands and holding it between both of hers.

"I'll do some research tonight. Thanks for your input, and for the tree house, and—well, for understanding him." Fiona threw her arms around Pete, and they embraced for a moment. "Now go work on your art."

Pete gathered her things and leashed up Turtle. "I'll talk to you tomorrow, Fi," Pete said before kissing her good-bye, leaving Fiona with an appetite for more.

☆☆☆

Pete came early Wednesday morning to continue the construction project. The two of them enjoyed working together, and as talkative as Mack was, there were portions of the day the two of them spent in blissful silence, each doing a particular task that didn't require them to communicate.

The major components of the tree house were finished just as it was starting to get dark. The roof needed shingles, and the two windows didn't have their shutters on yet, but it looked amazing. Mack couldn't wait to "ice the cake," as Pete called it; he was eager to paint it.

Fiona had approved the blue he chose for the outside of the simple yet elegant structure because it went nicely with the bluish-gray of the house. The interior would indeed have lime-green walls and a bright-orange ceiling, as Mack envisioned it. With its graceful ladder, sturdy and symmetrical bracing, and clean lines, the tree house was a thing of beauty set harmoniously into the great tree. Mack could barely contain his excitement as he climbed up into it, surveying the yards on either side of them.

Initially, Pete worried the boy wouldn't think it was high enough off the ground, but she was pleasantly surprised at how delighted Mack was to stand a foot and a half higher than the fence line. Perhaps it was more about a different perspective than how extreme it was.

"It's incredible, Pete! Come on up!" Mack urged.

Turtle barked as Pete ascended, sensing there was something to be excited about.

When they were both inside, Mack jumped in place to test its sturdiness. "It doesn't even wobble!"

Pete grinned broadly and suddenly thought of her father and how he would have loved it up here.

"Pete!" Mack looked up at her, his brown eyes charged with energy. "This tree house is unbelievable! You're good at so many things, and not just normal stuff. You have special-heavy-magic-superpowers, and you use them for good. Thank you for this."

She opened her mouth to respond, but instead took a moment to let the power of his simple words sink in. No matter how many tricks time played on her, she stood undeniably in the sweet now of the present tense. All the random information about other people's lives that the gift and curse of seeing flooded her brain with could not drown this feeling of hope. The terrifying voice capable of filling her mind with noise was quiet right now, but even if it dared to speak, Pete was certain all she would hear was happiness.

Fiona had gotten out of work a little early and came out into the yard just then. There in the twilight, Pete saw her radiance from a new angle and smiled at the sight of her.

Mack called to his mother, urging her to come up. Fiona told him she'd be up in a second. She walked all around it while Turtle followed her, then stopped in front of it so she could take a picture.

"There's just enough light on your gorgeous faces. I want to always remember this!" she sang up to them before taking a few photographs.

Mack stuck his arm out the window and waved her up. She slipped her phone into her pocket, petted Turtle, saying she was sorry he couldn't join them, and then mounted the steps.

"Wow. I love it," she marveled. "I love it up here. This is an amazing place to be. I hope you thanked Pete sufficiently, Mack Theodore Angeli," She draped her arm around him.

"I did, didn't I, Pete?"

"Yes, Mack, you certainly did," she answered. "I had a great time building this with you. You're an excellent worker, truly." She put her hand on his head lovingly.

"It's so strong, I bet it would stay up in a hurricane!" he boasted.

Fiona looked up at the ceiling and then the walls, knocking on one. "It *is* strong, Mack. This tree house is strong, unique, and beautiful, just like you and Pete."

Pete and Fiona studied each other over Mack's head while he looked down at Turtle, who was pacing back and forth and looking up at them. "Thank you for this," Fiona whispered to Pete.

Pete blinked at her in silent acknowledgment.

Mack suggested they celebrate the tree house with a special dessert after dinner and asked if Pete was staying over.

She hesitated.

"Please, that way we can have our own little Thanksgiving breakfast before you go see your family, and we go see ours. Please, will you?" Mack pleaded.

Fiona looked down at the floor because she didn't want to influence Pete's decision.

"Okay, Mack, how could I say no to an invitation like that?"

She also didn't say no to the massage Fiona offered to give her after Mack went to bed. She was sore after all the hard work and grateful that Fiona wanted to make her feel better. About twenty minutes into it, Pete fell asleep and didn't wake until morning. She could still smell almond oil on her skin when she saw Fiona's striking red hair on the pillow next to her. Something felt different to her; she didn't know what it was at first—she just knew something had shifted. Then she realized that, although she had not yet landed in a place of certainty about their relationship, her anger toward Fiona had taken flight.

After bacon, eggs, and homemade biscuits, Pete and Turtle went west to Springfield, and Fiona and Mack drove north to Maine. Time with her mother and Rudolph was more pleasant than Pete expected.

She had planned to spend the night at her mother's, but came back to be with Sheila in the evening after receiving a text message saying how depressed she felt after visiting her mother, who'd been mostly incoherent. She and Turtle camped in at Sheila's place for the night, and the two old friends stayed up late talking, laughing, and at points crying.

☆☆☆

Calvin had been urging Fiona to get Mack started with some type of volunteer work and suggested they participate in the monthly beach cleanup at Castle Island and Carson Beach at Fort Independence the Saturday after Thanksgiving. Both he and Fiona thought this was the easiest place for him to start. Mack was reluctant at first because he wanted to spend the day in his new tree house, but when Fiona reminded him that the paint inside was still drying, saying he couldn't play in it until Sunday, he agreed to go.

They invited Pete and Sheila to join them. They all met up there at nine in the morning, armed against the cold with Thermoses of hot coffee, warm bagels, and lots of winter clothes. Luckily, the sun was out, making the windy weather more tolerable. Dogs had to be on leash at the beach, so Sheila brought Fred, the calmest of her dogs. Turtle was thrilled to see his pal.

They checked in with the organizer of the cleanup, an elderly woman named Chloe, who thanked them and gave them each a bag for trash. She cautioned them not to touch any needles, broken glass, or used prophylactics, saying to point them out to her and she would pick that sort of stuff up with a scooper she had. As soon as they started combing the beach, Mack asked Calvin what a prophylactic was.

"Do you know what a condom is, Mack?" Fiona asked him.

"I've heard the word. Isn't it a *sex* thing?" He squinted in the morning sun, looking so much like his father to her in that moment.

"Yes, it's something that men wear on their penises when they have sex." She was hoping that would be the end of it as she bent to pick up a soda can.

"Why?" Mack inquired. Calvin chuckled. The boy looked in his direction.

"You're a man. Maybe you could explain it better," Mack said.

"Yeah, Uncle Calvin, please do," Fiona said, grinning at him.

"Well, the condom keeps the man from making a baby or spreading germs that might cause disease."

"Oh," Mack said, bending to grab a candy wrapper. "I think I get it." Then he sprinted over to where Pete, Sheila, and Turtle and Fred were.

When he was out of earshot, Calvin and Fiona burst into laughter.

The sunlight grew brighter as they all combed the beach, bending over to pick up debris from the sand. Sometimes they were spread out away from each other, and other times they were a team of five. After about a half hour, Mack got excited and showed Pete, Fiona, and Sheila what was in his bag. Calvin was way ahead of them, talking with Chloe.

"My bag's almost full! Look!" He opened it wide for them to see. Inside were bottle caps, some large pieces of a shoe, cigarette butts, a few coffee cup lids, various bits of paper, and a rusty piece of twisted metal that caught Pete's eye. She reached in and pulled it out.

"That would be cool in one of your collages," Fiona commented.

"I was just thinking that," Pete said. Their eyes met in silent appreciation of each other.

"People are like fish!" Mack blurted.

They both stared at him, awaiting an explanation.

"They're free but if they can't resist the bait, they lose their freedom. But like us, they're drawn to shiny things, so they're kind of helpless. Maybe in another universe, fish use poles to catch people." Then he took Turtle and darted off toward Calvin.

He set down his bag and picked up Mack, playfully slinging him over his shoulder, which made the boy laugh loudly.

"Did that make sense? Am I missing something? Is it something only you and Mack get?" Fiona asked, putting her free hand into Pete's coat pocket playfully.

"He's a deep thinker," Sheila said, bending to pet Fred. "This world needs deep thinkers. I'm gonna catch up with the boys." She smiled and headed in their direction because she sensed Pete and Fiona might want some privacy.

"That," Pete said, "was pure Mack. I sort of know what he means, but only he knows exactly."

Fiona pulled her hand out to link arms with Pete. They walked down the beach like a four-legged, two-armed beast, searching for more litter that sullied the shoreline.

They stopped walking and stood close, facing each other. Pete turned to look into Fiona's eyes, which were like twin microcosms, and saw herself reflected, a tiny human profile in front of the sky, sea, and shore. She beheld herself there, thinking of her own imperfections, Fiona's addiction, the flaws in their relationship, and the unknown that lay before them.

Pete knew in her heart that their love was bigger than all of that when Fiona gazed back at her soulfully, wordlessly echoing the desire to mend their relationship. In that moment, they exchanged the gift of seeing each other clearly and honestly. Pete and Fiona leaned into each other for a kiss, then embraced, holding tight against a sudden gust of wind.

# About the Author

Medella Kingston fell in love with writing at an early age and published articles, poems, and stories when she was growing up. She wrote, performed, and sold songs for movie soundtracks, and continued writing short stories for her own pleasure. She currently sings in the band Omnesia, which has aired locally on UC Berkeley's radio station and been heard as far east as Goa and the Mumbai University. *PeopleFish* is her first novel and like her main character, Pete, Medella was a house painter, makes art, and has had several inexplicable experiences in her life that fall into the realm of psychic. She lives with her partner and their two dogs in the East Bay.

Facebook: https://www.facebook.com/medella.kingston
Website: http://www.medellakingston.com/
Email: medella.kingston@gmail.com

NINESTAR PRESS, LLC

www.ninestarpress.com

www.ingramcontent.com/pod-product-compliance
Lightning Source LLC
Chambersburg PA
CBHW021949170626
46808CB00001B/77